STAR OF HOPE

BOOK ONE OF TALES OF SEA & SKIES

BRIGITTE CROMEY

YARROW LEAF PRESS

Formatting by M. H. Woodscourt

Cover Design by Luisa Galstyan

Interior maps by Annamarie Dunne

Published by Yarrow Leaf Press

www.wordsinmyblood.com

ISBN: 979-8-9850208-1-6

To the inhabitants of the Nuthouse, especially Dad.

And to Noah Anne. It's been years since that birthday that began everything, but this book is still for you.

CONTENTS

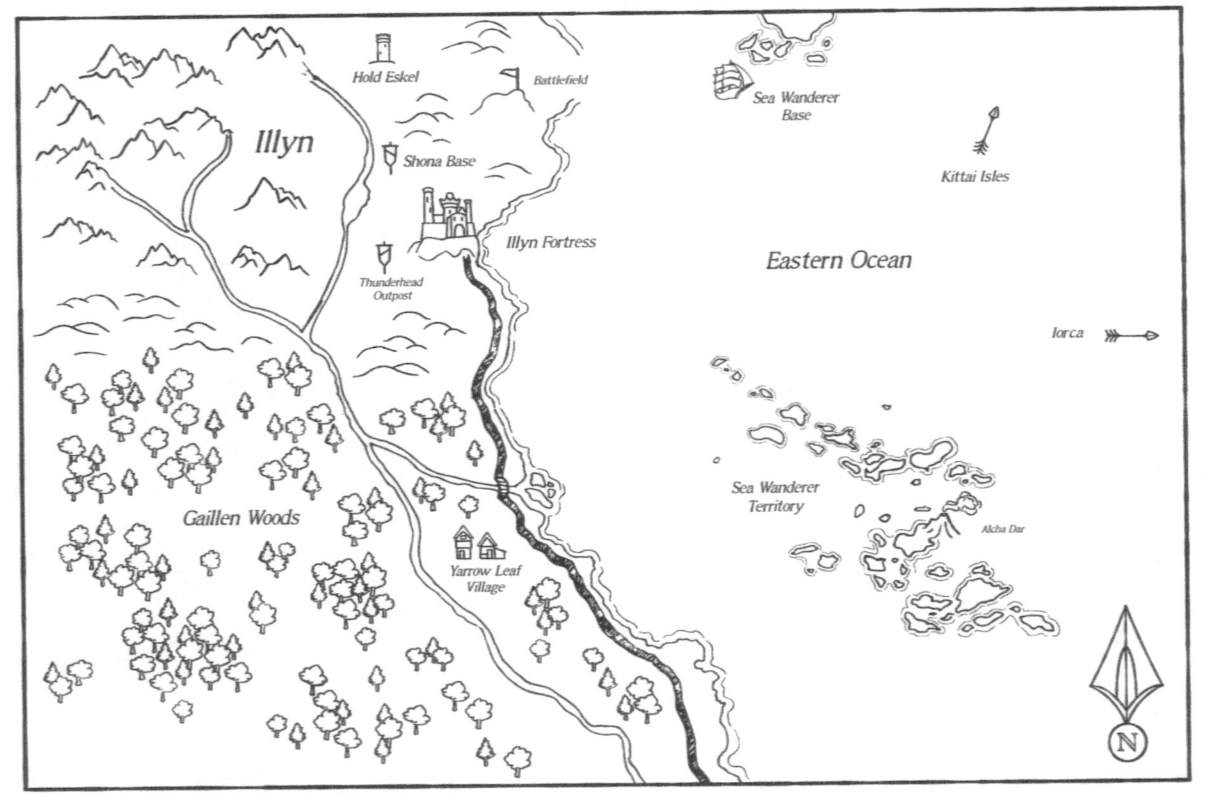

Illyn
Hold Eskel
Battlefield
Shona Base
Illyn Fortress
Thunderhead Outpost
Gaillen Woods
Yarrow Leaf Village
Sea Wanderer Base
Kittai Isles
Eastern Ocean
Iorca
Sea Wanderer Territory
Alcha Dar
N

TO THE READER...

Yes, this is a second edition.

In many ways, this is also a first edition.

You see, this is the book that seventeen-year-old me dreamed of—from the words inside, down to the art on the cover—when she sat in front of a computer with dial-up internet and began writing. This is the story that she saw through to the end, even after years of learning, mistakes, and triumph.

We've come full circle, she and I, because this is the book that made me an author. I've come to realize that it'll always have deficits, but such is the paradox of first books—they always set the benchmark upon which there will only ever be improvement. Yet, no matter how many more stories I write, this will always be the firstborn; the book that started me on my journey.

Some of you will have read the first printing of Star of Hope, and to you come undying appreciation and thanks. This story was never meant to be of just one chosen person, but of many incredible, ordinary people—and you are my 'many'.

Thank you for every message you've sent, every comment on my social media posts, every gracious review and recommendation, and every time you've said 'I want this signed'. Jumping into the publishing world was like leaping out a plane without knowing if the parachute would open—and it did, because of you.

To you who've never read this tale, welcome. Here you'll find a gaggle of friends who love each other enough to move mountains and shake seas. You'll find a people desperate for hope and a girl who was born to lead them. You'll find a father's love displayed in practical ways, and a rebel with a sacrificial heart. Above all, you'll find a story written to comfort and encourage (maybe even entertain). This is the heart of noblebright fiction, after all—to shed light in the darkness, to spread hope to souls who have none, and to instill fierce courage in faint hearts.

Welcome to the adventure.

~ BCC

STAR OF HOPE

1

FRIENDS INSEPARABLE

The stars were always peaceful.

Rose pulled her knees tight to her chest as she leaned against the chimney, still warm from the day's work. The cold in her chest loosened as she peered between the branches of the chestnut tree overhanging her parents' home, a perfect patch of sky visible where two boughs intersected. Stars crowded the tiny square with pale light, twinkling despite the smoke from the kitchen fires. On quiet nights, when the forest shimmered under the full moon and peace reigned within and without the tiny house, the stars felt close enough to touch. Most of the time, however, the stars remained distant; promises of a peaceful elsewhere that was as far removed as the sky.

Rose carefully shifted positions against the chimney, hoping the scraping sound wouldn't be noticed by anyone in the rooms below. She needn't have worried. The sounds of an argument still percolated through the thatch, mixing with the wind rustling in the chestnut leaves. As a shooting star streaked across the patch of sky, the clamor from inside grew louder, and something shattered.

Not again.

She clapped her hands over her ears with a shudder. *I wonder what it is this time.* The raised voices from below were too muffled to make out the context of the argument, but she was certain that it would rapidly become her fault, were she to appear at an inopportune moment.

Another crash almost made her jump out of her skin, this time that of the door opening with enough force that a vibration went through the thatch. A harsh voice called her name from the front side of the house, sending shivers of tension through every muscle. Rose slithered off the roof, landing in a pile of wood shavings near the back door. Dusting herself off, she hurried to the sheep pen. If she moved quickly enough, it would look like she'd been feeding the animals instead of hiding. The freezing ache in her chest reappeared as she took one final glance at the stars before disappearing into the work shed.

Tomorrow will be better. And if not, there are always the stars.

THE FOLLOWING MORNING, the late-spring sun filtered through the trees and fell upon Rose's neck with caressing sweetness as she knelt in a patch of madder plants. She wiped a chunk of clay from her hand, and dropped a handful of roots into the basket. The next handful proved more difficult to extricate from the ground, and she gave a huff as one of the brittle roots snapped off.

Again with this. Why am I so clumsy?

"It's all right," her best friend Violet said, moving over to work with her digging stick in the damp earth. "It's always hard to get them out." She gave a sigh that quickly turned into a chuckle. "Sometimes I wish they didn't make such a pretty color. I'd happily never dig these again, but it's such a nice red!"

"I know," Rose sighed, brushing dirt from her immaculate green dress. In the sunlight, her skin glowed almost white; testament to a complexion that hardly ever tanned, even in high summer. She tugged a long sleeve over her wrist and apologized, "I'm sorry I'm not myself today. I know you'd been looking forward to today."

Violet raised her head, a concerned furrow appearing between her sky-blue eyes. The apprentice healer was a bit younger than Rose—having just turned sixteen—built the perfect height for hugging, and possessing of a peaceful demeanor that was a welcome solace in the face of last night's turmoil. Her voice softened as she asked, "What's the matter? Did something happen?"

Rose turned her head away, the sun warming the edge of hair not quite covered by her tightly wrapped head scarf. "It's nothing. Mother and Father were having another argument last night."

Violet patted her knee. "You could have come to the cottage and stayed with us."

Dirt sprayed as Rose shook off another tangle of roots. "I tried." She brushed her dress again, uncertain if the shadows across it were stains or sunlight playing tricks on her. "Mother noticed me trying to sneak out and ordered me to stay home." Her voice lowered, even though there was no one nearby save Violet's younger siblings. "She says it would reflect badly on her and father if everyone knew their daughter had left the house again."

"So, what did you do?"

Rose shook her head. "I waited until they weren't paying attention, and went out to the roof."

"Again?" Violet sat back on her heels, her digging stick drooping in her hand. "Did you get in trouble?"

"Not badly." Rose thought back, piecing together the events that had led up to her mother catching her in the back yard and ordering her to bed with a voice that cut like jagged wood. "I don't even know what the argument was about." She pressed her lips together, tension stabbing at her temples. "I don't understand it," she confessed. "They're always fighting, and whenever I try to say anything, they both look at me like I'm responsible."

Violet gathered her digging tools, brushing a lock of mousy brown hair out of her eyes before offering Rose a hand up. "You aren't to blame. They're just difficult."

Rose accepted her offered hand, and they set off through the woods. "I know they're difficult," she said as they crossed a glade, the voices of Violet's younger brothers echoing between the trees. "But I can't help but wonder if it's something I'm doing to make it worse. Even if it's not, the way they look at me makes me wish it was, just so I could make things better." She found herself unconsciously twisting the edge of her apron, and dropped the hem with a huff. "I just don't know how to say it—or anything. Every time they fight, I keep telling myself I need to speak up, or say something, or even walk out and let them yell at each other."

Violet shifted the basket of madder roots and tools to her other arm, a questioning look in her eyes. "And?"

"And every time, I sit there like a frog on a rock." Rose shook her head. "One of these days—" A thread of warmth went through her chest, a tiny coal of defiance that only ever flickered to life when surrounded by her closest friends. "One of these days, I'll stand up for myself."

Violet wrapped dirt-covered fingers around her hand and

squeezed it. "You will. I know you will." She smiled. "And until then, I'm here."

THE WALK WASN'T long to the Yarrow Leaf Tribe's village, where the trees of the Gaillen Woods hemmed in the tiny community on all sides. The two girls parted ways at the gate of Violet's grandmother's home, Violet entreating and Rose promising to reunite as soon as their respective responsibilities would allow. After seeing her siblings safely inside the split-pole fence, Violet made her way towards the healers' cottage. The afternoon was warm for spring, and the thatch roofs of the village shimmered under the rays of the sun as she crossed the square.

The healers' cottage was a three-room house not too far from the center of town, its garden a glorious tangle of medicinal herbs and flowers. Violet's mentor, Kalina, was attending to the bees in their straw skep at the rear of the garden, and Violet greeted her cheerfully before going inside to put away her and Rose's harvest. After the sunlit forest paths, the whitewashed interior of the small house was dark and cool, and she breathed a sigh of relief that quickly turned to a stew of worry over what Rose had said that morning. The rest of that day was absorbed in tending the garden and preparing salves for sale during the upcoming Trading Week, and it wasn't until evening that she was able to unburden herself to her beloved mentor.

"—don't even know what to say, when that happens," Violet confided. The windows were shuttered against the night chill, and the fire crackled subtly in time with the creaking of Kalina's rocking chair. "Whenever they fight, Rose always ends up getting the worst of it. And I can't even do or say anything to help her."

"Mmm. It's difficult for us as well," her mentor confided.

"Ever since—well, ever since she was a babe, they've been at each other's throats." An unexpectedly guarded look flickered across Kalina's weathered face. "The war had its effect on many throughout the tribes. Sometimes, I wonder if we were so grateful for peace that we forgot that not all wounds can be seen."

Violet nodded, tightening her grasp on the ends of her knitting needles. She'd wondered as a child why Trading Week was the only time anyone from outside the woods visited the village, but no answer had ever satisfied her curiosity. It hadn't been until later in her adolescence that she'd understood the truth. The fall of the country immediately to the north of the woods—leading to the borderland skirmishes commonly referred to as 'the war' by those old enough to remember—had been enough to drive her people into self-isolation.

"I wonder what her life would've been, if it hadn't ever happened," Violet said, setting her knitting to the side and taking a sip of tea. Though she and her siblings had lost their parents several years previous, she was certain they had never treated any of their six children the way Rose's parents treated her. *Almost like they don't want her at all.*

"Rose's life?" A guarded smile crossed Kalina's face. "Very different, I assure you."

ON THE FIRST day of Trading Week, Rose was awake before the sun. She plaited her long, dark hair, wriggling into a work-day dress and apron before wrapping a head scarf to completely cover her pinned-up braid.

"Outsiders will be here," her mother had warned her the previous night, casting a scathing look at the black hair escaping her scarf. "They don't know us or our ways, and you'd be best to keep yourself inconspicuous."

It was an old reminder, the progeny of a long line of reminders. *Stay hidden. Don't draw attention. Don't embarrass us.* Rose tugged at the sleeves of her dress—their length hiding skin much paler than the rest of the tribe's. She'd bowed her head in acquiescence to her mother's litany last night, but now, as the first rays of morning sun peeked through her shutters, Rose found herself wondering if being noticed was such a bad thing. *Maybe if more people noticed her trying to keep me hidden, things would change.*

"Don't cause trouble," she warned herself as she hurried to feed the sheep and pigeons. "Don't jeopardize anything for yourself."

The atmosphere downstairs was every bit as tumultuous as she'd feared, clattering erupting from her father's workshop as he gathered his stock of carved-wood goods for the short trip to the center of the village. He cast a brief, distracted glance her way as she came into the open-fronted shop.

"Oh, good, you're awake." He pointed to a folded blanket and bag bulging with wood shavings. "Go take those and reserve our spot."

Rose nodded soundlessly, gathering the items into her arms and hurrying out of the yard before her mother could see and object. As she turned a corner into the lane, Rose took a grateful breath of cool morning air. With luck, it would take her parents another hour to collect themselves and their goods. For now, the morning was hers.

A cacophony of sounds greeted her as she stepped into the village square. Even at this early hour, there was activity everywhere as the villagers scurried about; setting up booths and blankets, haggling with the traders in their painted wagons, and carrying armloads of trade goods.

"Rose!"

Rose yelped and turned barely in time to avoid getting flattened by a pair of sisters; one tall and lanky, the other built stockier. "Heather! Clover!"

The two curtseyed dramatically, and the taller one doffed an imaginary hat. "Large as life and twice as scary, Your Grace!"

Rose resettled the bag in her arms, the tension in her shoulders relaxing at the sight of her friends. Heather had chestnut hair tumbling in untidy ringlets to brush the shoulders of her dress. At sixteen, she was still all elbows and knees, having grown faster and taller than the rest of her figure could match. Clover was fourteen, her hazel eyes snapping with mischief. Her skin never lost the kiss of summer, staying tanned long after everyone else's had turned pale during winter. Combined, the two girls were responsible for most of the mayhem in their circle of friends—though somehow, had never managed to drag Rose into trouble.

"You scared me," Rose confessed. "I didn't even hear you coming."

"Aye, and Heath', *you* almost knocked her over." Clover elbowed her older sister. "Take her bag; it's the least you can do."

Heather put an offended hand to her chest. "I almost knocked her over? That's rich, Ducky." She brushed past Clover to neatly lift the bag of wood shavings from Rose. "But never let it be said that I'll stand by idle while I can help a friend—oh, *frogs*, Rose, what did you fill this with? Bricks?"

"I think Father packed his smaller boxes into it," Rose said, a smile tugging at her mouth. She tucked the blanket under an arm to accept Clover's enthusiastic hug. "Hello, Ducky." They set off towards the edge of the square, Rose directing their steps towards a space in between two wagons where everyone would see her father's wares. "Where's your sister?"

Clover jerked her thumb over her shoulder. "Right there. Or have you already forgotten?"

Rose sighed patiently. While loving and cheerful-spirited, Clover wasn't always the brightest. "I meant your other sister."

"Hmm? Oh, I don't know. I think she was helping Mother and Father with our things." Clover scanned the crowd around the traders' wagons. "Ah, there she is. Willow!"

Rose looked where Clover was pointing to see a girl with blonde hair weaving through the villagers. Two inches shorter and as many years older than Rose, Willow was a slim, strong girl whose dry sense of humor was only matched by her strength of will. She sidled up next to Rose and linked arms. "Hallo, dear. How are you?"

Rose smiled. With Willow's family, she didn't have to worry about hiding her differences—no one noticed a girl with darker-than-usual hair when there was someone nearby whose hair turned gold when the sun hit it. "I'm quite well. Your sister kindly offered to carry my things for me."

Willow nodded wisely. "Of course she did. All of her free will, too."

"Naturally," Rose agreed, stifling a laugh at Heather's bemused face. "What are you selling this year?"

"Ehhh, spoons, scarves, mittens, bowls, and bread—with nuts in." Willow glared at her two sisters on the last few words.

"Wait, now," Heather croaked. "The nuts were not my idea."

"I'm sure," Willow agreed with an eye roll. "Yet, even though you're the one who suggested it, *I* was the one mother picked to spend the night cracking nuts and baking."

Rose gave her friend a cursory look. Willow enjoyed cooking, to be sure, but the idea of her sleep-loving friend staying up late was unheard-of. "You? There must have been a mistake."

"That's what I thought too," Willow frowned at something across the square. "Was your mother planning on coming early?"

Rose jumped despite herself. "No. Why?"

"Ah, nothing." Willow dropped her stormy blue gaze to the blanket clutched in Rose's arms. "Let's get your blanket set up, my love."

THE GAIETY of Trading Week seeped into everyone, so that not a moment passed when music did not ring in the square. The inn —a carryover from bygone days when the village had stood on a major trade route—did a good business selling drinks to the traders and their guards, and the common room on the ground floor was almost always full. The rest of the tribe also prospered, and the village breathed a collective sigh of relief at the knowledge that they were well-stocked for the next winter. The day after trading ended, preparations began for a celebratory feast.

Violet brushed her hair carefully, pulling it away from her face with a carved wood clasp that had once belonged to her mother. She smoothed her best dress and took a shawl from its peg in her room. Although summer was well on its way, the night air was still chilly. The sounds of distant revelry filled her ears as she cut through the woods to join her grandmother and siblings for the walk into the village. Greeting everyone with hugs all around, she swung her youngest brother to her hip and followed her grandmother toward the square.

She heard the festival before she saw it. Flutes, fiddlers, and drums blended together with the hum of many voices to urge her forward. A bonfire in the center of the square illuminated the buildings with crackling light, casting jumping shadows across the forms of a juggler and acrobats as they performed for the gathering crowd. Casting a look across the square, she noticed Willow, Heather, and Clover watching the acrobats, and—bidding her grandmother a quick goodbye— Violet hurried to join them.

"I wasn't sure I'd find you lot." She wrapped an arm around Willow. "Heather told me you might not be here this evening."

Heather pulled a face in her direction. "A joke, that's all. Have *some* faith in us."

"Violet!"

"Rose!" She set her brother down to embrace her friend. It only took a moment's glance to tell that things had been diffi-cult in Rose's home. Even though it was a festive night, Rose's hair was bundled tightly in a scarf, and she stood as if expecting a blow at any moment. "Were your parents able to sell the last few boxes?"

"All except that biggest one. You know, the one big enough to hold a small child." Rose's smile flashed for a moment, but vanished almost in the same heartbeat. "Father's quite offended that no one wanted his 'work of art'."

Heather looked down with mischief in her eyes. "I'm sure *someone* would. But what peddler is going to break his arms hauling that 'art' from village to village?"

"Be nice," Willow ordered before turning towards Rose. "Love, is everything all right?"

Rose shook her head. "Nothing. It's nothing."

"It's not 'nothing'." Willow's eyes snapped with frustra-tion. "What happened?"

Rose's shoulders hunched. Her eyes darted towards Willow's younger sisters, who were currently engaged in making faces at Violet's younger brother.

Ah.

Violet bent down to the little boy. "Little Tree, would you like to go see the juggler?" She gave a meaningful look at Clover as he nodded enthusiastically. "Clover and Heather will be *very happy* to take you over that way."

Clover took his hand. "Oh yes! We'll see you in a bit, eh?"

"Yes, yes." Heather took his other hand, tipping a wink at Violet. "'Scuse us a mo'."

Violet tugged both Willow and Rose into the shadow cast by a nearby house as the others trooped away. "There, there're fewer people about now. What happened?"

"Aye, explain," Willow said. "We'd like to help, but we can't if you don't tell us."

"All right, all right!" Rose said, shaking off Violet's hand and taking a step backwards. "I was trying to help Father by putting away his tools while he packed what he didn't sell, and I dropped one of the chisels. It made a big scratch across one of the boxes. Mother was furious." Rose twisted the corner of her shawl, not seeming to notice that threads were popping out of the hem. "She started yelling. Father was trying to talk her down. He said it wasn't my fault, and that he'd be able to fix it." She glanced over her shoulder, her words tumbling out faster and faster. "It only made her more upset. I don't think she knew what she was saying."

Willow raised an eyebrow with an expression that promised vengeance. "What *exactly* did she say?"

"I heard her say—" Rose's voice broke, and Violet had to lean closer to hear her. "She said I was worthless—that no child of their blood would ever be so clumsy or stupid—and it proves all over again that they made a mistake taking me in in the first place."

A sickening pang shot through Violet's chest, and she exchanged a hasty, panicked glance with Willow. The theory of Rose being adopted had been discussed by the three of them before—no one else in their tribe had black hair, for one, and her willowy build was far different than the other children they'd grown up with—but no one else had addressed their suspicions so publicly.

"What?!" Willow demanded. "She's insane." She glared at Rose's parents, who were taking seats at the tables near the fire. "Just let me handle it. I'll set my Da on them."

"Willow, calm down," Violet pleaded. "It won't help anything." She looked at Rose in disbelief. "That's really what she said?"

Rose's face had gone red. "Aye," She crossed her arms tightly. "I mean, I *know* she lost babies before I was born, but that has nothing to do with me. And—and it wasn't only me that heard." Her voice shook as she explained, "S-she said it right in front of some of the peddlers and their guards."

"Of all the stupid, unkind, heartless—oogh! When I get my hands on her, I'll—" Willow clenched her fists.

"Please, no. It's not going to help." Rose's eyes were reflecting the firelight glassily as she pulled her shawl tighter. "She didn't know what she was saying, but I think she already regrets it." Something hardened in her expression, and her jaw clenched. "Besides, it does confirm what we were already wondering."

Willow sighed. "And it does at that." She uncrossed her arms. "Look, we'd better go. They'll know something's wrong if they notice us hiding."

"If they haven't noticed already," Rose muttered.

"You can stay near us for the evening," Violet offered.

"Aye, do," Willow frowned. "And if she says a single word more to you tonight, I'll strangle her."

Heather and Clover rejoined them on their way towards the fire. "Have a nice chat?" Heather asked as they took their seats.

Violet nodded. "We'll tell you in a moment, don't worry."

"Aye, and you'd better," Heather eyed her. "I don't distract small children for free, you know."

THE DANCING and laughter continued long into the night. Rose's friends walked her home that night, bidding her farewell at the gate of the woodcarving yard. The house towered above them, cold and quiet in contrast to the whirl of light and color that still occupied the square. Rose twisted the edge of her shawl, an icy knot hardening deep inside at the thought of being alone with her parents after the events of that morning.

"You'll let us know if you need anything, yes?" Willow said from outside the yard. "We'll take her to the laundry if she goes off on you again."

"Aye, we're happy to do something unsavory," Heather added with a ferocious grin.

"I don't think it'll come to that, but thank you." She'd seen her parents talking and laughing with one of their friends near the casks of ale, the activity a promising indicator of peace for the remainder of the night. "I'll be all right."

"Are you still able to help me dig up the rest of the madder?" Violet asked, brushing a lock of light brown hair away from her face. "The dye merchant said he's staying another night, and he'll buy whatever I can scrounge."

Rose pursed her lips. "I forgot. Thank you for the reminder." She stopped and considered the state of her father's workshop and yard. Heaps of shavings spilled out of packing boxes, and sawdust made a trail into the house. "I'll sweep the yard tonight, and chances are, they won't notice anything else. I'll come tomorrow morning, early."

"Right then," Willow shrugged her blouse straight over her

shoulders, giving Rose a casual wave. "We're off home, then. Coming, Violet?"

"Coming!" Violet pressed a kiss to Rose's cheek in a swirl of peppermint and lavender. "Goodnight, Rose."

"Goodnight!" Rose called. As her friends disappeared into the darkness, she took a deep breath and retrieved a broom from the corner of the yard. The repetitive motions of sweeping settled her mind, but nothing could undo the knot now formed deep in her stomach.

Not theirs.

Somehow, the thought was a relief as well as a burden. *Not their daughter. Not their blood.* She tipped her head back to look at the stars.

So then, who am I? And who could I become?

2

THE PEACE SHATTERS

The following morning, Violet and Rose returned to the madder patch deep in the forest. Rose didn't speak again about the shocking news of the previous day, but Violet could see that something had shifted in her friend's heart. There was a hardness in the set of her jaw, and a dangerous light in her eyes that suggested the revelation hadn't been nearly as devastating as Violet had expected it would be.

The day passed peacefully enough, and evenfall saw them gathered with Willow and her sisters in the healers' cottage, washing and cutting that morning's harvest. Violet was in the middle of blotting dry a handful of roots when a knock fell on the door.

"I've got it!" Clover exclaimed, darting to the door and opening it a crack. "Halt, who goes there—friend, foe, or food?"

"Clover, open the door." The voice coming from beyond the carved wood was deep, and Violet recognized it as one of the sisters' many older cousins. He stepped over the threshold, ducking his head under the lintel as he said, "I'm sorry to disturb you, Kalina, but you're needed urgently at the inn."

"It's no trouble, Rowan," Kalina said, already gathering her bag from a peg by the door. "Violet?"

Violet nodded, her nerves jumping as she went to retrieve her own satchel from her room. She returned in time to hear Rowan and Kalina in hushed conference near the door.

"Will you stay with them until we find out what's going on?"

Rowan nodded. "I was planning on it."

"Thank you." Kalina's countenance settled into determination. "Violet, come with me."

"Are you sure?" Rowan glanced out the door, and sudden foreboding stirred in Violet's chest. "She might be better off with me."

"She's still my apprentice, and I need her. Violet, let's go." Kalina pushed the door open and stepped into the night, Violet following on her heels.

Violet actually had to quicken her steps to keep pace with her mentor as they set off towards the center of the village. "What's wrong?"

Kalina frowned. "Those merchants who stayed burst into a Council of Elders meeting. They're making some wild threats, and evidently they took hostages until their demands are met."

"Demands!" Violet exclaimed as they came into the village center. Ordinarily, there would be peace at this time of night. Now, the place was ablaze with torchlight. As the pair approached, someone burst out of the inn and waved them over.

"Kalina, hurry!" It was one of the innkeeper's sons. He pushed through the crowd inside the common room, raising his voice above the clamor. "Kalina's here!"

The crowd parted to reveal one of the elders standing next

to a table, steadying someone whose face was covered in blood. Violet realized with a start that it was Rose's father. She took a deep breath as her stomach churned. Most calls to the healers' cottage involved illness, or minor injury; all things that she'd trained for until she could attend to them with her eyes closed. But an actual *injury?*

"What happened?" Kalina demanded.

The councilwoman rounded the table, her hands clasped tightly at her bosom. "Their leader came with several of the caravan guards and demanded a hearing."

"He was making such wild claims!" someone else chimed in. "Stories about a search for someone, that they finally tracked her here, and demanding that we turn her over."

The churning intensified in Violet's stomach. *Who's 'she'?*

"I don't even think those were caravan guards," the first woman commented. "Their weapons—I've never seen caravan guards so well-armed."

"When we told them she wasn't here, their leader got angry and ordered his men to grab Ash."

"Who's 'she'?!" Violet asked again.

Her frightened voice was lost in the hubbub as Kalina pulled her to the table where Rose's father lay unconscious. "Here," Kalina pulled bandages from her satchel, guiding Violet's hands to place bandaging against the cut on the man's brow. "It's just like any other cut. You know what to do for those." Her voice sharpened as she asked, "Where are these men now?"

An unsympathetic voice cut through the confused babble of answers. "They're gone." Willow's father Alder had pushed his way through the crowd and was giving the onlookers a steely glance. "If you don't have business here, get out. You'll only get in the way."

"Why are you here?" one of the older men asked grumpily. "This doesn't concern you."

Violet tried to keep her mind on her work as the room emptied, but found herself wondering the same thing. Her friends' father had led their tribe to battle many years ago, but he wasn't part of the Council—in fact, according to Willow, he wasn't even well liked by most of the elders.

"I was locking up when they went past my house," Alder said. "They threatened my son when he asked what they were doing. I think that makes this my business." He turned a stormy gaze much like his eldest daughter's on Oak. "What happened here?"

Rose's father had come around. He winced as Kalina peeled the blood-soaked bandage away to swap it with a fresh one. "They wanted to know where my daughter was."

What? Violet squeezed her hands so tightly they ached. *Rose?*

"He said they'd be back tomorrow, and if we didn't agree to hand her over, they'd kill us all." Oak, the village storyteller, spoke from the head of the table. "I don't know where the rest of their men came from, but there were enough to make good on his threats."

Alder crossed his arms, a deep sigh settling his shoulders in a straight line. "But they *specifically* asked about Rose?"

He doesn't seem surprised. Worry pulsed in the back of Violet's head. *Maybe we* aren't *the only ones who had suspicions about her.*

"Their commander said someone was shouting about an adopted daughter—a girl not of forest blood. He was reasonably forthcoming about why he was here, and on whose behalf." Oak handed Alder something that gleamed silver. "He's here in the name of the warlord of Illyn, and he's looking for the daughter of the Thinar line."

Violet's spine stiffened as Alder's hand tightened around the coin.

"When Illyn fell to the northern raiders, her conquerors were greedy," Kalina said. *"They turned their eyes south—to our forest."* Her voice hushed. *"We kept our home safe, but at such a price."*

"Has no one left the woods since?"

Kalina shook her head. "No one."

No one had left, and no one entered. Violet swallowed hard. *I thought it was fear of war that kept us isolated. What if it was for another reason altogether?*

Fifteen minutes later, Rose sat anxiously on a bench before the Council, taking deep breaths against the knot of ice under her breastbone. Her parents sat across from her, stiffly apart despite sitting on the same bench. Rose had barely spoken a handful of sentences to her mother since the words in the marketplace that had shattered her world into fragments as sharp and sparkling as the stars. At the memory, she leaned farther into Violet, seated next to her. The healer's presence was calming, sturdy in a world where she wasn't sure what was stable anymore.

The Council quieted as Oak called order, recapping what had occurred that night before turning his attention to her. "Sixteen years ago, our men were returning from the war on the northern edge of the woods. While they were camped next to the river on their way home, a boat grounded on the shore. You were in that boat, Rose."

"We found this in your wrappers." Her mother pulled a cloth bag from her apron and upended the contents on the table.

A necklace fell to the polished wood with a tiny clatter, two pendants tangled in their delicate chain. Rose picked them up with trembling fingers, an unusual familiarity settling in her heart at the sight of a silver leaf and a gold, five-pointed star. *I've never seen these before, so why does it feel like I've known them my entire life?*

She raised her eyes to her parents, suddenly craving the answers only they could provide. "What do these mean?"

A second, unspoken question lurked at the base of her tongue.

Who am I?

Neither of them met her eyes, turning instead to look imploringly at Oak. He sighed and said, "The kings that ruled Illyn before the war were of the Thinar clan. Their banner was a golden star on a field of blue." An ancient piece of parchment crackled as he passed it to her. The ink was faded beyond readability, and the edges charred, but the half-melted seal at the bottom portrayed a star that matched the pendant. "We'd hoped that secrecy would be enough, but somehow, your family's enemies have found you."

Rose's fingers tightened around Violet's, and she let the parchment fall to the table. "Is this true?" she finally asked, voice miraculously steady against the ice in her chest.

"It's true." Alder's voice pulled her to look at him, leaning in his chair against the wall. "I was the one that pulled you out of the boat. That document confirmed your identity, back when it could still be read." His keen gaze flicked to the others surrounding the table. "The question is, what do we do? Council?"

One of the men shrugged. "What *can* we do?"

"I am *not* turning my daughter over to these thugs!" her father exclaimed.

"If what they said is true, she's not really your daughter."

Her mother's shoulders slumped as she gazed at the tabletop. "You don't have to tell me that."

Deep inside her chest, the ice cracked to spill out in fire. Rose dropped Violet's hand and shot to her feet. Her parents blanched and leaned back in their seats as she shouted, "You don't have to tell anyone that! You said everything you needed to when you *yelled* it in the marketplace! You told me all my life to cover my hair, hide my skin, never draw attention to myself, but you never thought to say why?!" Her voice cracked, eyes hot and dry as she demanded, "Did you *ever* care about me, or was I only ever an embarrassing second best to the children you could never have?"

"I did!" her father stammered.

Her mother huffed. "Of course I did."

"Well, one thing's for certain," Alder's chair legs scraped the floor as he came to stand behind Rose. His next words to her parents matched the certainty in her heart. "It *was* a mistake, entrusting the two of *you* with this secret. No matter how well you kept our trust in the past, your stupid, unfeeling words brought Rose t'this man's attention now." His voice dropped threateningly. "If I were you, I'd think very, *very* hard b'fore opening your mouths again."

Rose sat slowly, her heart racing. *Not theirs. Not now, not ever.*

"Well done," Violet whispered in her ear.

She squeezed her friend's hand as the debate resumed. "One of us or not, we cannot let a girl go to her death."

"What are the other options?"

"They threatened to kill us all!"

"Handing Rose over undoes everything we've done over the last fifteen years," Alder insisted. He'd remained standing, his tall figure a bulwark against the gazes of everyone in the room. "It's clear she needs t'leave. *Tonight.* Along with anyone else who'd be in danger."

Surprised exclamations from the Council overlapped in a

cacophony of dismay, broken by Alder's voice. "What's so surprising about that? I have daughters of my own, and a wife and son. I'd not have them anywhere near while we try t'negotiate with a madman." He shrugged. "If I'm too cautious, so be it."

One of the other men stood amid the flurry of worried chatter and questions. "I'll go start alerting them."

"Quietly. And tell Willow and Heather to get t'gether whatever they can't live without." Alder's hand was warm as he put it on Rose's shoulder, his voice lowering as he told her, "I'm sending them with you."

"I'll come too, if Kalina lets me," Violet murmured. "We won't let you go alone."

"All right, all right!" Oak commanded over the turmoil. "Everyone, quiet!" He pulled a bag from under his chair and dumped a round of polished ash wood onto the tabletop. The Council members' chatter subsided as it rattled against the table, Oak stopping the movement by laying his hand flat on the polished surface. "Are we agreed?"

Rose's mother smiled unsteadily. "If it will save my daughter's life, yes." Her eyes flicked to Rose. "Isn't that right, love?"

She's giving me an opportunity to fix this. Rose steeled herself against the eyes of the woman who'd raised her—already, the word 'mother' hung heavy and wrong at the base of her throat —and looked resolutely at the opposite wall. *It's too late.*

The other adults reluctantly touched the wood as well, those who couldn't reach touching the shoulders of those who could. Alder gave a significant glance at her and Violet as he put a hand on each of their shoulders. "You as well."

Rose took a deep breath and reached to brush the edge of the wood with her fingertips, Violet's hand slipping up to touch her forearm. *No going back now.*

"Council, you have heard the plan." Oak eyed her parents.

"The two of you have some real thinking to do about your actions. Give your ayes now, or hold your peace."

Violet's mentor was the first to agree. "Aye."

From around the circle came more agreements. "Aye, aye." "Aye."

"And the girls?" Alder asked.

Rose and Violet exchanged a single, wide-eyed look. Finally, they answered together. "Aye."

VIOLET PACKED her things hurriedly into a bag on her bed. Taking her cloak down from a hook, she joined Rose in the sitting room. Her friend had already said goodbye to her parents in a tense conversation, and was staring into the fire with a taut, worried face as Violet joined her. They'd barely sat in the silence for a minute before the latch on the door rattled, and Kalina opened it to admit Willow and her sisters.

"G'evening, ladies!" Heather tipped an imaginary hat, gesturing grandly with the half-eaten apple in her hand. "How's the poisoning business? Going briskly, I assume?" She took a crunching bite from the apple before gagging dramatically. "Ack! Maybe a little too briskly!"

"Are you all coming with us?" Violet asked, getting to her feet to hug the newcomers.

"Only Willow and I." Heather eyed Clover, who was greeting Kalina's cat enthusiastically. "Ducky and some of the others are going to take our siblings to that cave where we found the salt that one time."

"Da's idea," Willow said. "Most of the others are going to hunting camps—well, those that are listening."

"Those who are *listening*?" Violet asked with a frown. "There are people who *aren't*?"

Willow's cloak rustled as she shook her head angrily. "A

handful; not many. They're saying this is all being taken out of proportion, or maybe these fellows are being misunderstood, or the Council ought to try and reason with them first—argh!" She threw up her hands. "They've got heads thicker than hazelnut shells."

"This is terrible." Rose hadn't said a word since she'd arrived, and now she refused to meet anyone's eyes. "I should have said I'd go with them." She shivered. "Then no one else would be in danger."

"Frogs and toads, Rose," Willow's stormy eyes took on a steely hue. "No one is blaming you for this. I'm not even sure anyone's surprised! It's been sitting right under our noses this whole while, and the only people who're acting stupid are the ones who want everything taken care of for them."

"She's right." Heather tucked the remains of her apple into the belt pouch she wore over a russet-colored dress. "And if anyone wants to blame you, they'll go through all of us first. I mean, that's what they'll have to do." She rubbed a hand through her curls. "Da's pulled out his bow, and it's not even hunting season."

Rose didn't look convinced. She'd wrapped her arms around herself, and Violet wondered if she was about to try and run.

Luckily, Clover seemed to have noticed too. The younger girl looked up suddenly from the fire. "I say, Willow, while you're gone, can I have your bed?"

"We *share* a bed!"

Amid the laughter that followed, Violet gave her a grateful smile. Clover winked as the door opened to admit Alder, unstrung longbow in hand. The sight of the weapon doused the laughter as effectively as a bucket of ice water.

"Girls, you know Blackthorn, yes?"

The girls nodded seriously at the older apprentice with Willow's father.

"He's going to take you northwest, deeper into the woods. When it's safe, we'll come get you." Alder handed Blackthorn a folded paper. "There's a letter for the innkeeper. She's vaguely related to us, and she'll know where you can stay safely until it's time to come home." Gesturing to the door, he said, "You'd better say goodbye, Clover."

AFTER SEVERAL HOURS OF WALKING, they stopped for the night. Violet tossed and turned on the lumpy ground for a long time before finally sitting up in irritation. Heather, Rose, and Blackthorn lay asleep in the shadow of a guelder rose thicket, but Willow's space was empty. Peering around, Violet caught sight of her; sitting on the ground a dozen feet away.

"Good eve." Willow leaned back on her elbows to look at her as she approached. "You couldn't sleep either?"

"No, I tried." Violet sat with a huff and stared into the night sky. Between the gaps of the tall, dark trees, the sky stretched out like a great canopy of sable cloth.

"Neither could I." The silence stretched for a long while before Willow asked, "Do you think it's true?"

Violet let out a sigh. "I don't know."

"I don't know if I want it to be true." Willow rolled to her elbow. "I love Rose, and I don't want anything to happen to her."

"Neither do I," Violet confessed. "But, look, Willow. She's changing. In the Council meeting, she stood up to her parents. She's barely even *disagreed* with them before." Her voice dropped. "I've never seen her like that."

"I have, once or twice," Willow said. "But not when it

mattered." She gazed searchingly into the sky. "Sometimes, all it takes is one moment of courage to start something that will change the rest of your life. That could have been her moment."

Violet snorted. "You didn't come up with that yourself."

"No, Da said it once." Willow shook a hand free of her cloak. "Look, *if* it's all true, then she's destined for bigger things than either of us ever dreamed about. We need to help her, any way we can." She spat on her palm and held out her hand, a habit she'd gotten from her sisters that Violet found disgusting. "Are you with me?"

Hoping her friend wouldn't see her grimace, Violet clasped Willow's hand.

"I'm with you."

Spurred by worry that none of them wanted to acknowledge, the travelers pushed themselves to put distance between themselves and their home. As they began their second day of travel, Rose pulled her shawl tighter.

It's almost summer, she told herself. *I shouldn't feel this cold.* She glanced at the sun. *And it's not about to storm. Then*—she craned her neck to see beyond the next bend in the path—*what's bothering me?*

A twig snapped. Not ahead of them, but behind them.

Rose jumped and looked back. In an instant, her unknown feelings crystallized. *Fear.* She turned to Blackthorn, whose eyes were also busy probing the forest. "Did you hear that?"

He nodded wordlessly and returned to scanning. Another noise came, this time from the right. Ahead of them, Rose saw Willow begin to turn—her eyes widening as they locked on something behind them.

"Rose!"

A flicker of movement darted from behind a tree, the

sudden tramping of many pairs of feet resounding in her ears. Violet yelped in terror, and Blackthorn whirled to snatch a tree branch from the ground. Faster than she could draw breath, they were surrounded by men dressed in dark, travel-worn clothing, and bearing weapons of types she could only guess at. Hair as dark as a crow's wing contrasted pale skin and blue eyes—the combination as familiar as her own reflection.

They've been following us this whole time.

"Rose, run!" Willow yelled. "It's you they're here for!"

Rose shook her head frantically. "Not if it means leaving you."

"Go!" Blackthorn growled, brandishing his branch.

For a moment, Rose stood torn, as the dark-clad men charged and sounds of panic split the air. Then, her feet moved on their own, and she sprinted for the trees. She'd only made it a few steps when something caught the back of her shawl, yanking her backwards for a terrifying moment before she tore herself free.

Violet screamed somewhere nearby. Rose glanced back just in time to see her friend hurl a rock into a man's face, before another grabbed her arm.

"Let her go!" Rose yelled, grabbing a clod of leaf mold from the forest floor and hurled it at him. It showered uselessly around his head as he cursed at her.

Someone grabbed her arm, and she screamed. She twisted her arm hard, wrenching the man's hand as she broke free. The man cursed and pulled a knife from his belt, lunging toward her as she stumbled towards Violet.

With a shout, Blackthorn jumped between them and met the man's charge with his branch. He struck a hefty blow on the man's forehead, knocking him backwards a pace before shouting, "Rose, get out of here!"

The man cursed and wiped blood out of his eyes. "Enough of this. Take them all, men!"

"No!" Rose wheeled to see Violet's captor bludgeon her friend with a short wooden club. The healer sagged in his arms, unconscious.

Someone's arms closed on her waist from behind, and a dark piece of cloth fell over her eyes. Before she had time to wriggle away, something impacted the side of her head. Stars exploded through her vision, followed by blackness, then—suddenly—silence.

AWAKENING CAME SLOWLY, and vision even slower. By the time both were restored, Rose could tell night had fallen. She was sitting—slumped, really—against the wall of a rattling, jouncing compartment, moonlight occasionally filtering through a grated door at the far end. Blackthorn was nowhere to be seen, but Heather and Willow were piled together against the opposite wall with Violet curled at their feet.

She wasn't sure how long she'd sat in the gloom when the others started stirring. Violet was the first to sit up, holding her head and moaning as she awoke. "Rose? Are you all right?"

Even though she knew there was little reason to feel comforted, Rose found the anxious fluttering in her nerves calming as she reassured Violet, "I'm all right. My head hurts, but I'm all right."

"Good." Violet scooted over and curled up next to her. "Where are we?"

"I'd say we're still somewhere in the woods," Willow answered from where she leaned against the wall with Heather's head and shoulders on her lap. "Apple, anyone?"

"You're awake?!" Rose said, a surge of relief speeding through her limbs.

"No, I'm dead."

"Is Heather all right?"

Willow bounced her knees, jostling her sister. "I think so. And I suppose that's 'no, thank you' about the apple."

Heather stirred with a groan. "Perfectly safe, they said," she muttered, "They'll never find you, they said. Also, your knees are awfully bony, Old Thing."

Rose began to smooth the tangles out of her hair and froze, a terrifying realization occurring to her. "They took the necklace." Her voice went squeaky. "The aspen and star; your Da gave them to me before we left. I'm so stupid, why didn't I hide them?"

"It's not your fault," Willow said. "We thought we were safe."

Violet patted Rose's leg. "Aye, we thought everything was all right."

"I'm so stupid," she mourned. "This never would have happened if—"

"Shh!" Willow exclaimed as the cart rattled to a halt. Outside, a handful of men's voices raised in conversation.

"...here until daybreak. Only for a few hours."

"Can't we wait for the others?"

"Too risky." The first voice had the hard edge of a commander. "We can't risk anyone coming after us. Though I doubt there'll be anyone left to follow once the others're done with them, the lucky bastards."

"I'm not so sure," This man sounded like he was right next to the cart. "They say the foresters are hard to keep down. The others might've had a fight on their hands."

"'Specially if they put up as much a struggle as that one lad did. I've never seen anything like it." This third voice had a nervous edge to it. "You think it's true what they say about the forest blood?"

There was a snort. "You've been sitting around your granny's fire too long! They're just as human as we are. Trust me," The men's voices were growing fainter. "No forest spirit ever screamed like he did."

The girls sat in shocked silence as the voices faded completely.

"Blackthorn?"

"Probably," Willow said.

"They're attacking home too!" Violet's voice had gone thin and shaky with panic as she sobbed, "They're going to kill us all!"

"It's possible." Willow pulled Heather close to her, her younger sister not even protesting. "We can't control that. What we *can* control is how we respond to whatever happens."

"I'm so sorry," Rose said. She put an arm around Violet as her friend's shoulder's shook with quiet sobs. "This is all my fault."

"Nonsense," Willow answered. "None of this is your fault."

No, it really is.

Rose opened her mouth to correct Willow, closing it with an uncomfortable sigh as her friend snapped, "No! If you blame yourself for this, I'm never speaking to you again."

"Tell us a story, Old Thing." Heather's voice sounded small in the darkness. "There's nothing else we can do, and we'll only fight with each other if we keep on like this."

Rose pulled Violet closer and scooted as close as she could to Willow and Heather. The night slipped away as Willow's voice spun the story, until one by one, the girls fell asleep. Before nodding off, Rose caught sight of the night sky through a knothole in the ceiling.

Stars are always peaceful. She settled farther into the corner, measuring her heartbeats by the quiet breathing of her friends. *At least if I die, I'll have seen the stars one last time.*

3
FOREST BLOOD

South of the Yarrow Leaf village, Willow and Heather's younger sister Clover balanced on a rock deep in the forest. Her brown hair, never quite as tidy as Willow liked, stood in a ruffled corona around her head, and her fern-colored skirt was hiked to her knees. Unusually, a red felted hat sat askew on her head, a gift for Heather that she had promptly annexed as the perfect accessory.

She tipped the hat to sit even more rakishly as she turned to survey the clearing behind the rock. They'd often come here in more peaceful times, but now, three days after the night her sisters had left, the novelty of living outside was starting to wear thin. While her mother and younger brother had fled to a hunting camp, she and most of her friends' siblings had come here on her father's orders. They hadn't heard anything from the tribe since then, and Clover had a creeping suspicion that they'd been left on their own.

I'm too young to be a mum. She scanned the clearing again, mentally counting children. Several small girls knelt with their friends around a game in the dirt, their assorted brothers chasing each other about the nearby creek. *Good thing I'm not in charge here.*

"Clover!" Violet's older sister Juniper called from where a tangle of blankets and cloaks could be seen in the mouth of a cave. "I need a hand here!"

Clover slid off the rock with a tearing of moss and side-stepped children to arrive at Juniper's side. Though Clover would never admit it aloud, she felt safer with the presence of the young woman. Even if Juniper was only five years older than Clover, she acted like the type of capable adult that would take good care of everyone. "All present and correct, ma'am!"

Juniper paused slicing bread to gesture in the direction of the creek. "Get them washed, would you? I'm almost finished."

"Glad to." Clover swept a curtsey, hooked a heel of bread, and breezed off. Collecting children from the edges of the clearing, she propelled them towards the creek, neatly tucking one under her arm as he tried to bolt. "Where do you think you're going?"

He kicked ineffectively at her ribs. "Pumme down! I don't wanna get wash!"

"That's 'washed'," she corrected. "You don't want to get *washed*, and I'm so sorry, but you don't have a choice."

He kicked a few more times before resigning himself to being carried—and washed. Once at the creek, Clover scrubbed the littlest boys and cleaned her own face and hands before running to join the crowded mob around Juniper.

"'Scuse me, fatties," Clover announced, elbowing her way through the children to hand out chunks of cheese alongside Juniper. "Calm down, everyone! There really *is* enough for all of you."

"Noisy lot, eh?" Juniper asked over the din as the last child was served.

Clover nodded, her mouth full of bread. "Not as loud as

they used to be when Heather was here." She pointed towards the hill looming behind the cave, where, somewhere, Juniper's husband was keeping watch. "Sedge says we'd better keep them quiet, though. Don't want anyone hearing us—Hoy!" She returned her attention to the children just in time to catch one stealing his brother's cheese. "Little'un, you can't do that! Give that back at once." She plonked down between the two boys, seizing the cheese and returning it to his brother.

His lower lip quivered. "It's mucky!"

"You were just as mucky earlier—Oh, all right." She handed him her cheese, plopped her hat on his head, and set to work on the dirty piece. "A little dirt never hurt anyone."

Lunch had almost finished, and most of the children were happily playing when a sliding, scraping sound announced the reappearance of Juniper's husband from the rocks above the cave.

"Welcome back," Juniper commented, handing over a portion of lunch that they'd saved. "Anything?"

Sedge shook his head. "Nothing. Smoke, and that's it. And this lot is getting too loud." He sighed and set aside the food. "It's been three days. I have no idea what's happening at the village, but it may have been a bloodbath."

"Shh!" Juniper admonished, waving a hand at the children. "Do you *want* them to hear?"

"You know I don't," he argued. "I'm sorry, but it's been weighing on my mind. And you can't pretend the littlies smell so bad you haven't caught the smoke on the wind." He sat back on his heels. "We *need* to find out what's happened."

"Is it safe?" Clover interjected.

"I don't know."

"Well, we can't stay here for long," Juniper said. "We don't have enough food to last us more than another day or so." She brushed her skirt again. "Someone's going to have to go back home."

Clover pulled off her hat and held it over her heart. "I'll do it."

The couple looked askance at her. "You're too young!" Juniper exclaimed.

Clover gave her a haughty look. "My Da thought I was good enough to help here, didn't he?"

"She does have a point," Juniper told her husband. "Look— I'll go with her tomorrow and we'll scout out the village. If we can, we'll get supplies." She smoothed out the patch of sand that Clover had been digging in. "Or at the very least, we'll know what's happened."

"That's about the best we can hope for." Sedge glanced around the cave. "I'm going to go take over the lookout. Can you try to quiet this lot?"

"Naturally." Clover clapped her hands in rhythm that was repeated by the children. "Come over here," she called. "I have a story for you."

The children began crowding in, their young faces open and filled with curiosity. "A Nightrider tale?"

"No. This is a new one. It's about the faeries of the forest."

"Here?"

Clover wriggled her eyebrows mysteriously. "Maybe. These faeries are beautiful, strong, and fast. They have green hair and greener skin, pointed ears, and even pointier arrows. It is said their blood runs free through the blood of the people of the woods." She stuck her tongue out at Juniper as Violet's older sister rolled her eyes. "Now, many years ago, there was a great disturbance in the north. A warlord came and swept down upon the mysterious forest, determined to take it as his own. His whole army went into those woods, and only half came out."

"What happened?"

Clover dropped her voice spookily. "No one knows. Some say the forest itself is haunted, others say that elves live in the trees and the ground, and kidnapped the men. But many say that the secret lies in the blood of the people of the woods."

"Us!" One of the boys exclaimed.

"Can't be," Clover scoffed. "None of *you* have green hair."

MORNING along the eastern coast dawned sleepy and mist-covered. Out at sea, a bird wheeled over a trim sailing ship, riding high at anchor along the coastal road. Its two triangular sails were furled, and a light green ensign of a shell between two breakers flew from the prow. Lines of brightly colored washing hung between the aft cabin and mainmast, a hand-painted sign at the prow declaring her to be the Sea Wanderer ship *Fire Dancer*.

At the railing, a young girl watched as a boy in an amber-colored shirt held up a handful of breadcrumbs. Settling into his hand, the carrier bird chirped softly and began stuffing itself. With a smile, the boy set the bird in its coop and returned to the railing, squinting at the shore before calling, "Father! Father!"

A man with curly brown hair opened the cabin door, letting out a sound of sizzling and smell of food. "What?"

The boy pointed at the shoreline, where the glow of a tiny fire could be seen through the early morning mist. "There's a signal on shore."

The man followed his children over to the rail. "So there is! Well done for spottin' it."

"Are we going t'take her in?"

"Yes. They've clearly been tryin' t'hail a ship." The man

glanced at the sky. "Go get your mother. We need t'find out who set that signal an' why."

THE SAND GRATED under their hull as the little dinghy came aground. "Stay in the boat, Tiren," the Sea Wanderer captain ordered, surveying the group on the beach in one long look. "I don't know why these lot've summoned us, but I don't trust them."

The boy's brown eyes reflected the morning light as he moved seats to hold the tiller steady. "Yessir."

Bysar shook water from his boots as he crunched ashore. The men awaiting him were black-haired and blue-eyed, their clothing drab and cut in the style of the northern country of Illyn. He was familiar with the bands of bandits that roved this stretch of coastal road, but this crew didn't bear the same hungry and desperate appearance of ordinary brigands.

"We saw your signal. I presumed y'needed help." *I should have come armed.*

Luckily, the man in charge of the group seemed disinclined to attack. He gave an obsequious smile. "I hope you didn't come too far out of your way to answer. Come, sit by the fire and warm yourself."

Bysar reluctantly followed him to the fire, now diminished in height. There were several stones nearby, smoothed from years of travelers using them as seats and tables. He warily sat, eyeing the wagon behind the fire. *Slaves or prisoners. But with these many guards?*

"I'm busy, mercenary. Say what you have to and let's be on with it." He shook his head at the drink one of the other men offered.

"Suit yourself." The leader took a seat near him. "Here's my problem. We're under contract to Lord Kuma of Illyn to deliver a specific person to him, and we had some trouble in the getting."

"I'm not sure I understand." Bysar glanced at the wagon before scrutinizing the leader again. He noticed now that the fellow had a newly minted cut across his forehead. "What type of trouble?"

The leader—*No, soldier*—shrugged expressively. "Speed is of the essence, and we ended up with too many captives for that type of pace. I need to reduce the load on the wagon, and I thought we could come to an arrangement that'll benefit both of us." He cast a sharp glance at the *Fire Dancer*. "Your people aren't known to stay within the law at all times, and everyone knows you'd never turn down a chance at profit."

I think I see where he's going with this. Bysar mentally counted the coins in his strongbox on the *Fire Dancer*. *I don't know if I'll be able t'pay his asking price.* "Save th'accusations for another day, mercenary. How many're you talkin' about? And how much're you asking?"

"Three. At a low price, given my current predicament." The soldier scratched a number in the sand at their feet.

Bysar raised an eyebrow at the runes, and his guts twisted as he calculated the space of the *Fire Dancer's* hold. "I c'n only spare supplies for two." He hoped he'd kept his displeasure out of his voice as he rummaged in his belt pouch. "I'll not beggar myself t'assist you."

"Good enough. I'll have my men get them into your boat." The soldier snapped his fingers at the man nearest.

THE SOUND of waves washing against their hull brought Willow softly awake. Her mouth tingled, a bitter layer coating her tongue as she blinked slowly at the lantern-lit ceiling.

Violet! Rose!

She swung her legs over the side of the hammock she had been lying in, unceremoniously tumbling to the floor as the ship heaved beneath her. "Oh, fish." The floor heaved again, and Willow steadied herself against the bulkhead with a sigh. Her last foggy memory was that of a sickening, ashy-acrid smell and a jostling as someone pulled her from the cart. *No question about it—they've separated us.* A few tears leaked onto her cheeks before she dashed them away fiercely. *Not even a chance to say a proper goodbye.*

Rubbing a bruised shin, she unsteadily got to her feet. Heather swayed in another hammock, wrapped in blankets from her head to her feet. Willow looked into her sister's face, reassured to find her breathing evenly—with a tiny hint of a snore.

"Well, you're no use for now." She straightened her shoulders and listened for the signs of anyone else. No sound greeted her ears, save the swishing of water past their hull. "Well, then," she told her sleeping sister, "let's find out where we are."

The door opened after a swift tug, Willow's confident manner immediately disappearing into a surprised squeak as boy toppled backwards into the room.

"Sea and skies," he yelped, gangly limbs flailing as Willow jumped backwards in shock. He was about Heather's age, with darkly tanned skin and brown curly hair. As he rolled to his feet, a streak of sunlight from abovedeck caught his face, illuminating his eyes with all the colors of the forest in autumn.

They stared at each other for a long moment before Willow broke the silence. "Good—morning." She frowned at the sliver of sunlight piercing the deck above their heads. "If it is morning. Ahm—if you don't mind my asking, who are you, and where are we?"

The boy brushed dust off his amber-colored shirt as he got up. Although younger, he was several inches taller than she was. "You're on the *Fire Dancer*, my family's ship. My name's Tiren. Who're you?"

"I'm Willow, of the Gaillen Woods. The other girl is my younger sister Heather. Why are we here? Where—" she swallowed hard. "Where are my friends?"

He leaned against the narrow hallway's siding nonchalantly, body easily accommodating the rise and fall of the ship. "An Illyn mercenary signaled my father, and they made a deal." A frown crossed his face. "I don't know about y'r friends, though. You two were th'only two they brought aboard." He ran a hand through his hair, making his curls stand on end. "Y'look ordinary. Why on earth are mercenaries messin' with you?"

"They kidnapped us, and—" She stopped, eyeing him cautiously. "You said your father struck a deal. What *kind* of deal? Are you going to hurt us?"

The boy stiffened, offense in every line of his lanky frame. "We're *couriers*, not pirates! And Father assumed you were *in* trouble, not the cause of it!" He gestured at the deck above them. "And he wants to hear your story, if you're able t'tell it."

Just then, Heather appeared, swaying as the ship rode over a swell. "Odd," she said, tugging her curls into order. "I didn't expect to wake on a boat. My expectations were a jail, or a castle, or maybe slung over some horses." She made a face. "Even tied to a block of sandstone and talking to the fish."

Willow raised an eyebrow, affectionate sarcasm lacing her voice. "If you stay with a face like that, you won't have to worry. The fish'll toss you out of the water."

Heather's observations had the young Sea Wanderer laughing within moments, and the two of them began talking animatedly as he led them on deck. Willow clambered up the ladder a fraction behind them, a cool breeze brushing her face as her head crested the deck. The sight that greeted her eyes was enough to stun her into complete silence, as a crimson-robed sun sank into an expanse of more water than she'd ever imagined.

We've been asleep a whole day? She shielded her eyes and peered in the opposite direction of the setting sun. There was no coastline to be seen—no land, no trees, no road. Willow's heart sank as she let her hand fall to the railing. *And no sign of the wagon.*

"Willow?" Heather's hand encircled her elbow and drew her away from the railing. "Come on, Old Thing. It's time to eat." She pointed towards the aft cabin. "And you can tell the captain what's going on."

OVER DINNER, Willow and Heather told the Sea Wanderer family everything that had happened. When they were finished, Tiren's father Bysar leaned against the bulkhead and sighed. "That's quite the story, though I almost believe it after having spoken with th'caravan leader." A thoughtful frown crossed his face. "Where'd you say y'were from? The tribe, I mean?"

"Yarrow Leaf, Sir."

"Mmm." He placed an elbow on the table. "Of th'Gaillen Woods. There's legends about that place, y'know."

Heather and Willow exchanged glances. "What type?" Heather asked.

Bysar propped his chin on his hand. "Oh, you know; that your children're born from trees, you talk to squirrels, you're invisible unless you want t'be seen, that sort of thing."

"Also that y'lure travelers off th'road, and th'forest eats your enemies," his young daughter added.

"Sea and skies," Willow exclaimed. "That's a load of squirrel tripe. Though, if hardly anyone's seen our people for so many years, it makes sense." She shook the musing away and addressed Tiren's father, "Look, I appreciate your kindness. But we need to help our friends. Is there anything we can do? Can we go after the caravan?"

"You've been listening t'to many peddler's tales." He propped his chin in his hand. "In stories, pr'haps a group of normal folk can bamboozle their way through rescuin' captives from a secured caravan guarded by more'n a score of armed men—"

"All right! All right!" Willow rubbed her throbbing temples. "Then what *can* we do?"

"We'd have t'send for help from other Wanderer vessels. Urgently. But—" Bysar gave her an uncomfortable look. "Look, the current ruler of Illyn's had revolt on his hands ever since he ascended th'throne fifteen years ago. Before I summon anyone, are you *certain* Rose—it is Rose, yes?—is who everyone thinks she is?"

Willow clasped her hands on the table, staring at her interlaced fingers as she tried to collect her thoughts. To be certain, there was the immediate 'yes' lodged firmly in her heart, but the explanation—the evidence—churned somewhere far beyond.

"I'd say yes immediately, Sir," Willow said. "But you might take that as merely a girl's stubborn loyalty to a childhood friend." She stared at the grain of the table, her mind's eye looking past the weathered wood to innumerable moments from the past. "You don't know Rose the way we do. You wouldn't see the years we've spent taking care of her broken heart when her own parents didn't acknowledge that she might have one *to* break." She sighed. "I mean, yes, Sir, she's the right age, she *looks* exactly like the mercenaries who captured us, and our own father says he was the one to discover the proof in her swaddle." Her eyes met Heather's, and she saw her own certainty mirrored in their cloudy blue depths. "Yes, Sir. I believe it with my entire heart."

Bysar let out a long, slow breath. "The Almighty must've directed your course to us, then. Sea and skies, you might have ended up *anywhere*, if someone else had seen their signal." He rubbed a finger along his chin. "If Rose *is* the last of the Thinar royal line, her capture could tip th'balance of power in Illyn towards their warlord's favor. *Or* it could incite th'rebels to finally do something other'n throw eggs at their overlord."

He held up a hand, forestalling Willow's sputtered questions. "I'm not a political man. I carry messages, and this's about the length of my knowledge." He stood up. "But I think I might have t'write a few messages of my own, tonight. We can't be certain of where they're going, an' we're too few t'do anything even if we knew." Bysar met her eyes solemnly. "Until we get help, your friends're out of reach."

4
ASHES

A grey, clouded dawn came over the Gaillen Woods. Juniper and Clover had left the cave several hours previous, slipping through the woods like a pair of foxes. Both girls dove for a tangle of bryony bushes as they crested a rise, the treetops sparse from this height. In the distance, Clover could see clear curls of smoke rising. "Look over there."

Heedless of keeping hidden, they pelted through the woods toward the village. The smoke only thickened as they went; a heavy, choking thing tinged with something even more foul. By the time they'd reached one of the well-trodden paths into town, both Juniper and Clover were doubling over every few steps, coughs racking both of their throats.

"Here," Clover gasped, pulling out a pair of handkerchiefs and offering one to Juniper.

"Thank you," Juniper wheezed before hurrying into the outskirts of the village. Clover hurried to follow, tying her handkerchief as securely as she could around her mouth and nose.

Clover knew what lay before them even before they rounded the final stand of trees, and the first sight only confirmed her worst suspicions. The Yarrow Leaf village had been burned to the ground. Stone homes were missing their roofs, timbers caving into the bellies of the charred buildings. Other buildings had collapsed into piles of smoldering timbers, thatch sending trails of thick grey smoke into the sky. Elsewhere, coals smoldered fitfully under ash blankets, the occasional breeze swirling flurries of white and grey across scorched ground.

"C-check the houses," Juniper ordered, her voice shaking. "See if you can find out where it started."

Clover nodded and went to obey, blackened grass crackling under her boots as she did. A squeal escaped her, prompting a rush of tears as a roof collapsed over what had once been a goat pen. After skirting the outside of the empty square, she final found her way to the place where her house had once stood.

"No!" She smeared a hand across her eyes, tears leaving blackened smears on her skin. "No, no, no!"

There were crunching noises as Juniper joined her. "It's all gone." A cloud of ashes rose as she kicked a crumbling timber. "No wonder no one sent us word. They're dead."

Clover cast a glance over where Juniper was staring. Closer to the square, embers still glowed near a charred white-and-black something inside the cave of a collapsed house. She clenched her fists. "Father tried to warn them! Why didn't they listen?"

Juniper gently pulled on Clover's elbow, drawing her away from the sight. "I don't know."

After what seemed like a year, they'd circled the entire village and stood on the outskirts of the devastation. Here, several bodies lay scattered like crumpled autumn leaves.

"Look at this." Juniper stopped next to one of the bodies. "Fire didn't kill this one." She pushed the man's corpse over and pointed to a messy wound on his stomach.

"S-someone fought back?"

"I think so." Juniper brushed her hands on her skirt. "There's another. And there, too."

Clover swallowed hard. "Oh—I recognize that one. It's Jute, the cooper." Her tears left another smear on her hands as she wiped her eyes. "Did anyone survive?"

Juniper walked into the forest fringe, her boots leaving ashy marks on the unburnt ground. "The fire didn't spread to the woods." She pointed at the fresh stumps of several trees, and places where bushes had been torn out of the ground. "Someone survived to push it back." Hey eyes turned northwest, in the direction of one of the tribe's hunting camps. "Come on, we need to find them."

"You go," Clover insisted, "I'm staying here."

"Don't be ridiculous." Juniper grabbed her sleeve and towed her into the woods. "There's nothing left here. No people. No homes. *No life!* When the tribe comes back—"

"If they come back," Clover snapped.

Juniper pointed in the direction they'd come from. "We have a responsibility to our children. Someone survived; we just have to find them. Come on!"

"Fine." Clover followed Juniper into the trees. Deep inside, she welcomed the anger. It stopped her from thinking about what she had lost.

They didn't make it far from their destroyed home before finding the soldiers' trail, easy to spot leading away from the carnage. Despite their efforts to avoid it, it kept crossing their path. Finally, it snaked away, and the girls were able to turn to the west. Another hour later, they had reached a narrow creek that they both agreed was near the hunting camp when a shout startled them.

"Clover!"

Clover spun around. She relaxed as her cousin stepped from behind a tree, slackening the string on his bow. "Rowan! Don't scare us like that again."

He slid the arrow into his quiver. "Why are you here?"

Clover's smile left her face as she asked, "Has anyone told you how things were at home?"

Rowan scowled. "We guessed it was bad. How bad?"

Juniper shook her head. "We can't tell you yet. Is there a Council member here?"

"Aye, Nyssa."

Both girls sighed in relief. Nyssa was like a grandmother to many children throughout the tribe. Juniper asked, "Is there anyone else?"

Rowan frowned. "Clover's da was there, but I think he's gone again."

Clover pursed her lips in surprise. "How long ago was he here?"

Rowan led them upstream, walking right alongside the water's edge. "He arrived late last night. Looked terrible, but didn't say anything about what happened." He brushed aside the boughs of a weeping willow to allow them through. "Now that you're here, maybe we can hear some news."

The refuge was not nearly as well situated as the cave they had taken the children to. Bedrolls dotted the ground in the shelter of a stand of elder bushes, and other signs of human habitation scattered the ground in between. A campfire glimmered in the evening shadows as they entered the camp, its inhabitants calling out greetings.

"Ro, where are your da and the rest of the men?" Clover asked.

He patted a child on the head as she ran past him. "Your da kicked them all out. They're keeping watch."

Da must've told them what happened.

Rowan led them around the edge of the camp to a cooking area. To Clover's great relief, she saw her father sitting against a beech tree. "Da!" She yelled, running towards him. She hadn't realized how worried about him she'd been until this moment.

Alder stood to meet her hug. "I thought the two of you were at the cave."

"We *were*," she muttered into his jacket. It smelled like smoke. *I don't think I'll ever get that smell out of my nose.*

"That doesn't explain why the two of you are here and not there." Alder looked up. "Rowan, you're free to return to your post."

Rowan nodded to the girls and left. Juniper watched him go before settling cross-legged. "We were running out of supplies. No one had come to give us news, and we were worried."

"You've been to the village?"

Clover gulped. "It was awful."

Her father knelt next to the makeshift hearth. "And then you've been..."

"Coming here," Juniper continued for him. "To see if anyone survived."

"Hmm." Alder rolled two roasted groundnuts out of the ashes of the fire. Pulling leaf wrappers off the roots, the girls gingerly nibbled at the steaming flesh. "Well, as you can see, some of us did." He frowned. "Not only that, some of them did, too."

"We know." Juniper pointed in the direction she and Clover had come. "We found their trail. It's going everywhere. They don't seem to know what direction is what."

Alder raised an eyebrow. "Wait here. I'm getting Nyssa."

The girls did as they were bidden and remained seated. Clover took a healthy bite of her groundnut, fanning away steam. "It's good to have real food again."

Juniper flicked a bit of ash away. "It isn't real food, just cooked food. There's a difference."

Clover shrugged as Alder returned, the village elder Nyssa following him. The girls greeted the old woman, who crushed them in a hug that was stronger than expected. "Welcome, daughters. I'm sorry you had to see what happened at the village."

Clover bit her lip as she pulled away from Nyssa's embrace. Alder stepped in on her behalf. "We need to decide what to do about the soldiers. I expected they'd return to Illyn now that their work is finished, but it looks like they're making for the village northwest of us."

Nyssa pursed her lips. "Where we sent Rose?"

"Exactly." Alder resumed his seat against the tree. "I was going to let them go, but we have to stop them before they get to her."

Clover leaned against her father and waited while he and Nyssa continued their debate. Eventually, their words stopped meaning anything as she drifted in and out of sleep. She woke with a start as her father shook her shoulder gently. To her surprise, silver moonlight greeted her bleary gaze as she sat up. "How long was I asleep?"

Her father chuckled as she rubbed her eyes. "Quite a while. I'm sorry to wake you; the men and I are leaving, and I'd like you to come with me."

Clover yawned. "Not Juniper?"

Alder shook his head. "She's asleep over there."

Clover turned to see Juniper sleeping in a bedroll under one of the trees. "Why?"

"She's going to take supplies to the others at the cave. And she wants to be with her husband." Alder shifted a pack on his shoulders. "I can't say I blame her. The only reason *you're* coming with me is so I know where you are."

Clover gave her father a sly look. "Mum will kill you if she finds out."

He pointed open-handed at her. "That's if she finds out." He handed her another pack. "Take that."

Alder set off through the camp. Clover trotted alongside him as they stepped outside the protecting bramble hedge and into the group of Yarrow Leaf sentries. There was more than a dozen of them, all dressed in subdued colors and carrying packs and weapons. Clover looked around the group in wonder, hardly recognizing her neighbors and friends under the stern faces.

As Alder and Clover joined them, the men's quiet talk hushed. Alder accepted an unstrung bow from one of the men. "I know you've all been told why we're leaving. We can't allow these men to live after what they did." Alder put his hand on Clover's shoulder. "They're likely frightened, being in unfamiliar territory. Use that fear against them if you can." He eyed the moon. "And they've had several days' head start. We need to move fast."

With few other words, the men began their march. The moon was sinking near the treetops as they moved along deer trails traveling northwest. Soon, they had found the trail and were gaining ground.

Clover kept pace with her father, taking one and a half steps to every one of his. After an hour or so, she quietly asked, "Da? Is everyone all right?"

Alder sighed deeply. "We got as many people out as we could." Frustration and grief tinged his voice as he said, "Some people didn't want to listen to us. They wanted the Council to protect them and negotiate. They didn't realize the type of force these men were willing to use."

"But is everyone all right?" Clover's breath was coming harder, and tears welled in her eyes. "There were bodies, and—"

Alder stopped, gathering her into his arms. "Kalina. And Rose's parents."

"Ohhhh," Clover wailed. "What will Rose say?"

Her father bent so his head was level with hers. "I know it hurts, Ducky. There's no way to pretend it doesn't, and that's all right." His arms tightened. "But if we take the time to grieve properly, we'll be allowing those men to hurt more people the same way."

Sadness settled into the hole in her stomach, like a lump of porridge gone cold and stodgy. "Yes, Da." She tried to stand straighter around the ache in her middle. "I understand."

Despite the reassurance, he still let her hold his hand for a while as they walked through the darkened woods to catch up with the rest of the men. Pale points of early morning light showed through the leaves as Alder commanded a halt. Clover curled into a ball with her head on her father's leg. Both her stomach and head pained her and she fell deeply asleep within seconds.

SEVERAL DAYS LATER, the sun beamed down on Clover's head as she followed her father through the undergrowth. Once coming abreast with the slow-moving war party, the Yarrow leaf tribesmen had taken to the tactics that had served them well in previous conflicts. Ringing the encampment, the woodsmen made sentries disappear and horses spook at nothing. The grief in her stomach had stopped aching as much, replaced by determination, and she'd done her best to help whenever her father wasn't looking. The night before, when two of the men pulled the corpse of a sentry past her hiding place and discovered her, her father had finally marched her to where they had left their packs.

"I thought I told you to stay here!" he exclaimed.

Clover crossed her arms and sat down at the roots of a tree. "I can help!"

Alder sighed and sat next to her. "If this was only about making silly noises in the dark, I'd let you, your sibling, all your cousins, and the local foxes help." He gripped his hands on his knees. "It's all fun now, but there will be fighting eventually. I don't want you anywhere near that."

"I can help!" Clover was annoyed to hear her voice break as she said it. "And I can keep myself safe!"

"You think that." Her father took her hand. "But trust me; these men are smarter than the others are letting you believe."

Tears leaked from Clover's eyes as she muttered, "Then why didn't you send me back?"

He smiled. "I want to know exactly where you are. I don't sleep well if I don't know where all my ducks are."

Clover had to smile. The phrase was a term her mother had coined when pregnant, her three daughters following her like duck-lings. "All right. I won't go off on my own. Can I at least come with you?"

He ruffled her hair the same way Willow usually did, a gesture as unusual for him as it was common to her older sister. "If you listen to me, you can come with. But not tonight. Tonight, get some sleep."

They'd doubled their time that day, and gotten ahead of the soldiers by late afternoon. The men slung their packs to the ground beneath a weeping willow and began unspooling trip lines around the area. As the light began fading, Alder came over to Clover. "Tonight, you play squirrel." He indicated the tree, "Take your pack and mine up there, and stay there until I come get you."

Clover brushed aside the weeping branches and clambered into the tower of the tree as her father gave her a boost. Kicking her feet free of her skirts, she scaled higher until she found a comfortable branch. "I'm all right here. Can I have your pack?"

"Here." He looped a rope through the straps and tossed the other end to her.

Clover hooked his pack on a dead limb close to the trunk. "Can I watch from here?"

The smile lines around Alder's eyes deepened. "If you can see out, you're too far from the trunk. Any more questions?"

"Can I eat your food?"

He laughed. "Yes. Just stay quiet and don't attract attention. And don't fall out; your mother would kill me."

She gave a cheery salute. "Yes, Sir."

The branches below fell into place as he walked away. Clover hunkered on the tree limb, the sounds of the men below distracting her well into the darker portions of evening. Finally, after eating most of a piece of bread, she settled against the tree and fell into a light doze.

Her rest was broken several hours later by the sounds of violence. The clearing resounded with chaos below her, clashing metal and dull thuds sending tremors of panic through her limbs. Frozen with fear, Clover shrank against the tree trunk as shadows danced across the willow's branches. Then, a scream sounded, and a body crashed through the veil to fall against the tree trunk.

Clover bit the back of her hand to stop her own cry. Just as she was certain she'd never see another knotberry harvest, another tall shape parted the branches.

"Clover?"

She let out the breath she'd been holding in a sob. "Father!"

"It's safe to come down now."

Without further ado, she threw the packs to her father and scrambled down to him. Falling into his hug, she started crying into his jacket. "I was so scared. And there was that man, and there was a fight *right here*, and I was so afraid."

He tightened his arms around her. "It's all right. It's all over now."

She didn't know how long he held her, but after some time she pulled her face out of his jacket. The Yarrow Leaf men were gathering again, talking in subdued tones. She looked up at her father. "Did you win?"

Alder released her with a sigh. "Yes, but at a cost. Some of the others are out digging graves."

The knots tied in her stomach started to loosen. "But you stopped them? They're all gone?"

"That's right." Her father sounded weary. "We were lucky we only lost two of our own. We're going to rest a while here and then continue on to bring Rose and the others home. I think the north village is only a day or two from here—those Illyn men had no idea how close they were." He sighed. "Incidentally, Clover, the man who commanded them is dead. His own men killed him as the fighting started. I think they blamed him for the forest turning on them."

She nodded grimly. "Good."

"I hate to agree, but yes." He gave an almighty yawn. "I'm going to take a nap. You might want to as well."

"I'll try." Clover wrapped her cloak tightly and huddled next to her father as he began snoring. The stars glimmered through a tiny patch of sky, silent witnesses as tears began trickling down her face. *Almighty, I'm young. I'm scared. I'm tired.* The cold ground pressed unfeelingly against her limbs as she hunched into a smaller ball. *A week ago, things like this only happened in stories. A week ago, all we had to worry about was what winter would be like. I just want things to go back the way they were.*

Clover remained staring into the night sky as the rest of the Yarrow Leaf force slept, and, as thousands had done before, appealed to the Almighty over and over for peace.

It was a long night.

AFTER THE SKIRMISH with the war party, they rested a day and a half in the clearing near the willow tree. Now, Clover and her father were walking alone into the village where they had sent Willow and Heather. "It's simpler," he'd explained, "The men wait in the woods to keep intruders out, you and I find Rose and the others, and we go home to start rebuilding."

She supposed this was so, but as they went through the village she began to wonder. Her father, confident as always, was making for the inn. She caught up to him and whispered, "Da, it's so quiet."

"I know, I noticed too. Of course, it *is* nighttime."

The inn was a two-story building at the edge of the square, recognizable by the pint pot hanging above the door. Alder stopped at the door. "Normally, you would not be going into a place like this, this late in the evening. And don't tell your mother, because—"

"—she'll take you to the laundry. I know, I know." Clover grinned.

"Exactly." He pushed the door open and they went in. Clover followed Alder over to the bar, where he asked the serving man, "I'd like to see the landlord. Is he about?"

The fellow laughed. "He's not, but the land*lady* is. I'll fetch her."

He vanished through a door into the kitchen. A few moments later, a harassed looking woman came into the taproom. "How can I help you?"

"I'm Alder, and this is my daughter Clover." Alder rested a hand on her shoulder. "About a fortnight ago, I sent my other daughters Willow and Heather here, along with some of their friends. We're here to collect them and bring them home."

The innkeeper startled like a child caught in a lie. She cast a hasty glance around the taproom before beckoning them behind the bar. "Come into the kitchen."

Clover and her father followed her into the steamy kitchen, where a pot of something sat low over the coals. "Sit down and have something to eat," the innkeeper admonished, dishing out bowls of stew. Clover gulped a too-hot bite of rabbit in surprise as the woman explained, "Your daughters aren't here."

Alder tensed next to Clover. "What happened?"

The innkeeper's face was strained. "Maybe a week ago, a pair of herdsmen found a young man in the woods."

"Blackthorn?" Clover said in surprise.

"Was that his name?" The woman twisted her hands in her apron. "He never said. He—he was too far gone for our healers to save. He couldn't say much, but he told us what happened. They were attacked less than a day from here." Her voice cracked. "Attacked and captured by the Illyn soldiers."

Her father's face grew stormy. "Illyn?"

Clover put her head on the table in despair. From overhead, she heard the woman say, "Aye, there's been a garrison of them here for a year or so now. Every few months, new ones arrive from Illyn and swap the old. Right now, with the lot that took your girls gone, the garrison's pretty empty." The woman's voice turned helpless. "They're pitiless, they are. If they're bored, and someone crosses them, well—" Clover felt her father tense beside her and, he shook his head at the innkeeper. "Anyway, that's why it's so quiet 'round here. Our folk are afraid to venture out when it's not broad daylight."

"Great snakes, woman, you didn't tell us? Or anyone?!"

The innkeeper turned away. "Not by our choice! They threatened to destroy our homes."

"They did that already to ours," Clover muttered into her stew.

"What?"

Clover swallowed a lump of gristly meat. "They burned it. It's gone." She glared at the innkeeper's back. "And they're coming for you."

"Clover!" Alder snapped. She looked guiltily at him, but he had already turned to the innkeeper. "They *were* coming for you. We stopped them two days ago."

"You really stopped them? They're gone?"

"Gone and dead. They won't bother you any longer. Not those ones, anyway." He shook his head. "Not that it helps our girls at all. Heavens above, don't you realize what's at stake here?"

The innkeeper shook her head. "The way things've gone, we've only focused on ourselves."

"One of those girls we were trying to keep safe—Rose?" Alder said briefly. "She's the only child of the last king of Illyn."

"Fate preserve us." The woman sat down hard on the bench next to Clover. "What can we do?"

Alder set his spoon down. "I'll leave some of my men here to help you get rid of the garrison. The rest of us will follow that caravan. If those men took them to Illyn, we're going to Illyn." He quirked an eyebrow at Clover. "And you're staying with me."

She sighed and dug her spoon into her bowl again. "Oh, fish."

That night, the Yarrow Leaf men congregated quietly in the inn. Their wounds were treated, they ate real food, and slept a full night. The following morning, newly provisioned and clothed, seven men and a fourteen-year-old trekked into the woods towards Illyn.

5

DIAMOND EYE

At first, Willow only participated in shipboard chores out of a need to distract herself. However, as the days passed, she began to enjoy working alongside Tiren and his younger sister Kyli. After sending messages off to the Sea Wanderer authorities and any other friendly ships nearby, Bysar took them on a course due north in an effort to catch up to the caravan. Despite it being summer, the wind and weather were against them, and the *Fire Dancer* was forced to tack as they struggled north.

Their progress was cautious, and much slower than Willow's anxious heart preferred, but she couldn't deny that the *Fire Dancer* had not been prepared to house two additional people. Once they'd caught sight of the caravan and marked its position, Tiren's father changed course and made for a little island. "We need water, and I'm not sure when our next chance is t'resupply."

They anchored off the coast of the island, and spent the next few hours rolling their empty water casks overboard and tethering them behind the small dinghy. After rowing the water casks ashore, Tiren returned with the boat to collect the girls.

"Are y'ready?" he called.

"You're taking the boat ashore?" Heather asked with a crafty grin.

He shrugged. "Naturally."

"So, it's a race, then."

Willow only had time to voice a startled squawk as Heather plunged overboard. Spitting water, she resurfaced and yelled, "Come on, you're not being sporting! Hurry up!"

With a sigh, Willow slid down the rope into the boat. Once they landed on the island, Tiren led the way into the undergrowth, Heather squelching as they went. After helping fill the water casks and loading them aboard the ship, the four swashbucklers went to fish for dinner. Tiren knocked Kyli into the water before plunging in after her, everyone except Willow returning to the *Fire Dancer* dripping wet and with tangled hair.

That evening, a carrier bird returned. It flew directly to Heather, perched in the rigging. She whooped as she clambered to the deck, where the other three crowded around. Tiren gently removed the capsule from its foot and headed to the bow.

Bysar was kneeling on a mass of netting so messy that Willow didn't know how he could even find, let alone mend, a hole. As they approached, he stood, stowing a bone needle in his belt pouch. "That came quickly."

Taking the capsule Tiren offered him, he wiped his hands on his tunic front. "Well, sit down." They arranged themselves along the inside of the railing, Kyli taking the coveted seat at the prow. Frowning at the cramped writing on the parchment inside, he read silently for a moment before looking up. "Well. Seems like whomever wrote this was sittin' on an urchin."

"What's an urchin?" Heather whispered to Kyli.

"A round fish with pokies all over it."

"Oh."

"What's that supposed to mean?" Willow asked "Do they believe us?"

"I think so. Though," Bysar folded the message in half. "Could be news has already reached them through other currents. They want t'talk t'you. Urgently."

"Did they say anything else?" Willow squinted at the tiny slip of parchment. "Is anyone else able to help?" She fidgeted with the edge of the net. "It's been almost a fortnight since we were kidnapped; I don't know how much longer we have." She bit the inside of her cheek. *How much longer Rose and Violet have.*

The message crumpled into Bysar's fist. "There's a trader—Th'*Diamond Eye*—comin' from Illyn. She has a full crew of traders an' guards." He gestured at himself and his children. "Not just a family boat. If they reach us sooner'n not, we *could* stand some chance."

"If we keep sight of th'caravan," Tiren added.

Willow pressed her lips together. "How soon can the *Diamond Eye* reach us?"

He examined the sky. "My guess, with this weather? It'll be another day or two b'fore we can make any meaningful threat. We'll have t'be patient."

THE *DIAMOND EYE* met them off the Illyn coastline a day later. The two vessels pulled within hailing distance of each other, and Willow accompanied Tiren and Bysar to the larger ship.

After relating the whole story—and then relating it once over for those that hadn't caught it the first time—she took a seat by the railing to listen.

"I think we caught sight of them this morn," the captain of the trading ship said, scratching his beard thoughtfully. "This time of year, that road's heatin' up with trade all along th'coast."

"Only saw one with a slave wagon, though."

Willow had been astonished by the sheer range of ages in the Sea Wanderer crewmen. The fellow who'd spoken was no older than her sister Clover.

"True enough," the man agreed. "Bad news, though. They've been joined by a squad of guardsmen from the next garrison up th'road." He spat on the deck. "N'cluding a few of those Iorca mercenaries."

Based off the general swearing and spitting that followed, Willow gathered that this referred to soldiers from a country at odds with the Sea Wanderers.

"Was there any indication of where they're bound?"

"Th'capital would be my guess; Westhaven, it's called." The captain scratched his beard again.

"Looking for fleas?" Heather whispered to Kyli on the other side of her.

"Shhh." Willow patted her sister's arm.

The brief conversation had been noticed by Bysar. He frowned at them before saying, "We'll have t'make a move before they get to a town with more'n a few soldiers garrisoned. Th'farther they get into Illyn, the harder it'll be t'do anything." He checked the sun. "We'll have t'wait another day. Are you steady on supplies?"

The *Diamond Eye's* captain raised a bushy eyebrow at one of his crew. "Are we?"

"Aye, we're steady for now." The sailor shook a hand a little. "In another few days, ehh."

"We'll have t'plan on moving fast, then." His captain also examined the sun. "We'd better get the lot of you back t'your vessel. We'll sneak closer once th'sun sets. Wouldn't want t'lose them now, would we?"

UNDER COVER OF DARKNESS, the *Fire Dancer* and *Diamond Eye* had come in close to the shoreline. Under the brilliantly colored clothing and nonchalant manners, men she'd met from the *Diamond Eye* had transformed into keen-eyed fighters before Willow's eyes. She found the change striking in a way that she couldn't quite place, as Bysar came to collect his son from the aft cabin some hours after sunset. They were all busy— Heather and Kyli playing cats-cradle while Tiren watched and Willow working on a string bag for collecting shellfish.

"Ready, son?"

Tiren bent to retrieve a sheathed sword from a locker. "Yessir."

Willow stopped winding cording into a ball. "Wait, you're taking him? I thought—" She stopped herself.

"I have reason t'believe this'll be hairy enough t'require everyone with trained hands." Bysar's voice was firm but kind. "I'm not comfortable risking you or your sister."

"Glad to know I'm expendable, Sir!" Tiren gave his father a cheeky salute before banging the door behind him.

"Lower the boat an' fasten your lips!" Bysar called after him before dropping his voice. "I'm sorry, Willow. I don't want t'leave you out, but this's too dangerous."

The door rattled again as he left. Willow tightened her hold on the ball of cording and bit hard on the inside of her cheek. *He's right. There's no reason to cry over it.*

"Sorry, Old Thing," Heather said, sliding along the bench to press her shoulder against Willow's.

"I'm *fine*," Willow insisted, rubbing her nose as she got up to leave. "He's right. You and I would only get in the way." Her breath caught tightly in her throat. "I'm going to bed."

She squinted towards land once out on deck. A few blurry lights dotted the shoreline as the men from the *Diamond Eye* made landfall, their figures swallowed up in the dusky twilight. A last evening breeze tugged at her loose sleeves and made the furled sails creak overhead as Willow descended the ladder to their sleeping quarters.

"No point in staying up," she muttered. "There won't be news for hours yet." She brushed her hair and braided it, scalp aching from the tight bun she'd been wearing that day. "No reason to stay up." She changed clothes for bed. "No reason at all." As Willow reached for the lamp, her hand stopped. With a sigh, she pulled a blanket out of her hammock, and the ladder creaked as she returned to deck.

The voices of men returning woke her. She and Heather, who'd joined her on the pretext of not being able to sleep, almost tumbled over each other in their urgency to clamber down from the aft deck. Tiren was the first over the railing, his eyes red-rimmed and curls windblown. His voice tumbled out in a stammering rush. "I'm sorry, Willow. We tried our best."

"What?" A chill streaked through her chest—the cold nothing to do with the early morning. "What do you mean?"

"Tiren, find your mother." Bysar said as he climbed over the railing after his son. He came straight over to Willow and Heather as Tiren scrambled belowdecks. "Girls, the news is both good and bad. Once I get the boat stowed, I can tell you th'whole thing, but for right now let me put your minds t'rest. Your friends—as far's we c'n tell—are alive."

Willow reminded her frozen lungs to take a breath. "Alive

—but not with you?" She crossed her arms, almost worried more about his answer. "Are they safe?"

The morning sun threw patterns of light onto his face as he turned to the railing. "Let me get th'boat, then we can talk."

Around the table a half hour later, the entire female population of the *Fire Dancer* was all ears as Bysar explained, "We made excellent time towards where we last saw th'caravan. Before we got there, though, we ran into trouble—there was another caravan between us'n our target."

"Another?" Heather looked up from an artful arrangement of breadcrumbs on the tabletop. "More slavers?"

"Merchants." Tiren's voice echoed inside his cup. "A supply train."

"Right," Bysar agreed. "We had t'slow our progress t'skirt around them." He pushed his empty breakfast bowl away and propped an elbow in its place. "It was a bit odd that th'caravan was awake at that time of night, so me'n some of th'men from th'Diamond Eye went t'go see what'd put th'cat amid th'chicks."

"Alone!?" his wife gasped. "Are your brains riddled with barnacles?"

He laughed. "You'd think so. It wasn't th'brightest move," he admitted. "They could've killed us on th'spot, if they'd seen us. They were on edge, too. Someone'd just stumbled into th'camp, a survivor from some attack up th'road."

"What attack?" Willow interrupted. She cleared her throat. "I mean, who attacked who?"

"Bandits, they thought. But th'fellow that came running in made it sound like it's a group of rebel fighters."

"So—"

"So we white-waked t'where th'caravan should've been." Tiren said, brushing crumbs off his jacket. "He was right about an attack."

"Th'*Diamond Eye's* captain said he recognized the wagon at th'campsite," Bysar continued. "Whoever it was that attacked hadn't done much t'cover their presence. Th'slaving wagon's door was open, an'most of th'guards dead."

His wife stopped clearing empty bowls. "Someone was still alive?"

Bysar nodded with a tight expression on his face. "They were interested in bein' fast, not tidy."

Willow and Heather looked at each other, then at Kyli. The Sea Wanderer girl's eyes had gone wide, and her face drawn with tension as Willow meaningfully nudged Heather.

Heather sighed and rose from the table. "Let's go, ducky." She took hold of the end of the younger girl's sash. "I've got a lure I need to finish, and I need someone else's hands to hold it while I glue."

Willow turned her attention back to Bysar as the door clattered shut on Heather and Kyli. "So, were there survivors?"

"Aye, a few of th'soldiers were still alive; 'nclunding one of th'guardsmen from th'next town." He shook his head. "All we could give was th'mercy strike. Th'ones that were more lucid told us that th'attackers were part of the rebel group called 'the Shona'." Bysar let the word hang in the air for a moment before adding, "They said th'Shona broke loose the prisoners who'd been inside th'wagon. As far's we understand, they're alive and free."

"Whew," Willow sighed. "I wish you'd started with that part." She slackened her jaw, suddenly aware that her teeth were aching from being clenched too long. "I know it's silly to complain about rain in a drought, but I wish that they'd been rescued by someone—I don't know—nicer?"

"Don't be too hard on them," Bysar said, compassion softening his face. "The *Diamond Eye* crew heard rumors when they were in harbor last week. For a rebellion force, they don't seem that bad."

"But to leave men suffering—" she swallowed the rest of her words. *It sounds horrible.*

"It happens sometimes." The Sea Wanderer handed his empty cup to his wife. "If they were in a hurry, they might not've had time t'give the mercy strike. It *was* dark too."

"Still, it's miserable." She stood to finish clearing the breakfast dishes. Chores weren't action, but it was still better than sitting and doing nothing. "I'm glad Rose is safe, though."

"Me too," Tiren agreed. He yelped as his mother slung a wet rag in his direction, peeled it from his head and started to swab the table.

"What now, then?" Willow steadied a precarious stack of bowls alongside the washtub. "How can we help?" Her mind churned with ideas—most involving harried treks through the wilds and more than one faceless person wielding sharp objects. "Can we go after them?"

Thin paper crackled as Bysar pulled a message slip from his vest pocket. "Now that she's free—and by freedom fighters' hands—there'll be th'kraken t'pay for the rebels in Illyn. If the powers there want her back, they'll hit hard 'til she's theirs again."

"So, she's still not safe," Willow said, her half-formed plans dissolving like spring snow. "I'd hoped we could find her and bring her to safety. Now that she's with these rebels, I don't know *what* to do."

"Well, our people wanted t'talk with you in detail even b'fore this." Bysar unfolded the paper and inspected it. "An' another message came from them this morning. I think they've been keepin' a close eye on things in Illyn, and this'll interest them even more now. There's nothing meaningful we can do here, but we might be able t'put Rose's story in th'ears of those who'll be able t'help." He raised an eyebrow at her. "How'd you like t'see our capital?"

Action is better than sitting and doing nothing. Willow dropped a mug into the washtub. *Even if it's taking me even farther away from the people I love.*

"I'd love to."

6

THE SHONA

After waking from a nightmarish sleep to find Willow and Heather gone, Rose and Violet sank into a depressed haze for their remaining journey. At night, Rose pressed her face against the splintery surface of the wagon box and watched the sky through the cracks between boards. Over their journey, the stars had begun to change, warning her that they were getting farther away from home with every day traveled. The only difference came when their guards' boisterous moods indicated they were near the journey's end. From the discussions the girls were able to hear, word had been sent on ahead of their imminent arrival, and plans set in motion for public festivities.

Festivities. The word, chance-heard a day or two previous, churned in Rose's mind one day as the wagon lurched to a halt. *What kind of miserable, twisted person creates a festival to surround someone's death?*

Violet's murmur of surprise drew her from her grim contemplation. "We've stopped early."

Rose blinked at the sunlight filtering through the cracks in the roof. It *was* too early to be stopping for the day, yet shouts of greeting and the sounds of camp being made could be heard outside. She scooted closer to Violet and pressed her eye to a knothole in time to see the heralded newcomers as they arrived—men dressed in hunter green uniforms over chain mail. A few seemed out of place amid the pale skinned northerners, clad in colorful uniforms and with coppery-hued skin.

"From another country?" she wondered out loud, her voice rasping with disuse.

"Maybe," Violet agreed. "Their voices sound strange. I'd never know which one, though." She peered through the crack again before sitting back with a sigh. "Are they—what's the word—mercenaries? Why are they meeting us?"

Rose sat away from the side of the cart and rubbed her temples. "I heard someone say we're near the mountains. They're worried about bandits."

"When was this?" Violet scooted close enough for their shoulders to touch. "I don't remember."

"You were asleep," Rose sighed. "One of the guards mentioned a resistance group that keeps blocking their way to the mountain passes. The other guards are probably here to make sure we get to where we're going safely." As much as she tried, she wasn't able to keep the dread out of her voice.

Violet took her hand. "I know. I'm scared too."

The next night, the two girls were huddled together in the cart when they both awoke to the sounds of fighting. Men were shouting, swearing, giving orders, and running past the cart in a confusing jumble of sound. Elsewhere, there were screams and yells, swishing sounds, and thudding. Occasional whistles could be heard, high-pitched and urgent—the commands of an enemy neither of them could see.

Rose and Violet shrank against the wall, staring into the darkness and clutching each other's hands. Eventually, the noises died down, to be replaced by footsteps and hushed voices. They both jumped as several people spoke nearby.

"What's this?"

"Not supplies. Wrong type of wagon." The voices were young and male; a far cry from the rough voices of the career soldiers and mercenaries they'd been hearing for over a week. "Damn! This isn't the supply caravan, is it."

"Prisoners?"

"Could be. Go check the lieutenant for keys."

A short while later, footsteps sounded as someone returned. "Here."

Something metallic rattled, and the door vibrated. Finally, the hatch creaked open to reveal a handful of people silhouetted against the dying fire, all dressed for travel and carrying weapons. Their leader, a tall boy with a quiver slung across his back, leaned into the cart. "Are you all right?"

"Yes, thanks to you," Rose said. She accepted the hand one of the boys offered her and slid to the ground outside the cart. Her legs ached, and she winced as she stretched for the first time in days. "Who are you? What happened?"

"We're the Shona." The boy gestured at the rest of the group, which she now noticed included several girls. "We guard the mountains against that tyrant and his outsiders."

"Soren." Another boy appeared from the darkness outside the camp ring. "We'd better go. A few got away."

"Which?"

"Some of the greens. One of the jungle crawlers."

The leader of the Shona patrol scowled. "Go after them!" he knelt next to Rose. "Are the two of you able to travel?"

Violet was sitting on the ground beside Rose, rubbing her

calves and wincing. "I suppose," the healer hesitantly said. "It's been days since we were out of that wagon."

"Well, we'll have to test out your legs. The caravan we were waiting on is still due to come this way any time." He pulled a whistle from his jacket and blew a high-pitched command. Several more of the freedom fighters emerged from outside the circle of light. Now that they were in the light, Rose noticed that their physical features were mostly homogenous—dark hair, eyes that glinted blue or grey in the torchlight, and builds much taller than the foresters she'd grown up with. By contrast, Violet's petite height looked even shorter, and her mousy hair outrageously light. For the first time in her life, Rose blended in without even trying. *Is this what it would have been like if I'd grown up here?*

"Soren, what's wrong?" one of the girls asked. "Why're there so many guards?"

"Wrong caravan." Soren gestured at Rose and Violet. "They were the only ones in the wagon, and no supplies."

"Need those supplies, though," one of the others said from the edge of camp.

"I know." Soren rubbed his chin thoughtfully as he got to his feet. "And these two need to go to the main camp. Thunderhead doesn't have time for new recruits." He turned to address one of the girls. "You're due to return, anyway. Take them with you?"

A scowl crossed the girl's face. "I expected I'd be here another day at least. Erven didn't give me a timetable."

Rose hastily looked away to cover an unexpected smile. There'd been a note of a pout in the freedom fighter's voice, sounding almost like Clover on her more petulant days. Luckily, no one else seemed to notice her amusement, as the disagreement continued over her head.

"He *told* you you'd be under my command, didn't he?"

"Well, yes—"

"Then that's that." Soren tucked the whistle into his pocket and offered Rose a hand up. "If any survivors reach the caravan, they'll be on their guard and we can wave at those supplies as they disappear into the fortress. I can't have anyone slowing us down."

Violet brushed down her bedraggled skirt, her eyes round as she peered into the darkness surrounding the camp. "Um— If there's trouble, I'd personally prefer to be out of it."

The girl huffed. "All right, all right." She flicked her hood over her head and jerked her head towards the trees. "Let's go. Stay close."

They followed the girl into the darkness, the torchlight and smoke fading into the crisp, piney scent of a high forest. Above them, the edges of mountains could be seen, cutting into the stars like jagged teeth. As Rose's eyes adjusted fully to the darkness, Violet's hand slipped into hers.

"We're safe."

"Free, yes," Rose agreed, eyes still dry despite the relief washing through her limbs. "But not safe yet."

THEY FOLLOWED THE SHONA GIRL, who identified herself as River, through scrubby bushes and willows. Eventually, the undergrowth gave way to pines as they kept going uphill. As they kept going inland, the hills began growing higher until they were in mountains. They crossed a meadow, slipping between bushes and jumping over a creek before taking a break.

Violet leaned against Rose's shoulder, her initial burst of energy long faded in the chilly mountain air. River's form made a dark shape at the water's edge, her black and charcoal clothing blending into the undergrowth as water gurgled around the mouth of a flask. "How are you feeling? Do we need to stop for the night?" Her form resolved once more as she stood, offering the water to Violet. "There's still several hours until sunrise."

"If you're sure it's safe—" Rose said, a shiver apparent even in her voice.

"It's as safe as it can be," River said reassuringly. "Anyone who wanted to follow you would have to get through Thunderhead's patrols. There's a village nearish, and I know the healer well. We can get a few hours of sleep there." She yawned. "I'm used to this, and I'm *still* tired."

Violet smiled. River had briefly sounded exactly like Willow—though she was certain that Willow wouldn't *ever* have been caught awake at this hour. "I won't say no to sleeping, if you're sure it's safe."

"Safe as anywhere else," River said. "This way."

They walked for another half hour before finding themselves on the fringes of yet another meadow. The blurry outlines of sheep could be seen in the grass, and the sparse lights of a hamlet were beginning to show through the gloom. "Thank you, Almighty," Violet sighed. There wasn't much to the tiny thatch-and-timber homes, but something about the place sang to her heart of safety and comfort.

"Told you it wasn't far," River said, leading them towards a house that stood at the edge of the meadow. A stand of aspen trees clustered around the back of the building, their white and black trunks glowing against the darkness of the pines beyond. Nudging open a gate, River led them between garden plants to the door and boldly knocked.

Several long moments passed before a light bloomed behind the door and the latch rattled. The woman who appeared in the doorway was in her forties, a shawl with long fringe wrapped over a nightgown and a long braid dangling over one shoulder. Despite the sleepiness leaving furrows on her face, she smiled at the sight of their guide—a welcoming expression that spoke clearly of years of love tangled with hardship. "River! I wasn't expecting you." She glanced at the sky behind them. "Sea and skies, it's not even dawn yet. Did Erven send you? Is everyone all right?"

River stood on tiptoes to give the woman a kiss on the cheek. "Morning, Miss Arielle. Everyone's fine." She reached back and grabbed Violet's hand, pulling her over the threshold and into a room filled with the comforting medicinal smells of peppermint, lavender, and sage.

Violet looked around, eyes unexpectedly welling with tears as they swept over bundles of herbs hung in the corner, a stone mortar and pestle, and a shelf lined with pottery jars. *A healer.*

She jumped as River squeezed her hand and explained, "I've been with Thunderhead for the last week. Just pulled these two out of a transport wagon, and thought we could rest here before I take them on to Hollow."

The healer's eyes lit with sudden understanding. "Of course, of course. Here, sit down, you two." She drew the door closed behind them before bending to stir up the fire. "Erven passed through this morning, but he didn't mention you'd been at Thunderhead. He was a bit preoccupied. Are you staying, or do you need to go back?"

Inside the lit home, Violet could see that, as she had suspected, River was younger than either her or Rose. "I'll sleep a bit, and I won't say no to food. Soren made it clear that I was supposed to go straight to Hollow." She rolled her eyes— dark, and tilted slightly under bluntly cut bangs. "He said he didn't have time or patience to mess with newcomers."

Arielle gave an exasperated sigh. "Of course he did. Come sit here, girls." Arielle pointed to a sheepskin-covered bench near the hearth before pulling two blankets from a drying rack and handing them to Rose. She swung a cauldron from over the fire and began ladling water into a teapot. "Warm up, and we'll get some food into you." Her face creased with a smile as she added, "And I'm sure some tea wouldn't go amiss, either."

Violet settled next to Rose on the bench, the fire warming her face pleasantly. "Thank you. Sorry to disturb your sleep."

"I'm used to calls in the middle of the night." Arielle set the teapot aside before adding oats to the cauldron. Dropping a chunk of honeycomb into the porridge, she turned her attention to them. "More often, it's because someone's encounter with the soldiers or taxmen didn't end happily." Her eyes had gained a curious sharpness as she asked, "Why were you in the transport wagons? Normally the warlord gets his slaves from pirates."

Violet had been prepared to answer, and was on the verge of spinning some unconvincing story when Rose spoke up. "They were going to kill us—well—" Her hands tightened around the edge of her blanket. "Me." Her eyes didn't leave the fire, voice almost toneless as she said, "According to what your warlord believes, I'm the daughter of your previous king. I'd offer you proof, but the only proof I had was taken by—oh, fish!" Rose's voice jumped back into its normal cadence as her hand flew to Violet's knee. "The necklace! The lieutenant still had it!"

"Necklace?" River interrupted. "What did it look like?" She dug in her jacket pocket. "I think I took some off the—aha!" she triumphantly produced a grimy handkerchief.

Arielle gave the girl a stern look as she poured tea into mugs. "I thought Erven taught you better than that."

"He *did*!" River retorted. "I was getting the keys for Soren, and these were in the same pocket." She unfolded the handkerchief to reveal the aspen leaf and star pendants, their chain tangled around them. "And they were too pretty to leave, with him dead and all—here." She tipped the necklace into Rose's palm.

"Thank you." Rose carefully untangled the chain and held the necklace to catch the firelight. The delicate aspen leaf shimmered like moonlight alongside the golden star, its points sharp and dangerous-looking against the flames. "I was told that these were found with me as an infant. I don't know if these are enough proof, but—"

"It's enough proof for me," Arielle whispered from the table. Her eyes shone unexpectedly with tears, and her hands were clasped so tightly around the teapot that they'd gone pale. "The queen's family was of Hold Brynjar, who fought under the silver leaf. And The star was the emblem of the house of Thinar—given to the queen for her betrothal." She blinked hard, and set the teapot down on the table with a thump. "And they gave them both to their daughter Brielle after her christening, over fifteen years ago."

"If this is a fake, it's a bloody good one," River commented.

"It's not a fake!" Violet insisted, her tea sloshing out of its mug. "We wouldn't be here if it was! We'd be—" To her dismay, tears began spilling down her cheeks. "We'd be home, in our beds, with nothing to worry about except whether Rose's parents would be fighting again. We didn't ask for any of this!"

"She's right," Rose said tightly beside her. Her eyes had taken on the same flinty cast as they had during the council meeting as she turned to the older woman. "Our Council of Elders was very careful to keep my lineage a secret from everyone—including myself." She crumpled the necklace in her lap, desperation lacing her voice. "I never asked for this to happen, but it has. And I still don't know what I'm supposed to do with it all."

"Easy, now," Arielle knelt in front of them, her dark hair

edged with gold by the firelight. "I know it's a lot to take in. You don't have to waste time convincing me of your truthfulness. I was there the day of the princess's christening; I saw the gifts myself." She gently gathered Rose's hands into her own, bringing them together in a globe around the crumpled necklace. There was something wistful—even affectionate—in the healer's voice as she said, "It's been many years, but I still remember the joy on your parents' faces at finally being blessed with a child."

"I've been out of place my whole life," Rose confessed, her eyes locked onto Arielle's. To Violet, it was apparent that both women had completely forgotten her and River's presence in the room. "Hidden, and resented. And I never knew why."

"I know." Violet was reminded of Kalina's bedside manner as Arielle squeezed Rose's hands. "But late nights with no sleep make for terrible understanding, and even less peace." She released Rose's hands and sat back on her heels. "This moment, it's most important for you to rest. Tomorrow, if River doesn't object, I'll take you to the Shona myself once you've had time to sleep." She raised an eyebrow at the young freedom fighter. "I assume you'll be off soon?"

"Aye, Erven'll want to hear about what happened. Hopefully, Soren's got his head buried deep enough in his quiver that he won't put it together on his own." River leaned against the wall. "But I'm not in a hurry yet. You mentioned food?"

THE NEXT MORNING, Violet woke to a rain-whipped meadow and steely grey sky. After a good breakfast and conversation with Arielle, the healer led her and Rose along a hunting trail deeper into the mountains. They'd been walking for several hours when the valley widened to reveal a lake. A beach ran along most of the shoreline, wind-driven waves lapping at the sand, while a man-made dike held back the water from an area of swampy land at the far end. Huge piles of nature-sculpted boulders stood in the water, their forms bringing to Violet's mind sentinels from old stories.

"The warlord's men rarely get this far into the mountains," Arielle said as they rounded a bend. "The Shona do an excellent job at guarding the passes."

"I'll assume that was said for my benefit," a boy's voice said from somewhere nearby them.

Violet jumped, looking between lake, trees, and rocks before seeing a boy perched on a rock above Arielle's head, water dripping off his dark hair. Despite the rain, he wore only a thin jacket over his grey shirt and trousers.

"Good morning to you too!" Arielle said, shielding her eyes against the thin rain as she looked up. "Is Erven here?"

The boy shook his head. "He's on patrol. I think he'll be back later today."

"What about Lena?"

"Aye, she's here."

"I'll take these two to her, then." Arielle beckoned them to follow as the boy slid down from the rock. "We'll be able to dry off once we get inside."

They followed Arielle and their new guide along a trail leading from the lakeshore into the pine forest. Several rock pinnacles loomed over the trees as they approached a steep hillside. As willows and underbrush gave way to trees, the arched mouth of a passage opened onto the trail. It was formed of branches and layered with canvas, the pattering of rain mixing with voices.

Violet blinked with surprise, instinctively drawing closer to Rose as they stepped out of the passage. At the feet of the rocks, the bushes and trees had been cleared and a roof constructed over all, raftered with pine poles and insulated with more canvas. A cave mouth opened between two rocks at the back of the space, glowing from a campfire somewhere in its depths.

The Shona were everywhere. Most looked old enough to remember the war sixteen years previous, though a handful seemed barely over a dozen years old. Most were taller than Violet, and had the dark hair and vivid blue eyes she'd come to understand were typical of Illyn natives; though a few bore the slanted eyes and crow-black hair she'd first noticed on River.

"Violet! Rose!" The younger girl's familiar voice broke the low hum of chatter, and Violet turned to see her approaching alongside a few of the other Shona. "Are you feeling more rested now?"

Rose nodded beside her. "Much better now."

"It's wonderful what unbroken sleep can do," Violet agreed. "And Arielle's tea is lovely."

"Speaks the healer," River laughed. "I knew the moment the two of you met, you'd be swapping remedies. Now, once you meet Lena, you'll be insufferable."

"Where is she?" Arielle interrupted. "I know you're eager to introduce Rose to everyone, but I'd like Lena and the rest of the command to meet her first."

"I think she's in there." River gestured towards the cave, ushering them that direction while calling, "Lena? Arielle's here!"

A waifish girl came out the low opening, brushing a swoop of dark hair out of her face and under a band of blue cloth. She had the coltish look of someone who'd just begun growing to an adult height, and her thin face lit up as she saw them. "Arielle! You're back!"

Arielle smiled and opened her arms for the girl to rush into. "Lena. You get prettier each time I see you. Where's your brother?"

"He's out, but he'll be back soon. I think." She let go of Arielle but kept talking, words tumbling out of her mouth like water running over the edge of a rock. "I'm so glad you came. We had an *epidemic* of coughs, and I completely depleted my coltsfoot—you know how hard it is to find up here, and I was hoping you'd come soon and bring more. And I collected and dried the spruce tips, and we're out of honey but I need to make more syrup—"

"Lena, Lena, slow down," Arielle laughed. She looped an arm around the girl's shoulders, gesturing towards Violet and Rose. "I'd like you to meet some people. Girls, this is Lena. She's one of the healers here. Lena, this is Violet. She's also a healer."

The young girl bounced on her toes. "Another healer! Good. We need more healers." She looked them over, sharp intellect showing through the stream of chatter as she commented, "River told me how Thunderhead found you. You don't look like you're from Illyn, but Rose—where'd you say you were from?"

Rose's hand tightened over the pocket of the apron Arielle had lent her. "It certainly is an interesting story," she began after a panicked glance at Violet.

"And one that will raise many feathers. River might have —" Arielle glanced back as River shook her head. "Oh. Perhaps it should wait for a smaller audience. It's important for Erven to hear as well."

"Oop! Yes." Lena agreed, sweeping her hair back over her shoulder. "Later, then." She tipped her head to one side, suggesting, "My brother's gone for now, but I'm sure he'll be back in no time. Perhaps you'd like to clean up while you wait?"

Both Violet and Rose turned their heads anxiously to Arielle, who had been holding a whispered conversation with

River. The younger girl nodded and stepped back as Arielle reassured them, "I'll explain things here, if you'd like to clean up. Then I need to get back to my work." She came to clasp Rose's hand. "Don't worry, this is the safest place for you in Illyn right now."

"Thank you for your help," Rose said. "I don't know what we'd do without you."

Arielle inclined her head, a twinkle starting in her eye. "It's a joy, my lady."

"Come on," River said from behind them. "Let's get you cleaned up and looking respectable."

THEY FOLLOWED the girl to a hut near the river, where rock-lined pools clustered under a canvas-and-wood roof. There, they were finally able to wash away the sweat, grime, and fear of the last fortnight. The water was freezing cold, and Rose couldn't hold in a squeak of dismay as her toes hit the pebbled floor.

"What do they do in the winter, I wonder?" Rose commented as she dragged a brush through her tangled hair.

"I don't know. Maybe heat the water somehow." Violet picked through the pile of clothes that River had left, wrinkling her nose. "No skirts here, I notice. Heather would throw a party if she saw me wearing trousers."

Rose laughed as she pulled out a shirt and pair of much-patched trousers from the pile. They fit—almost—and were at least cleaner than her filthy dress had been. "It's probably best to blend in." She gathered a scarf into her hands and was folding it to hide her hair before a sudden realization dropped into her mind. *I don't have to hide it.* Her hands froze at the thought, as River stepped into the shelter.

"All done?" The girl gave them a cheerful grin. "That's

much better. Rose, you look like you could be one of us already!"

Rose took a deep breath and began braiding her hair from her temple—a style she'd often envied on Violet and Willow but had never bothered trying for herself. Something stirred in her chest, almost like the same hope that rose when watching the stars.

I don't have to hide anymore.

River led them back towards the main hollow once they were finished dressing, keeping up a lively commentary as they went. It was somehow even easier to talk with the young freedom fighter than it had been with Arielle, and Rose found a myriad of questions pressing at the back of her mind.

"How did you end up here?" Violet asked. "And why are there so many children?"

"Most Shona were orphans," River said. "Or runaway slaves. It's difficult for villages to take them in, especially the ones closer to the fortress." Grim hopelessness tinged her voice as she explained, "It's hard to feed a foundling when you can't even feed your own."

Rose hopped over a rock, her feet protesting the activity after their time in the wagon. "Doesn't anyone fight back? Or are the Shona the only ones?" She winced as her ankle turned under her. "I don't see how you can hope to defeat anyone with so few numbers."

"We can't." River held a branch back to let them pass. "The warlord's men are too well armed. We'll steal supplies and stop tax collections, or raid slave caravans. Sometimes they'll send patrols against us, and we have to stop them." She shook the rain out of her eyes. "We hold these passes against them, and that's all we can hope for. It would be easier if the highlanders would help, but so long as we keep the soldiers away, they don't bother."

They descended into the hollow, River leading them to an alcove in the side of the brush wall. "This is normally for storing supplies. Unfortunately, supplies are short." She grimaced. "When Erven comes back, I know he'll want to talk to you. You might want to rest before then."

Rose unrolled her damp dress and spread it out in a corner. Suddenly exhausted, she pulled out a bedroll and snuggled into it. Weariness swept through her veins as her eyes closed. *Whoever their leader is, I hope he returns late.*

7
I CAN'T RISK YOU

"Violet? Vi, wake up. There's soup, and bread." Rose's muscles protested as she bent over Violet, holding a bowl of soup. They were still in the side room in the Shona outpost, cloaks and blankets tumbled about on the earth floor.

"What time is it?" Violet groaned, opening one eye.

Rose smiled. "It's almost noon."

"Noon tomorrow?"

"I guess their leader got here last night, but said to let us sleep." Rose handed her friend the bowl before starting on her own, surveying the hollow as inconspicuously as she could while finishing her meal. Many of the Shona were about; eating their food, cleaning weapons, talking, and playing games on the floor.

River sat cross-legged a short distance away, her hands busy braiding fibers into cording. She looked up as Rose approached. "Did you sleep well?"

Rose sat uneasily on the floor beside the girl. As content as she had been to don trousers the previous day, she still felt like every eye in the hollow was trained on her. "It was wonderful to sleep without being bothered. I didn't even feel the lumps in the floor." She looked around the hollow again. Lena had appeared from somewhere, and had struck up a lively conversation with Violet. "What are we supposed to do now?"

"Nothing, for now." River made a face as one of the strands of fiber snapped in her hands. "You'll have to tell your story again later today, but for right now you can do whatever you like."

"Can I help you?"

River nodded towards the basket of supplies. "Help yourself."

Working with the unfamiliar fibers was not that different from the cordmaking Rose had done for her parents, and the rhythm of twisting and tying helped settle her nerves. After a while, Lena and Violet joined them, Lena with willow bark that she was pounding in a mortar. They each took a turn with the heavy stone pestle, methodically reducing the bark into powder. The rest of the Shona in the large room came and went as the afternoon passed, going about daily chores and normal life.

After a few hours, an older boy joined their group. Rose paused her work to look up curiously as he joined them. He seemed about nineteen; an Illyn native with vividly blue eyes. A belt crossed his shoulder to hold a hunting knife and pouch at his side. Lena smiled as he took the seat next to her. "Did you have a good patrol?"

"Decent. Saw mountain cat signs near the south creek, but I think they're old." He fished in a pocket of his worn, charcoal-colored jacket and pulled out a knob of resin wrapped in leaves. "I found this and thought you might need it."

"Thank you; I did need some." Lena crinkled her nose. "It's just so sticky."

"Sticky, eh?" the boy wriggled his fingers dangerously close to her hair.

"Erven!" Lena squealed, squirming to her feet and fleeing around the circle.

Erven? Rose and Violet exchanged a surprised look. "*You're the Shona commander?*"

Amusement crossed his face. "Does that surprise you?"

"Umm, no. I—I thought you were older." Rose fidgeted with her handful of cording. Across the group, Violet raised a skeptical eyebrow.

"When you grow up fighting, responsibility comes early," River said defensively. "He's been on his own for almost as long as I've been alive."

"That's true." Erven unsuccessfully swatted at Lena with sappy fingers. "And Arielle always says that I look younger than I ought to."

With a squeal, Lena tumbled to land half in, half out of Rose's lap. Erven stopped chasing to help her up, handing her the resin. He scrubbed his fingers on his jacket and extended his hand to Rose. "I spoke with Arielle last night, and she told me who you are. Welcome, Your Majesty."

Rose frowned at his sticky hand. "I hardly think the title is needed."

"Even if not, we've waited too long for someone who deserves to carry it." He gestured towards the cave. "If you're feeling better, we need to talk."

"Can Violet come?"

"Of course." Erven offered Violet a hand up, and Rose stifled a giggle at the height difference between the two of them. Despite being somewhat shorter and less muscled than the other older Shona, Erven was still more than a head taller than Violet.

They followed Erven across the hollow and into the cave,

other Shona calling greetings or stopping him to ask questions as they went. Their progress wasn't quick, but Rose didn't mind. It gave her an opportunity to see how the Shona's leader interacted with them. She'd been worried that his manner would be more like the curt, hurried outpost commander they'd met two nights before. Instead, Rose was struck by how Erven maintained a sense of easy-going attentiveness, even when answering questions or talking with the others.

Finally, they reached the cave, and Erven struck a spark to a lamp set in a niche over their heads. The light illuminated a jumble of equipment, blankets, and baskets filled with clothes. He sat on one of the blankets, gesturing for them to do likewise. "Ah, that's better." Erven ran a hand through his dark hair wearily, making some of it stand on end. "I was out late last night and took the dawn patrol today."

"Heavens," Violet muttered.

Rose had to agree with her. Between River's unbridled cheerfulness, Lena's constant chatter, and Erven's admission, it seemed all freedom fighters subsisted on starlight alone.

"I wanted to let you sleep, but there are some things that we need to get started on." Erven's expression shifted to something calculating. "With you here, we have half a chance to unite the highlanders, but we need to figure out how best to approach them."

"I don't understand," Rose said. "You're acting like you were expecting this. Why are you so willing to believe me?"

"I *was* surprised when I heard." Erven smoothed the edge of the blanket he was sitting on. "Over the last five years, four people have announced themselves as heir, then been captured by Lord Kuma's men within a few days. He dealt with them brutally, and in public." An edge crept into his voice. "He's not known to tend towards mercy, and he likes to deal with dissidents publicly to warn others not to try him."

I wonder if the dissidents he's talking about were his people. "I'm sorry," she whispered. "I didn't know."

"You didn't know, and that's what makes the difference. You neither announced yourself, nor did he wait for you to." Erven met Rose's eyes with a level gaze. "From what I understand, Lord Kuma found you. That alone makes me want to believe your story." He tipped his head to one side, the gesture remarkably like his younger sister Lena. "But then, I also spoke with Arielle. Her knowledge of the royal family goes back decades. If she believes, so do I."

Rose shifted uncomfortably. Hearing what type of man was after her had put a chill in her blood that no blanket could soothe. "The Shona who rescued us said that some of the soldiers had escaped. By staying here, we're putting your clan in danger."

Erven sighed and rubbed his face. "Even if no one survived, Lord Kuma would have eventually found out you escaped. This country's waited long enough for someone to rally behind. If the Shona can keep you safe by any means, we will."

She shuddered. "What if they come after us?"

"They will. But we're not defenseless. We've shown them often enough that these mountains have teeth." Erven stood and stretched. "Let's get some food. Violet, I heard you're a healer?"

Rose squeezed her friend's shoulder. "She's very talented."

"I suppose so." Violet smiled gratefully at her before looking up at Erven. "Is there any way I can help?"

"Can you to help in the infirmary? Lena has some training, but not much."

Violet dusted her hands in a businesslike manner. "I'd be honored. I'm not fully trained either, but I'd still like to help."

"Good! Wonderful!" Erven stepped out of the cave. "Let's eat."

. . .

Despite Rose having only told her story to Erven, Lena, and River, the rest of the Shona seemed to know all of it by the following day. Some acted suspicious, going out of their way to watch her every movement. As she went about work in the hollow—carrying out chores in the hollow, tending the littlest children, joining a patrol to learn the area, and sharing meals—Rose felt the eyes constantly on her. On their third day in the hollow, she mentioned her uncertainty to Violet.

"Do they feel like they're watching us?"

The healer's cloudy blue eyes flickered around the hollow for a long moment before she said, "They're like that no matter what's happening. I think it must come from living on edge all the time." She motioned with her head towards the far edge of the hollow. "Like him. Tait, I think?"

Rose frowned at the boy Violet had pointed out. Despite being engrossed in a conversation with one of the girls, the patrol leader's eyes were always moving—watching, she supposed, for danger. *I never realized how much this life would change you.*

She was helping Violet and Lena take stock of their stores of herbal products when Erven popped in to remind them of dinner. As they followed him towards the kitchen, a girl burst into the hollow carrying a slate with writing on it. Her appearance sent a ripple of surprise through those gathering for dinner as she ran straight to Erven. Her face was bright red and her hair stuck to her forehead as she gasped, "Erven. Thunderhead patrol runner."

"Here, sit." Lena handed the slate to Erven before calling, "Water, someone?"

Erven's eyes darted across the cryptic writing. "Hmm. Whoever wrote this was in a hurry." He scooped a handful of ash from a trash pile and scrubbed it over the marks on the rock, dusting his hand on his jacket before turning to Rose and Violet. "It would seem the warlord's making his move."

The hum of conversation immediately died down as Erven called for attention. "There's a group of about fifty soldiers nearing the Thunderhead outpost. We think they're looking for Rose."

Rose's breath caught in her throat as her face warmed. *This is my fault.*

"If Thunderhead falls, their pass into the mountains is open. We have to draw the forces away. Carina, Tait, River, gather your lot. You have five minutes."

The hollow buzzed into activity as Shona hurried to gather weapons, warm clothes, and supplies. Erven crouched next to the runner. "Has Soren already sent a runner to Whitecaps?"

The girl shook her head. "No, and he doesn't know I'm here either." She pulled Erven closer and lowered her voice so only the few of them heard. "He told us not to interfere. He said if we tried to stop them, we'd *all* end up dead."

Erven's shoulders went tense. "Thank you for taking the risk to come here anyway. There's more at stake here than Soren realizes. Stay as long as you need to."

The runner nodded as Erven stood, calling one of the patrol leaders over. "Carina!"

The girl he'd called ran over, pulling a hood down over a face scarred from cheekbone to hairline. Concern settled over her face as Erven ordered, "Send our fastest runner to White-caps. Thunderhead says that the soldiers are making for the pass towards us. There's a meadow right before the pass, and that's where we'll have to stop them. Have Whitecaps send as many as they can."

"Will Thunderhead be sending their own?"

Erven's brow furrowed. "I—" He took a deep breath. "I

don't know what the situation at Thunderhead is like, at the moment."

"I'll send someone now." The girl dashed off, calling to someone as she went.

Erven turned back to Rose and Violet. "Violet, can you come with us?"

Violet straightened her shoulders. "If you think I can help."

"Thank you. Lena will show you which supplies to take. Lena?"

Lena had been standing uneasily at the edge of the hollow. "Me as well?"

"I have no idea what we're walking into. I think we'll need both of you. Can you show Violet what to take?"

Lena's eyes lit up. "Of course!" She took Violet's hand and pulled her off to the infirmary.

Erven watched them go before turning to Rose "I need you to stay here."

I can't let them go into danger on my behalf while I stay behind. Rose swallowed the fear that had immediately welled up in the back of her throat and insisted, "I've been hiding from them my whole life. I want to come."

Erven sighed. He wrapped a firm hand around her elbow, pulling her aside to the edge of the hollow. "Do you not understand what will happen if you're captured again or killed?" he whispered. "You're the best hope this country has for freedom, and Lord Kuma knows it. But right now, the Shona are the only ones outside of the fortress who know you're alive."

She shook her head. "Please, I have to do something."

"We need you to stay alive. Sea and skies, this is the first chance we've had to retake the country—if we fail here, there's no hope left." Erven's jaw tightened. "I can't risk losing you in battle."

His voice was so earnest that Rose found all her desire to

argue draining away. She sighed, stuffing the whispers of *useless* to the back of her mind. "If you think it's for the best, I'll stay here."

"Thank you." Erven released her elbow, eyes taking on a dangerous light. "I've got to go."

Rose watched him walk off towards the cave, weaving between the Shona as they began assembling. Most carried slings and knives, but many had proper swords that looked salvaged from previous battles. Some of the older boys carried bows and quivers over their shoulders. *They look like they're used to this.* Rose gave an encouraging smile as Violet went past, carrying a pack tied with strips of blue cloth. *They're used to this, but she isn't. Almighty, keep her safe.*

Erven reemerged from the cave, wearing a sword with a swept-back cross guard at his hip. "Attention, please." The talk died into a respectful silence. "We're making for the meadow near the arch rocks. If the soldiers get past us, they'll have a clear route to this base *and* Rose. Don't over-extend yourselves. Listen to your commanders and fight safe. Captains, I'll have you at the front with me so I can give you your orders. Let's move."

With a low buzz of conversation, the Shona flooded out of the hollow. Rose watched Violet's head disappear into the tunnel with a pang of loss. *I wanted to say goodbye.*

8

A TERRIBLE EXCHANGE

The Shona had left the lake behind them some time ago. Moonlight silvered the edges of the trees as they followed a creek towards the foothills, halting at the foot of a rise. Mountain willow bushes grew along the creek's edge, and the water rippled softly over smooth pebbles. In low tones, Erven gave his orders. "Thunderhead is defending their outpost. We'll have to hold this area until Whitecaps can get here. Under no circumstances should the enemy find it easy to reach this pass."

As the Shona spread out, Lena beckoned for Violet to follow her to a glade by the water's edge. "We'll set up our supplies here." The girl set her bag down and began unpacking. "Erven will call when it's time to go, so we need to have our things where we can reach them quickly."

Violet unslung her pack. A noise from behind her sent her heartbeat pounding in her ears, and she wheeled only to see River emerging from the willows.

"Easy, Violet!" The girl pulled a dark scarf from around her face. "I brought a few of my command. What can we help you with?"

Think. What do we need? What would Kalina say? She pressed her lips together and surveyed the creek and the rise beyond. "We'll help getting the wounded to us."

"And lookouts in case soldiers get this far," Lena added.

"Not that they should, right?" Violet asked nervously, her stomach churning. *This won't be like the injuries you've seen before,* she warned herself.

Suddenly, cries rang out from the meadow below.

"Oh no," Lena gasped "I hope Erven had the clan in place in time. They're much earlier than we expected!"

River grimly looked at the sky as an arrow zinged through the air. She gestured at the pack that Violet had yet to open. "Better keep that ready. Lena, stay under the trees. That was a long shot, but there could be more. Violet, let's go up the rise."

They reached the top and ducked behind a tree as a crossbow bolt arched toward them. Violet peered around the tree as more arrows screamed through the night air. The soldiers were indistinct blobs across the meadow, their dark shapes darting from tree to tree and—occasionally—falling under a hail of Shona sling stones. Narrowing her eyes, she finally made out the Shona; slinking like foxes from patches of moonlight into dark shadows.

Two archers joined her and River atop the ridge, each carrying a hefty bow almost as tall as they were—longbows, used by her own tribe for generations. Violet had only ever seen them used in hunting, but she knew their devastating potential in battle. Drawing their bows, the pair began picking off targets on the other side of the valley. As they did, another wave of soldiers burst from the trees on the far side of the meadow. The dark figures pressed forward, overwhelming the few Shona that had ventured too far from the trees. Screams ricocheted through the trees as the smaller fighters went down under the onslaught.

RIVER TUGGED VIOLET'S SLEEVE. "Let's go." The girl's voice had gone grim. "You'll be needed."

They turned and stumbled down the slope, Violet awkwardly keeping her footing on the slippery pine needles and rocks. River skidded to a stop near the creek, Violet almost cannoning into her. "It's not good," she told Lena. "More soldiers showed up."

Erven appeared from the trees, a ribbon of blood trailing from a cut high on his cheek. "We're retreating into the woods. The longbows are helping, but they can only pick targets one at a time."

"Have you heard anything from the others?" River asked as Lena passed Erven a bowl of water.

"I haven't seen anyone from Thunderhead. And it's still too soon for anyone from Whitecaps to be here yet."

Lena took the bowl from her brother's hands and reached up to swipe at the blood with a cloth. "Do you know how we stand with injured yet?"

Erven shook his head. "That's why I came. They might be hurt, but can't get to you."

Just then a boy staggered in, half carrying a girl. Erven swore and helped support the girl over to the healers. They laid her gently on the blanket that Violet had unrolled, and the boy handed River the girl's sling and stone pouch.

"What's happening?"

"I don't know, but there're too many for us." The boy's voice—unbroken and still squeaky—caught on the words. "Tait heard a horn call, too. I think there're more coming."

Violet turned her attention to the girl they had brought in.

She was young, thin with hollows around her eyes. An arrow had gone through the muscle atop her shoulder. Violet's hands froze at the sight, so different from any injury she'd ever seen in her training.

The girl screamed as Lena pulled the arrow free, her voice piercing through Violet's fear. *It's just an injury. Don't panic. Stop the bleeding. Keep it clean. Let the Creator do the rest.* Violet grabbed the girl's hand as Lena pressed bandages into the wound. "Hold my hand. Tight. Don't look away from my eyes."

Violet wasn't sure how much time had passed before the girl began to relax, her breathing evening out. As she straightened and went to gather more supplies, Erven's hand caught her shoulder. "If you can leave, I need you in the meadow."

"Why can't I go?" Lena asked. "I can help too!"

He shook his head, voice stern. "I need you to stay here."

Lena scowled. "But you're letting Violet go! She's no Shona!"

"She has more years of healing experience." Erven rested a hand on his sister's shoulder. "Lena, trust me. It's better for you to stay here."

Violet scooped her bag from the ground, settling its strap over her shoulder in the same way that she carried her satchel back home. The darkness of the willows as she followed Erven made it easier to say the words that had been simmering in her heart. "I'm glad you think I'm qualified to help you, but I don't really know if you've chosen the right person. I'm sorry—I'm a healer, yes, but I've never treated battle injuries."

Erven stopped in the shadow of a bush. "You're able to stop bleeding? Able to bandage? And able to tell how badly injured someone is?"

"Y-yes," Violet stammered. "I can do those things, but that's not all there is to it!"

"It's enough," Erven said. "Besides, you don't seem like you'll panic the first time you see someone die."

Violet's jaw gaped open at the implication behind his words. "She's *that* sensitive? What were you thinking, letting her become a healer?"

He turned away. "She *wanted* to be a squad commander. I didn't want her to get hurt." A horn sounded in the distance, interrupting whatever else he'd been about to say. "That's not good. Come on, let's get down there."

Don't panic, she reminded herself as she stuffed bandages into her bag and followed him. *They need you too much.*

Kalina's training had not prepared Violet for the sights and sounds of a battlefield. Whistles and shrieks of slingstones echoed eerily between the trees, coupled with the high-pitched yells of the Shona and deeper shouts of the advancing soldiers. She did her best to keep her eyes on Erven, following as closely in his footsteps as she could as projectiles tore through the pines above them. They'd almost reached the edge of the trees when Erven rushed forward, waving her urgently on.

"Violet, here!"

A boy writhed in the shelter of a juniper patch, gasping cries growing faint even as she slid to a halt beside him.

"Oh Almighty," Violet gasped, the desperate exclamation a prayer in its own right. She grabbed bandages from her pack and pressed them into the cut, but they soaked through within seconds. It took a sudden rush of fluid against her hands for her to realize that the wound went much deeper than she had first thought. Her first instinct was to reach for more bandages, but as she reached into her bag, the boy convulsed and went still.

Her stomach clenched. "I'm sorry, Erven." She swallowed against a lump choking her voice. "There's nothing else I can do."

Erven's voice came into her ears as if from a great distance. "It's all right. You did what you could."

River joined them as they stood from the boy's still form, the younger girl putting a reassuring hand on Violet's arm before telling Erven, "They're still advancing. Are we getting reinforcements?"

Erven's voice came grimly from the shadow he'd stepped into. "Whitecaps is too far for anyone to make it here yet, and no one is coming from Thunderhead. I don't know what Soren was thinking!"

All three of them jumped as a volley of crossbow bolts struck barely a dozen feet from them. The urge to run seized Violet's limbs, and only the screams of those stuck prevented her from taking to her heels. She barely heard River and Erven's continued conversation, continuing in growing urgency behind her.

"We need to retreat," River insisted. "If we wait any longer, we're going to get massacred!"

There was a slither of steel as Erven's sword went into its scabbard. "You're right. You and Violet help get the wounded out."

Violet didn't have time to process the words before a whistle pierced the darkness. It must've been a signal, as the Shona fired a mighty volley of stones and javelins before taking to their heels.

"Come on," River shouted, grabbing her sleeve. "Get everyone back to Lena that you can!"

Violet blindly obeyed, making for the ridgeline that blocked the way back to the creek. She pulled one boy to his feet, then a girl to hers; babbling some nonsense about retreating and running as Erven appeared again from the darkness.

"Have you seen Lena?"

"What?" Violet passed the girl she was helping to another Shona. "Isn't she at the creek?"

He pushed sweat-soaked hair away from his forehead. "No. And she wouldn't have retreated that far. I can't find her anywhere."

"She must be out here somewhere," Violet said, a sinking feeling growing alongside the terror in her stomach.

"That's what I'm afraid of."

They ran through the retreating Shona towards the meadow. Just as she wondered what else could possibly go wrong, a very young voice cried out in terror.

Ahead of her, Erven froze.

"Lena?" Violet whispered.

"This way!"

Violet pelted after him as Lena screamed again. Coming around a boulder, she saw that a burly soldier had cornered the girl against the rock.

"Lena, run!" Erven broke into a sprint, his sword gleaming in the moonlight. He crashed into Lena, knocking her to the ground as the man lunged.

Scrabbling backwards, Erven regained his feet. His blade met the soldier's with a clang, rapidly followed by another as the man swung again. Erven planted his feet and deflected the blow, turning to slash at the man's unarmored upper arm. The soldier growled and brought his sword up to block, forcing Erven back a pace. The swords slid against each other with a screech.

"Look out!" Violet cried.

Lena had a dagger poised to throw, her eyes wild with terror. Her scream was bloodcurdling as she hurled the dagger end over end. It hit the soldier in the throat and stuck, the hilt quivering. With a yell, Erven disengaged, twisting and jumping backwards as the soldier's sword glanced off his side.

Erven crumpled to the ground at the foot of the boulder with blood already spreading across his tunic. The soldier wheezed and staggered backwards, his eyes closing in death.

Violet stumbled over to Erven's side, planting a hand on each of his shoulders as he took a shuddering breath and screamed. Her voice sounded muffled to her own ears. "Erven! Erven, try to stay still."

He cried out again, spine arching against the ground as she frantically ripped open the ties on her bag. Linen met her fingers, and she wadded the bandages into the wound. "Lena," she called, looking up to see the younger girl standing, frozen, a few feet away. "Lena!"

Lena jumped, her breath coming rapidly as she asked, "Is he all right?"

Violet returned her gaze to the Shona leader. Erven's bright blue eyes were unfocused, and his breathing rasped in his throat. The sudden lack of sound after his earlier cries made her heart sink. "I—I don't know."

Footsteps pounded nearby, and River appeared out of the darkness. "They're not stopping their advance; we're going to get overrun—" she stopped abruptly. "Sea and skies," the girl whispered, "what happened?"

Lena's voice was rapidly approaching a wail. "Erven saved me—he's hurt—Violet said—"

Violet heard a curse from River as she moved her bloodied hands to add more bandaging. Erven gasped under her hands, chest heaving and awareness painting his face with pain as he tried to sit. "Lena!"

"Don't move!" It took all of Violet's strength to hold his shoulders down against the ground, the movement sending another rush of blood to soak the bandages she'd just placed. "Hold still, please. You can't move; you'll—"

The awareness of what she'd been about to say suddenly sunk in, as Lena started sobbing in River's arms.

I've never seen a wound this bad. I don't know what else to do. I'm helpless here—one look at Erven's eyes told her everything she needed to know. *And he knows it.*

"Violet, how bad is it?" Erven whispered, his voice hoarse.

She matched his tone, hoping Lena wouldn't hear. "It's bad."

"Am I going to die?" At her hesitation, his hand wrapped around her wrist. "The truth, Violet."

"There's no time. I—" She swallowed against the lump in her throat. "I think so."

Erven took one shaky breath, then another. Tears sparkled in his eyes, crystalline in the moonlight. "How soon?"

"I don't know!" she protested, her words blurring together in her haste to get them out. "An hour; a few hours maybe? If you don't move, and we can fix it—"

His grip tightened on her wrist. "Don't." He took a deep breath before releasing her, eyes flicking to the other girls. "River, get Lena out of here."

Lena twisted in River's grasp. "Erven, no. You can't—"

"Go!" Erven shouted. He struggled upright, pushing Violet away as she tried to stop him. "Whatever happens to me, you need to survive. You have to help Rose reclaim her country."

"Are you mad?" River snapped.

"You won't get out alive," Lena sobbed. "They'll kill you!"

"They'll take the pass if something doesn't stop them. But they'll stop chasing you if they know who I am." Erven held his sister's gaze steadily and scrambled to his feet with a gasp. "You *need* to get back to the others. Here, take this." His hands went to his sword belt, quivering as Violet helped him undo the buckle.

River's voice shook as she took the sword. "Are you sure? We could—"

"I'm sure. Now get my sister to safety." Erven's voice dropped. "That's an order."

Violet bit her lip as River wrapped an arm around Lena's slim waist and dragged her into the darkness. The girl's shouts were soon lost in the overarching clamor of an enemy yet to be withstood—or pacified.

As soon as Lena was out of sight, Erven sagged against a tree. His breath started coming harshly, and one hand went to the blood-soaked bandages around his torso. "Violet?"

"Here," She pulled the last of the bandages from her satchel and wrapped them as tightly as possible around his chest and stomach. "I'm sorry—I don't know what else—"

"It's all right," he said. A tear ran down his face. "Will you take care of my sister?"

She nodded, a rush of hot tears coming to her own eyes. "I promise."

"Thank you."

Erven set his shoulders stubbornly and stepped out of the shelter of the trees. Violet watched, frozen, as he limped across the open space with hands extended in surrender. He disappeared into the blur of torchlight that marked the soldiers' lines, before vanishing from sight.

Violet blinked away the tears and forced her feet to move. With pounding heart, she darted around the rocks, beneath the trees, and into the darkness of the pass before pausing at the top of the little ridge. Already, the torchlight was receding.

It worked, but at what cost?

9
GRIEVING

Rose had spent the evening trying to keep herself busy. Even though she hadn't told anyone but Lena and Erven her story, everyone who'd remained in camp knew who she was, and why the soldiers had dared to press into the mountains. Their curious stares unnerved her, and she had to force herself not to hide. She'd stayed up late into the night, staring at the stars and hoping to with each rustle of footsteps to hear the war party returning. Finally, she looked up from stirring a pot of oatmeal the next morning as the first of the Shona came limping into the hollow.

As the fighters trickled in, it became apparent that something terrible had happened. Many of the returning Shona were wounded, staggering under the weight of their comrades and stumbling from exhaustion. Others, it became apparent, had not returned. The expressions on the faces around her ranged from disbelief to grief, pain, and horror as they heard who had survived and who had not. One set of younger children burst into tears as an older Shona knelt in front of them and broke the news that their brother had been killed.

Rose bit her lip and looked away. *If it hadn't been for me, this wouldn't have happened.* She pushed her way towards the entrance, reaching it as Violet walked in with Lena and River.

"Rose." The healer's eyes, normally clear and calm as the sky, were filled with anxiety and a restlessness that Rose hadn't ever seen before.

Rose hugged her friend tightly to her. "What happened?"

Violet brushed a strand of hair out of her face. "There were far more than we expected." She pulled away from Rose's hug to cast a worried glance at Lena; swaying against River's shoulder next to her. "The others are saying that we've been betrayed."

"Not by me!"

"No, not by you." Violet rubbed at a crimson stain on her sleeve. "By the commander of the outpost that first called for help." She took Lena's elbow gently. "Lena, I'm sorry, but the wounded need to have a place to lie down."

Lena gestured toward the infirmary. "Over there." She wiped her eyes with her sleeve. "I'll come help you."

"Violet can handle them," River said. "Let's get you resting." With a bare nod to Rose, she guided the younger girl into the cave where they had held conference with Erven the afternoon before.

Instantly, Rose knew what was wrong. Something clenched inside her chest. "Violet, where's Erven?"

Violet took a deep breath before looking squarely into her eyes. "Erven's been captured."

For a long moment, Rose was conscious only of her own breathing and the chill spreading across her heart. Her voice came out as a croak. "That's impossible."

"It's possible, and it gets worse," Violet said helplessly. "He's dying."

Rose covered her face. "I can't believe it."

"Believe it." Lena's shaking voice came from just inside the cave. Peering into the darkness, Rose saw that her face was streaming with tears. "It was my fault."

"I don't know how it happened." River knelt next to Lena with a stunned expression. "He's usually so quick that no one gets the chance to hit him. When he knew he was dying, his last command was to make sure you had a chance to unite the clans. And then he surrendered to buy us enough time to escape." River winced as Lena started sobbing. "I need to go tell the others. And scramble a patrol to cover our trail." Dirt scraped as River stood. "Can you two stay with her?"

Violet rubbed her hands on her trousers, apparently unaware that they were as bloodied as the rest of her. "I have to get to the infirmary, or we'll lose more of the wounded. Rose?"

Rose nodded mutely as she and River switched places. Violet's footfalls disappeared behind her as Lena's sobs began dying into shuddering silence. The responsibility of what her friends had said rested like a stone on her shoulders. *This is all my fault.*

"Lena, I—"

"DON'T." Lena's shout was muffled in the folds of her bedroll. "Don't say you're sorry!"

Rose scooted closer and put a hand on Lena's thin shoulders. "I wasn't going to." *Liar.* "I just wanted you to know I'm here."

They were quiet for a long time, Rose steadily rubbing her hand in circles over the younger girl's back. Finally, Lena's breathing settled into the steady rhythm of sleep.

Under the circumstances, it's probably the best thing for her. Rose stood as quietly as she could and left the cave. The hollow was eerily quiet, and even the more hardened Shona's faces were tear-streaked. She'd meant to find the infirmary and help

Violet—though how, she had no idea—but even the short journey across the hollow was filled with so many curious and resentful gazes that she found herself fleeing out the tunnel instead.

Emerging into the sunlight, she found her way to the edge of the lake, feet slipping on the polished rocks at its edge. With the pressure inside building to a silent shriek, she snatched a rock from between her feet and hurled it into the center of the lake.

He's dead, they're hopeless, and it's all my fault! Another rock followed the first, then another. *He called me the best hope for freedom, but look where it's gotten them!* Another rock thunked into the water.

Useless, her foster mother's voice spat in the back of her mind, the word an echo of all the times Rose had said the wrong thing, made a mistake, or drawn the wrong kind of attention. *What makes you think you could have made a differ-ence, anyway?*

"I'm *not* useless." She clamped her hand around the last rock before setting it deliberately down in the shallows. She took a deep breath of piney air, her chest heaving under the weight of the single word. "And I can't hide any more, either."

Rose pulled the aspen and star pendants from her trousers pocket.

Brielle. Brielle Thinar. The name rang strangely in her mind, but something still felt familiar about the syllables. *I don't know her, but everyone thinks we're one and the same.*

Less than a month ago, I wondered who I might become. Rose carefully untangled the chain on the necklace and clasped it around her neck. The metal felt cold on her skin at first, but gradually began feeling comfortable as she watched the sun begin to set. *This was Brielle's home. Her birthright*—a tinge of smoke from the Shona's cooking fires sent a stab of guilt through her stomach—*and her people.* Rose settled her shoulders and eyed the distant snow-capped peaks with new resolve. *Even if I don't feel ready, I can't turn away.*

ROSE RETURNED to the hollow in the middle of dinner, joining River and Lena in a quiet corner. Lena's eyes were bloodshot, and she hunched over her bowl of dinner with a blank stare. Rose eyed her with concern, asking River, "Violet couldn't leave the wounded?"

River was still wearing her armor. The sadness in her deep brown eyes was joined by exhaustion as she shook her head. "There's just too many."

As they finished eating, Tait came over. His jittery nature was even more pronounced as he said, "Lena, we've got to find out from Thunderhead what happened. I'd like to take an extra patrol out tonight."

"What?" Lena looked up from her untouched bowl, her eyes glazed with tears.

As Tait repeated himself, River and Rose exchanged a worried look. Lena shook her head and sighed. "I don't know, maybe? Is there anyone who's not exhausted? Can't it wait until tomorrow?"

"I think it's important," Rose said, catching the frustration on Tait's face. *With as upset at he is, he's likely to yell at her; and that's the last thing she needs.* "If something happened to them, we could have more soldiers coming any time?"

"Do whatever you think is best. I don't care." Lena left her bowl on the ground and walked away.

"Is she all right?" Tait asked, frowning in the direction Lena had gone.

"No," River curtly answered. "Erven's all she's had since she was a baby. You think she's all right?"

He groaned. "We're vulnerable without him. She's going to have to pull herself together."

"Look, let her have her time to grieve." River picked up Lena's bowl and stood to see eye-to-eye with her fellow commander. "We can figure things out."

"Can I help?" Rose asked, immediately regretting it as both Shona turned to look at her.

"You?" Tait snorted. "What can *you* do? You're the reason we're in this mess."

"That's not fair," River elbowed him. "She didn't ask for any of this, either." She raised an eyebrow at Rose. "Did you have any suggestions?"

Rose pressed her lips tightly together and bowed her head. *No, he's right. It's not my place, and I shouldn't meddle.* She was about to wave off the question when Lena's stunned face came back sharply in her mind's eye. *She's lost so much. They've all lost so much. If I'm going to be the person they all believe I am, this is the place to start.*

"Once the shock wears off, we might want to do what we can to strike back," Rose finally said. She tugged the cuff of her shirt nervously. "It would send a message that the warlord failed."

"Maybe," Tait said, his expression softening a little. "It *would* help morale."

"We can talk about it tomorrow," River promised. "I've got to get these patrols sorted. Can you stay with Lena tonight?"

Rose took the bowl of food from River. "I'll see if I can get her to eat."

THE NEXT MORNING, and the following, and the following after that, Lena stayed in her bedroll long past sunrise. Many of the other Shona were slow to get moving as well—patrols were long in returning from their routes, daily chores were neglected, and meals were solemn. Each day, new graves dotted the hillside cemetery, as more victims of the meadow skirmish succumbed to their injuries and joined their commander in death.

Erven's absence gaped like the cavity left by a missing tooth, to the extent that even Rose and Violet noticed. It became apparent how much he'd quietly shouldered when unexpected things were left undone, patrol ranges overlapped or missed areas, and supplies began running low. Rose found herself gradually assuming more of Lena's—and by proxy, Erven's—duties, as the younger girl rarely retained enough concentration or attention to detail to fulfill them. Giving orders still didn't come naturally, but the disorder that occurred when she didn't was even worse.

It became apparent that the patrol commanders recognized Lena's weakness when they began referring questions to Rose rather than the younger girl. Soon, the daily meetings that had begun in grief became times to lay plans for the Shona's future.

"We still haven't heard much from Thunderhead since that night," Tait huffed. He pushed his hair out of his eyes and leaned against the cave wall. It was getting cramped with the four of them, plus a captain from the Whitecaps outpost, and Rose wondered if they could tidy out a storage alcove for a better meeting place. "Normally they're open about who's travelling nearby, but there's been nothing from them in days."

"They've had a shock, just like everyone else," River reminded him.

Carina, the third captain, rubbed the scar running across her face and right eye. "It'd be nice if we could get our paws on a few caravans." She squinted her good eye to examine the piles of pebbles they were using to keep track of their supply inventory. "If we don't show our faces soon, supplies will be getting awf'ly low."

"You said we should think about striking back," River said to Rose. "There's a handful of less-defended garrisons in a few of the outlying villages. If we knock them about a bit, they'll think twice about trying to come after you again."

"This is your area of experience, not mine." Rose fidgeted with the end of her belt. Even with it, her trousers fit too large around her waist. "I can keep track of supplies and remember who's been on night patrol too many days in a row, but planning attacks is beyond me." She looked over at the Whitecaps commander. "What do you think?"

The girl stretched double-jointed arms elaborately and yawned. "They need to clear the mud out of their ears and remember why the mountains are dangerous." She gave Rose a smile with the sharp edge of grief in it. "And they need to know we won't take the deaths of our own lightly. We'll be with you."

"Everyone's angry," Tait said, the emotion evident in his voice as well. "It'll be good to remind Lord Kuma that the mountains have teeth, and we'll use them to avenge what we've lost."

Rose nodded, a new, sharp-edged version of grief stirring in her chest. *They've lost more than I could ever hope to understand. Maybe it is time to strike back.*

"Hurry, get him on the table!" the man's voice was harried, nervous. "I can't work with him on the floor. Hurry, you fools! It's our skins if he dies."

Something was wrong. Erven swam through blackness, eyelids cracking open as he was lifted and set on something hard. Pain consumed his left side, each breath tearing at his ribs. Like it or not, consciousness was returning. Men swarmed around him, voices shouting about beds, bandages, medicines.

He gasped as the bandages sticking to his side were pulled away. His skin warmed under a new rush of blood.

"Bring me that tray. Hurry!"

Hands clutched at his limbs. Terrified, he thrashed in the unfamiliar grasp. This wasn't supposed to have happened.

"Hold him still!"

Pressure. Tearing pain. Erven screamed as something stabbed his side afresh. He didn't know how long it was until the pain dulled, and the hands let him go. He weakly swung a fist at the first person he could see. The man jumped. "Whoa! There's still fight in this one!"

"Good." It was the first voice, somewhere behind him. "He'll need every bit of it." Bandages tightened around his chest and belly. Pain forced his eyes closed.

"Milord wants to know how soon he'll be ready for questioning." It was a new voice, hard edged.

"Well, it won't be for a while," the first person answered curtly. "This wound would have killed him if he had arrived here any later. He's barely conscious now."

"But he will recover?"

Fingers dug into the pulse in his neck. When words came, they were hesitant. "Yes. I think he will."

He was lifted again, carried down stairs and through a door. Someone laid him on a blanket, spread on a cold floor. Crushing despair overwhelmed him. He hadn't counted on living long enough to reach the castle. If he recovered, the enemy would certainly torture him until he died in agony or gave up the location of the Shona and Rose. Weakened, he knew he would not be able to hold out for long.

· · ·

IN THE MORNING LIGHT, the fortress of Illyn rose above the seaside cliffs to meet the sun gleaming off the ocean. Ships came and went from the harbor below, a steady stream of carts bringing their cargo to the town huddled at the foot of the rise. Within the stern walls, the fortress crawled like an ant hill as countless soldiers and slaves went about their duties. Anvils rang in the smithy as armor and weapons were repaired and horses shoed. The cadence of drills could be heard from practice grounds, punctuated by the bright uniforms of Iorcan mercenaries in a sea of drably-clad soldiers.

In the courtyard buildings, and in the warren of cellars and workspaces belowground, the slaves hurried about their duties with the urgency of the expendable. As fires were stoked, food cooked, uniforms washed and mended, and stores counted, the workers exchanged whispers in stolen moments. Amid the whispers was constant talk of the skirmish a handful of days previous. Even for those who'd already heard them, the stories bore repeating.

"I heard they lost."

"Lost? You're daft, you are. They turned back."

"They never!"

"—Never found her?"

"Not her, but they took the Shona leader."

"The Shona…"

As talk circled round him, one of the errand boys emptied his twenty-third bucket of water into the giant cauldrons in the long, high-ceilinged kitchen. He adjusted his hand on the rough rope handle and made for the door. At the cistern near the wells, he paused to tip his face to the sun, the first full rays of morning shining over the courtyard walls. The bucket filled for the twenty-fourth time that morning, he made for the kitchens once more.

· · ·

"Hey, errand boy!"

Merald set the bucket on the flagstones and went over to the cook, ducking his head and wondering what new unpleasant task needed done. To his surprise, the man pointed towards a basket and jug. "That'll do for the water for now. Take those to the guards in the cells right away."

That's not so bad.

Merald hurried from the kitchens and across the courtyard with the food and drink. The flags above the watch commander's office snapped in the breeze as he entered, taking a set of winding stairs to the level of the basement that housed where the cells and interrogation rooms. He slowed his hurried steps upon nearing the cell block and poked his head in through the door. The guards were, as usual, sitting around in the little room off to the side. One of them looked up with interest as Merald set the basket and jug on their table. "Wasn't there more?"

Merald kept his gaze studiously on the ground. "No, Sir. That's all I was given."

"All right," the man sighed. "To your work, then. Sharpish, now!"

As Merald turned to leave, one of the regiment healers came out of one of the cells with a sergeant. "He needs someone to feed him. Milord wants him healthy enough to talk, but I don't have time to mess with prisoners."

"All right... ah! You, boy!"

Merald stopped as the healer brushed past him on the way out the door. "Sir?"

The sergeant beckoned him over and handed him a bowl of porridge and flask of water. The cell door opened with a screech of damp hinges as the man ordered, "Go in and give the prisoner his ration. Bang on the door when you're through."

Merald swallowed hard and stepped into the cell, the door closing behind him with another ghastly noise. Once inside, his eyes widened with surprise. The prisoner was a boy not much older than he was. A healing scratch traced along one side of his face, and bandages circled his ribcage and stomach. The whispers of the other slaves circled through Merald's mind.

Shona.

As Merald stood quietly in the doorway, the boy stirred. Caution—tempered by pain—sparked in bright blue eyes as he stared at Merald. "Who are you?"

"Merald." He held out the bowl. "I'm just here to give you your food. Can you sit on your own?"

Defiance flashed through the prisoner's face. "I'll try." He pushed himself to one elbow, his arm shaking.

"Hang on." Merald braced his back and pulled him upright before passing him the bowl. "What happened to you?"

"My clan walked into an ambush. I turned myself in to buy time."

Merald gave an impressed whistle, sitting back on his heels. "So, *you're* the Shona leader—Erven, is it?" By the boy's narrowed eyes, he guessed the name was accurate. "The uncatchable shadow—all of us were amazed they got you."

"Am I the *only* one they caught?" At Merald's nod, Erven sighed in relief. "Thank the Almighty." He let the spoon fall into the porridge with a sigh. "Do you know what they're planning?"

Merald shook his head. "The regiment healer said they're letting you recover before they interrogate you."

"I'll die too fast if they try now." Erven's snort came out as a cough.

Merald grimaced, eyes going to the bloodied bandages. "How bad is it?"

Erven coughed again and winced. "Our healer didn't think I would live more than a few hours after surrendering. I shouldn't be alive now."

"Is that good?"

"It is if they want me to recover—"

Understanding struck with painful clarity. "—but now they can do whatever they want to you."

The Shona leader looked bleakly at him. "I was supposed to have died in the forest. Now, it'll be on their terms, in a way that they choose." Erven set the bowl on the stone floor with a clink of spoon against pottery. "Sorry—I don't think this'll stay down if I try to eat." He gave Merald a hopeful look. "Will you be able to come again?"

Merald's hand tightened around the water flask. "I'll try. Just—hold on as long as you can."

10

ONE WEEK ON

Rose stood with the Shona who had led the southern dawn patrol. After over a week, Lena had stopped trying to make decisions, silently returning to the infirmary to help Violet, and most of the Shona had grown accustomed to Rose's way of asking questions and solving problems. Sensing the change, Rose had tried to be everywhere at once in the younger girl's absence—cooking and counting supplies, taking patrols alongside the others, and doing her best to learn the names of everyone she interacted with.

They're beginning to get comfortable with me. I can't let them down.

She looked up as River approached, Violet a step behind. The healer was wearing skirts again, trousers too much of a stretch for her friend's sensibilities. "You managed to pry her away? I'm impressed."

River smiled, a rarely-seen dimple appearing in her cheek. "It took three of us and a jug of oil, but we managed."

"Very funny," Violet said. "What's wrong, Rose?"

"I'm not entirely sure yet." Rose turned to the waiting Shona. "Go ahead, please. Sorry to make you wait."

One of the two leaders, a shortish boy with the bad skin of adolescence, cleared his throat. "We had our patrol out near Thunderhead." He shrugged. "We usually do that, to make sure the overlap between our ranges gets covered. We ran into a Thunderhead patrol."

"Oh, good!" River exclaimed. "Finally, we hear something from them."

The boy frowned. "I wouldn't call it good. They were very rude."

"Right," his partner chimed in. "They wanted to know 'who are you', 'who sent you', and 'why are you here without permission'. Their leader told us that no one is allowed in Thunderhead territory without Soren's permission."

"Hmph. Thunderhead *territory*," Rose snorted. Not even the pleased feeling of finally understanding one of Erven's cryptic notes on the patrol schedule could erase her annoyance at the news. She sighed, stuffing the frustration to the back of her mind. "Thank you for reporting in; you can go rest now. If I have any more questions, I'll let you know."

Rose waited until the patrol had walked well out of hearing range before turning to the other girls. "Well, that shakes the oaks."

"Sorry?"

Rose waved away River's confusion at the idiom. "It's all right. I'm just annoyed. Vi, what should I do?"

Violet showed her empty palms. "I'm still trying to figure out what's wrong."

"We've been trying for a week to get Thunderhead to talk to us. Now it's obvious," River explained, scratching patterns in the dirt with a twig. "Soren didn't like Erven to begin with.

Now that Erven's dead, he doesn't feel like answering to anyone."

Rose rubbed her forehead, uncertain if her headache was from not sleeping enough or from this most recent bad news. "I couldn't tell any of that when they rescued us. Is he jealous?"

River grimaced. "Competitive. And charismatic. He's older than Erven, but Erven always had the Shona's support."

"So now I have a warlord who still wants me dead, a clan who's still accepting me, and a competitive, *charismatic* outpost commander. Violet, do you see any problems here?"

"Sarcasm, for start," Violet snorted. "What are you going to do?"

"Violet!" Rose huffed. "I need advice, not for you to let me decide and agree to whatever it was I decided. If you were me, what would you do?"

This time, the snort was one of annoyance. "I don't know. Kill him?"

A pang of shock went through Rose's stomach. "I didn't think you'd say that."

VIOLET WAS ABOUT to start her last round of bandage changes when Rose ducked through the curtained doorway a few hours later. Her heart was still reeling from her cold-hearted statement of earlier, and she didn't meet her friend's eyes as Rose crossed the room. *She's going to be so angry with me. I probably sounded just like her awful mother in that moment.* Her hands shook as she reached for a bowl of salve, Rose's feet appearing at the edge of her vision as her friend stopped just in front of her.

"Violet, I'm sorry." Rose's hands were clutching the hem of her shirt, fingers turning white in Violet's periphery. "I knew I was getting more callous as time went on, but I didn't realize you were too. This is all my fault."

"It's not your fault. You didn't do anything wrong." The knot in Violet's chest loosened, replaced by the urge to make things right. "I didn't mean it, really."

"I know." Rose stepped back, her eyes uncertain but determined as she looked around the infirmary. "Is—" she paused, her face uncertain but determined. "Is there anything I can do to help you?"

Violet was on the verge of refusing—previous experiences with Rose and blood hadn't gone well—but something else stopped her words.

This is her version of an apology.

Violet passed her friend a jar of antiseptic vinegar. "Here, you can carry this—oh, and wash your hands."

Once Rose had cleansed her hands, they did Violet's rounds together. Miraculously, Rose managed the grisly work with only a slight paling of the face and tremor of the hands. As they finished, she said, "I really *am* sorry, Vi. I hadn't realized how much sadness you encounter every day."

Violet tossed dirty bandages in a basket to be washed. They landed with a dull thump as she agreed, "Too many people have died over this already."

"That I understand." Rose rubbed her eyes, color seeping back into her skin. "In case you were wondering, River agreed with what you said. She's still bitter over losing Erven."

Violet turned away. "Most of us are."

Rose caught her elbow. "Stop second guessing yourself. We have to move on."

"I'm moving on in my own way," Violet answered, pulling her arm away. "What else did River say?"

Rose sighed and began folding blankets, left tumbled in a stack after being brought in from drying in the sun. "She agreed that killing him *would* solve things. But you can't simply kill someone because they don't agree with you."

"I wasn't thinking. I'm sorry." Violet took a blanket from her. "There must be some other way to deal with him; we just have to find it."

OVER SEVERAL DAYS of delivering food to the dungeons, Merald was able to keep in contact with Erven. The Shona leader's condition had improved, but this afternoon Merald was worried as he entered the cell. Erven huddled in the corner under his blanket, face flushed. As soon as the door closed behind him, Merald set the food down and rushed over. "Are you all right?"

Erven shook his head, drawing his arms tighter to his sides. "The healers haven't b-been here for days. I'm freezing."

Merald set a hand to Erven's forehead. The skin felt wickedly hot. "Sea and skies," he whispered. "I need to get a healer."

"I don't know if you should."

Merald unwrapped the binding around the Shona leader's torso. "Why not?" He studied the sloppily sewn gash and swallowed hard. "Even I can tell that this is not right."

Erven blinked dizzily. "Lord Kuma. If he finds out I'm sick."

Merald frowned as he replaced the bandaging. "He might have forgotten you. The healers certainly have." He shook his head. "The guards should have taken better care of you. They'd be in trouble if they let his pet Shona die."

"And if I get well? Then what?" Erven shivered, a flash of fear running through his eyes. "They'll kill me anyway."

"You'll have to trust me. I'm sorry." Merald banged on the door for the guards to let him out. As the door closed behind him, he asked, "He's getting worse, Sir. Could a healer look at him?"

The guard snorted. "Again? Those healers are always here. Aye, go on then."

Merald hurried up the stairs to the healer's hall, stepping into a sea of confusion. The medical ward was packed with men, and more continued to stumble in. Many were helping comrades over the floor to cots as the healers scurried past breathlessly. One grabbed his arm and ordered, "You, boy. Go to the kitchens and tell them we need hot water—lots of it— here immediately."

"Yes Sir," Merald answered, already turning to obey. "What happened, Sir?"

The healer swore as another man staggered in, clutching a muddy bandage to his face. "Another attack by those blasted Shona. Curse their innards; they're coming after us in broad daylight now."

"Um, Sir, I was sent by the jail guard. One of the prisoners is sick."

"We can't spare a man to look at him. It'll have to wait. Go! Get the water."

"Yes, Sir." Merald ran towards the kitchens. Once this errand—and the four more that the healers added on—was complete, he directed his steps to the courtyard, looking for anyone he could trust. A squad was drilling on the parade grounds, and he recognized one of the more compassionate captains amidst the spectators.

"Sir? May I have a word?"

The man turned to him, expression going from average boredom to one of confusion. "What do you want?"

Merald's guts twisted, but the memory of how hot Erven's forehead had been loomed against his mind. He dared to look the man in the eye. "S-sir, the Shona prisoner is very sick. It's been over a week, and he's not getting any better. None of the healers have been to see him for days."

The captain cursed, his eyes narrowing. "I warned them this would happen. Do they listen to me? No." He regarded Merald more closely, a measure of respect in his gaze. "And you feel so responsible to come and talk to me?" He gave a hint of a nod, like something had been decided for him. "For that, I'll help you." The captain gestured to a heap of logs next to a chopping block. "Stay here and stack this firewood. We're so short on healers that they've sent patrols to round up more from the other towns. When the next one arrives, I'll escort you both down there."

Merald bent to begin collecting logs. "Yes Sir."

Scarcely an hour later, several guards trotted through the main gate on horseback, one with a woman riding behind him. Merald paused his work long enough to see the captain approach from inside a barracks. The man dismissed the guards before leading the woman over. "Let's go."

They descended to the dungeon, where the captain's appearance made the drowsing guards look alert. "Hey, lazy loafs! This lady is here to look at the prisoner. Don't annoy her, or you'll be mucking out the latrines for a week hereafter." He snatched the keys off the ring on the wall. Unlocking Erven's cell, he said, "Report to the infirmary when you're done here. Boy, come let me know how he is."

"Yes, Sir." Merald ducked his head in thanks before following the healer into the cell.

The woman was kneeling over Erven's still form, an accusing tone lacing her voice as she demanded, "Why didn't they take care of him?"

Merald shrugged helplessly. "The Shona stepped up their attacks. There was one several days ago, and another yester-day. They forgot about him."

"Barbarians," the woman cursed, a tear running down the side of her nose. She took a deep breath, her expression hardening as she began numbering items on her fingers. "Go and get me these things, please—hot water, another empty bowl, rags, and a clean blanket."

Merald obeyed promptly, returning with the items she'd requested. The healer took the bowl of water from him. "Thank you. Come over here and help me."

As she began cleaning the wound, Erven began to stir. Finally, he blinked at the ceiling, then at Merald and the healer. Recognition lit his face, and he whispered, "Arielle?"

The woman gasped. "You're awake! What happened? How'd you get this way?"

Erven's breath caught with a gasp as she began unwrapping the bandages around his torso. "They did what they could, but I think something's wrong." Another breath hissed from between clenched teeth. "Is Rose all right? The Shona?"

"They're all right," Arielle said, dampening a rag and swabbing it across the wound. "Rose is helping them stay together, and they're attacking the soldiers with a new vengeance. They all believe you're dead." She wrung out the rag in the dirty water and soaked a new one in fresh. "I thought so, too."

"He should be, for all the help the healers gave," Merald said hotly. He gritted his teeth against the sight of the swollen gash revealed by the healer's ministrations. "They don't care about anyone other than their own men."

Arielle clicked her tongue. "Whoever stitched this was in too much of a hurry. I have to open it again." She put a hand to Erven's shoulder. "Can you bear it?"

His jaw clenched. "Do I have a choice?"

Arielle shook her head. "It'll certainly kill you if it stays like this." Pulling a vial from her bag, she dipped a thin knife blade into the solution within. "This will hurt," she warned.

"Understood," Erven gasped.

Merald gulped before asking, "What should I do?"

"Hold him still." Arielle made a face. "If you can."

A trickle of yellowish fluid emerged as she began to cut the stitches in Erven's side. Blood drained from Merald's face, but he took a grip on Erven's shoulders as the healer tipped disinfecting solution into the wound. A scream ripped out of Erven's throat, and he fought against Merald's hands as Arielle swabbed out the wound with another cloth. Despite her swift work, it was long seconds before Erven relaxed, shuddering in Merald's grip.

Once the wound was clean, Arielle began stitching, every jab of the needle making both Erven and Merald cringe. Merald's arms shook from the effort of keeping the Shona leader still throughout, and it was a relief when Arielle finally set the needle down.

Once the wound was wrapped in a layer of clean bandage, Arielle pulled a glazed pottery flask from her bag and instructed Erven, "Here, open your mouth. I can't kill the pain entirely, but this might help."

"That's terrible," Erven muttered after a single swallow of the liquid. Merald had to agree—the smell had been sharp and resiny, and the drops clinging to the mouth of the flask were dark and sticky-looking.

"You won't think so when it lets you sleep," Arielle informed them both. She unrolled a clean shirt and passed it to Merald. "Help him with that?"

"Are you going to tell the others I'm alive?" Erven asked as his head emerged from the neck of the shirt.

"Your sister's stopped eating out of grief; of course I'm going to tell them."

"They'll need to move fast," Merald warned. "Once the soldiers find out he's getting better, they'll kill him."

"I'll get word out as soon as I can." She pursed her lips, a shadow crossing her face. "Conscription officers arrived at my village and told me I could consider myself in service here until I was no longer needed. With as stern as they were, I couldn't really argue."

Merald banged on the door to get the guards' attention. "Will they let you go at all?"

"They'll have to." Arielle shouldered her bag. The lady's eyes were determined as she said, "And if they don't, I'll make sure my supplies run out and can only be replaced by myself."

As they left the cell, she addressed the guards, "I'll be back this evening. I can't believe you barbarians would treat him that way." Unsatisfied at the grunt she received, the woman pulled open the door with a muttered curse.

Outside the jail, Merald asked in an undertone, "His clan *will* want to rescue him, right?"

"Of course." She snorted. "I think my greatest difficulty will lie in convincing them to do things *properly,* instead of rushing in and getting killed."

11

ALCHA DAR

"Da? How much longer?" Clover rubbed an insect bite on her leg and sighed at the state of her skirts. At this point, they'd been dragged through enough mud puddles and streams that they were chafing against her socks.

"I don't want to move in until we're sure the coast's clear." Alder picked up his bow, leaning against the stump she was perched on. "The others'll be back soon, and maybe we can get something to eat."

The rocks they were hiding amongst stood at the top of a little rise near the coastal road. Despite the warm summer sun, the breeze that blew from the east was cool, bearing a hint of salt and humidity. Clover wrinkled her nose against the wind, not wanting to say she hadn't meant 'how long until we move again'. The weeks of travel had stretched into a fortnight, and her feet and mind had grown so tired that the home of a month ago now seemed like a half-remembered dream.

After realizing how many Illyn troops frequented the border where the woods met plains, Alder and the other Yarrow Leaf men kept to the sparse trees along the road, scouting each human habitation before approaching openly. So far, all they'd learned was that slaving caravans often passed along this road towards the Illyn capital—including on with a single wagon and twice the number of guards.

"*Including some of those foreign bastards,*" *the wheelwright said, spitting into a pile of sawdust.*

"*Foreign b—*" *Alder glanced at Clover, making friends with the shop dog and pretending she wasn't listening.* "*Hmm. Which foreign are we speaking about? Kittai Islands? Sea Wanderer?*"

Clover forgot that she wasn't supposed to be listening. She'd heard her father mention the names of countries across the sea in passing, but had never put too much thought into them otherwise.

The wheelwright scoffed. "*Do you live under a barrel, man? You can't even go a fortnight without running into some of those jungle crawlers.*"

"*Ahh, that type of foreign. Fascinating.*" *Evidently, something had ticked over in her father's mind.* "*And you said they were guarding that caravan?*"

The man spat again. "*Seemed so. There was some to-do about it, thought I.*"

"*Could be.*" *Alder dug in his pocket for a coin and flipped it to the man.* "*Cheers. Clover, let's go.*"

The wheelwright's story had been confirmed by others along their route, and as they'd neared the Illyn capital it became clearer that the caravan had passed by. No one said anything, but Clover knew that the closer they got to the Illyn capital, the lesser the chances grew that Rose, Violet, and her sisters might still be alive.

Alder raised his head from checking his bowstring as one of the other men came around the rocks. "Anything?"

"Nothing but the usual farmers, herdsmen, and layabouts."

Alder coiled the bowstring and slid it into its bag. "Just as well. Let's go see if we can get any news." He smiled at Clover. "I'm hungry, too."

WILLOW WORRIED that her eyes were about to pop out of her head from staring too much as the *Fire Dancer* nosed her way into harbor. As they'd forged their way south, the air had grown warmer, and the water clearer. When they began seeing more and more islands, Bysar was able to confirm that they were coming quickly to Alcha Dar, the Sea Wanderer capital. He sent and received messages almost every day, up to the day that mountains on the horizon proclaimed their arrival. As they drew closer, Willow learned that the entire island chain was comprised of ancient volcanoes, now devoid of fire and breaking down into the sea. The tallest, Tiren explained, had been the seat of Sea Wanderer government for generations.

A town spread along the lower slopes of the mountain, houses terraced into its side or teetering on stilts. A bustling market grew around the edges of the harbor, merchants hawking their wares alongside houses and livestock pens. The air was filled with the sounds of people speaking more languages than Willow had ever heard, mixed with the sounds of blacksmiths at work and animals complaining as they were unloaded from ships. The crews of the motely array of ships hailed from an even wider range of countries, all clothed in colors that made her eyes ache.

"Heather," she whispered as they passed a ship crewed by men with skin so dark it was almost black. "I had no idea people came in these colors."

Heather patted her hand approvingly. "I'd no idea either. See?" Her younger sister pointed at a pair of boats unloading baskets of shellfish. Several of the women working on the docks had hair even lighter blonde than Willow's. "I thought *you* were the strange one. How can all these people be the same?"

"The Sea Wanderers aren't all one people," Tiren's mother said as she joined them. "Anyone who swears t'obey our law may claim allegiance." She pushed up bright orange sleeves to lean against the rail. "My family's ancestors hailed from th'deserts far south of your woods." She tousled Kyli's curly hair as the girl went past. "Our children can't claim t'be anythin' but Wanderers."

Willow gave her sister a significant look. "Our family doesn't match our tribe either."

Heather was about to reply when Tiren's father hollered from the bows. Everyone worked to secure the ship before following him to a house on stilts at the edge of the forest. "My cousins," Kyli explained, as a girl and boy a few years younger than her jumped off the platform and ran to hug her parents.

At dinner, they sat outside with Tiren and Kyli's cousins on the edge of the platform, their legs dangling off the side. The ships bobbed at their moorings below, cries of seabirds filling Willow's ears. She balanced her bowl on her knee and scooped the food with her piece of flat bread. Sea Wanderer food was spicier than anything she'd ever eaten, but the strong tastes were growing on her. As the others went to explore after dinner, Willow went into the house. The adults had also finished their food and were sitting around the low table talking.

"Oh, Willow. I was about t'come find you," Bysar said. "A message came right before dinner from th'intelligence agent that's been receiving our messages. He'd like t'see you tomorrow."

"Oh? Oh." Willow glanced out the door. "Just me?"

"Heather too, if it'd make you feel better," Bysar smiled

understandingly. "He said he'll send someone t'bring you to him tomorrow."

"Ah." She tugged the hem of her shirt straight across her hips. "Is it all right if I excuse myself? I have some thinking I need to do."

THE FOLLOWING AFTERNOON, Willow returned to the *Fire Dancer* with a face like a thundercloud. Tiren and his father greeted her with smiles that quickly turned to confusion as Bysar asked, "How was it? I expected you—" he stopped as Willow shoved past Tiren to kick a swab bucket across the deck. "Oh."

Heather trailed a few steps behind her, explaining, "It didn't exactly go well."

"No, it certainly didn't." Willow's face burned as she forced back the venom in her words. "I thought your people really cared about this! You made it sound like they'd have some kind of interest in what happened outside their bloody horrible borders, but no!" She angrily tugged the hem of her shirt. "This 'intelligence agent' I was supposed to speak with was a patronizing clerk who didn't give one whit about what I had to say."

"Didn't he take your story?" Bysar frowned.

Willow gave a short laugh. "Oh, of course he did. He took down my details, certainly."

"I think it was a form he was filling out," Heather contributed.

"Exactly!" She was gratified to see both of the Sea Wanderers' expressions as she explained, "He wanted to know my background. He wanted to know 'where were you born, where do you live now, what brought you out of the woods'; *that* type of thing." She covered her face and wailed, "And I *told* him what happened to Rose and the rest of us, and where they are now, and all that, but he brushed it away and said it was in the reports you'd been sending. He said that since she and Violet seem to be safe, that's the last he needs to do with it, and that he'd 'pass the information on'."

Pain in the back of her throat warned that she was about to start crying in earnest. She stamped down the gangway, into the trees between the harbor and houses. Kicking her worn shoes off, she clambered up one of the rocks and huddled against an overhanging tree. Everything on the waterfront blended together in one glimmering haze from this distance, and any noise was drowned out by the hum of insects in the surrounding trees. Hidden from view, she felt safe enough to curl into a ball and cry until the tension in her shoulders lessened.

Once the tears subsided, she uncurled and pulled her report from her sash. Over the weeks of travel from the Illyn coast to the Sea Wanderer capital, she'd spent hours and several precious sheets of paper composing her report for the Sea Wanderers' intelligence office. The culmination of her carefully written document was a heartfelt plea for the Sea Wanderer government to send assistance to the rebels in Illyn. She scowled at the inky sheets.

"I should've stuffed these up his nose. Maybe he would've read them, then." She crumpled each sheet into a ball and hurled them violently into the trees.

As the last sheet disappeared, she swung her legs over the edge of the rock and sat kicking the air. *If they won't help us or take us seriously, I'll have to find someone who will.*

Before the rebellious conclusion had time to take root, a rustle sounded—just out of eyeshot from the top of the rock. Expecting to see Tiren or Heather's curls at any moment, she told the trees, "You can tell them I'm fine now. I just needed a minute."

"I'm glad you're feeling better."

The young man who came into view stopped below the rock, sunlight reflecting off blond hair lighter than her own. To her embarrassment, he was holding several of her crumpled notes. "Sorry if I startled you."

"You didn't," Willow lied. "I was just going back." Ignoring the scrapes that the rocks left on her palms, she slithered down and hurried to put on her shoes.

The fellow followed her to the other side of the rock. "My name's Ethan." He held out his hand. "And you're Willow?"

Willow paused halfway through pulling on her sock. "I am." She returned the handclasp suspiciously. "Did my sister tell you where I was?"

Her new acquaintance handed her the other sock. "I stopped at your ship t'see if I could talk t'you now that I've read th'report you left with the clerk." He scratched the back of his neck. "They mentioned you'd come this way in a less 'n pleased manner."

Only her mother's admonition to never let ones' mouth hang open stopped her from gaping at the young man, who was now smoothing the wrinkles from her notes. "You're—"

"Council Intelligence." He tucked the smoothed sheet into a vest pocket and started on another. "Sorry I wasn't able t'meet with you earlier. I meant to, but I had t'clear out a backlog in my reports first. You know, filing." A crooked eyetooth lent the smile he gave her a conniving twist. "Whosiswhatsit accuses his cousin Arno th'Smelly of poisonin' his shellfish beds, an' he wants t'make sure a proper report gets filed—" He flapped a hand. "I had t'file it all. In the dustbin."

AFTER STOPPING at the *Fire Dancer* to let the others know where she'd gone, Willow followed Ethan to an office deep inside

Alcha Dar. As he led her through rocky corridors, Willow had to concentrate on listening to his brisk descriptions of what everything was. The main corridor spiraled through the mountain, occasionally opening in arched windows onto a center hall. After leaving the main route, they walked through a maze of torchlit byways and twisting stairs. Even in an obviously utilitarian area, the floors were tiled in bright colors and silk draperies covered the doors.

"This is very different from where I had my last meeting," Willow said, thinking of the wooden building off the dockside where she'd been frustrated by the patronizing clerk.

"I was allowed t'pick where I wanted my office," Ethan said cheerfully. "Naturally, I picked a place that was th'hardest t'get to." He pushed aside a drape the same crimson color as his shirt and unlocked the sturdy door hidden behind it. "Come in, and make yourself comfortable."

Willow raised an eyebrow as she went inside, wondering what the unnaturally tidy Rose would make of the state of the little room. The light from several lamps dangling from the ceiling fell on a desk covered in documents stacked to the breadth of her hand. A sword leaned against the chair behind the desk, and a pair of boots tottered in a corner. The damp air from outside mixed with a dusty note from narrow shelves lined with battered books and scrolls. She swallowed the first few things that came to mind before saying, "I thought you said you'd cleaned off your desk."

Ethan closed the door behind them and gave the room an amused glance. "I guess it's not too tidy in here." He picked up a pile of documents from a second chair. "Here you are."

Willow tried to contain her chuckle as she sat. The room was exactly like how she imagined her sister Heather's office would look. "How do you find anything?"

"For me, it's easy." Ethan took the chair behind the desk,

setting his armful of papers atop one of the other stacks. "*I* remember where I leave things. It's when anyone else comes looking for something that there's trouble. The times when someone's tried t'snoop, *they've* been frustrated, an' I've noticed immediately when things're out of place." He pulled the wrinkled pages of her report from his vest and set them in the center of the desk.

"Right, then." Some of the jollity left his voice as he produced a bottle of ink from the mess. "I've read everything you told th'clerk, but there's a few things I'd like t'clarify. Bear with me if it feels like you're repeatin' yourself."

Willow settled her shoulders and took a steadying breath. "Whatever you need."

"Right." He dipped his pen and started making notes in shorthand across the top of a blank page. "I'll go through this first bit fast. T'start, your village is in the Gaillen Woods? Same village as Rose an' your other friend are from?" At her nod, he continued, "You have three siblings, all younger, parents both living?"

"Mum took care of all of us, Da—" Willow let her words trail, uncertain how to properly capture her father's nature. "Da is everywhere you need him the most. He led the tribe's forces when there was fighting along the Illyn border, and he's the one that found Rose shortly after."

"I think you put that in the clerk's account." Ethan stopped writing to consult a wrinkled page. "Yes. What happened the night after the festival?"

WILLOW AND ETHAN talked for hours, as she carefully explained everything that had occurred over the last fortnight. The intelligence agent—who upon further conversation turned out to be scarcely a handful of years older than herself—left few stones unturned, expanding his understanding to supplement what she'd already reported. An hour into their conversation, she stopped and asked, "Why care so much about where we're from and who our families are?"

Ethan had set down his pen and flexed the fingers of his left hand. "When information's limited, y'have t'make your decisions based off prediction. The more I understand, th'better I can guess what Rose an' Violet'll do now they're freed. It puts more weight b'hind my recommendations t'my superiors if I've put in my time doin' research."

He'd then picked up the pen again. "And as it happens, you're th'best source of information I have."

By the time her entire story had been laid out, picked apart, and gone over again, it was nightfall. Ethan walked her back to the *Fire Dancer*, explaining, "Now that I've heard th'full story, I can begin work on my own report t'my superiors. My thanks for takin' so much time t'make sure I've understood everything."

Willow pulled down her sleeves against the damp night air as they stepped onto the docks. "No, thank *you* for making sure the whole story could be told properly. I feel much better, knowing that someone with some power knows about the situation." As they approached the jetty where the *Fire Dancer* lay docked, she asked, "Um—is there any way I can help you?" She fanned a curious insect from her face. "This is so important, and so much time was lost in us getting here. I'd like to be able to help any way I can."

The torchlight from the jetties ringed Ethan's head in light. She almost missed the caution in his eyes as he regarded her for a moment. Then, just as quickly, he nodded. "I can certainly use your help. I'll have t'see about gettin' you an' your guardians guest quarters in a more secure spot than your vessel." He frowned. "Tomorrow, probably. I'll get t'work on things, and y'can expect someone t'show you all to your new accommodations by midday."

"She's baaack!" Tiren called from the *Fire Dancer,* and the cabin door banged open.

"I should go," she apologized. "Thank you again."

"Goodnight!" Ethan gave her a flick of a salute and turned away.

Heather, Tiren, and Kyli were waiting for her at the top of the gangway. "Top o' the evening, Old Thing!" Heather slung an arm around her neck. "Come on, we saved you dinner."

12

MOUNTAIN DUCKY

The raids had gone better than Rose had expected. Fueled by anger, the Shona had worked together better than ever, and shown little mercy. She had been grateful to realize that the Shona squad commanders were highly capable when it came to raiding. The storerooms were fuller, and morale higher after a series of well-timed victories. Less enthusiastic about their recent successes was the Thunderhead outpost commander Soren. That afternoon, Rose and some of the others went to try and talk the stubborn leader into working with them. The visit had not gone well, and the entire journey back had seen her seething inside.

She was in the middle of mending shirts with Lena when Violet came to join them. Rose had found long ago that the repetitive task of stitching helped settle her mind. It was one of the few things she'd been able to do so well that not even her foster mother had found fault with her work.

"How'd it go?" Violet asked, taking up a shirt and inspecting the threadbare edges.

"Soren's a tough one." Rose examined a frayed cuff. *Difficult to fix, but at least it's not an entire clan counting on me. Why can't everything be this easy?* "I'd hoped going to see him in person would make him a little more amiable, but he's resisting all attempts to talk sensibly."

Lena set down her mending abruptly. "I'm going to go see if the hunting party's back yet."

Violet's eyes followed Lena as the younger girl left. "Is she still not sleeping?"

Rose shook her head. "She was crying again last night."

"Oh," Violet bit her lower lip. "Maybe I should take another look at her."

"I don't think she needs a healer. She needs time." Rose held her needle in her teeth, speaking around it as she hunted for the thread. *Just like all of us.* "Anyhow, Soren admitted readily enough that he's always been jealous of Erven. He was—" She squinted at the eye of the needle. "Charismatic is a good way describe him." She twisted to stretch out her back, musing, "I don't think he realizes the danger of us being divided. He *did* agree to come here for another meeting tomorrow, so that's a step along the right path."

"Do you want me there?" Violet picked up the shirt Lena had been working on.

"Of course I do!" Rose set down the needle. "Depending on how tomorrow goes, the others may push to eliminate him, and—" She sighed. "And I don't know how I'll answer them."

It was midafternoon by the time Rose finished her mending. As had been happening recently, her journey across the hollow kept getting interrupted by questions. Dinner was a similar affair, and it was a long time before she was able to settle in to review reports from the day's patrols. *No wonder Erven hardly slept.*

She'd been working for almost an hour when Arielle's voice

startled her out of her study. "They told me you'd taken over some things, but I didn't realize how much!"

Rose looked up to see the village healer silhouetted against the light from the banked kitchen fires. "Good evening!" She stood and dusted herself down. "What brings you here so late?"

"I needed to talk with the commanders. And you, I suppose." Arielle glanced around the alcove where Rose had taken to sorting through reports. "Where's Lena? Has she been eating?"

Rose shook her head. "Violet and the rest of us are doing what we can. She's not sleeping either." She twisted the edge of her tunic. *And the nights when she does sleep, she wakes crying in the middle of the night.* "I've taken over all of her decision-making, but it's not helping."

Violet came in as she said it, the healer's face lighting at the sight of Arielle. "Arielle! How are you!"

"I'm well. I hear you've been doing wonderful things with your trainees."

"They're eager to learn whatever I can teach them." She sighed, and a shadow passed over her face. "I just don't have the answers for some things. Do you have time to speak with them before you leave?"

Arielle nodded. "I'll stay the night. Heavens above, my village can spare me another day." She turned to face Rose. "Though what I have to tell you might leave you awake along with Lena."

A chill went through Rose's stomach. "What is it?" She glanced into the hollow. Most of the Shona were already in their beds. "Do I need to get the others?"

Arielle pursed her lips. "Actually, it might be best that I tell you before Lena hears." She sat across from Rose, explaining, "Several days ago, I was summoned to the fortress. On the way there, my escort mentioned that their healers were overburdened with casualties from your attacks."

"I suppose so," Rose mused. "The clan is so bitter that they didn't show much mercy."

"As soon as I arrived, one of the captains took me down to the jail. One of their prisoners was suffering from an untended wound."

Faint hope began to grow in Rose's heart. *It can't be.*

"There's no good way to say it, girls." Arielle's voice dropped to a whisper, "Erven's alive."

Rose's eyes widened, and she quickly schooled her expression into submission. *How? What happened?*

"I didn't think he'd make it to the castle." Violet's voice had gone shrill. "How did he survive?"

"I can only assume their healers were able to save him. But the wounds went bad, and he was very ill when I saw him yesterday."

"Were you in time?" Rose asked, finally trusting her voice. "Is he going to live?"

"I believe so." Arielle took a deep breath. "The captain gave me a pass for the next week or so. I'm going again tomorrow."

"Going where?" River asked as she and Tait came into the alcove with Lena on their heels. "Evening, Miss Arielle." She nodded to Rose. "I hope you don't mind; we wanted to hear if there was any news."

Rose patted the ground next to her. "There is, and you'll want to sit down." She looked at Arielle. "Better just tell them straight out."

Arielle eyed her with doubt furrowing her brow. At Rose's insistent look, she finally said, "Children, I came to tell you that Erven survived capture. He's alive."

Lena started crying. "I thought—you all said—everyone thinks—"

Rose put an arm around her, her own heart heavy. "I know. We all made a mistake." Her eyes darted to Violet. *Some of us more than others. She's not going to forgive herself for that.*

"He's alive?" River said, blinking away tears.

"Alive," Arielle said, "but still in danger."

"Obviously," Tait scoffed. "What are we going to do?"

Violet shuddered. "We need to get him out. They'll torture him to death if we leave him!"

This statement made Lena cry harder and the others talk over each other.

Violet could have said that better. "Calm down, everyone." Rose's voice was pitched more for quiet conversation, and she had to repeat herself twice before her voice cut through the din. "How likely is he to recover now?"

"He was strong and in good health before he was injured," Arielle said. "And he's always been a quick healer. I don't think the wound will be our concern."

"We need to rescue him!" River exclaimed, Tait nodding at her side. "I'll start picking the force."

Arielle looked sternly at them. "You can't make that decision without your commander."

Rose's spine prickled as everyone turned to her. *Commander? Me?* "What do you say?" she asked Violet.

The healer tilted her head to one side. "I have no idea." She bit her lip. "And please, don't ask me. My mistake is what left him in enemy hands in the first place."

Rose got to her feet, pacing the room with the pressure of the others' eyes on her. *I can't decide this. I organize supplies and make sure everyone feels heard; I don't make military decisions! I should let someone else do this—someone who isn't totally useless.* She stopped with her back to the others, a hand going to the necklace tangled in her shirt. The star and aspen pendants were cold against her fingers, their edges as sharp as the thorns on the flower she'd been named for. As her mind calmed, one thought bubbled to the surface. *Erven didn't think I was useless, and he proved it by sacrificing himself. I can't leave him to die.*

As VIOLET WATCHED, Rose's shoulders straightened, and her head lifted. When she turned around, the light in her eyes had kindled into something Violet could only describe as 'dangerous'. "Start planning," she ordered, looking from face to face. "We've got to get him back."

STICKS CRACKED in the undergrowth as the Yarrow Leaf scouts returned, and Clover raised her head expectantly as her father greeted his men.

"Find anything?"

One of the men slung a flask of water down for Clover. "There's a town ahead, biggish. An inn, stables, a market. We can get food and news there."

Alder smiled. "Excellent. I'm so hungry I could eat a wolf."

Clover pulled her jacket into position under the straps of her pack. It was too big—loaned from one of the men and filthy from days of being slept, traveled, and eaten in. Despite the chilly nights, the days were warm, and she was sweating as they broke from the undergrowth onto a road.

Towns had been getting bigger the deeper into Illyn they went, and coming into the marketplace was a shock after so long travelling. The squat wooden buildings teemed with activity, from the shouts of merchants to the squeals of children at play.

"Try not to say where we're from," Alder warned. "We'll regroup on the other side."

His men acknowledged with grunts and sarcastic remarks before dispersing, some to buy food and others to collect gossip. Eventually, Clover and her father were left to themselves. "Let's go find a jacket that fits you," he said. "Your mother would take me to the laundry if she saw you looking like that."

"That's what you say about everything."

"It's true!" he protested, leading her to a ramshackle stall in the marketplace.

As they sorted through piles of second-hand clothing, Alder carried on a cheerful banter with the stall owner. Clover pulled out a floppy-brimmed hat with a ratty feather stuck through the hatband and promptly stuck it on her head. Her father gave her a despairing glance, but continued his conversation with the shopkeeper. From her eavesdropping, Clover learned that the warlord's men had come through the town twice to recruit men for the army.

"First, they only took volunteers," the proprietor offered, shaking out a faded tunic. "Then they came with a conscription notice. All the young men are gone, and I've heard the lot here now is under orders to take all battle-ready men with them."

"That so?" Alder asked. He tossed a jacket to Clover. "Try that on."

As she complied, the woman eyed her. "Hazel eyes on that one. You're from farther south?"

"Oh, here and there." Alder leaned against the stall and scrutinized Clover. "Might need a skirt, too. Or britches."

"Da!" Clover exclaimed, turning pink.

"Whaaat?" he threw up his hands. "You're so hard on your skirt with all that climbing and jumping and rolling in mud—"

"Mum'll take you to the laundry!"

He winked at her. "Don't tell her, then. If we're going to be in the mountains, Ducky, you'll want britches."

The stall owner snorted. "She might as well. Seems most of the girls around here want britches. The Shona are the reason, I'm sure."

Alder raised an eyebrow. "Ah, yes. I'd heard of them here and there. They're quite active then, these…?"

With an efficient flap, the woman shook the wrinkles from a pair of trousers and tossed them to Clover. "Shona. The rebellion group in the hills. I hear they've rallied to some girl they claim is King Alaber's daughter."

Clover pulled up her hat brim to stare at the woman, who nodded approvingly. "Ah, that's interesting, isn't it? Aye, she appeared a few weeks ago after the Shona lost their leader in battle. That's the reason His Mightiness is all of a sweat." She pointed. "See, there are the recruiters now."

Clover looked where the woman pointed. Several brawny men in dark green uniforms were moving purposefully through the marketplace, their expressions distant from the hostile glares thrown at them by the townsfolk. They stopped in front of a sign board and tacked up a poster.

"Hmmm." Alder squinted in the direction of the sign board. "Ahh, I can't see that far. Clover, go check that sign while I pay the nice lady."

Dropping a respectful curtsy to the woman, Clover dodged between sheep, carts, and passerby to join the other onlookers. Squirming between bystanders, she was able to make out what the notice said. "The lady was right," she muttered as she scampered back to her father. "It says that all men have to report by dusk or get forcibly conscripted."

The woman gave a satisfied snort. "There, what did I tell you? Take my advice, master," she addressed Alder, "Take your little-un and get out of here as fast as you can. If you need to hide, take one step too deep into the mountains. The Shona will find you." She spat on the ground. "Bloody wraiths, they are."

"We'll look into it." Alder said amiably. "I do have some experience with wraiths, myself. Let's go, Ducky."

They found most of the Yarrow Leaf men near the booths selling hot food. Others ambled back from a dice game in a nearby alleyway. Once they were safely in the sparse foothill trees, Alder called a halt. "If you were getting supplies, hand them out. If you have news, let's hear it."

"Lord Kuma's inviting the towns and farms to contribute food and supplies for the army. They're not happy, but they're too scared to refuse."

"I talked to a lady who said her husband left to avoid being conscripted. He'd heard rumors of a village in the mountains that was gathering forces."

"Do we know why all this is happening?" one of the others asked.

Alder tipped his head. "I have some ideas, but I'll hear you all first. Anyone?"

His brother-in-law eyed him. "I think it's Rose." As everyone turned to look at him, he explained, "I bought the recruiting sergeant a drink. He said the warlord had captured a surviving heir to the ruling line." He raised an eyebrow meaningfully. "She escaped. Now he's assembling men to hunt her down."

"Most of the men in town are being conscripted tonight."

Alder nodded. "We heard the same thing. That's why we left when we did." He scratched his head. "It might be Rose who these rebels are rallying to, or it might not. The Shona might be our best chance to find out either way. I was told that they patrol the lower mountains, and that we might find them if we go deeper in." He shouldered his pack. "Or they might find us."

Clover devoured the food one of the men had brought her, slipping an apple into her pocket as they began walking again. Despite their adeptness at woodland travel, the foresters found the terrain of the Illyn Mountains a challenge. By late afternoon, everyone was tired and eager to find a campsite for the night. They were moving along a small stream when something rustled in the undergrowth. Clover froze, hands tightening into fists.

"Wild animal?"

Alder took a slow breath. "Human, I think." He rested a hand on Clover's shoulder, asking for quiet as they started moving again.

They'd barely taken a dozen steps before another voice rang out. "Stop right there, hooligans!"

Clover chortled despite herself. "Hooligans."

The men clustered tightly, their weapons out. Alder pushed Clover behind him. "We're not—" he frowned. "Whatever a hooligan is, it's not us. We're looking for the Shona."

The tribesmen found themselves surrounded by hard-faced youths dressed in layers of grey and black clothing. The leader, a bony boy with smoldering eyes, stepped from behind a tree and slackened the string on his bow.

"Who are you, and why are you looking for us?"

Alder shifted his weight to his back foot and put his hands in his pockets. "We're looking for some of our tribe that were kidnapped and brought here. We were told the Shona knew everything that goes on in these mountains."

Clover tried not to grin at her father's tone. In spite of their present situation, he spoke like the Shona leader was just someone he had met at the tavern.

"That's so. But I'm sure they forgot to mention that

outsiders are not welcome." The boy eyed the weapons in their hands. "Especially armed ones."

Alder laughed. "In these parts? We'd be insane not to go armed." He gestured at the boy's bow. "Stop straining your bowstring and let us talk like civilized men. I'm sure you can see we aren't here to threaten you or your tribe."

"The warlord has many spies, outsider." The boy slackened his string and replaced the arrow in his quiver.

"Thank you." Alder sat on a rock at the foot of a tree. "I don't know about you," he said to the boy, "but we've been hiking for a long time today."

With a small smile, the leader agreed, "We're the farthest out patrol today."

"Bit young for that." Alder pointed out, pulling a bag of dried fruit out of his pocket and offering some to Clover.

"No younger than your tagalong."

Clover spluttered on her fruit, causing her father to thump her back. "True. She's the only of her siblings that I have right now, and I didn't want to let her out of my sight." He tugged on her earlobe. "She gets in too much trouble otherwise."

Clover glared equally at her father and the Shona leader, who were both chuckling. "I'm not a little girl. Stop gabbling and ask him about Rose!"

That sentence—or maybe the name—did the trick. The Shona stopped laughing and looked hard at her. "Who?"

Alder sighed. "Rose. She's the reason we're here. There are rumors that she's escaped and is somewhere in the mountains."

The boy gave him a flinty look that Clover wished she could replicate. "Our clan leader was killed when the warlord's men came for her, and she's taken over."

"But you're not happy about that," Alder noted.

"She's just another outsider; like you and your men and

your tagalong." The boy's hand drifted to the hilt of a long knife. "I'll have to ask you to come with us. Our outpost leader Soren will want to speak with you."

"Just as well." Alder said easily, offering a hand to Clover. "I want a word or three with him myself." He called to the rest of the men, "All right sluggards, let's go!"

Amid groans and grunts, they followed the Shona deeper into the mountains, Clvoer eavesdropping on her father's conversation. Sure enough, her father's innate talent for making people at ease showed itself immediately. *Even if their outpost leader hates us, there'll be at least one of the Shona who likes Da.* The rest of the men weren't doing terribly either, befriending the younger Shona and trading stories and food as they marched.

It was close to nightfall when a pair of massive rocks blocked their path. As they approached, several Shona stepped into their path. "Who goes there?"

The boy leading them spat on the ground. "Don't be stupid, you can see it's us."

"Aye, I see it's you, Arrick. What I don't see is who these others are." The sentry gestured at the Yarrow Leaf men. "They're armed, and outsiders. We've had enough outsiders here today."

"I know, but they have business with us. Let them in."

The boy shuffled his feet and clasped his spear tighter. "I can't without permission."

"Are you forgetting your place?"

The sentry looked at the ground. "No, sir."

"That's better."

They straggled between the rocks to enter a sheltered valley. The mouths of ancient mining tunnels opened into the hillsides, crumbling timbers shored up with new logs and broken piles of rock. A few small buildings stood around the center of the valley, and more of the grey-clad freedom fighters bustled around the encampment.

"You all can dismiss," Arrick told the Shona escorting them. "And don't go gossiping."

"They're practically children," Alder pointed out as the patrol disbanded. "They can't stop themselves from talking any more than the moon can stop itself from waning."

The patrol leader acquiesced with a sigh. "True enough. But this way they know they can't go shouting about you to anyone who'll listen. At least, not until the commanders decide what to do with you."

"Are we prisoners, then?" one of the other men asked, his hand going to his knife hilt.

"Do you really think they could keep us here if we wanted to leave? Stand down." Alder chuckled. He shrugged at Arrick. "No offense."

Clover expected the Shona to be angry, but he only gave a grim smile. "It's hard to convince anyone that undersized troops have a chance in a fight."

As the men began setting down their things in the mouth of one of the tunnels, Alder pulled the boy closer and lowered his voice. "I helped you out there. But *I* would also like to know what you people plan on doing with us. I didn't bring my daughter all this way to lose her in the Illyn Mountains."

The Shona captain sighed. "I realize that, Sir. But Soren has to be the one to decide."

"Ah, yes. The chain of command at its unhurried best. Where is he?"

Arrick ran a hand through unruly hair. "Who knows? He's rarely here. He'll be back tomorrow, at least. He has to visit our main base and talk to Rose."

"Aha. Is she in charge of many rebel groups?"

The boy's expression turned grim. "She's leading the

Shona, and the highlanders are trying to decide if they support her or not. Some of the men from the coastal towns are spreading the word to assemble in one of the villages." He fidgeted with the end of his bow. "But it won't last. She can't even keep the Shona together. Soren, our outpost commander, hasn't sworn to her yet, and I don't think he ever will." He lowered his voice. "He's trading in information with Lord Kuma."

"And you have no difficulty with that?" Alder questioned.

The boy frowned. "I'm sure he thinks that it's the best way to ensure that we stay safe."

"All right. I can see I'll get nowhere with him for now," her father sighed. "Is there any way to get some food? We're all starving." He winked over the boy's head at Clover. "And I, for one, could eat a whole wolf."

13
UNDER NEW LEADERSHIP

Clover didn't see the meeting between Soren and her father. She fell asleep in a nest of sheepskin, her new hat pulled firmly over her eyes. When she awoke, the rest of the Yarrow Leaf men were readying their belongings. Bolting upright and shoving her hat over her filthy hair, she asked, "What's going on?"

"Oh, good, you're awake." Her uncle handed her a dense piece of bread. "We're going to the Shona main base. I believe your father and the camp leader came to an agreement."

Stuffing bread in her mouth, she rubbed sleep out of her eyes as her father came into the cave. "Ready to go!"

"Just in time, too." Alder turned to the Shona waiting outside the cave—the same as had escorted them the night before. "Are your people ready?"

"We're ready." As they left the camp amidst the patrol of Shona, Clover overheard him tell her father, "To tell the truth, Sir—"

Clover giggled. *Da hates being called 'Sir'.*

"—I'm glad you and your men are with us. Soren doesn't

like Rose, and I'd hate to see any of the Shona hurt. The last time she was here, he lost his temper and it almost got bloody."

Alder grimaced. "Don't call me Sir. Exactly whom are we supposed to be protecting here?"

The boy banged his knuckles against a passing rock. "Yourselves, I suppose." He shrugged. "I guess that includes Rose. She's one of yours, after all."

"Exactly," Alder confirmed. "Don't forget it."

The journey to the Shona's main base didn't take as long as Clover had expected. They stopped once, during which she took the opportunity to observe the outpost leader Soren. He was amiable enough, laughing and joking with his command as they sat on rocks and shared water and food. His manner suggested that he could easily laugh, but could just as easily be turned to anger or jealousy. He was around twenty-one, with broadening shoulders that suggested he had not yet reached full maturity.

Clover kept an eye on him as they broke their rest and began hiking again. *He seems nervous,* she thought as they skirted the edge of a lake. *But if he's cooperating with their enemies, he might have good reason for nerves.*

"We're getting close now," one of the Shona warned as they stepped back into the trees. The wind whipped the girl's ragged sleeve as she pointed. "It's just near that slope."

"Awfully close to the castle, isn't it?" Alder asked.

"We're farther into the mountains than you might think," the girl informed him before smiling at Clover. "Love the hat."

Clover tipped the brim of her floppy hat. "Thank you."

They passed a swampy area and stopped for sentries to recognize them. If Clover strained her ears, she could hear voices in the distance. It wasn't unlike the noise she had unsuccessfully forbidden her refugees from making. She was just looking for the source of the camp noises when they walked down a sloping tunnel of brush and vegetation into a hollow roofed with timbers and brush.

As she had seen in the other outpost, the people going about their business ranged anywhere from twelve to their early twenties. As his people moved to mingle with the rest of the Shona, Soren turned to address Alder. "We'll meet with the commanders now. Your men are free to rest, so long as they mind their manners. Don't forget that these fighters are more than your equals, and they're all on edge around newcomers."

"I won't forget," Alder mildly replied. He looked around at his men. "You lot, go take a nap. And try to blend in."

Clover giggled before her father turned a stern gaze on her as well.

"You too."

"Da!" she yelped. "I want to come!"

He shook his head. "We might have to leave as soon as I'm done with my meeting. Rose might be here, but the others are still missing."

She pressed her lips together in annoyance and flounced over to the men in the corner. "Da says we might have to leave soon."

One of the younger men happened to be one of her many older cousins. He nudged her in the ribs. "You don't like being sent to wait?"

She crossed her arms and watched the Shona try not to stare at them. "I don't like being treated like a child. I was *responsible* for children back home." She slouched against the wall, sticks poking her in the back. "I just want to hear what they're talking about."

"You could wander around and make friends with some of the others here," he suggested affably. "You know, get to know the area. And if you happened to end up near where everyone is talking…"

Clover allowed a devious smile to spread over her face. "Not bad," she admitted.

He settled back against the wall and closed his eyes. "Don't mention it."

Clover began wandering the hollow, gradually getting closer and closer to the tunnel that Alder and the other Shona had disappeared into. As she went past a group of younger children playing on the ground, one tugged on her skirt. "Hey!"

"Yes?"

"You're dressed funny. You're not from here, are you?"

Clover shook her head, her hat brim flopping at the movement. "No, I'm not."

"She looks like that other girl." One of the other children put down his toy. "The healer."

She raised her eyebrows. "What healer?"

He squinted at the tattered hem of her skirts, worn over the trousers she'd been given earlier. "Our healer isn't from here either, and she wears those skirts like you do."

Clover's heart pounded against the walls of her chest. "Can you take me to her?"

"Sure." He scrambled to his feet and grabbed a handful of skirt. "Come on!"

Clover followed him into an infirmary, hung with blankets and filled with the smells of herbs. The child ran across and returned with another girl. Clover squealed with delight. "Violet!"

VIOLET CAME out of her dosage calculations fog to see a skinny, filthy Clover running towards her. She could hardly believe her eyes, but her heart moved her feet for her. They met in a tangle of skirts and a rush of laughter, squealing and hopping in a dance all their own.

Violet was the first to recover, holding Clover at arm's length and examining her friend. The most arresting aspect of the girl's appearance was the hat. Huge and broad-brimmed, it flopped in some places and stuck out at others. A tattered pheasant plume protruded jauntily from the brown hatband.

"Where *did* you get that hat?"

Clover swept the hat off, revealing hair much rattier than usual. "It came to me. I think it likes me." She replaced it haughtily. "And it says you look like a squirrel in a rainstorm."

"I'm sure," Violet answered soothingly. "You're clearly hearing things. Come this way, and I'll get you some nice tea and you can lie down."

Clover answered with a burst of laughter such as the Shona had not heard in a long time. "Eat my socks, healer." She hugged Violet fiercely with another squeal. "Healer! You're the healer now! I'm so happy! I knew you could do it!"

Violet groaned as her ribs protested. "Yes, but it isn't easy."

"I guess not." Clover let her go. "Willow always said that nothing is ever as easy as it looks." She frowned. "Where is Willow? Isn't she here?"

Violet took a deep breath. *She's not going to want to hear this.* "Let's talk somewhere else. Tora," she called to one of her assistants, "I'm going to be in the meeting room if anyone needs me."

Tora frowned as she unloaded herbs into a basin. "There's a big group from the other outposts in there."

"Ah, right." Violet took Clover's hand. "Then I'll be in the cave. Let me know if you need anything."

Tora saluted casually. "Naturally."

As they went towards where she and Rose slept, a thought occurred to her. "How... did you get here?"

Clover pointed as they came out into the hollow. "With them."

Violet's heart settled more than she'd thought possible at the sight of her neighbors. Against the slight figures of the Shona, the grown men appeared powerful, steady, and reliable —all things she'd sorely felt the lack of among the younger freedom fighters. "And how—"

"My Da," Clover explained. "Looking for you and the others."

Violet frowned at the group of foresters, the distinctive lanky figure of Clover's father conspicuously absent. "I don't see him. Did he go into the meeting with Rose and the others?"

"He's there, but he didn't let me come." Clover stuck out her lower lip. "He's trying to *protect* me."

"Well, I have to be there." Violet winked at her. "Coming?"

Dimples appeared in Clover's cheeks. "Of course!"

CLOVER DID her best to be unobtrusive as she and Violet stepped into the meeting room. She needn't have worried. *It can't be easy, arguing while sitting on logs,* Clover thought as she hunkered beside Violet in the corner. *But they seem very interested in trying anyhow.*

Her consideration of debate seating shattered as she caught Rose's voice, raised over the hum of discord. "It doesn't matter what you thought of him before he was killed. What matters is us staying together!"

Clover's jaw dropped in amazement. Now that she knew where to look, she could pick out her friend among the other dark-haired Illyn natives. Rose's hair had been left uncovered, twisted into a braid hanging over one level shoulder, and the edge in her voice carried a firmness Clover had never heard before. Clover shook her head in wonder. *A few months ago, she wouldn't yell at us even when Heather and I gave her a scare.*

"I didn't like Erven, but he was the glorious leader of the Shona," Soren was saying as she finished contemplating the change in Rose's demeanor. "It would've ripped the clan apart if I challenged him. But he's gone now, and his death makes way for change." He glared in Rose's direction. "I can't let you drive the Shona to obliteration by coming in and acting like you know what you're doing."

"She's kept the Shona together," one of the boys snapped. "That's more than you've done!"

Soren's log seat scraped on the earth floor as he stood to point at Rose. "You shouldn't be here. If it wasn't for us, your head would be on a pole right now. If you keep this up, those stupid enough to follow you will end up dead." He waved an accusing hand at the rest of the Shona. "You won't get any help from Thunderhead. When the soldiers find you, you'll wish you had listened to me."

A rumble of voices greeted this statement. Clover's eyes flickered nervously from face to face as several of the Shona shot to their feet. The woman sitting nearest Rose joined them, her cool voice cutting through the clamor. "What's the outsider's take on this?"

Clover cautiously got to her knees to see her father, reclining against the wall on the other side of the room with his eyes closed. "Hmm? Oh, you want my opinion." He sighed and stood up, an edge of sarcasm and hostility running through his voice. "Funny, I thought outsiders didn't have a say here."

Clover's eyes widened. *Da's angry. Da* never *gets angry.*

She shrank closer to Violet as Alder addressed Soren, "So, you think without your leadership, th'Shona will certainly be destroyed?"

Soren waved a dismissive hand at her father. "Stay out of this. You'll be heard in your due turn."

"No, Sir." Alder took a step forward, towering over Soren's unfinished height. "I've a few things t'say, and when I'm done, I'll sit down and you can continue your argument." He pointed a hand at the young man. "I don't know who Erven was, but you respected his position even if you hated him. Now that he's dead, you feel you deserve his place."

"Well, yes!" Soren sputtered, crossing his arms over his chest. "He was the—"

"I'm not finished," Alder said. "T'be a leader requires that you have th'liking and trust of those under you." He glanced around at the Thunderhead Shona. "Your reputation among your own command is that of a leader with an uncontrollable temper. You don't spend enough time with them t'know *what* they think of you. Even if none of this were th'case, your talk of how concerned you are for the Shona is ridiculous. Everyone here knows you allowed safe passage to the enemy t'put yourself in power."

Judging by the shouts of surprise, most of those in attendance had not heard this information. Alder raised his eyebrows. "Hm. Well, if they didn't know, they do now."

As the room erupted into shouting, Soren rounded on Alder. "Who do you think you are, anyway? Who gave you the right to come in here and throw around accusations?"

"Who gave you the right t'decide the Shona succession?" Alder asked significantly. Clover stifled a giggle as he continued, "When your master attacked our home, I led our men to battle. *I* am the one who ensured that this girl—" he pointed at Rose, now standing among the rest of the Shona with her eyes narrowed and jaw tight, "—would stay alive long enough t'challenge you." He stepped forward, driving Soren back. "And

I'm tired of hearing you lie about how virtuous you are in order t'get what you want. Only a coward does that."

As Soren reached the wall, his face turning pale, one of his own commanders demanded, "You did what?"

"I knew you were jealous, but you abandoned us in battle to get rid of Erven?" one of the others exclaimed.

Another girl with black hair and slanted eyes leaned towards Violet, her voice low and grim. "Should we tell them?"

Violet shook her head. "Not while Soren's here—"

Her next words cut off as Rose's surprisingly strong voice cut the din. "Everyone quiet!"

Clover hadn't expected that a room of people would quiet so rapidly, yet quiet they did. Alder was once again lounging against the wall, his posture decidedly different from Soren's. The Thunderhead commander had his back firmly against the wall, eyeing them all like he was prepared to go down fighting.

Rose's shoulders straightened as she stepped towards the traitorous leader. "Soren, the Shona have had enough. It's clear that you're not angry at us, but at the leader you never had the decency to confront yourself. Regardless of your feelings towards him, Erven is gone. With the backing of the commanders, I demand that you step down." She lifted her chin to look him in the eye. "Now."

Soren spat on the ground in front of her. "I refuse. And if you knew what's right, you wouldn't ask it."

"You heard the woman," her father's voice rumbled as he moved to stand behind Rose. Clover scrambled to her feet as he ordered, "Leave now, boy, before the rest of your tribe drives you out."

Soren's eyes flicked, panicked, from one of his officers to another as the rest of the Shona slipped from their places to range behind Rose.

"The southerner's right, *gajin*." The girl with slanted eyes stood powerfully at Rose's left elbow. "You've lost our trust."

"Ours too."

"And ours." One of the Thunderhead captains joined them.

"Soren, give this up," the older woman urged. "It's obvious no one believes you."

"Because the Shona take orders from anybody now," Soren sneered. He'd lost any appeal that Clover had seen in him as he shifted angrily from one foot to the other.

"No," Rose drew herself to her full height as the Shona gathered behind her. "Because your clan orders it."

His jaw clenched, and he turned away. Then, a dagger flashed in his hand as he turned and sprang towards Rose with a yell.

Clover closed her eyes in horror, her hands going to her ears. *No! Rose, run!*

There was a gasp, a roar, and a thud. Then, chaos.

"Clover!" Violet's voice broke through the clamor as strong hands gripped her elbows. "Ducky, open your eyes."

She reminded herself that Violet was a healer and did as she was told. "Rose?"

Rose stood frozen a few feet away, a pool of blood soaking the dirt in front of her feet. Before her stood Alder, the blade of his hunting knife crimson as he retrieved it from Soren's fallen body. Clover's mouth had gone terribly dry, and it took several tries before she was able to get the words out.

"Da?"

He turned, fear flitting through his eyes as he dropped the knife. Her feet moved on their own and she crashed into his open arms, burying her face in his worn vest as the Shona buzzed with arguments and stunned chatter. "Da."

"It's all right. It's over." He raised his voice over the din as his arms tightened around her. "Milady, your clan will become suspicious if they don't know what's happened."

"Oh—right." Rose's voice shook slightly as she asked, "Do I have all of your backing before I tell them?"

Someone snorted, and Clover turned her head to see that it was the girl with tilted eyes. "You've been in command since we realized Lena couldn't be. Now you have the title that goes with it. Go tell the others."

Rose took a deep breath as Clover pulled away from her father. Her shoulders straightened, and her chin went up. "All right, then."

The Shona began streaming into the main hollow, Rose letting them pass. Her expression held a strange mix of uncertainty and gratitude she turned to Clover and Alder. "Thank you, Sir."

Alder's voice was matter-of-fact at Clover's back. "You're still one of us. Just don't call me Sir."

"Then please, don't call me Milady." Rose gave Clover a sad smile and walked out after the rest of the Shona.

VIOLET RETURNED to her work in the infirmary as the hollow buzzed all around her. The tasks were mostly busywork, but they soothed her troubled heart and brought distraction from the dozens of questions brought by those who hadn't been in the meeting room when Soren was killed. By the time she'd finished everything that needed doing—and some things that hadn't—she realized that Rose had been conspicuously absent since her announcement earlier. Dodging more questions, Violet crossed the hollow and ducked into the cave. The noise of someone crying echoed off the rocks, and the gloom soon revealed Rose, kneeling on her bedroll with tears streaming down her face.

For a long moment, Violet stood shocked. Over all the years of their lives together, she couldn't recall a single instance of seeing her friend cry.

Finally, she found her voice. "What's wrong?"

"I hate it."

Violet settled to her knees beside Rose. "Hate what?"

"He's dead. He's dead, and I don't care. And Clover's da told me that Mother and Father are dead, too—the soldiers burned the village, and they never made it out of their house. It's terrible, and I *don't care*." Rose looked up at Violet, her eyes so wide that Violet could see edges of white around the blue. "Violet, what's *wrong* with me?"

Violet put her arms around her friend. "Nothing's wrong with you."

"All this time, I've been telling myself I didn't care about them, or Soren, or anyone else that hurt me. But now, they're dead—and I *should* care, but I don't! I can't!" Rose's hands clutched at Violet's skirt, her voice hushing. "How can I lead anyone if their deaths don't matter?"

There was silence for a long while as Violet pondered the question. Her thoughts kept going to the terrible reality that they'd always suspected.

Home is gone. We're all each other has, now.

Her circling thoughts settled on the thought, and she bit her lip. *Whatever happened at home, Rose needs me right here, right now.*

"I don't know," she began haltingly, "I don't even know if there's anything *wrong*." She rubbed a hand in circles on Rose's back, wishing she could push comfort through her touch. "And I don't think you actually don't care. I think," she stopped and tried again. "I think, maybe, you feel it so deep that it'll take a long time to come out."

"Like with Willow," Rose muttered.

Violet nodded. "With Willow, you argue with her, then have the real fight later once she's figured out why she's angry with you." She leaned her cheekbone against Rose's shoulder. "*You* don't feel things right when you hear about it, because it takes too long to figure out what you think about it."

"If you say so." Rose didn't sound convinced, but her breathing had evened out. "But not feeling anything about Mother and Father—" Rose sniffled. "I mean, they raised me! We had some lovely times when I was younger." She pulled away and buried her face in the knees of her patched trousers. "They're dead, but I can't feel *anything!*"

Violet sat back on her heels, at a loss. Rose's parents had always been cold and on edge with most people, with their daughter—*foster daughter*—getting the worst end of the stick. "It's been a long time coming," she finally said. A very unkind feeling stirred in her chest, and for a moment she wished she could spit on the spot where the woodcarver's shop had once stood. "You've had to seal yourself off from them for years, to keep yourself safe. Even *with* the lovely times, all of us could tell that your heart was hurting." She bowed her head. "We did what we could, but none of us knew how to help. I don't know what to tell you, other than that it might take years to sort out how you feel about them."

"And I don't have years," Rose muttered through her crossed arms. "I don't have any time." She looked up with red, puffy eyes. "I can't do this. I can't have everyone counting on me." She scrubbed the handkerchief across her face and returned it to Violet. "I don't know how I've fooled them all, but it's only a matter of time before someone figures out how lost and useless I am." She buried her head in her arms again. "And I can't leave, either, because then they'll be hopeless."

Violet ran gentle fingers across Rose's hair. "You aren't

doing as badly as you think. You're a good study, and you read people well. When's the last time you got time by yourself?"

Rose raised her head. "Not working? I don't know."

"Go for a walk," Violet urged. "Or go watch the sky like you used to. Maybe it'll give you some time to think."

"Maybe."

Violet tucked her handkerchief away. "You could probably also use some tea."

"I suppose I could," Rose agreed.

"Tea. And some food," Violet said, pulling Rose up with her. "Let's go and see what we can find."

The hollow echoed with laughter as they left the cave, its source easily found in Lena and River sitting atop Clover. The laughter quickly changed to battle cries as a pair of little boys tore past the knot of girls, one of their sisters in hot pursuit with a washrag.

"You see?" Violet gestured at them. "Not everything has to be sad."

The smile Rose gave Violet was brief and pale as the first stars of twilight, but genuine. "I suppose you're right."

Hot food and tea followed, along with a story from one of the Yarrow Leaf men. At some point in the meal, Violet noticed Rose slipping out of the hollow. When she returned almost an hour later, her face was relaxed, her manner easier, and her voice lighter in tone.

Violet hadn't expected how the change in just one person's demeanor could alter the mood of the entire camp. The remainder of the evening passed with far less tension than she'd feared, and everyone bedded down with contentment.

THAT NIGHT, Violet had nightmares of her village burning.

· · ·

T HE FOLLOWING MORNING, Alder approached Violet and Rose as they were sending out the morning patrols. "We're going to stay; all of us."

Rose sighed. "Thank you."

Violet could see that she meant it. The addition of seven mature men could do no harm among the younger Shona. *Besides, Clover can stay too.*

"It's nothing," Alder shrugged. "You need someone who doesn't look like an underage forest wraith to help you with the other tribes. And," he added, "helping you is the best way to find Willow and Heather."

14
THE MISSING PIECE

The new quarters were light and airy, with windows overlooking the harbor and enough space that Heather and Willow had their own small room. After giving the place a thorough investigation, Tiren had emerged and commented, "I think it's rooms they'd allocate for an ambassador and their staff, but I'm not going to complain at sleeping in servant's quarters."

He'd immediately ruined the image this statement lent him by sprawling to play a game on the luxurious rug with his sister and Heather. Willow would have joined them, but her days had become filled with ink and slightly mildewed documents. She wasn't sure if this type of work was what she was best suited to, but it was better than sitting in a worried stew.

True to his word, Ethan allowed her to help him prepare a report on the situation in Illyn for the Sea Wanderer leadership, and the last few days had seen her leave their suite early and return late in the evening. From digging through the reports sent to him by other intelligence operatives—Sea

Wanderer and otherwise, she'd begun to grasp the enormity of what she'd need to request of the Sea Wanderer government.

"I had no idea so many factors were in play here," Willow commented one afternoon, upon reviewing the most recent draft of their report. "Highland tribes, the Shona, army recruitment, mercenaries—where are you even collecting this information from?"

Ethan continued rummaging through his piles of paperwork. Despite his insistence that he knew where he kept everything, Willow had noticed that he spent significant amounts of time looking for lost items. "The Sea Wanderers have informants all over th'map. Most eventually comes to me, and I pass it to my superiors." He found the document he was looking for and began to copy the text into a ciphered notebook.

"I didn't realize how unsteady the balance between you and Illyn is," Willow continued, scrutinizing a crudely drawn map. "And it's not only them you have to worry about, it's the —" she hesitated, trying to get her mouth around the unfamiliar word. "The Iorca, is it?"

"Right." Ethan scattered blotting sand over his notebook. "They like snappin' at our eastern edges, and they're bedfellows with the Illyn warlord." He blew away the excess sand. "We've never gotten along. It'd be interestin' if they could be persuaded that alliance with Illyn is only going t'cost them in th'long run. If he can't get control of th'whole country, he'll never be able t'make good his debt t'them."

"Is that what this is all about? Money?" Willow looked up from her map.

"Everything is." Ethan's crooked smile showed at the corner of his mouth before disappearing. "It's one thing t'conquer a country, it's another thing t'hold onto it. Though,"

Ethan picked up his pen again. "If he *does* manage t'bring the highlanders under control, pay Iorca what he owes, *and* send Rose to an untimely demise, it creates more problems for us. If Illyn an' Iorca join forces against us, we're table scraps."

Willow rubbed her temples. The long days of reading and writing had given her a headache that tea wasn't taking away. Watching him write, she noticed thin scars on his hands and wondered where they'd come from before pulling herself back to catch the end of what he was saying.

"—that it's in our best interest t'help Illyn rebels, no matter their leaders." He stopped. "Were you listening?"

She shook her head. "I'm sorry. I don't know where my mind goes sometimes."

Ethan propped his pen against an empty plate covered in mango peelings. "I was saying that our trouble isn't in gettin' supplies or reinforcements t'the rebels'n Illyn. It's in convincin' our leadership that it's th'right thing t'do."

"But surely, they'll agree, won't they?" Willow's jaw twinged, and she reminded herself not to clench it. "Surely it's obvious that Rose needs help."

"They'll say we don't know where she is, or what she's doin', or even if she's alive at all." Ethan flexed the fingers of his writing hand. "All they—and us—know is that she an' Violet were taken from th'caravan by the Shona rebels. For all we know, they could've been slain by *them*."

"You don't know that!" Willow snapped. *Is he right?*

"All I'm tryin' t'say is that getting our council t'commit to anything quickly is hard, even in th'best of times. Getting them t'commit t'supportin' a rebellion when they've no stake in th'matter is even harder." His chair scraped on the floor as he leaned to pull another notebook off the packed shelf behind his head. "Getting them t'willingly step into a conflict when there's a good chance at pissin' off our own enemies? Harder still. An' when you're in charge of not only compilin' the report, but defending it as well? Hardest of all."

He set the pen down and looked straight into her eyes. "If we don't get this across their skulls first time, we'll get no second chance, and you'll be better off sailin' for Illyn yourself."

A FEW DAYS LATER, the tropical sun beat down on Willow's head as she and Heather returned from a visit to the market with their friends. She hadn't been out of the mountain for several days, and her friends and sister had unanimously ganged up on her to "Get outdoors, before you grow mold!"

With baskets full with fruits neither she nor Heather had ever seen, they crashed into their rooms in high spirits. While the others pulled a table and cushions onto the rug in preparation for a game tournament, Willow retrieved the book of the Iorcan language that she'd begun studying. Most of the informants from the eastern side of the Sea Wanderer territory wrote their reports in a combination of both languages, and she was tired of handing over reports to Ethan with only half a summary. Despite her continued dislike of paperwork, she hated only being able to complete her tasks halfway.

Somehow or another, studying became napping, and she awoke an hour later to a heavy weight on her chest. "Are y'going t'nap the whole year away? We've been waiting!"

Willow swatted at her sister's face. "Go away."

Suddenly, her pillow whisked from under her head. With a growl, Willow followed her sister out to the sitting room. Tiren and Kyli were eyeing each other over a dice game, a pile of rambutans in front of each.

"And what have you been doing while you were so patiently waiting?" she asked, taking a seat beside Tiren.

Heather lounged on the floor. "Watching these two gambling for rambutan. And chasing a lizard."

Willow helped herself to one of Tiren's rambutans. She wasn't sure which she liked more; the spiny outside or the taste of the fruit inside. "I shouldn't be surprised."

"No, you shouldn't." Heather began scooping pulp from the inside of a passionfruit, flicking seeds at Tiren. "Besides, it seems like chasing lizards is about the only other thing we'll be doing today."

Willow frowned at her. "Heather, stop." She squinted at the dice. "And what game is this?"

"Oh, this is just us wasting time." Kyli pulled a carved wood box over. "We wanted t'teach you'n Heather Sails an' Shores once you woke up."

They spent the next hour playing the game and eating fruit as the sun shone through the west-facing windows. After two games, Willow pled indifference and sat in a corner with her books. Soon after the others started yet another game of three-way Sails and Shores, the door rattled and opened to admit Ethan.

"Good afternoon!"

"Good evening, actually," Willow corrected, glancing out the windows. The sun was beginning to sink into the horizon, and she wondered if he'd left his office at all that day. "I got pressed into service for a market run, and here we are now. Will you sit? There's fruit."

Ethan shook his head. "I really don't have time, I just— ooh, rambutan?" His ink-stained hand hovered over the bowl. "May I?"

Tiren passed him one of the baskets they'd been using to

collect the fruit peelings. Ethan took a seat against a cushion, stretching his legs out in front of him.

"Is everything all right?" Willow asked. "I thought nothing could pull you out of the office."

He flicked out a knife from his boot top to snip through the rambutan husks. "That's only when I'm workin' on something with lots of paperwork." He popped the fruit in his mouth and spoke around it. "Being behind th'desk is a part of th'job, but it's dull after too many days. I usually spend more time out than in. I actually came t'find you and Heather." He smiled. "There's news."

Willow raised her eyebrows. "News? Heath', come over here, please."

Her younger sister slammed a warship down on the board in front of Tiren's fleet. "Consider y'self challenged, fiend."

Tiren shook dice in a carved wooden cup. "You can go." He spilled the dice out on the floor and surveyed them proudly. "You're losin', anyway."

Heather flicked a rude gesture his direction before sitting next to Willow. "What's happening?"

Ethan sheathed his knife and set the bowl of fruit to the side. "I've had word from one of our courier vessels. Th'Sea Wanderer ambassador to Illyn was tossed from th'capital."

"That screams 'We're frightened'," Willow mused.

"Aye," Ethan agreed. "But they'd kept their ears well sharpened prior t'that. The first thing y'might like t'know is that there's been an uproar in th'Illyn fortress. Seems the men th'warlord sent out t'meet a slaving caravan returned without their cargo."

"We knew about that," Willow said, waving a hand impatiently. "What else?"

"Soon after that, a massed search party had a run-in with th'Shona." Ethan shook his head. "It was evidently big enough that even th'townspeople'd heard of it. Despite th'Shona leader bein' killed—some say captured—in that battle, th'Shona have since stepped up their attacks on patrols, taxmen, and local garrisons."

"Riight." Heather frowned. "I'm not following your line of thought."

"Someone's still leading the rebels," Willow explained. "And we didn't think the Shona had more than one leader."

"What, really? Not very smart of them." Heather sat up straighter. "What else?"

"Ah, I haven't mentioned th'most interesting bit." Ethan pulled up one knee and clasped his hands around it. "Right as our courier was leaving, they started hearin' whispers of th'heir apparent gathering forces. Men were leaving their homes t'join the rebels in th'mountains."

Tiren and Kyli looked up in surprise as Heather loosed a war whoop. The three of them began an impromptu dance on the carpet as Willow pressed her hands to her face. *This is it. This is the piece we were missing.* When she could breathe again, she asked, "You're serious?"

"Yes." Ethan chuckled at the mayhem occurring to his right. "Once they'd heard that part, they sent a message here as fast's they could. It happened a little over a week ago, I think."

Willow couldn't contain the smile that spread over her face, or the relief speeding through her limbs. "She's safe."

"As safe as we c'n confirm." Ethan gave her an apologetic look. "I came t'get you so we c'n put th'finishing bits on that report. Our council needs t'hear it as soon's possible."

Willow stood and put her book on a shelf. "I guess it's just as well I took that nap, eh Heather? This sounds like it'll be a long night."

• • •

THEY WORKED for hours that night and the following day, going over and over the report until it fulfilled Ethan's standards and Willow's needs. "Do you put this much energy into every report?" Willow asked sometime after their tenth hour of revising.

Ethan rubbed his eyes, disgustingly cheerful even after a night of minimal sleep. "Not much. I've got a system for how much time things warrant." He nudged a pile of papers on the corner of his desk. "All these're quick little jobs—read them, condense, pass them on t'the people in charge of that area." He gestured at the scribbled-out copies and maps on the crowded work surface. "This's a big job, containin' information pertaining t'multiple areas of our organization."

"But it's close to done?"

"Sure," he said. "More, I don't think we've any more time." He stretched arms over his head with a yawn. "I'll get it into th'speaker's hands tonight, and they'll discuss it at their next meeting."

Willow stacked the papers neatly. "And when will that be?"

Ethan sighed. "They'll have t'read it themselves first, t'decide if it's worth their time t'call a special session t'hear you present."

"Present?!" Willow squeaked. "Isn't the report enough! Heavens above, we've spent enough time on it."

Ethan pushed the door open for her and reached over to snuff the lamps. Outside, the corridor was dimly lit and smelled of dusk. "I told you, there's only going t'be one chance t'get it across their heads and t'their hearts."

"I thought *you'd* present it!"

The faint light in the corridor caught a gleam of teeth as Ethan laughed. "They need t'hear your words from your mouth." Keys rattled as he carefully fastened several locks before setting off in the opposite direction from her. His voice trailed after him, echoing in the stone corridor. "If I were you, I'd spend some time figurin' out what t'say!"

15
SHOULDERS BACK AND CHIN UP

A few days later, Willow woke with nerves fluttering in her stomach. She dressed carefully, fussing with her sister's unruly curls until Heather swatted her away with a growl. To her consternation, Ethan was nowhere in evidence as a guardsman escorted them to the audience hall. Here in public areas of the mountain, the mosaics on the floor were polished and immaculate, and the walls resplendent in carvings and ornaments. She smoothed her washed and mended dress over her hips, taking comfort in the quiet blue color. After long thought, she had returned to the *Fire Dancer* to retrieve her old clothes, reasoning that it would only make sense to represent her people well.

The corridor opened into a reception hall, filled with sunlight from windows high in the walls. One of the walls of the chamber was entirely filled by a huge arched doorway, covered with layers of gold-tied blue and emerald curtains. The guard handed them over to a steward, who greeted them courteously and took their names before vanishing behind the curtains.

Willow and Heather stood close together, both awed and entranced by the grandeur. Heather eyed the guards flanking the doorway, armed with gold tasseled lances and sporting heavily tattooed arms. "It's not exactly jolly ol' teatime at home under the roses, is it, Old Thing?"

"No, it's not," Willow whispered. "I thought I'd finished being surprised by how big and colorful everything is here." She sighed. "I wouldn't mind that tea, though."

Heather squeezed her hand. "I'll make you some when this is over, eh?"

Both of them jumped as the guards, responding to some command neither of the girls had heard, tapped the butts of their lances on the floor. The sound echoed through the reception chamber, fading as the curtains whooshed aside. Somewhere inside the hall, Willow heard the steward announcing them.

"Right, then." Willow took a deep breath.

"Shoulders back and chin up, Old Thing."

They stepped into the hall.

The ceiling was nearly hidden by a fine mist of incense smoke that curled between the columns of the outer perimeter of the hall. Columns lined the long carpet from the archway to the dais, inlaid with gems that Willow had only heard about in stories—amethyst, topaz, agate, tiger's eye, moonstone, and more—all arranged in a swirling motif of waves crashing on a shore of hammered gold.

Willow's attention was immediately drawn by the man sitting in the position of honor on the dais—the Speaker for the Sea Wanderer Council. She guessed that standing, he'd easily be taller than her father and much, much broader. His deep-set black eyes probed hers from all the way across the hall, mouth framed by a short-trimmed black beard. In keeping with his people's tastes, his clothing shone richly with brown, green, and gold. A thick band of twisted silver, gold, and copper circled his head, leaving indents in his bronze skin. At one glance, she knew that—no matter who really ruled the Sea Wanderers—this was the man who would need to be convinced in order for anything to be done.

"Willow, of th'Yarrow Leaf tribe from th'Gaillen Woods. You, your sister, and your guardians are welcome in our court." His voice reverberated through the hall. The accent so apparent in Tiren and his family's voices was lessened in the ruler's voice, its depth reminding her of childhood legends.

Willow cleared her throat. She'd thought long and hard about what she was going to say, practicing on Heather until her sister had thrown a pillow at her and demanded silence. "Thank you, Majesty." She swallowed hard, reminding herself of what was at stake. "I have come on behalf of Rose, the daughter of the last king of Illyn. Some time ago, the current warlord sent men to kidnap her from our home. Her bloodline represents a threat to his rule. We have seen that he will stop at nothing to remove that threat and solidify his grasp on the country he conquered years ago." She took a deep breath. "I know that he intends to kill her. When I—" she glanced at Heather. "*We* learned that she had escaped captivity, we made our way here as quickly as possible."

Now that the fluttering in her stomach was calming, she found her confidence growing. It had been like this at home, when reciting memorized legends in school. "Over the last few days, I have worked with your intelligence agents to compile all the information we have regarding Rose, her bloodline, and the state of affairs in Illyn. While Rose's initial situation was dire, things have the potential to rapidly develop one way or the other for her and the rebels that we believe have now rallied around her. I beg you, and the entire Sea Wanderer Council, to consider our request for assistance most seriously."

She swallowed hard. "Illyn has been too long in the grasp of someone who'll stop at nothing to get what he wants."

There was silence for a long moment as the Speaker looked to the men on either side of him. It was only then that enormity of her audience sank in—the entire Sea Wanderer Council sat in a row of chairs behind the columns flanking the hall on either side. Her heart jumped as the Speaker said, "Thank you for your earnest words. This matter was brought t'my attention shortly after your arrival, and your report has been th'subject of much discussion prior to this audience."

Willow curled her fingers around the insides of her cuffs, trying to keep her nerves in check as he continued, "We've been aware of th'growing instability in Illyn for several years now. Your report on the current state of things was very informative and indicates that th'situation's growing more volatile by th'day. If what you've said is true, your friend and any with her could be in grave danger."

He shifted on his throne. "However, in the last decade, there've been no fewer'n four attempted revolutions within Illyn, all led by those with many years of experience in war an' command. From what we've read, your friend is young, sheltered, inexperienced, and fearful. Like the local warlord, we've no proof that she is who th'people believe her to be. Without some kind of compelling evidence, it'd be foolish for us t'intervene in th'affairs of another realm. If we interfere in matters that don't concern our people, we run th'risk of endangering ourselves t'no purpose." He sounded sympathetic as he added, "The Council will discuss your petition, and decide what help, if any, we can offer." The man added, "If at that time y'receive an unsatisfactory answer, you're free t'return t'your own people and mount an effort from your woods. I wish you well."

It seemed that the interview was over. *Wait, that's it? No wonder Ethan didn't come. He knew all along this was a fool's errand.* The memory of all the hours they had put into their work was enough to push Willow's temper beyond containment. The Speaker had turned his attention away from her, talking to one of the attendants taking notes at the back of the dais.

"Wait!" She balled a fist and took several steps forward. "Your Majesty, I think you're making a terrible mistake."

"Oh?"

Several of the council members looked astonished, others angry, and their combined expressions made her quail. *No stopping now.* She straightened her shoulders and stood tall in her mended clothes. "Yes, sir. I'm here not just on behalf of Rose, but on behalf of my entire tribe. This rebellion's success or failure will determine the direction Illyn will take for the future. They're all that stands between this warlord and uncontested rule over a whole nation."

She scanned the faces of the council members nearest the dais, pinning each of them with her eyes. "If he succeeds in uniting Illyn, he will once again turn his eye to the south and our home. We defeated their forces when they were weakened from conquest, but against Illyn's full strength, our forest will splinter like matchwood." Willow thought of her father's javelin, propped against the doorjamb in her home. They used it to hold the door open in nice weather, but she could remember a time when he had routinely checked the blade and oiled the wood.

"And what makes you think that they'll be content? As the country destabilizes, the bond between Illyn and your greatest adversary grows stronger. If you're worried about your enemies now, you'll be even more worried when they've settled their accounts and combined to attack you." Some of the council members were starting to look worried. The

Speaker himself leaned on one elbow, staring intently in her direction.

She knew her face was turning red, but she kept going. "My friends and family will be the first to die, but not the last. I was told that the Sea Wanderers valued justice. You have the greatest force at your disposal in the entire ocean, and you could use it to guarantee peace." She caught her breath and looked straight at the Speaker. "It's a coward's trick to hide in the hopes that others will keep the peace for you. If you don't take this moment seriously, it will be a decision you will regret for years to come."

In the silence that followed, someone cleared his throat. The ruler tipped his head to address someone standing behind her. "Ethan, you have something you'd like t'add?"

Willow's heart thumped hard. *He's here?*

She nervously turned to see him walking to join her in the center of the hall—and by his trajectory, he'd vacated one of the council seats behind the columns. Gone were the ink-stained cuffs and cheerful manner of the intelligence agent, replaced by a shirt of flame-colored silk and vest of fine, soft leather. A sword dangled from his belt, and suddenly the practice scars on his hands made sense.

Ethan took a knee in salute. "Your Eminence, you've heard me speak of Illyn's ruler often." At a nod from the Speaker, he got up and walked past Willow to stand before his ruler. "Over th'last few months, reports from our agents in Illyn have grown distressingly dire. They speak of taxes raised b'yond bearing, mercenaries keepin' a peace marked by fear, men conscripted from their families, slavery, an' other ills. It bears the image of a nation shakin' itself t'pieces under a ruler who doesn't care who he tramples in th'pursuit of control." The hilt of his sword flashed as the intelligence agent clasped hands behind his back. "He's allied with the Iorca, and th'only reason he's not already come against us with their support is his unstable grip upon his own throne. If he succeeds in wipin' out Thinar's line, he'll've removed th'last obstacle between us and an allied enemy."

"You sound awfully certain about this," the Speaker said with a touch of humor.

Though she couldn't see his face, Willow heard the crooked smile in Ethan's voice. "I've said it for years, M'lord. With as eager as we are t'bicker with each other, you'd think we'd jump at th'chance t'scrap with someone else once'n a while." He shrugged. "We've been so wrapped up in our own conflicts, it's a miracle we haven't already been attacked from all sides. It's time we stopped hiding behind neutrality."

"Indeed," the Speaker sighed. He turned his attention to Willow, a tired cast appearing over his features. "You've shown boldness, Willow of the Yarrow Leaf tribe. Th'Council an' I will carefully consider your request and our response to it." He gave a slight smile. "You'll have an answer by the end of th'week."

Willow sensed from the stifled gasp behind her that Heather was as pleased as she was. "Thank you, Majesty."

"Go in peace."

Willow made her very best curtsy before stepping back. As they left, she caught sight of Ethan walking closer to the throne, no doubt to continue the conversation in private. She clenched her jaw. *He'll have some other explanations to make later.*

"You're a noble? You sit on the Council?"

"Yes?" Ethan frowned. "You couldn't tell?"

"No!" Willow snapped, tightness growing across her skull. They stood in the corridor outside the guest suite, the midday sun bright and hot outside the windows. "All those times you talked about your superiors, and now I find out they're the Council. I can't tell who's anyone here! We don't have nobility at home, and with you people everyone just does what they feel like, and dresses however they please, and how was I supposed to know?" She ended with her voice an uncomfortable several measures higher—and louder—than usual. "And it would have been nice if someone had given me an idea of how things worked before surprising me!"

Too late she realized that Ethan was laughing. "And don't laugh at me!" Her nose was starting to prickle. Willow fled towards the docks before anything worse could happen.

An hour or so later, after a good cry in the privacy of her hammock on the *Fire Dancer*, Willow was hanging clean washing on a line between aft cabin and mast when Ethan approached along the dock.

She snapped a wet shirt in his direction. "I'm not interested in talking right now. Would you please go away before I say something I'll really regret?"

To her frustration, the young nobleman didn't go away. Instead, he sat with his legs dangling off the side of the jetty. "I owe you an apology." He looked up sheepishly. "It didn't occur to me that you wouldn't know my standing with th'Council. You've been so quick to adapt that I forgot I should've warned you."

Willow snapped another shirt and pegged it to the wash line. "Yes, you should have." Her throat had gone tight again. "To you this is just another part of the job. You forget that I don't do this every day." The line bounced as she pegged up the last pair of Heather's socks. "To you it's just another report, another faceless person across an ocean from you." She brushed past the washing to lean over the railing and point an open hand at him. "This is personal for me, *mate*. If this goes wrong, it's death for everyone I love. Remember *that* the next time you wonder if I need to know something."

"I understand." Ethan's eyes narrowed, like something else was taking his attention. "Are we still friends?"

She plucked a pair of Tiren's trousers out of the washtub. "It depends. Are you going to be more forthcoming with me?"

"My job is keeping secrets, y'know. I'll be as open with you as I can."

"Good." She ducked a last spray of water from the washing. "Come aboard and help. Friends don't sit around while others're working."

ROSE HADN'T EXPECTED how relieved she would be to have Alder and his men staying with the Shona. With their unwavering support, the remaining Shona who weren't certain about her leadership were finally coming around. Breakthrough finally came when they began to come to her with questions and issues first, rather than going to one of the captains.

With conscription mandatory in the lowland towns, the Shona were having almost daily interactions with men fleeing conscription. With the addition of the Yarrow Leaf men at her side, the deserters were more likely to stay.

"We can't stay here much longer," Rose commented one afternoon, after no fewer than five newcomers had arrived to join the Shona.

"Of course not." Alder spat a chokecherry pit into his lunch bowl. "They've survived here as long as they have by staying hidden. It's impossible to hide this many people."

They were sitting a short distance from the others, on the hill above the Shona camp. Tents had sprouted outside the entrance to the hollow, and smoke trailed into the sky from several cooking fires. Below them, Lena, Clover, and River sat shoulder to shoulder on a log, the feather on Clover's hat flapping as she laughed with her new friends.

"There're villages in the highlands." Annika, the Whitecaps commander, lounged against a rock nearby. "Whenever anyone's made it to us, we've sent them uphill to Hold Eskel."

"Does anyone here know how to find it?" Rose asked. She nodded at the tents below. "If we had a central point to tell them to gather at, more might come."

"We *all* need to go there sooner than later." Alder had slid down and propped his head on the rock they'd been sitting on, his hat over his eyes.

"Pardon?" Rose was getting used to Alder treating her like an equal, but politeness died hard.

He sat up with a sigh. "Your predecessor. He's regained his strength, yes?"

"I don't know." She set aside her bowl with guilt squirming through her stomach. "Arielle said so the last time she was here, but she wasn't able to see him after they released her from service last week." She slumped with her palm cupping her chin. Even amid their growing forces, several raids on foothill garrisons, and day to day tasks, rescuing Erven had not ceased to gnaw at her mind.

Alder squinted into the sunlight. "If the warlord knows who he has prisoner—and he does; we heard about Erven's capture in the villages—he'll not be willing to wait long before trying to get information from him."

"He's right," Annika agreed. She ran a hand through closely cropped hair in frustration. "If they want to get to the highlanders, they go through us first. If they find out where our outposts are—"

Clover yowled like a strangled cat from below, as some of the Shona littlies piled onto her amid shrieks of laughter. Rose watched the mayhem, the stark description Alder had given of her old home filling her with a sense of dread. "Think we can send some of the little ones with the new men?"

"We can," Alder answered gently. "Though, if I were you, I'd start making preparations to move more'n just the little ones. If there's a chance they could find out where we are, I'd much rather give ground rather than lose lives."

ERVEN SWORE and shielded his eyes as his cell flooded with torchlight. Someone yanked him up by his arm, sending a tearing sensation across his side. Blinded by the torchlight, he had to let the guards march him out of the cell. His vision cleared as a barred door clanged open, and he was shoved to the ground in an open cage. Trying to fight away fear, he scrambled to his feet.

They mean business, he realized as one of the guards kicked him down, breath driven from his lungs in one painful gasp. *I don't know how much I can take.*

AN HOUR LATER, the captain received a report from the interrogation officer.

"He's not giving us anything, Sir." The man looked uncomfortable. "D-do you think we're going to succeed?"

"Do you, Lieutenant?" the officer asked quietly.

The man swallowed. "He's very strong-willed, Sir. Does Milord still want him?"

"Yes, he was specific about that. And he wants the information to be clear, so I suggest your methods allow the prisoner to still be able to speak." As the man saluted, the captain added, "And I'll summon that healer. Just in case."

Captain Ricar buried his head in his hands as the door closed behind the soldier. The slave boy who had first brought the prisoner to his attention peered anxiously at him from the corner. *I saved him from dying when it was our negligence that was threatening him. This time, if I carry out my duties, he will die because of my actions.*

"Don't think that this will make your life any easier," he told the boy. "If anything, it's been made worse." He poured sealing wax on a written order and stamped it with his seal of office. "Take that and go to the supply hall. You're an errand boy, yes?"

The boy mutely nodded as he took the paper—an order for a serving man's uniform.

"You're now my personal groom. The stables will send you and a guardsman to fetch that one healer. You ought to pray to whatever god you worship that she's still where we left her."

"Yes, Sir." As the boy turned to go, he asked, "Sir?"

"What?" He rolled his eyes. "You want to know why, I'm sure. Why would I help a pitiful prisoner?" The lad jumped as he barked, "Maybe it's because no man deserves torture! Get out!"

The boy fled.

It's probably wise of him, the captain thought. *I've seen too many men lose their temper over a slave's question.* Even as he sat, he contemplated the lad's question and his answer one more time. *That was the answer. I've killed so many. Hurt others by not helping them. But no one deserves that.* Struck by the realization, he muttered a prayer he wasn't even sure would be heard.

"If you're listening, keep him alive."

16

DEATH BEFORE BETRAYAL

Erven was six, huddled in a ruined building with the gang. He clutched his sister closer, afraid that she would start crying again and wake the others. The gang had made it clear—he'd found her, so she was his responsibility.

A noise startled him and he lurched to his feet, only to look defiantly into a woman's face. They examined each other for a long moment. Finally, she held out a hand. "Are you hungry?" He swallowed hard and looked at the baby. With a sob, he put his hand in the lady's and the three of them walked away from the gang.

"You don't have anything to gain by this!" one of the men roared.

Blood coated Erven's tongue. He focused on each breath as his ribs stabbed with pain. Something struck his stomach and the world swam before him.

. . .

"I want to help! Why can't you let me go on the raid?" Lena demanded, her face misshapen with barely concealed tears.

"I can't. You'll get hurt." He ground a hand into his temple.

Lena's face relaxed into concern as she knelt beside him. "Headache again? Can I help?"

"If you want. Arielle left something, but she didn't say how I was supposed to take it."

"I'll bet it's a tea. I'll need hot water, and a clean rag, and..." *Her voice faded as she scurried away. The pain behind his eyes lessened as an idea sparked. Maybe there was something she could do that wouldn't place her in danger.*

WHEN HE OPENED his eyes again, Lord Kuma was there. Erven flinched; terrified, confused, and knowing that it showed. Strangely, the warlord didn't seem as angry at him as he did at the guards. "Keep trying. Let me know as soon as he breaks."

He tried to gather enough strength to spit, but a boot slammed into his side and the world spun as he blacked out again.

He'd taken wounds before, but never this bad.

Violet's voice was the first thing in his ears as he gasped back to life. "Erven, try to stay still." The healer kept adding more bandages, pressing them into his side as blood soaked through.

"How bad is it?"

He knew her answer even before she spoke, and the words only confirmed his decision. "It's bad."

More blood soaked the bandages even as he stepped onto the field. If things went according to plan, he wouldn't be alive long enough to worry about the enemy torturing him.

A blow cracked across his shoulders and pulled him into the torchlit room. He had time to realize that there was rage on the face of the guard before another sent him back.

He took a shaky breath. "Will you take care of my sister?"

"I promise."

THE NEXT TIME CONSCIOUSNESS ARRIVED, Erven thought he was still dreaming. His eyesight swam with spots of light, and a wave of dizziness swamped his senses as Arielle shook his shoulder. "Wake up, boy!" As his eyes slid shut, he heard her say, "Officer, you've gone too far."

Arielle bent over him as the soldiers started arguing with each other. Her whisper carried to his ears alone. "Erven, if you're able to hear me, make a fist."

His entire body throbbed, and his hand felt stiff as he forced it closed. From a distance, he heard her voice, relief carrying through every word. "Thank the Almighty. Follow my lead. This is your only chance."

"I don't know what information you possibly needed," Arielle's voice said above him. "But whoever told you that brutality would work is an idiot. There's nothing I can do for him. See?" She thumbed his eyelid, and it didn't take much effort to let his eye go blank and roll back. "If you were sensible beasts, you'd let him die in comfort, but I can tell that's too much to ask."

"But will he live long enough to talk?" This was a chilly voice that he recognized as the lieutenant commander. "Perhaps you should prove it before we take your word."

"If you command."

Behind closed eyelids, Erven gathered strength to respond to whatever it was she would need him to do. He heard Arielle fumble in her bag, and suddenly a strong-smelling rag was thrust under his nose. Light stung his eyes as he opened them for a brief moment, breath rasping as he coughed blood before lying still.

Arielle sounded satisfied as she said, "I've seen this before. I'm telling you, milord, he's finished."

He was expecting the kick when it came. His stomach churned at the sudden burst of agony in his ribs, but he bit down on the inside on his cheek and made no movement or noise in response.

After a long moment, a defeated order came to his ears. "Someone get a blanket."

"What will you do now?" Arielle's voice asked.

Folds of blanket muffled the man's reply. He felt himself lifted and carried away before the soft darkness enveloped him again.

MERALD WAITED NERVOUSLY with the horses as the sun slanted towards the west. The captain had conducted the healer down to the jail, both of them attempting to act like they saved prisoners every day. Finally, they returned, this time with a pair of soldiers lugging a body wrapped in a blanket. One of the men passed a tiny bag to Arielle, mumbling, "Thankee for taking care of it, ma'am."

"Aye. Toss it over here," Arielle commanded, taking the bridle of one of the horses. The men threw the body over the back of the horse, and the blanket slipped to reveal Erven's pale, bloodied face.

Merald's heart sank. *Were we too late?*

Captain Ricar gave Merald a hard look. "Help the lady mount and see her home. I'll tan your hide if I find out you've dawdled on the way back."

Merald bobbed his head anxiously before giving Arielle a boost into the saddle. She looked down frostily. "Captain, thank you for summoning me. And gentlemen, thank you."

The two soldiers walked away, the set of their shoulders plainly telling of their relief to be dismissed. As they passed out of earshot, Arielle's tone changed, and hope flickered in Merald's heart once more. "Thank you, Captain, again. I hope you won't be in difficulty yourself."

He shrugged. "I'll be able to blame my way out." His gaze shifted to Merald. "Lad, this is your only opportunity. If you see a way to stay out there, do so. I'll cover your absence."

Merald nodded, the hope surging as fast as despair had a moment ago. "Yes, Sir." He met the other man's eyes squarely. "Thank you, Sir."

Arielle gave Merald a sharp glance as he hefted himself uncertainly onto the other horse. "Hold onto him, lad."

He fumbled in the saddle until he got a good handful of the blanket. Even with the jostling, Erven didn't move. Merald bit his lip. *Hold it together. He'd be disappointed if you broke when you were on the verge of freedom.*

"I wish you a good night, Sir." Arielle nudged her horse's ribs, turning it towards the gates. Merald followed her, trying to keep hold of Erven and stay in the saddle. As they were waved out of the gatehouse, she increased their pace. Swearing quietly, Merald clung to the saddle and prayed that the bouncing would get easier to stand.

They were out of sight from the castle when Erven sputtered to life, spitting blood and starting to slide off the horse. Merald grabbed the blanket just in time, shock running through his limbs as he yelled for Arielle to stop.

Erven's eyes opened as they laid him on the ground. "We got away?" He blinked at Merald. "Who let *you* go?"

"The captain," Merald answered, more stunned than

relieved. "But you were dead! The blood all over your face—I thought—" He glared at Arielle. "You knew this whole time?"

"Yes," she admitted, "it was easier than explaining on the spot. Erven, we have to get you to the Shona. Lord Kuma may not swallow the story that you died, though you *did* make it convincing."

Erven gave her a ghost of a smile. His eyes shifted across to the horses. "You'll have to tie me onto the horse."

"That much I knew from the beginning." Arielle exchanged glances with Merald, and he sighed. His no-more-riding resolution seemed to already be broken.

They stopped the night with a trapper Arielle knew. Merald slept in front of the man's fire, dreaming restlessly. He woke once to hear Arielle whispering with the trapper, and several times to hear Erven moan in his sleep. They stayed for another day, which Merald spent splitting logs while Arielle watched over Erven. The Shona commander slept fitfully the whole day, only waking briefly to eat. The next morning, after Arielle had tended to Erven's injuries again, they set off deeper into the mountains.

It took them most of the day to get through the passes and into Shona territory. Merald stopped matching wits with his saddle, choosing after several hours to walk and lead the horse behind him. He envied Arielle her cool composure in the saddle. Erven fell asleep after an hour or so, held fast in the saddle by sturdy ropes despite the bumpy path.

It was late afternoon when a voice halted them. "Hold and be recognized."

"It's me, Lisbet," Arielle called as she dismounted. "How do things stand?"

The girl swung down from a pine, her sling dangling off her belt. Merald goggled in surprise at the sight of a girl in formfitting trousers, remembering belatedly to close his mouth. "All well. The lowlanders left a few days ago for Hold Eskel."

"That's a relief." Arielle scanned the area. "Is anyone else with you?"

The girl shook her head, eying Merald suspiciously. "My trainee has a head cold."

"Glorious." The healer placed a hand on the girl's shoulder. "Listen, now. Run ahead and warn Rose that we're coming. We need someone to hide the horses, a patrol to hide our trail, and a bed in the infirmary."

"I'll be fine," Erven started to say.

"Quiet," Arielle snapped. She looked at the girl, who had gone pale under her tan at the sight of Erven. "Go, girl! Fast!"

The girl scrambled backwards, stammering a 'yes ma'am' as she went.

Arielle looked at Erven with disapproval. "I thought you were asleep."

"I was." With a groan, he plucked at the knots holding him in the saddle until he could slither off and stand next to Merald. "We'd better get in there before Lisbet spills the news to everyone." He limped towards a clump of aspen. "There's a bolt hole this way."

"Why are you walking?" Merald asked firmly. "Shouldn't you be more careful?"

Erven gave him a defiant look. "It's my ribs that are broken, not my legs."

"Just leave him," Arielle muttered, tying her horse's reins to a branch. "He's too stubborn to listen. He'll feel that pain again once he stops moving."

They followed Erven into a brush-walled room full of covered baskets and heaps of wood. "We'd better—" Erven's hand went to his side and he took a shaky breath. "Better find Rose and let her know what's happened."

Arielle pulled open a drab curtain. "Only if you agree to get some rest."

Violet and Rose were in conference with the new Thunderhead commander when commotion broke out in the main hollow. Rose set down her notes, scratched on a smooth rock in charcoal, and commented, "I haven't heard that much noise since Clover fell into a basket of feathers."

Violet grinned. "I wonder what it is this time."

As they returned to their discussion, River burst into the room. The girl's eyes were sparkling with tears. "Rose, he's back!"

"What?"

River pushed her bangs away from her forehead. "Arielle's here." She caught her breath and added, "And Erven's with her."

Rose had thought she was past being surprised by anything, but this news stunned her into complete silence. She bolted to her feet and out of the meeting room, Violet close at her heels. Out in the hollow, the rest of the Shona were gathering with excited chatter.

They burst into the cave, where they found Arielle helping Erven wrestle his head through the neck of a clean shirt. "I'm fine," he insisted. "Just let me rest."

"You're back!" Violet sputtered.

"Really, Vi. Anyone can see that." Rose caught her breath and knelt next to him, heart shuddering at the sight of dark bruises mottling his limbs. "What I want to know is how."

Erven ran fingers through his hair, revealing another bruise on his temple. "One of the captains discovered that there was a line he couldn't cross."

The commotion increased in the hollow, and a squeal fell on Rose's ears as Lena pushed through the gathering Shona. The girl's face had gone red with tears of joy.

"Erven!"

AFTER THE EMOTIONAL reunion with his sister, Erven slept through the rest of that day and into the next. He awoke with much of his old personality restored, immediately asking to talk with Rose. She found him in the storeroom where she and Violet had spent their first night in the hollow, leaning against the wall and surrounded by the reports she'd saved from the last few days of patrols.

"Why did you move your things in here?" she asked as she sat across from him. "I was going to let you and Lena have your space in the cave back."

Erven set down the slate he'd been reading, the bruises around his right eye standing out purple against his skin. He looked exhausted, and Rose wished he had given himself another day to rest. "Except that the cave is for the Shona commander." He smiled. "Don't think that just because I'm back, you're going to get out of your responsibilities."

Her pride stung, Rose retorted, "I assumed you'd be in charge of the Shona." She crossed her arms. "They're your people, after all."

"Yours too," he said, pushing a stack of reports aside with his foot. "And if you're going to lead these people, you need to get used to giving orders."

Rose sighed and propped her chin in her hand. "It's been a fast education," she admitted. "There's so much that I don't know."

"Though you've done very well, considering how fast you

were thrown into things." Erven shifted position against the wall, wincing. "I'll help you, certainly, but the command is yours."

"Thank you," Rose said uncertainly. She grabbed one of Lena's tunics from a basket and passed it to him. "Do you want me to explain what's been happening?"

Erven stuffed the tunic behind his back and gave a sigh of relief. Gesturing at the reports, he said, "I think I've got an idea of how things've been going. My worry is that we're getting too extended with all the raids we've been making."

Rose sighed. "The clan was so angry when you were captured, they wanted to take risks." She looked down, ashamed. "I was angry too, so I let them."

"Well, risky or not, I think Lord Kuma's tired of tolerating the Shona. He *was* content to keep us penned in the foothills, but now he's preparing for war." Erven gestured to the bruising on his face. "This was because he wanted me to give up the locations of our outposts."

Rose grimaced. "I'm sorry. This—all of this—it's all my fault."

Erven shook his head emphatically. "This was not your fault. I knew the risks when I made my decision, just like you need to know the risks surrounding your decisions." He picked up another report. "I'm afraid that he's close to finding us."

She gave him a careful look, worry looming large in her mind and driving out the guilt. "Did he find out anything from you?"

She immediately regretted her suspicion as soon as she saw the look on Erven's face. "Of course not. This is my family. You are my queen." He set the report down with a clatter of stone. "I expect to die before I betray you."

"Thank you." She picked up one of the slates, shaking her head at herself. *What else can I possibly say to that?*

Erven smiled reassuringly. He took the slate from her and dusted the report off, returning it empty. "Here. You probably want to make notes." The smile took on a sheepish look. "I always forget important things if I don't write them down."

After that, they spent hours in conference. That evening, they called all of the leaders present to the council room. After recapping once more what had happened to him, Erven concluded, "Lord Kuma is supposed to believe that I died during interrogation, but that won't fool him for long. And with our growing forces, we can't expect to stay hidden for much longer."

Rose stood to join him. "It hasn't been easy, trying to decide what to do. We've already sent on most of the men who've joined us from the lowlands to Hold Eskel, but it's coming time that the rest of us join them."

This revelation was not unexpected, though there was still a rumble of surprise. Sonya, one of the Thunderhead captains, voiced the question on everyone's mind. "What about the passes?"

Erven answered her grimly as he sat down, leaving Rose standing by herself. "The passes will be open, but I think Lord Kuma will be reluctant to move without more forces at his disposal. He knows he'll be out of his depth fighting in the mountains."

The boy who'd arrived with Erven and Arielle cleared his throat hesitantly. "They're expecting reinforcements from Iorca soon."

Rose nodded at his comment and turned her attention to Alder. Clover's father was—as usual—lounging in the back row, attentiveness sharp in his stormy eyes. "He's right, but would you mind elaborating?"

He spoke from his seat, his voice carrying across the assembled Shona with confidence. "Just based off how many of you are already carrying Iorcan weapons, I think it's safe to say you already know they have mercenaries here. But from what we heard on the way here, and since, there's more coming. And we can't stop those combined forces, mountain fighting or not. We'd need allies of our own." He sat straighter against the wall. "I've a few ideas regarding that. I suspect that—if we addressed them the right way—we might be able to get the help of some of the local Sea Wanderers."

From there, the meeting went long into the night, as plans were laid to move supplies and hide trails before the Shona vacated their outposts. As Rose dismissed the meeting, most of the Shona were yawning. She finally rose from her seat, reluctant to leave but feeling the need to sleep. Alder and his second talked quietly in the corner, inaudible to most of the others. Arielle and Violet concluded a similar conversation, and approached her as she left the meeting room.

"We're going to move the injured to my village. They won't be able to make the trip uphill," Arielle told her as they crossed the darkened central hollow. "I'll mind them for however long I need to."

"You aren't coming with us?" Rose asked with concern. "I hoped I could rely on you for help with the highlanders."

"If you mean to rule, you need to be able to do it on your own," Arielle answered bluntly. "I'm needed in my own village, and you have ample resources here to draw from."

Rose drew a quick breath, tamping down feelings of panic at the idea of Arielle leaving. She turned to catch Clover as her friend went past, hat brim flopping over her eyes. "Tomorrow, dear? Will you help Violet get her patients ready to move?"

Clover flapped a hand at her. "Consider it done, Milady."

She tugged the brim of the massive hat up to grin cheekily at them. "I'll expect payment, of course."

"I'll give you a new feather for your hat," Rose offered.

Clover departed with a whoop, chased by shushing from those already falling asleep. Rose smiled at her friend's unflappable enthusiasm and told Arielle, "She's a breath of fresh air. I'm glad her father brought her."

"He has his own reasons to volunteer to contact the Wanderers," Arielle said, casting an appraising look at the woodsman. "I believe he thinks he'll find his other daughters with them."

"What do you mean?" Violet asked, tucking the ends of her hair more securely into the scarf she'd taken to wearing.

"Well, did you not mention that your friends were sold to a passing ship?" Arielle neatly stepped around a pair of children tossing jacks in the dirt.

"Yes." Violet patted the head of one of the children. "Go to bed, you two! They've been gone for so long that no one knows where to start looking."

"To a father like him," Arielle gestured at Alder, who had followed them out of the council room and was talking with the few of his men who were still awake. "No rumor is too small or a journey too long to get his children back."

Violet had been uncertain of who would give orders, now that Erven was restored to them. He laid these uncertainties to rest by displaying an uncommon partnership with Rose. Between the two of them, the Shona were prepared to move within several days of his return. Through necessity, Rose took charge of most of the everyday quarrels, problems, and crises. Although Erven didn't say much to any of them, both Violet and Rose could tell that he was slow to recover after his ordeal.

Alder left more than half of his men with the Shona, as he and the rest made for the coastline to attempt contacting the Sea Wanderers. Much to Violet's dismay, Clover departed with her father. "I'm sorry," Alder told her and Rose. "I've brought her this far with me, and I don't want to leave her. You'll see us again. We'll return with allies."

17
ALLIES AND LEGENDS

Willow and Heather were cooking dinner. Despite the luxurious accommodations inside the mountain, both agreed that there was something lacking in having meals delivered day after day. Willow was also nursing a headache from staring at documents too long, and was beginning to wonder if any of the work she'd done would make a difference. *At least I know what result I'll get when I cook. And keeping other people's bellies full makes my heart happy.*

The sunset found them onboard the *Fire Dancer*, bustling back and forth with aprons over their trousers and loudly disagreeing on what certain ingredients were.

Heather examined the assortment of produce the girls had collected from the dockside market. "I think this'n's a potato."

"I doubt it." Willow stirred a pot of water briskly. "It's not the right shape."

Heather swung a cleaver expertly, bisecting the tuber and examining the inside. "It looks like a potato—" She sliced off a piece. "Feels like a potato."

Willow had turned her attention to chopping onions, and didn't see Heather pop the piece in her mouth. "And?"

A strangled noise from behind made her spin around. "It is *not* a potato." Heather stuck her tongue out, examining the end from crossed eyes. "My tongue's gone numb."

Ethan burst into laughter from the other end of the table. "It's close enough." He took Heather's pile of vegetables to the pot of water. "You have t'cook it."

"Well how was I s'pposed t'know!" Heather demanded, brandishing her cleaver before attacking the rest of the pile of produce. Her muttering was soon lost as Willow clanged her spoon on the edge of the saucepot.

"Is that how you tell the food's done?" Ethan asked.

Willow peered down her nose at him. "The pot will tell you when it's ready."

Tiren clattered across the deck from the gangway. "There's th'chicken!" He flung a parcel on the table. "Is it done?"

"How'c'n it be ready if you've just brought the chicken?" Heather asked crossly.

"Thank you," Willow said, snipping the twine on the parcel.

Tiren pulled a pair of document tubes from his sash. "Some fellow in uniform gave me these as I was coming aboard, too."

Willow and Ethan exchanged looks. "Who's it for?" the intelligence agent asked.

Tiren shrugged, taking a cube of mango from Heather's cutting board. "Could be for either of you. Though it wasn't a standard guardsman who brought it."

Ethan snapped the seal on one of the tubes and slid out the document. "I'm curious how they knew I'd be here."

"You're getting predictable," Heather chortled.

"That's not a good thing." Ethan's brow creased as he examined the message.

"News?" Willow asked as she slid chicken pieces into a pan of onions.

"Mostly for me." He leaned over and lit the end of the document in the stove, holding it gingerly until only the rim was unscorched.

"Secrets and darkness, then." Heather thumped her cleaver against a coconut. "No need to be dramatic about it."

Ethan dropped the charred paper into the flame. "There's one for you, too, Willow."

"My hands are covered in chicken," she complained. "What's it say?"

"It's from th'Council." He snapped the seal on her message. After reading it silently, he announced, "They want t'see you and Heather tomorrow."

"Is that what yours was?" Willow clanged her spoon on the pan again. "Did you know ahead of time?"

Ethan barely rescued the message as Heather's coconut split open in a spray of juice. "You know you're s'posed to do that over a bowl, right?" He sighed. "Yes, my message was related. And yes, I knew they were coming close to a decision."

"Excellent," Willow commented. "When tomorrow?"

"Two hours after noon." Ethan stuffed the paper into its tube. "I'm sorry, but I need t'leave. There're some things I need t'attend to."

As the door clattered behind him, Heather remarked, "He's an odd one, Old Thing." She levered a piece of coconut meat out of the shell and popped it into her mouth. "Here one moment, and gone the next, and no one knows what he knows or doesn't know."

"You aren't wrong," Willow agreed. "And I'd love to know what it is this time that's making him disappear."

• • •

THE NEXT AFTERNOON, the knock came two hours after the midday gongs. Willow and Heather followed the guardsman to a meeting room. Upon entering, Willow saw that it held a table covered in papers and inkwells. The Council—a dozen of them at least —sat around the room, the Speaker occupying the seat at the head of the table. Ethan sat to the left of his ruler, looking preoccupied.

"Ladies, please sit," the Sea Wanderer ruler commanded. He wasn't wearing his circlet, and his clothes were plainly colored, but his voice still held the power that Willow had heard in their audience. "It'll be much more comfortable than standing, I assure you."

They sat in the two empty chairs. Willow noticed with a little discomfort that she was short enough to make the chair feel too low.

The Speaker cleared his throat. "Your report and presentation created much discussion over th'last few days. While we've been aware of Illyn's troubles for some time, it's becoming apparent that things're developing more rapidly there than we foresaw."

"Is there news?" she asked, suddenly worried that Ethan had been keeping information from her again.

"Neither bad nor good news, but news. I'm assuming you knew about Illyn's recruitment drives?"

She nodded. That news had come a few days ago, and she had condensed the report for Ethan's file. "They're gathering forces for a push into the mountains." She was glad that the Sea Wanderer network extended off the sea and into the coastal towns. "That's the last I'd heard."

"That's right." The man to the Speaker's right inspected a sheet of paper. "This week, we've also received reports of mobilizing of Iorca troops within their borders. We suspect they're preparing t'send more troops to Illyn."

Willow shook her head. "I didn't know that."

"We suspected this'd be their next step," Ethan said.

"We don't know for sure they're bound for Illyn," one of the others said. "It could be they're mobilizing t'reinforce the military in some other part of their country. They're known t'have unstable politics within their own territory."

"Reports aren't in keepin' with a local uprising or civil unrest." Ethan propped an elbow on the table. "Iorca's been reasonably peaceful. These mercenary troops're th'only ones movin within th'country."

"But there's always a chance—"

"Aye, sure an' there's always a chance they could be going to a sunset day parade followed by drinks'n'snacks under th'mango trees."

The man ignored Ethan's sarcasm. "Maybe, but y'can't know that for sure. We can't assume they're always going t'be predictable. And for another thing, those informants of yours aren't always as reliable as y'say they are."

"They're as reliable as they can be in their conditions!" Ethan spat, his face flushing. "If you think you can do better—"

"With reinforcements coming to Illyn soon, we can't dither much longer." The Speaker's raised voice cut through the argument decisively, and Willow was glad he'd moderated his voice to suit the small room. Ethan sat back in his chair with a glare at the councilman as the Speaker continued, "After days of deliberation, this Council's reached a decision. Now that there's th'possibility of a new ruler rising in Illyn, our people must take action."

Willow hesitated before breaking the silence that greeted the Speaker's words. Heart pounding, she asked, "What type of help can you provide?"

"Couriers'll leave within th'day, gatherin' our troops from

th'waters closest t'Illyn." One of the men pulled another sheet of paper from his pile. He ran a finger down a column of figures, his lips moving silently. "Between volunteers 'n' regular navy, that's close to five thousand men."

Willow raised an eyebrow. "So many?"

The laugh from the councilmen broke the tension in the room, and Willow's throat tightened as Ethan laughed with the others. *Don't laugh, just tell me what's so funny!*

"Lord Kuma commands more'n two thousand, *without* recruitin' from Illyn." The councilman with the roster flipped over a list, making hash marks on the back with the pen he'd been playing with. "With Iorcan troops, and th'possibility of more coming," he slashed his pen across the hash marks. "Illyn needs every man we can give her."

"Iorca commands a fully equipped army big enough t'out-number th'fish in my granny's net," one of the other men remarked. "If they choose t'take this as an opportunity t'de-clare war themselves against us, th'forces would be twice ours and then some."

The man who'd been arguing with Ethan leaned forward. "If we send any more, we'd leave our own people exposed. You're getting more than you asked. Be happy with that."

Willow's face grew warm. Forcing down the frustration, she asked Ethan, "Are there no more in Illyn who will rally to Rose?"

He took a breath to answer, but was interrupted by one of the others. "That's not th'problem," the man scoffed. "Th'-mountain people are notoriously stubborn. *If* this 'Rose' is able t'unite them, they've a chance. But otherwise, the battle is hopeless."

Ethan slapped his pen down. "This battle isn't hopeless. Men have been deserting the towns for weeks now, vanishing with weapons and supplies into whoknowswhere. Wherever there's a tyrant, there're always rebels. If the clans unite, we have a chance."

"This is an awfully large gamble you're taking," Heather observed.

The Speaker sighed. "We've known for years that this problem needed t'be dealt with. Your coming just sped things along." He rose from his chair, causing a sudden scraping of furniture as the rest of the men also stood. "Council, this meeting's adjourned. I'm sure many of you'll be wishin' t'speak with me immediately t'tell me all the things I've done wrong. You may speak with me later."

The councilmen left the room in clusters, muttering as they went. Most kept their faces neutral, though some gave Willow and Heather disgusted looks. Soon the room was clear, and Willow and Heather turned to go.

"Wait, please." The Speaker had resumed his seat beside Ethan at the other end of the table. The man looked worn out.

I would be too, if I had to deal with that lot all the time, Willow thought. "Majesty?"

"There's something else we needed t'speak with you about." The Speaker pointed to the seats. "Come, sit."

Willow and Heather exchanged quizzical looks before taking their seats. "We're at your service, Sir," Willow said. "What—"

"Here's the thing," Ethan interrupted. "I'm shipping out with th'couriers for Illyn, to coordinate th'team who'll make contact with Rose and the Shona. I'd like you t'come with me."

"Certainly," Willow answered without pausing. "Heather too, of course."

"You don't lose me that easily." Heather agreed.

"That's th'problem." Ethan dug through his pile of papers and produced one that was wrinkled with age and damp.

"Something's come to light that makes us worried t'keep you together."

Willow gave him a sarcastic look. "We aren't littlies in woodcraft. You don't have to separate us for fear I'll get distracted from work."

"Thanks, Old Thing."

"It's not that." Ethan raised his eyes from his paper. "It's actually something that came up when we first met."

"Yes, with myself a sniveling mess atop a rock." She sighed. "And I'll thank you to not remind me of that moment."

"After that, actually. It's a combination of a few things." Ethan ticked off the list on his fingers. "Your story, where you come from, your mannerisms—even how you talk. It all bears a close resemblance t'one of our military commanders that went missin' almost twenty years ago." He tipped his head. "And if *that* wasn't enough, the pair of you even look like him."

Willow and Heather cast dubious looks at each other. "We're not a pair," Heather insisted. "I've got a brown mop for hair, and she's got, umm."

"Hay. Thanks." Willow raised an eyebrow at Ethan. "If he disappeared so long ago, how would you know? You're not *that* much older than me."

Ethan waved his sheet of notes at her. "You don't think I've done my research? This's something that's on th'list of constant reports I keep addin' to. Y'never know when you'll come across something that closes th'books on an old case. Can I finish now?"

Willow sighed. "Go ahead."

"Anyway, here's why we think it." Ethan glanced at his notes. "Years ago, there was a lot of piracy an' racketeerin' along th'coasts of Iorca an' our own islands. We were also havin' trouble with th'Iorca, as we always have." He raised an eyebrow, making Willow stifle a chuckle. She'd read some of the recent reports from agents within the Sea Wanderers' rival. "They'd send pirates out t'clear our islands an' make way for colonies; we'd send our navy out an' patrol very aggressively along th'border." He held his fingers an inch apart. "We came so close on many occasions, but no wars were ever officially declared."

Heather shook her head. "I don't understand."

"Politics."

Willow jumped. In her interest in Ethan's story, she'd forgotten the Speaker. He sighed, "It's when y'can't go t'war against your enemy without signing your intent t'do so in triplicate."

"An' until that point, you're required t'sit down t'tea with them an' ask after their families." Ethan threw up his hands. "That's why I chose espionage. At least as a spy, y'can assume everyone's lying t'you."

Willow laughed at this, and Ethan grinned. "So, there was this group—the Fishhawk's Nest—who did their own raidin' around the eastern edge of Wanderer waters. They frequently had run-ins with Iorca who liked t'do the same thing along their coast. One year th'conflict ignited into skirmishes along th'eastern border."

"It was tense," the Speaker said. "I was a ship's captain at th'time. We feared the hostilities would spill over t'spark full war between Iorca and ourselves." He leaned forward with a conspirator's manner. "Instead of hunting down the ruffians on our side like we usually would, th'Council made the decision t'bring them in t'help push back th'Iorcan forces. Unofficially."

"Sharp," Heather acknowledged. "Anyone who blamed you would get a 'Who, us? Pay pirates? Us?'"

"Right. We struck our deal and started supplyin' them with weapons and food." The Speaker smiled. "Soon they were targetin' slaving ships. Every ship they took, they recruited more people t'join their crews. They even went after mainland bases where the Iorcan pirates resupplied, traded, an' spent their plunder. Iorca actually sent us a message, accusin' us of attacking them while under a flag o' truce. To which we replied—"

"Who? Us? Send pirates? Us?" Heather laughed.

Ethan took up the thread of the story. "The Fishhawks were powerful enough that th'other Sea Wanderers stopped their raids, on account of bein' pressed by authorities on both sides of th'law. The Iorcan raiders stopped 'cause they were losin' too many ships along that border. Within a short time, our waters saw peace. We recruited their leader to a command in the official military."

"I'll assume he's the one that Heather and I resemble?" Willow clarified.

Ethan nodded as the Speaker finished the story. "That year he took command, we'd a short-lived war with Iorca. With him, we survived several attacks that would've cost us dearly under other circumstances. A few years later, he disappeared."

"It was probably for th'best." Ethan set down his paper. "Th'Iorca'd put a massive bounty on his head. We made out that he went t'ground somewhere along the coast, but we lost him after that. It's our assumption that he disappeared into th'woods—"

"—Where he settled into a tribe with a new name, got married, and had children." Willow finished.

Ethan raised his eyebrows in surprise. Willow shifted on her chair. "That's a pretty far stretch, you know. But I suppose it could explain some things about Da."

"Like how come no one knows where he came from before marrying Mum," Heather agreed. "And how he talks when he's angry."

"*And* why we look different from our cousins," Willow finished, tugging one of her sister's curls. "Thanks for the tale, but what does this have to do with us being separated?"

Ethan frowned. "This place's like a net. All kinds of things slip out when they aren't supposed to. We've an Iorca delegation here—they're good trading partners, even if we don't like each other. Some of the other Council members are beginning to come t'the same conclusions I have, and that piece of information's worth a lot in the right ears." He fidgeted with his pen. "I think it's safer for th'two of you t'be on different ships."

"Think all you like. I'll do my own thinking, thanks." Willow stood, wondering if she needed to cry, yell, or sleep. *Maybe all three at once.* "Let's go, Heath'."

"I'm with you, Old Thing." Heather's sleeve brushed hers as they made for the doorway.

"Willow, wait," the Speaker said.

Against her best judgement, she turned to face him. "Sir?"

"I wanted t'aplogize." The Speaker bowed his head. "It shouldn't take a person begging for help for us t'decide t'intervene in a dire situation. The Sea Wanderers're often misrepresented as pirates and rogues, but we allow our reputation t'be an excuse not to act." He looked up, dark eyes solemn. "I'm sorry my people've waited this long. I'm sorry your friends were taken. I'm sorry you had t'be the turning point for us in this matter. And I'm sorry we said anything about your father. I'm just very sorry."

"I'm sorry as well." Willow cleared her throat. "Our people hate war. And I'm doing all I can to make sure there's peace. I wish none of this had happened, but I can't control the actions of others. All I can control is my reaction to them."

"That's right." The Speaker smiled distantly. "I recognize that phrase. Did you learn that from your father?"

"Yes, Sir."

"We fought side by side, once. He was a good man."

Willow nodded. "He's my hero, sir. No matter who he was before." She curtsied again. "Thank you for your apology. I hope this ends well for all of us."

She left the room, Heather beside her. As they followed corridors towards the waterfront, Heather's arm sneaked around her waist. Her voice was small. "I don't want to be apart from you, Old Thing."

Willow stopped and patted her sister's hand. "I don't either." She set her shoulders angrily. "It doesn't matter, what they said. I won't let them separate us." In an instant, the tightness in her throat turned to tear, and she turned to bury her face in Heather's bony shoulder.

"There, there, angry face. It'll be all right," Heather said, her voice comforting in Willow's ear. "You've been working too hard." She let her go and pointed out one of the windows. The harbor below shimmered in the afternoon sun. "Let's go find somewhere to take a swim. Maybe find an octopus and dump it in Tiren's hammock?"

Willow sniffed, drying tears on her collar. "Let's." As they set off down the stairs, she added, "And let's not tell the others what they said about Da, eh?"

"Do you believe it?"

Willow wrinkled her nose. "I'm not sure."

"Good. Me neither."

18

HOLD ESKEL

A little boy tugged Violet's pack strap. "How much longer?"

"Not for a while yet," Violet patiently answered, tripping over a tree root. They had been on the march for several long days after leaving the hollow, and everyone was beginning to feel the effects of many nights in the open.

"We should be there very soon," Erven reassured her.

She stepped over a rock in the middle of the path. "That's what you said two hours ago."

In fact, it took them four more hours before Violet passed through a narrow ravine and saw Hold Eskel for the first time. Mountains circled a bowl-shaped valley, tall grass giving way to clumps of aspen and the dark fringe of pine forest. The hold itself stood sentinel over the village spread at its feet, running all the way down to the banks of a slow-moving river. Herds of goats and sheep grazed in paddocks along the river, the occasional horse or cow standing taller amidst them. On the outskirts of the village sprawled an encampment of tents and other makeshift shelters, where movement could be seen as the first Shona reached hailing distance. Violet wasn't certain which appealed to her more, the peaceful setting or the chance of sleeping under a roof again.

"So, there it is, eh?" Violet looked up to see Thorn, one of the Yarrow Leaf men that had stayed with the Shona. He winked at her. "Personally, I think there are too few trees."

One of the Whitecaps captains agreed with him. "But you have to admit, there's plenty of room." She pointed at the tents far below them. "That's where we sent everyone who came to join us. I didn't realize how many had come."

The sky had taken on the cast of evening as Violet reached the camp. The Shona were preparing fires for the night, organizing their gear, and setting up sleeping spaces. She sighed. It appeared they would be sleeping under the stars once more. With a wary glance at the sky, she claimed an area near their supplies to set out her things. It had rained each afternoon since they had left the Shona base, but tonight had thus far remained fair.

As she unpacked, she watched the others in the camp come to greet the new arrivals. As some of the older Shona began building cooking fires for dinner, she was approached by some of the Thunderhead healers who wanted to know where they should station themselves. After pointing them towards her spot, she got a mere ten steps before a pair of children approached.

"He's not letting me sleep by him!"

The other boy pushed grimy hair out of his eyes. "He snores!"

She sighed deeply. "You set your things here." She pointed to a spot five feet away. "And you set yours there. Put your packs in between you, and you won't hear him snore."

As the boys settled their things, a broad-shouldered man

with a plaid tunic lumbered past. "Lassie, are you one of this pack of bandits?"

"Yessir. Well, sort of," she replied, inwardly groaning. "I'm their healer."

"Well, look here, healer. We're expecting more men from our hold any day now. Your people will be in our way, see?" He crossed his arms. "What're we supposed to do about that?"

"I'm not the right person to ask, Sir." She pointed across the camp towards Rose and Erven. "Those two over there are the ones you need."

"Much obliged, lass." He gave her a brusque nod and lumbered off.

Similar interruptions made her trip over to the dinner fires a long walk. She finally plopped next to Lena and accepted several slices of toasted bread and cheese. "Where'd we get the bread?" she asked through an oozy mouthful.

Lena likewise had her mouth full. "The village women saw how many children we had and gave it to us."

"Nice of them." She looked over at Rose. Her friend was still talking to the villagers, and more leaders from the other camps were joining them. "I wish they'd have let her take a break and get some food before they started pestering her."

"Erven too," River chimed in from the other side of Lena. The stocky captain had been unusually quiet ever since Clover had left. "He hasn't taken a rest since we started moving everyone here."

This reminder made Violet frown into her tea. "That he hasn't." Downing the dregs, she stood and brushed her bedraggled skirts free of crumbs. "I'll go see if I can lend them some sense."

"Good luck," River snorted. "You'll probably need it."

She found her friend sitting on one of a handful of barrels. From the people also sitting in the circle, she deduced that there were representatives from several tribes, men from the coastal towns, and Hold Eskel's leaders. As she approached, she heard Rose wearily say, "I know they're not in the best place, but I can hardly expect them to move now." She turned as Violet approached. "Yes, dear?"

Violet held out the food that she had brought. "If these gentlemen will let you, I brought you some food."

"Good idea, Violet," Clover's uncle said. He cast an appraising look over the company. "I don't know about you, but I'll be useless in any kind of conference without a nights' sleep. Is there anything stopping us from reconvening tomorrow?"

There were flickers of disagreement among the tribal leaders, all of whom seemed set on ignoring each other, but eventually they agreed. After some prodding, the village headman offered to open the inn for a meeting the following day, and the group disbanded into the evening.

"Thank you, dear," Rose said as they returned to the Shona camp. "I didn't know how long they'd go on talking. I thought dealing with the Shona was difficult, but dealing with four tribes, three towns, and one village council on an empty stomach is far beyond me."

Erven snorted as he walked beside them. The bruises from the beatings he'd endured had faded, but his shoulders slumped and his usual cheerful manner was wearing thin. "They'll calm down once they see we'll listen to all of them." He eyed the food that Lena offered him. "We'd better do what we can to get a good night's sleep. I feel like tomorrow could be a long day."

Despite everyone's desire to get an early start, there were a thousand and ten problems to be solved before Rose found herself commencing their meeting soon after lunch. Once everyone was present, she counted four tribal leaders, five citizens of the village, one Yarrow Leaf tribesman, two representatives of the lowlanders, and five Shona. The seventeen of them sat on an assortment of chairs and stools around a long table in the common room of the inn. Rose, wishing her chair was a little bit higher, sternly warned herself not to let her tiredness get the better of her as the men quieted.

"Well, is this everyone?" At the nods of the men, she said with relief, "Good. I'm pleased that everyone was able to come. As I've found out repeatedly over the last month, there's always something to occupy a leader's time."

By the chuckles and eye rolls around the table, she judged that her comment had found the right note. *Steady.* "And on a larger scale, thank you all for your support. There were more men here than I was told to expect. I expected we'd need to continue gathering forces, but you seem to have had an early start."

One of the men scooted his stool forward. "Well, Kuma wasn't exactly subtle about the fact that he'd found you." He propped an elbow on the table. "He posted notices to every town in the lowlands, and there was a big event planned." Her guts twisted, but she tried to keep the unease off her face as he continued, "Once we'd found out you'd escaped, most of us knew the mountains were the best place to find you."

Rose gingerly sipped from her cup of tea. "And what about the rest of you?" She carefully set the cup down. "I thought I was going to have to visit each hold in turn and beg for help."

The village leader—also the innkeeper—cleared his throat meaningfully. "We knew this was coming years ago. Didn't exactly start preparing recently."

"Really? Please, explain."

He looked uncomfortably at the gathered leaders. "When

that bastard's men attacked, we hunkered down and stayed put. No one expected he'd get as far as he did." His voice dropped. "That was our mistake. By the time we knew how bad the situation was, it was too late. A month after the castle fell, some refugees brought a woman to us. Very ill she was, almost out of her wits. Our women fed and clothed her, tended to her. Didn' take too long before we suspected she was the queen. Of course, we wondered how it could be, but in between ravings, she said her lord had sent her and the wee one away."

Rose caught her breath and tried not to let her sudden emotion show. *My mother. My real mother.* "What—" She cleared her throat and tried again. "What happened to her? Is she still here?"

The man shook his head gently. "Nah. She weren't strong to begin with. She died a few months after she arrived. To the last, she made us promise to help you when the time came. When we heard rumor you'd escaped, we began to prepare." He smiled crookedly, revealing a broken eyetooth. "That's why so many of us are here. We made one mistake, but we'll not make the same again."

Rose took a deep breath. "T-thank you."

"We knew as well." One of the other highlanders, a man with several black band tattoos circling his arms, spoke up. "Our fighters are ready to follow you." He glanced sidelong at the other tribal leaders. "As long as your other followers are willing."

"I'd hope you'd set aside your jealousy." Erven glanced over at Rose, who nodded for him to continue. She sat back from the table to collect herself as he said, "It's one thing to maintain rivalries in a time of peace, but in a time of war it's plain stupidity."

One of the other tribesmen snorted. "Why should we fight wi' them when we've been safe oursel' these past fifteen year?"

"You know the Shona," Erven said, looking around the table. "We've traded with your people, kept their secrets, and stayed out of your business." He leaned an elbow on the table, and Rose was struck by how pale he'd become. "It's been our blood that's kept the passes closed and let you enjoy your isolation. *We* stand behind Rose, and you ought to as well."

"We won't have a chance if we stay divided," Merald added from next to Erven.

"I suppose you would know that, wouldn't you?" Clover's uncle Thorn said. "Former slave, right?"

"And before that, one of the Aubron tribe," Merald said, tipping his chin towards a broad-shouldered tribesman with gold and green threads in his tunic. Rose raised an eyebrow in surprise, comparing his features with the other man. "Only, my family was exiled over a dispute of honor."

The man shifted in his seat, a flush creeping up his face. "Let the dead talk to the dead. We came here to discuss our support of the lady. The men who exiled your father are long gone."

"So is my family," Merald snapped.

"Please, settle old grievances later," Rose said with a warning look towards Merald. *I think I understand why Erven insisted he sit in.* "We're here to ask for the cooperation of *all* the highland tribes, regardless of honor. And the men from the lowlands." She turned to the weathered old fellow who had been named their spokesperson. "What do you say?"

He laughed, stirring honey into his tea. "Most of us left our families to fight for you. Don't fret, you have our support."

Rose smiled. "It's a relief to know that you're willing to fight on this side and not the other."

The man shrugged. "Few can stomach working with the

Iorcan troops milord hired. Their ways are too different, and they're only motivated by money. Besides, you're so outnumbered that it would've been wrong for us not to."

"As for that," Erven said. "There's some chance we could have allies of our own, if time works in our favor. Some of our men left more than a week ago to try and negotiate support from the Sea Wanderers."

"More outsiders? Why would they decide to help us?"

"We don't know," Thorn admitted. "If anything, probably just to protect their own interests."

"Well, help can hardly hurt," one of the remaining tribesmen agreed.

The fourth tribe representative resembled River, with glossy black hair and slanted eyes. He stayed silent until the Aubron leader glared over at him. "Everyone's spoken but you. Are you with us?"

The man hunched his shoulders. "I brought my men, didn't I? That doesn't mean I intend to enjoy working with you."

"I suppose that'll do," the Aubron leader chuckled.

The talk turned to discussions of training, communication, logistics and housing, and amid practical considerations the tension in the room subsided. After a break for dinner, they resumed, sending runners to and from the room to collect information or send orders. After many hours, Rose found herself losing the battle of staying alert. She blinked away drowsiness and proposed, "Let's adjourn. We can pick this up again tomorrow, once some of our plans have been put into effect."

Amid 'goodnights' and 'sleep wells', the leaders abandoned their seats and went to their camps. Over the course of the day, the Shona had moved to a rise above the main camp and erected several shelters to keep off the weather. Amid tired conversation, Violet and Erven followed Rose to one of several tents overlooking the camp.

"What's this?" Rose wrapped her hand around a javelin stuck in the ground outside the entrance.

Erven unfolded a piece of navy-blue fabric from his belt pouch. A gold star shimmered against the blue as he shook out the wrinkles. "One of the men gave me this. He says it was left over from the last war." Using some cording, he attached the flag to the javelin. "We'll get a proper flagpole later."

"Thank you," Rose said with a smile. *My parents may have touched this flag,* she thought, brushing her fingertips over the embroidered star. *I wish I could have known them.*

Violet eyed Erven. "Yes, thank you very much. Now *please* go get some sleep. I don't want you to die of exhaustion right as we've reached safety."

"Don't worry, I'll be fine," Erven laughed. He headed towards the Shona, sleeping in their bedrolls around their three fires.

Rose's hand found Violet's, and together they watched as the fires burned like the eyes of a dragon, sending smoke into the summer night. "It's really something, isn't it?" Rose said. "I didn't expect this many would come."

"But they did," Violet pointed out. "And they're ready to follow you."

Rose sighed, her eyes heavy and head aching with weariness. "They all think I know what I'm doing. I'm so afraid of what will happen once they find out I don't."

19
CAMP 'MUD PILE'

Cuttlefish was a funny name for a courier vessel. When Tiren had described the animal, she'd accused him of telling tales. Now that Willow had seen one in person, she decided that it wasn't a bad name. The vessel sailed in tandem with the *Skimmer*—another courier—and a larger military vessel, the *Seagull*.

After a week of frantic activity alerting close-by garrisons, life on the *Cuttlefish* was beginning to settle into rhythm. That afternoon, Willow had settled into the partitioned area she shared with Heather for a quick nap before returning to work. The gentle swaying of her hammock worked its magic, and she wasn't sure how long she'd been asleep when feet on the ladder announced an interruption.

"'ullo, Old Thing!" Heather abruptly hushed herself. "Oh, sorry. I'll come back later, eh?"

"It's fine," Willow croaked. She rubbed grit out of her eyes. "What is it?"

"It's really nothing," Heather apologized. "We're

approaching our next port. Also, Ethan got another message and asked me t'find you."

She swung out of her hammock, much more gracefully than when first learning how to use one. "I wonder what it is this time."

"Search me." Heather followed her abovedecks, ducking under lines as they made for the stern cabin. "I was in the middle of something. I'll be going." The ends of Heather's bright orange headscarf trailed in the breeze as she left to join the ship's birdkeeper along the railing.

Willow watched affectionately as her younger sister slid a glove onto one hand and whistled one of the birds down from the mast. *It's good for her to have something to do.* The aft cabin door was open, and she could hear Ethan talking with someone. "You called?"

He looked up as she came in, as did the *Cuttlefish's* captain. "We've gotten confirmation of the camp location."

She closed the door behind her and leaned against one of the lockers. "Will the island they were talking about work?"

"It seems like it." Ethan hunched over a map of the Illyn coastline, the end of his pen balanced over a dot of an island some distance away. "It's got enough deep harborage that our bigger vessels'll be able t'fit, and it's far enough from th'coast that it'll take some serious dedication for them t'find us."

She scrutinized the area, frowning at a cluster of larger islands outlined in a different color northeast of the dot. "It's not within the Kittai Islanders' territory, is it?"

"No," Ethan rubbed his forehead. "It's farther than it looks on th'map. And even if it was, they keep t'themselves."

"Mmm." She sat cross-legged on top of the locker. "Any sign of the Iorca fleet?"

"You'd better hope not," the captain snorted. "If they arrived this early, we'd be chum."

"If they follow the patterns they've established in th'past, it'll be another bit yet before they sail," Ethan sighed. "It'd be nice if we could catch them right as they're tryin' t'offload their men an' supplies." He held out both hands. "Alternatively, we could train th'local seagulls t'gnaw their rigging t'shreds. And when they're in confusion, we swoop in, dump them all in th'ocean, and ransom any that we catch!"

"That would be nice, but I'd rather put my hope in a sieve holding water," Willow laughed. "Let's focus on the work at hand, eh?"

Heather was on the fifth verse of 'The Great Grand Duke of Pern' when a glob of seaweed landed on the decking nearby. She glared at the forecastle. "If you do that one more time, laddie, I'll turn ye upside-down an' scrub this deck wi'yer head."

The Sea Wanderer mate—young for his post—threw another clump in her direction. "Stop that wailin', an' I will."

Heather wiped her hands on her shirt front. Pulling the knot tighter in her kerchief, she kicked her bucket of scrubbing water across the deck. It tipped and spilled murky water across the boards, and she went after it aggressively with her mop. "Ohhh, the Great Grand Duke of Pern had ten dozen wigs. He swung them in circles around his head—owch!"

Throwing down her kerchief, she charged the forecastle with mop brandished. The mate stood ready with another seaweed ball, and within short time they were chasing each other in circles round and round the deck of the *Cuttlefish*.

Having completed their mission to alert Sea Wanderer garrisons across the area between Illyn and Alcha Dar, the courier group had been given the command to make for the forward camp near Illyn. They were tacking along the coastline now, the commanders debating via signal flashes whether or not to go any closer to land. Heather was not privy to these discussions. She had been sentenced to deck chores after displaying a lack of dedication to military discipline.

"When I get my hands on you, I'll—oof!" Heather ran straight into the mate, sitting down hard on her rump. "What?"

He stared into the distance on the Illyn side of the vessel. "Shut up. Someone's signalin' us." His boots pounded the decking as he hurried to the captain's elbow. "Sir! We're being hailed."

"Hailed?" The captain sent a hold pattern to the *Seagull*, who responded with an acknowledgement flash. He turned to the other side of the ship. "So we are. Good work, lad."

Heather leaned over the railing, looking for the signal. It took several passes before she finally caught sight of the small boat. A green pennant fluttered from its masthead, and small flashes of light came from its bow. After weeks of contacting other Sea Wanderer ships, she knew that someone aboard the vessel was either a Sea Wanderer or knew their signals by heart.

The captain stowed his spyglass. "Tell them we're comin', lad."

"Who is it?" Heather asked.

Ethan answered from behind her, coming to lean on the railing. "It seems th'rebels've heard of us."

Willow joined them, the side of her hand smudged with ink. "It's from Rose!"

"How d'you know? Can you even see that far?" Heather demanded.

Her older sister made a face. "I can't, but he can." She tipped her head towards Ethan. "He says they say they're from the Illyn rebels!" Her face glistened with something Heather knew wasn't sea spray. "She's all right!"

The signalmen continued exchanging messages. By the time the faces of the people aboard the fishing boat could be seen, it was agreed that they were allies. "He says they're from th'Shona," the mate told Heather as they lounged against the rail. "Whoever that is. An' they've been hopin' t'get our attention."

"Shona, eh?" Heather tugged her kerchief down as spray hit her face. "I wonder what types they are." She eyed the crew as the ships drew closer. "Nice taste in headgear, though." She cupped her hands around her mouth. "You in the hat! Excellent taste, laddie!"

The answer came back on the breeze, as the figure whipped off a massive, broad-brimmed hat to let tangled brown hair blow in the wind. "HEATHER!!!"

"Someone must've put rum in my tea," Heather remarked. She belted out the next line of 'The Great Grand Duke of Pern' and was flabbergasted to hear it continued from the other ship.

When the men from the fishing vessel clambered up to the *Cuttlefish*, Heather and Willow pushed past the Sea Wanderers to clutch their sister. Clover shoved her enormous hat on Heather's head as they jumped up and down regardless of the heaving deck. Heather didn't think she could be happier until her father's arms surrounded them. The glee of meeting Clover turned to relief, and to her dismay she shed tears into Alder's weather-beaten vest.

Sometime later, the girls sat on the steps leading to the aftcastle, Clover and Heather flicking rice grains out of their lunch bowls at each other. They'd already exchanged stories, upon which their father had gone to meet with the captains of the Sea Wanderer vessels. Clover nudged her with an elbow. "He looks like he belongs with them, doesn't he?"

Heather raised her eyebrows. "Who does?"

"Da."

Heather and Willow met each other's eyes guiltily for a moment before hurriedly looking anywhere else. To cover her slip, Heather looked harder at the group of men. Unfortunately, Clover's innocent observation made sense. There was something in the men's manner, or possibly how they stood, that gave them all the same feel. Seeing her father interacting with the Sea Wanderers, she was starting to believe the tales she'd heard about him. Digging a chunk of taro out of her bowl, she decided not to let Clover in on her suspicions. "You're right, lassie. Though I've no idea why."

Clover took the taro. "I've no idea either. And why are you calling me lassie?"

Willow rolled her eyes. "That's the way they talk here. She's gotten completely entranced." She brushed crumbs off her shirt front. "Sorry, you lot. I've got to go. Duty calls."

"Bye, lassie!" Heather shouted after Willow.

"What's bitten her?" Clover set her empty bowl on the stairs. "She didn't even cry over what I said about home."

"Willow?" Heather shook her head. "If she's not with her nose deep in an inkwell, she's cooking. She's been wearing herself out."

"She always did think it was all her responsibility, eh?" Clover curled her legs under her. "Think she'll come with us?"

Heather sighed. "I don't know. She's wrapped up in what she's doing, and that intelligence fellow does make her laugh. I suppose it's good for her."

"Yeh." Clover leaned into Heather's shoulder. "I missed you."

Heather rested her chin on the top of her sister's head. "I missed you too."

. . .

THE TALK HAD BEEN GOING on for rather longer than Heather liked when their father returned. Heather and Clover had abandoned their steps after being trod upon by too many feet and were napping in a rope nest on the aft deck. Alder's whistle and yell from the lower deck startled them awake, and they tumbled out of the nest and down the stairs. "Present, Sir!" Clover giggled, trying to straighten Heather's kerchief.

"Take your ease. And don't call me Sir. We're here for another day or so, until one of the other military ships catch up. They want t'send an advance guard and some diplomatic fellow with us."

"What about Willow?" Clover took off her hat and straightened her hair under it.

"Willow's staying put," Alder sighed. "They said she's been helping coordinate their communication." His brow was furrowed, and Heather wondered how that conversation had gone.

Knowing Willow, there might've been shouting involved.

"You have your choice," her father said. "Do you want t'stay here, or do you want to come with us?"

Heather twisted the hem of her tunic. Stay onboard with the permanently distracted sister, or return with her father to an unfriendly country? She'd heard from Clover about the Shona, and it sounded more interesting than scrubbing salt off the deck. She shook curls out of her eyes. "I'd best collect my things."

THE SKIES LOOKED different here in high summer. As Rose walked to her quarters after yet another late night of meetings, she squinted at the stars through a veil of campfire smoke. The tent was high enough above everyone else's campsites to be able to overlook them all. *Just in case I needed reminding how many lives are at stake.*

She stopped before going into the tent and sat cross-legged outside the doorway, brushing dust off her trousers in disgust. The majority of the commanders knew exactly how old she was, and a few had gotten comfortable enough in the last week that they'd begun talking to her as if she were their daughter. She propped her chin in her hand and stared at the Shona encampment. *No one treats the Shona like they're children. At least, not to their faces.*

"Rose?"

It was Violet, no doubt wondering why she hadn't come inside and gone to bed yet.

"I'm out here." She uncrossed her legs and stretched them out, worn boots pointing down at the camp. "I'm just thinking."

Feet shuffled as Violet came out of the tent in her shift, pillow lines across her face. After a patient's flailing hand had caught and sent a slick of blood across her face, the healer had cropped her mousy brown hair short. A cowlick stood out over her temple as she pulled a shawl around her shoulders and sat next to Rose. "Too much thinking makes for long nights. Are you all right?"

"I wish there was another way to coordinate so many people." Rose rubbed one mud-stained boot toe against the other. "These nights of meetings feel like they're getting harder and harder to keep on track."

"Why?"

"Sometimes I think all they see when they look at me is one of the Shona." She sighed, "Or, worse, a naïve child. And not a particularly bright one, at that. I know I wanted them to get used to me, but I didn't expect this."

"Hmmm." Violet leaned back and took a long look at her.

There was something hesitant in her eyes as she finished her examination.

Finally, Rose huffed, "Just say it."

"Well," Violet let go of the ends of the shawl to carefully trace the edge of Rose's trouser cuff. "If they keep seeing you as part and parcel with the Shona, you might try looking different." She tilted her head to look at Rose's hair, which despite her care had started coming loose from her braid. "I know some of the girls here would love to teach you new ways to wear your hair."

Despite herself, Rose laughed. "That's your advice? Look like a lady?"

"Why not?" Violet answered sensibly. "If you're having trouble with them not taking you seriously, maybe it's better to look like you're already in power."

"It's worth a try," Rose agreed. "I wonder if I can find a dress or two that we can alter to fit."

"It'll be easier than when we were home." Violet gave a hiccupy giggle. "Here, no one will have to lengthen their pass-alongs so you'll fit them."

Rose ran her hands over her trouser legs again. "It *will* be nice to wear a skirt again." She craned her neck as a shooting star went overhead, barely visible through the campfire smoke. "Did you see that?"

She belatedly recalled that Violet's eyes weren't very sharp as the healer shook her head. "Sorry. Was it a dancing star?"

"It was." Rose leaned back on her elbows to examine the night sky. "They're different here than they were at home. It's taking me longer to learn them."

"You will, though." Violet shivered. "I'm going back to bed." She gave Rose a warning look. "You'd better get some sleep too."

Rose didn't take her eyes off the stars. "I will."

The moon had moved several degrees across the sky by the time Rose finally slid into her bedroll. The following morning, her request for a dress was greeted with enthusiasm by the women of Hold Eskel. Standing in one of the cozy homes while several women fitted the borrowed dresses to her frame, she had to be careful to not let her emotions show on her face. Something in the women's generosity and enthusiasm filled the aching hole that she hadn't quite been able to name. As they helped her into the last of three dresses—a soothing dusty pink with a carefully laced fawn overdress, she had to resist the urge to start crying.

River, pulled into the cheerful gathering after delivering a message from Erven, commented, "You don't look quite as young as you used to."

"That's rich, chickie," one of the seamstresses laughed. "And you're all of—"

"Younger than her, of course," River said cheekily. "But *I'm* still allowed to look it."

Rose turned to Violet, picking over a pile of dried yarrow stems in the corner. One of the girls had arranged Rose's hair in an elaborate braid pinned at the back of her head, and she wondered if it looked as nice as it felt. "Will this do?"

Violet's tired face lit up as she examined the results. "You look splendid! I think they'll listen a little better now!"

It had begun to rain. The sound on the cabin roof would have made it hard for Willow to concentrate on work, had it not been for the commotion outside. They were making preparations for landing at the newly established Sea Wanderer base, and the rest of the crew was busy bringing the *Cuttlefish* in. Exempt from these preparations, Willow was indoors, stacking documents into boxes and trying not to undo the work of several hours by smearing damp ink. Outside, there were shouts and hails from the men already ashore, and she could feel the vibrations through the deck as lines were thrown and boats lowered.

"Does it have a name?"

"What, this island?" Ethan was hunting through the document boxes on their worktable for his pen case. "We can come up with one. How's 'Mud Pile' sound?"

She noticed the case balanced precariously at the edge of the table. Tossing it to him, she commented, "You know, I think espionage has deadened your sense of humor."

"It's not that far off!" he protested, stuffing the pen case into a knapsack along with several maps. "The Kittai Islanders used t'have a logging outpost here, before pressure from pirates forced them out. Now there's just mud!" He dropped the knapsack on the table and banged the cabin door open.

Willow followed him out to the deck, sidestepping the crew as they made the mooring lines fast. The island rose steeply from the harbor, the sides of the bluff slick with mud and rain. She frowned at the sky. It had been fair for most of their journey north, but the weather had turned dismal. Retreating to her quarters, she retrieved a scarf and wound it around her head and neck before returning abovedeck.

From the opposite rail, Willow peered across the harbor to count more than half a dozen assorted vessels bobbing at anchor. All bore the green shell-and-wave ensign flown by the Sea Wanderer military. *So many are already here.* Just as quickly, a pang of worry struck. *What if this is all?* Her stomach sank, and for the first time in several days she wished Heather had stayed. *Heather would make me laugh, and I could forget.* A prickle at the back of her nose warned of tears, and she fiercely scrubbed at her eyes.

"Are you all right?" Ethan's boots clomped against the deck as he joined her. "Y'seem upset. Did I say something t'offend?" He reddened and went on before she'd had a chance to reassure him. "It's really not that miserable of a place, I promise!" He waved a hand generally towards the sky. "It's really muddy, an' I thought—"

"It's all right," she said. "I'm fine. I was just trying to count ships, and guessing how many men have come." She turned to face him, pulling the scarf farther over her head. "And I miss my sister."

"I did notice you're quieter without her about."

"Yes." She could barely see the low walls of camp from the harbor. "And I hope you don't mind me saying this, but I'm also starting to hate paperwork."

"What, you mean—" Ethan's words were drowned out amid the shouts from the dock. Another ship was making harbor. The *Cuttlefish's* crew were left to unload the remainder of their cargo and supplies themselves. With her belongings in her pack and a box under one arm, Willow followed Ethan up the slippery path towards the old logging camp. She was so intent on keeping the rain out of her face and her feet on the steep path that she hardly marked their progress until she was standing on level ground again.

"This is it, then?" She admired the sharpened points on the logs forming the walls. "Did we build this?"

"The Kittai Islanders built th'barracks and the other outbuildings." Ethan wiped rain out of his eyes. "The advance guard put up th'walls." He gave her a crooked smile. "It wouldn't do for just anyone t'saunter in without at least *some* kind of challenge. Let's go find where our things belong."

Willow pulled her heels free of the mud and followed, noticing the steeply sloped, ceramic-tiled roofs on most of the buildings. They put their belongings in the rooms allotted to them before taking their things to the command post.

Ethan looked appraisingly at the narrow room they'd been given for an office. It was already crowded with boxes of supplies, and document tubes covered the worktable. "I s'pose they heard I was on my way and decided t'leave it all for me t'untangle." He shook his head before eyeing the windows. "An' these're ground floor windows. Anyone could stand right there'n listen in t'whatever we're discussing." He set the lantern he'd been carrying down on the table. "Maybe we can move t'the second story later. Ready t'get started unraveling this mess?"

Willow shook her head, already weary at the idea of creating order from the mass of documents that they had walked into. "I'd like to look around."

"Go on." Ethan snicked the seal off a document tube. "I need to start, otherwise it'll annoy me th'rest of th'day."

Outside, the rain was wearing off into a chilly mist. The sparse trees surrounding the camp jutted against the leaden sky, rain dripping off their dull green needles. *It feels so gloomy. It must get very cold and lonely here.*

Most of the buildings bore the decaying roof tiles and mired paint of long years of disuse, but the sense of abandonment faded the farther she went into camp. Smoke drifted from chimneys and forges, anvils and carpentry could be heard, and there were voices everywhere. She stopped to say hello to a cage of messenger birds, their cheerful twittering reminding her of Heather. *There is some warmth here, I suppose.*

Ethan found her in the kitchens over an hour later. "I wondered where you were."

"I told you I was getting worn down with papers." Willow clanged her spoon against the rim of a giant pot of steaming water and vegetable tops. "That and having to triple-guess the motives of anyone who talked to me."

He leaned against the edge of a splintery work table. "Well, I s'pose I can spare you, now that there're more intelligence agents here." He shrugged. "Are y'certain this's where you'll be happiest?"

"I'm happy where I can be really helpful." Willow plonked a bowl of shrimp next to him. "Shell those, please. And save me the shells and heads."

Ethan held one of the shrimp at eye level, quirking an eyebrow. "And you're making?"

"Stock for soup."

"Mmm, tasty." He flicked out his belt knife. "Are y'saying communication isn't where you can be helpful?"

"You said it yourself; you have more experienced people here to help you," Willow pointed out, turning to see that her water was starting to boil. "I'm only useful condensing reports, or transcribing things for you to read later." She carefully swung the pot away from the fire before kneeling to rummage through a box of withered vegetables. "You can have anyone do that. And how many other cooks do you see here?"

Ethan looked up from the shrimp, his brow furrowing. "None, at the moment."

"Exactly!" Willow pointed at him with the frond end of a carrot. "No one else, because the others have had to do both cook and supply duties." She tossed the carrot onto the table amid a pile of other wrinkled vegetables. "And there're supplies coming in on every ship to be accounted for. For all command's talk about logistics and military, and who to send where and why, they haven't thought to make sure someone could feed everyone."

"It *is* a bit shortsighted. I need t'check on that," Ethan

mused, dropping a shrimp into the bowl. "I'll still need you t'split your time occasionally."

"And I'm still happy to help." Willow dumped the shells and heads into the pot, sending the rest of the vegetables in after them. "As long as I can decide how that split is allocated."

"Noted." Ethan laughed. "I'll see what command says. They might object. With your father not here, you're th'most expert person on Rose that we've got."

"Well, tell them that I'm as expert here as I am transcribing communications." Willow picked up the spoon. "If there's one thing you ought to know about me, Lord Suspicion, it's that I can't walk away from an opportunity to feed people."

20

UNEASY ALLIANCE

The camp had shed the hodgepodge organization that the Shona had arrived to. Now a central fire anchored the encampment, the tents of the various groups arranged like the spokes of a wheel. With a gift of dye from the representatives of Hold Thinar, more and more men donned navy-blue in addition to their clan patterns. Rose and Erven were kept busy meeting and working out agreements with the different tribes, leaving Violet and the outpost commanders to oversee the Shona.

More men kept arriving, continuing to swell the camp's numbers. Many brought women, and some brought their entire families. The air rang with the voices of excited children, the clanging of sword on sword and hammer on metal, the sounds of livestock, pipes and war drums, and shouts of men training.

Finally, the clashing sounds drove Violet to do something about the noise. She left her work apron hanging from a tent pole and went to go find Rose. As she approached the central fire where most of the leaders congregated, she found her friend attempting to reason with the Hold Aubron leader. She politely hung back until the man eventually left for his camp.

Shielding her eyes from the sun, she asked, "Have you been busy?"

Rose wiped a hand across her brow. "Everyone wants to double-check their orders against mine. And they're asking a lot of questions about the Sea Wanderers."

"I'd been wondering about that, too." In fact, she'd been more wondering about Clover. *She's still so young, to be pulled here and there.* "You've been so busy I didn't want to bother you."

"Oh, Violet, don't think that. If it wasn't for you, I don't think I could do any of this." Rose stood and stretched her back. "Erven helps me with diplomacy and strategy, but you keep me sane. You remind me why all this is worth the trouble."

"And—what is that, exactly?"

Rose had been looking over her head with a smile. "Oh, people that I care about. Like those, for instance."

Violet turned to look, catching sight of a party of men coming across the valley. Standing out amid the bareheaded men were a pair of girls; one wearing a massive hat, the other a brilliantly colored kerchief. As they approached, she could faintly hear the sounds of off-key singing.

"There once was a hat! A smelly, smelly hat. And the hat was on the fish, and the fish on the squid, and the squid in the barrel, and the barrel on the—"

"Shuttup!"

"Yooou shuttup!"

SHORTLY THEREAFTER, the Yarrow Leaf men and the Sea Wanderer delegate were sitting under one of the tents eating lunch. The rest of the Sea Wanderer advance guard had spread out to mingle with the Shona, forging their own relationships with the freedom fighters. The highlanders were keeping their distance for now, uncertain about these men who dressed flamboyantly and acted too cheerful for anyone's good.

Heather stood to one side with Violet, watching the reunion of Clover and her friends. She had commandeered her younger sister's hat, placing it atop her kerchief in a highly dignified manner.

"I think she should keep it," Violet said, eyeing the bedraggled headgear. "It makes finding her in a crowd very easy."

Heather frowned at the feather flopping into her eyes. "Aye, it makes her easy to find, but what if I don't want her found?"

"Well, at least yours is brighter." Violet touched a corner of the kerchief that was sticking out. "Do they all wear that bright of colors?"

Giving her a stern look, Heather observed, "You used t' like bright colors yourself. I recall y'used to like yellow." She braced her arms on the rock behind her. "Also pink, and blue, and purple, an'—"

"True," Violet agreed. It *had* been a while since she'd seen the rich hues of flowers, or spring leaves, or late-season strawberries. *Everything here is all green and grey and dark—like they've forgotten the flowers still bloom.* "They don't wear bright colors here." She forced her tone to lighten as she added, "The Shona don't even wear skirts."

"Neither do Sea Wanderers!" Heather slapped her thighs, raising a cloud of dust from her battered trousers.

Violet couldn't help a chuckle. "I think that's a fashion you enjoy a little too much."

Heather put her nose in the air. "Ridiculous."

Clover, River, and Lena finished tussling and came toward

them, straightening each other's appearances along the way. "Hello, squirrels," Clover said. "Having a nice chat?"

"Y'might say that," Heather said. "Violet doesn't like my trousers."

"I didn't say that!" Violet exclaimed.

A small boy ran up and yelled, "River, someone wants you!" He stuck out his lower lip. "They said they wanted 'someone in charge', not me."

River sighed. "I'd better go deal with that. Coming, Lena?"

The pair walked off as Clover piled onto the rock with Violet and Heather. "Where's Da?"

Heather pointed towards the central ring. "Talkin' with the fancy britches."

Violet chuckled. "With as important as they act, I agree with the name." She sighed. "I'm glad you're here, I only wish Willow had come too."

Heather plucked a blade of grass and started shredding it. "I wish she had, too. She's got a *job* now." She rolled her eyes. "She doesn't want this to fail if there's any way she can push it along."

"Da understands," Clover said. "He wanted to stay with them too."

"What makes you say that?" Violet asked. As she did, she caught a suddenly evasive glance from Heather; squinted eyes and deliberate nonchalance suggesting that there was more to Clover's innocent statement than the girl was letting on.

Clover shrugged. "I think he was one." She plucked her floppy-brimmed hat from Heather's head. "Their sense of humor is the same."

"Not that he'd ever admit it," Heather grumbled. Her stomach answered with a similar growl. "I'm hungry. Is there food?"

"Certainly." Violet stood. "Come on, I'll show you around."

As they went towards the cooks, Violet noticed that another party of highlanders had arrived and were making camp near the others. She sighed as a Shona pointed several of them towards her and the sisters. She indicated the fire. "You two go on without me. It looks like someone needs directions again."

Heather gave her a playful buffet. "Don't take any cheek, lassie. Just pretend they're your little brothers." She and Clover linked elbows and began skipping off towards the cooks.

During and after lunch, question after question drew Violet's attention until she belatedly realized that her friends had disappeared. A worried search of the camp revealed that they had joined the smelly, messy work of dyeing uniform tunics at the giant vats on the edge of the village. Both girls waved her away when she went to check on them, Heather inspecting her stained hands and proclaiming herself 'Bluefingers the Mighty'.

Violet was ill-content to leave her friends to their own devices, but her attention was soon drawn to the tension growing between the highlanders and the Sea Wanderer advance guard. Despite working out the differences between their own tribes, some highlanders found their new allies unbearable. They ridiculed their laid-back mannerisms, their weapons, and their manner of dress until finally the tension boiled over. During what ought to have been a neutral mealtime, fierce words became blows that left one man with a broken nose and another with his arm in a sling. Quelling that brawl proved to only delay more conflict, and the resultant bad tempers set Rose on edge. In a conference around the central fire, the young woman took them to task.

"I understand that your codes of honor make it very difficult for you to work with others." The firelight illuminated Rose's hair, braided in a style that Violet had helped her perfect. "It's difficult under any circumstances, especially if tradition demands you seek in blood an apology for insult."

Violet, Heather, Clover, and the Shona captains all sat in a row on a log seat. Violet leaned forward with elbows on knees as Rose continued seriously, "Every man is valuable. Rivals or not, we've gone too far with this to retreat now."

Erven joined her as the fire popped. The Shona leader had —finally—succumbed to Violet and Lena's admonitions to rest. His face had gained color, and he was moving as he had before imprisonment. "Like it or not, we need more forces or we don't stand a chance." He gestured towards the Sea Wanderer commander. "I challenge you to listen to this man without your usual prejudice and hear what he has to say."

The Sea Wanderer crossed his arms powerfully as sparks flew into the darkening sky. "You know something of the Iorca from th'men already here, but the Sea Wanderers've dealt with them for centuries. We know their fighting inside an' out. Between your knowledge of th'land and our knowledge of our enemies, we've a fighting chance if we work t'gether. We're not here t'patronize you, and we've come with something at stake." He stared down the gazes of the tribal leaders. "If we lose here, the alliance between Iorca and Illyn grows stronger, and they'll reach t'attack our own homeland."

"Be assured, the Sea Wanderers know war." The man smiled, showing a broken eyetooth. Bracelets around his wrists flashed as he pointed towards their camp, set a short distance from the rest of the tents. "Our advance guard contains some of th' best fighters in th'Sea Wanderer navy. I can speak of them, but I'd challenge you t'come see for yourselves. Tomorrow, we invite you t'test our mettle. Prove t'us how fierce of fighters these mountains breed!"

To Violet's surprise, the tribal leaders responded enthusiastically with growls and shouts to the challenge offered.

Heather leaned over and whispered, "Stark mad, the lot o' them."

VIOLET WORKED LATE that night over a child with a high fever. The boy was finally sleeping when she crossed the open space between tents. Halfway along, she heard a sound. Investigating, she almost crashed into Lena around a corner. The girl yelped and stumbled.

Violet caught her. "Don't worry, it's only me."

The girl gasped, "Oh, Violet! I was coming to get you." She pointed to her tent. "It's my brother."

Violet stepped through the doorway, the problem immediately making itself clear as she did. Erven was tossing and turning in his bedding, eyes wide but empty. "Oh dear."

"Usually I can wake him," Lena explained. "Or he wakes himself —"

"I understand," Violet said, already digging in her apron pocket. "Get some light?"

Lena hurried to light a candle as Violet pulled out a vial of peppermint oil. Unstoppering it, she gripped Erven's shoulder firmly and held the vial under his nose. "Erven! Wake up!"

The Shona leader jolted awake with a yell, and Violet ducked a flying elbow as he shoved her away.

"Erven! Erven! It's all right!" Violet leaned back, quickly stoppering the vial. "It's safe. You were dreaming."

Sanity flooded into his eyes. "Where's Lena?!" he gasped.

"I'm here." Lena brushed past Violet, falling to her knees and wrapping her arms around her brother. He buried his face in her shoulder with a sob, hands tensing on her back. "I'm sorry," Lena whispered as his breathing calmed. "I'm so sorry."

Violet replaced the vial in her apron pocket. "Are—are you going to be all right?" she asked after a moment.

Erven sat back with a sigh. "I think so. Sorry, it's just—" One of his hands went to his side, and he stopped with a haunted expression.

"It's all right," she hastened to say. "I was awake. Are you certain you don't need anything? I could—" She scrambled to find the right words. "I suppose I could find something to help you sleep better."

He shook his head, wiping sweat away from his hairline. "I've tried." His voice softened. "It only makes things worse."

There's nothing else I can do, Violet realized. Amid stammered assurances and offers of help should they want it, she bade the siblings goodnight and left. Finding her sleeping space amongst the Shona, she crawled into her bedding. The soft breathing—and snoring, on Clover's part—of her friends calmed her as she lay back and tried to relax.

I'm sure Erven isn't the only one who fights monsters in his sleep. She shoved Heather's encroaching leg away as foreboding stirred at the back of her mind. *There must be others; and after this is over, there's no telling how many will be broken right through the middle.*

21

THE ROGUE SCHOOL OF UNDERAGE MINIONS

For Merald, it had been a startling and painful moment to realize that one of the tribes answering Rose's call was his own. His family had been exiled from the tribal village over a dispute his father had with some of the powerful leaders. To a young child used to the openness and simplicity of the mountains, the bustle of a port town was an overwhelming flood of sound and sight. When his father perished in a gambling brawl, his creditors had made up for the loss by selling Merald, his mother, and his brother. After years of hoping, he had reconciled himself to the fact that they were gone for good.

Upon arrival in the camp, he had struggled to contain his temper at the sight of his old tribe. Even hearing that a bloody feud had resulted in the deaths of those responsible for his family's exile did little to help his anger. One of the few sources of comfort was Erven, who took time to train him in sword use.

"It's good for both of us," his friend said, carefully pulling on quilted practice armor. "I need to get into training, and you need to learn. This way, neither of us looks bad in training with the others."

The rainy season was over, and the mud of last month had turned to hard-packed dirt. Weighted practice weapons in hand, they faced off.

"All right, simple blocking," Erven commanded.

Merald nodded. His muscles had needed little building up from years of hard labor, but the movements of swordplay were still new. They alternated blocking and striking, pausing after several sets to rest. After warming up, they began free sparring. Even though the sword had become more comfortable in his hands, he felt himself giving way after a few exchanges.

Erven tapped Merald's breastbone lightly. "Dead."

"All right, you win." Merald flexed his shoulders stiffly. "That's two for you."

Erven clicked sword tips with him. "Better luck next time. You're improving." He undid his leather helmet's chin strap and sat on a rock, holding his side gingerly.

"Are you all right?" Merald asked, setting down his sword.

The Shona leader waved him off. "I'll be all right. Ribs don't heal overnight, and I need to stay in practice." He grinned. "Are *you* all right?"

Merald began taking halfhearted punches at a practice dummy. "I'm all right. It's strange being in the mountains after being gone for so long." He overshot and missed the dummy's head by several inches. "And I worry about what's going to happen."

Erven pulled off his helmet. "I worry about the Shona. They're not exactly suited to pitched battle." He ran his fingers through his dark hair.

Merald sat on the rock with his friend, wiping sweat off his face. "Makes sense. You always fought from the cover of trees, but this time we'll be out in the open."

"How did you hear that?" Erven asked. "I didn't think it'd become common knowledge yet."

Merald rubbed his hands over the quilting on his sparring armor. "Some of the men talk."

"That's not ideal." Erven shook his head. "But it's true. We have the advantage in the highlands, but standing our ground here would mean years of trying to wear each other down little by little. We have to be decisive." He sighed. "I hope the Sea Wanderers are as good in battle as they are in practice. We'll need them. Fighting in the woods, the Shona are able to use being small and fast to their advantage. Against fully armed men on an open field, I don't think they'll stand a chance. Well," he amended, "not the younger ones."

"So, what are you going to do?" Merald asked. The quilted tunic was becoming hot and heavy on his back.

"I'm still working that out. I'd give a lot to come up with something that would at least get the youngest out of the direct fighting." The confidence that Erven normally wore easily faded as he added, "Please don't say anything to anyone about this. I'd hate them to think that I don't believe they're capable of holding their own."

"I won't say anything," Merald reassured him. "I know how much they care about what you think." He raised an eyebrow. "But you know, they'll probably figure things out on their own once we get our orders."

Erven sighed and put on his helmet. "Probably. And even if they do realize they're at a disadvantage, it won't stop them from charging in anyway." He offered Merald a hand. "Let's start again."

• • •

AMID THE BUSTLE OF TRAINING, packing, and planning, Heather and Clover were bored. Their father had left them in camp before leaving to carry orders to the Sea Wanderers, giving them strict instructions to behave, be helpful, and not get in trouble. They'd attempted to train with the Shona, only to have their uncle see them and order them to go away. A mishap with one of the dye vats resulted in a wholly blue little boy and a scolding. Finally, they had been helping count uniforms until they had tried on too many helmets and were ousted from the supply tent.

As Clover observed dourly, "With so many people here older than us, we've gone from being responsible to being scum-nosed children."

"You certainly proved *your* maturity." Heather pulled her sister's hat over her eyes. Clover had been the one to drop a helmet on the supply master's toes.

"At least I didn't leave a trail of blue behind me for hours," Clover replied coolly as she pushed the hat farther up her forehead.

"You're right."

Clover sighed. It had been much easier when the only people to lead were their friends' younger siblings. "So, now what should we do?"

"We could see if Violet wants help," Heather suggested, leaning an elbow on Clover's shoulder.

Clover made a disgusted face. "I hate sick people, and injuries, and medicine smells. Bah!" She pulled her hat off and started crumpling the brim. "Besides, Violet is only ever with us for a few minutes before she gets called off to fix something. River's busy." She hooked a thumb towards the practice field. "And I have no idea where Lena went."

"Rose is long gone," Heather added, looking gloomily

towards the flagpole. "I'm not even sure she remembers who we are in the first place."

"Should we just strike out for home?" Clover asked. She had meant it as a joke, but it came out sounding serious.

Heather gave her a disappointed look. "Don't be ridiculous. You and I would get one day into the mountains, get horribly lost, and end with dragons chewing on our bones. Arrrk!" She slumped over dramatically. "And then Da would kill us."

"Forget Da. *Mum* would kill us."

Heather nodded. They sat in silence, watching as a squad jogged past with their sergeant bellowing at them in a mixture of languages. A pack of younger children followed behind, aping their elders in ridiculous fashion. Heather watched them pass, a mischievous expression spreading over her face. "We can't go home—"

Clover huffed, "That's what I've been saying!"

"But," Heather interrupted. "We can create a bit of it here." She rolled her trademark kerchief into a band, which she tied around her brow. "What were we known for most back home?"

"Getting in trouble."

Heather picked up Clover's hat and jammed it on her head. "Not always!"

"Stealing biscuits?"

"Ducky," Heather stood up. "There's no point in us sitting here with faces like boiled frogs when there're littlies who'll appreciate us." She grabbed a staff from outside a supply tent and began tying a second kerchief to it. "I understand Erven's been worrying about what t'do with the younger Shona."

"How d'you figure that?"

Heather winked. "Violet, in a moment of quiet before some very important person needed her attention."

Clover pursed her lips appraisingly. "Sooo,"

"So, we appoint ourselves Royal Headmasters of the Rogue

School of Underage Minions. I've got an idea." Heather gave her banner a practice wave. "Coming?"

Clover linked arms with her sister, and they sauntered off towards the side of the camp reserved for civilians. "I like it. Now, who should we hook first?"

HAD he known what his younger daughters were planning, Alder would have regretted his decision to leave them in the encampment. "It was a good day when I traded ships for trees." He remarked to one of his scouts as their feet touched the dock. "I only wish the change could have been permanent." He eyed the *Skimmer*, bobbing in the cove of the island base. "I'm surprised that thing hasn't dumped us in the brine already." They walked together down to the fires burning on the beach. Those who didn't have immediate business with the commanders were settled around the fires, warding off the dawn chill with mulled wine and cider. He claimed a spot next to one of his other men and accepted a cup of wine. "Any news down here?"

"Not much. Th'*Cuttlefish*'s coming in soon, with news of the Iorca fleet," one of the Wanderers answered him. "Other'n that, no." He frowned. "Weren't you supposed t'go straight t'command, Sir?"

"Yep. Don't call me Sir." Alder sipped at his drink, feeling the spices warm his tongue. He had missed the taste of spices. "I wanted my legs t'remember solid ground first." He wiped a drip with his sleeve as the men laughed. "No, if you must know, I'm waiting for my daughter's ship."

"Willow?"

He looked with concern at the fellow who'd spoken. "You know her?"

The man raised his glass. "She's the one who makes sure this's brought down for th'sentries. Good cook."

"That she is." Alder chuckled. "I thought she was aboard the *Cuttlefish,* working with that communications fellow."

"Don't think she's been with them since they arrive, Sir." The man pointed into the darkness towards their camp. "You'll probably find her near the kitchen."

THE COOKHOUSE WAS busy with voices, only some of which Willow could understand. The other cooks were from different areas of the Sea Wanderer's territory, and the number of dialects spoken made her head swim. She scraped chopped preserved ginger into oatmeal before turning to the laborious task of kneading bread. While kneading, she let her mind wander. The Iorcan fleet was due any day now, if the reports were correct. The Sea Wanderers would need to move soon after, or risk arriving late to rendezvous with the Illyn forces. The details of such an endeavor kept multiplying like mushrooms after a rainstorm; so fast that she'd lost track of how many new problems were created and solved with each passing day.

Amid the apprehension of the greater conflict was a smaller one—the question of where she could be the most useful. There was talk of a forward camp being set up near the front lines. As she punched the dough down, she wondered if the commanders would allow her to go with the advance guard. *At least that puts me closer to Rose, if only by virtue of being in the same country.*

She was startled by one of the others yelling, "Willow! There's someone here for you."

Muttering under her breath at being interrupted, she thumped the dough into a bowl and came out from behind the oatmeal pot. Waving a hand to clear away steam, she heard the other cook talking with someone who'd just come in. The voice of the newcomer was achingly familiar.

"Ah, here she is."

Willow shouldered past the other kitchen worker. "Da? What are you doing here? Is Heather with you? How's Rose?"

Her father raised an eyebrow. "I'm well, thank you. How are you?"

With an exasperated sob, she rushed into his arms. "I missed you." She planted her ear against his chest, his heartbeat comforting her as it had since childhood.

His voice rumbled next to her ear. "I missed you too."

After a long moment, she looked up at his face. "You wouldn't believe the things I've heard about you, Da."

He laughed as he let her go. "I probably would. When you're as old as I am, not much is unbelievable anymore." He eyed the trays of bread rising on a side table. "What do I have t'do t'get food here?"

The reminder sent her hurrying to make sure her oatmeal wasn't scorching. "Sorry! Here." She tipped a portion into a bowl and handed it to him. Getting the attention of one of the others, she called, "I'll be with my father, if anyone comes looking for me." Dishing up her own bowl and grabbing her jacket, she headed for the door.

Once sitting in the sunlight, she turned to get a good look at her father. "How are Heather and Clover? I've missed Heather so much."

"Wild as usual. Happy. Chatterin' like a pair'o magpies. They want to help in battle, but it's not going t'happen. Your uncle is keeping a few eyes on them for me."

Willow's shirtsleeve bunched around her arm as she put on her jacket. Shaking it straight, she said, "I'm glad they're together, at least. Oh," she added, remembering something her father had mentioned the last time they'd met. "How's Rose? What'd she say when she found out about her parents?"

He swallowed a bite of oatmeal. "She was quiet."

"Preoccupied?"

"That's what I thought at th'time." He paused and added. "But now I'm not so sure. Now, I'm wonderin' if she doesn't know *what* she thinks."

"Frogspawn. She's probably very upset."

"It's hard t'tell with her." Alder scooped up another bite. "I mean, even harder t'tell. You know she was always a hard one t'read, even before this."

Just then, the commanders of the *Cuttlefish* and several other ships came past. Recognizing Alder from a previous meeting, they stopped to exchange pleasantries. Willow sat back, listening to the cadence of talk between the men. As they left, she commented, "You're talking with your original accent again. I wondered if you would."

Alder raised an eyebrow. "Well, I suppose your tongue remembers, even if your mind doesn't." He stretched long legs out in front of him.

Willow felt a twitch of satisfaction. "So, you are a Sea Wanderer?"

"Was," he corrected. "And I don't know what you heard or who told it to you, and I don't want to."

"Why didn't *you* ever tell us?" She asked, pulling her jacket closed. The morning air was chillier than she had gotten used to.

He shrugged. "Those years are over, and I'm not exactly proud of anything in them."

She was glad she'd added the ginger to the oatmeal. She'd gotten used to the spices Sea Wanderers used in their cooking, and without it sweetened oatmeal would've been too bland. "I suppose I understand that, but it wasn't *just* the Fishhawks.

They said you had command in the Sea Wanderer navy. Why wouldn't you be proud of anything you did then?"

The wrinkles around his eyes deepened as he said, "I saw it as a chance to make things right from all the things I'd done wrong. But by that point I'd too many enemies within the Wanderers. Seeing a person who'd pillaged their farms now in charge was a little much for some to swallow." He unsuccessfully tried to catch a glop of oatmeal before it fell off his spoon. "And there was a lot of pressure from the other side, too. Going to ground in the woods was the best idea at the time."

"I didn't believe it when they told us. Heather didn't say anything?"

"She knows? She hasn't said anything to me."

"I guess that doesn't surprise me." Willow set her empty bowl on the ground. "When she decides to keep a secret, she *keeps* it. They told us both after I spoke before the Council."

"Glory…" he let the word hang in the silence while he finished his meal. Finally, he said, "I see you found some way to be useful."

"I speak Iorcan now. Well," she corrected herself, "I can muddle my way through. I'm not sure intelligence suits me, but I like working with Ethan."

All she received was a thoughtful 'hmm' as Alder scraped the inside of his bowl. "Your mother won't like the idea of you spying."

"What's she going to do, take me to the laundry in absentia? Besides, it's not my favorite. I like cooking and organizing more." She swallowed the last of her food. "What happens now?"

"Well, we're stuck waiting until command decides where to send us. I'm supposed to take orders to the army, but I think I'll be sending my men without me."

"What'll you be doing?"

Her father took her empty bowl. "Do you need a dishwasher?"

"Da."

"Whaat?" He winked. "I'm hoping they'll send me with the advance guard to help get things set. It'll keep me far away from any naval battles that might occur once we sight the Iorca fleet."

Willow stood and tugged her jacket straight. "Ethan will want to meet you."

"And I'm interested in meeting him. If I'm going t'be here for a bit, I'd like t'meet the young man who's occupied so much of my daughter's time." He smirked at her expression. "My only concern is what your sisters are getting into while I'm away."

22

A SHARP REMINDER

Mid-morning saw Violet directing a group of refugees to the civilian side of the camp. Pointing as she spoke, she said, "Privies are that way, the cooking fire is this way, and healer's tents are near the center of the camp." She glanced at one of the boys, his eyes bleary with fever. "You need to visit the healers." She smiled at his mother. "With your permission, Mistress?"

The woman gratefully set her load on the ground. "He'll be all right?"

Violet nodded. "I'll have one of my helpers return him. Or you can call at the tent."

"I'll have his sister come fetch him." The woman was already unpacking bedrolls as Violet took the child to the healing tents. Men from other villages had continued arriving, filling the ranks of the army until there were several thousand men in the camp. The healers' tents stood near the divide between the two sides of the camp, and the men and women there cared for civilians and soldiers alike. Leaving the child with one of her trainees, she went to find Erven. As she crossed the camp, she was accosted by Heather and Clover. The sisters had been helping make uniforms, if the blue streaks on hands and clothing were any indication.

"Hello, old girl." Heather draped an arm over her shoulders, leaving a damp blue splotch.

Some of the tension in her shoulders eased in the presence of the unflappable pair. "Hello, old girls. What have you been up to?"

Clover sighed. "Getting into trouble with Mistress Trout again."

Violet scrunched her nose. "Mistress Trout?"

"That's what River calls her," Heather said. "You know," she stuck out her chest and strode along with hands on hips, puffing, "I know children, I raised twenty of them. You scamps best keep to your work."

Violet laughed as understanding dawned. "You mean the lady in charge of the seamstresses?"

"Yeh," Clover answered. "Da put her in charge of us while he does important things." She frowned. "I didn't think we needed looking after."

"And we—erm—had a disagreement with her just now." Heather pushed her sleeve up to show Violet a spreading bruise. "We've been trying t'get uniforms for the Rogue School, but we don't have much to work with. She caught me dunking socks in the dye vats. Again."

Violet shook her head.

"So, we thought we'd come see what you were doing," Clover concluded. "What *were* you doing?"

"I was going to find Erven. The healers are getting overworked."

They'd crossed from the center of the camp to the edge, where the Shona had reorganized around their fire. The three girls picked their way between bedrolls and bundles to where

Rose and Erven were sitting and talking. Violet approached carefully, not wanting to interrupt. Heather and Clover exchanged glances before barging across to sit next to Rose.

"Hello, Your Highness!" Clover said, throwing a streaky arm around Rose's shoulders. "We were bored."

Rose patted her friend's arm absently. The young queen's skin was paler than usual, and the color was going from her lips. "That's very nice." Her gaze shifted up to Violet. "Hello, dear."

She must not be sleeping.

Rose had moved her things recently to the camp center, where she could be more easily available to the rest of the commanders. Since then, they'd seen and talked to each other less often. The change hadn't startled Violet—in fact she'd expected it. Her own duties kept her hours filled, and she'd tried to convince herself that it didn't matter. Seeing Rose after several days apart made her realize how much it did bother her, and the sharp awareness made her strangely mute.

"Hello."

Suddenly, the issue Violet had meant to bring up seemed pointless. Doubtless it would merely go down on the list of problems that both Rose and Erven kept on their ever-present slate tablets, new entries filling the space as fast as old ones were erased.

It seemed hers wasn't the only concern with the growing civilian population. "If they all bring their families with them, there will be thousands of people here." Erven was saying as she sat down across from him. In contrast to Rose, Erven had finally regained his health. Violet had seen him training with Merald and the rest of the Shona, indicating that his injuries had healed completely. "We can't move the whole population of Illyn into the mountains."

Violet crossed her legs and rested her chin in her hand as

their conversation continued. The noonday sun was pleasant, and her thoughts began fuzzing under its warmth. She had almost dozed off when she heard the scream. Jolting awake, she looked wildly around for her healing bag.

"Once a healer, always a healer." Heather tossed her the bag.

"If you say so. Erven, can I talk to you later?"

The Shona leader nodded with concern furrowing his forehead. "Just come find me."

"Thank you." She broke into a run towards the pasture where the scream had come from. Tora, one of the other Shona healers, caught up with her halfway there.

"Violet, what's happening?"

"I don't know," Violet shouted as she clambered over the railing to the pasture, where a group of men were gathered around someone. Others on horseback worked to corral loose horses in a corner of the field. "Follow me." Now she could tell that the person screaming was a woman, and she knew with a feeling of doom that the injured person was a child. "Move! Make room!"

Tora helped push through the men. "Move it, all! Make space!"

The men parted to allow them access to the toddler. As soon as she saw what had happened, Violet had to take several deep breaths to avoid vomiting. *It's just an injury—just an injury.*

It took a few awful moments to find her voice again. "Get the mother away from here. And anyone who doesn't need to be here, get out." As she fumbled for the child's throat, she saw that he was clutching a yellow flower in a bloodied hand. "What happened?"

Tora was ordering onlookers away as the drill leader

answered, "He ran across the field and spooked one of the horses. Took the hooves right on his head."

"Wasn't anyone watching him?"

"Got away from his mum," one of the men answered, wiping his eyes with a plaid kerchief.

"How is he?"

Violet's voice felt heavy, the weight of dozens of deaths piling into one single moment. "Give me a moment." She pulled a roll of bandage out of her bag and began cleaning gore off the little boy's face. Using another bandage, she wrapped his head to cover the fatal injuries. Eventually she rose, hardly even aware that her hands were covered in blood. "I'm sorry," she told the drill commander. "There's nothing else I can do."

He put out a hand to comfort her, but she brushed it aside, picked up her bag, and walked away. Behind her, the mother's wails split the sky as the men let her run to her son.

"How did this happen!" Rose's voice came out icy as she stared down the drill commander. "There's a reason the civilians stay on the far side of the camp!"

She supposed the man was unused to having his decisions questioned by a girl. His face was red and he seemed torn between apology and defense. "It wasn't exactly something we could control!" he blustered. "The straightest path from the civilians' area to the river is right through the drill ground. Even though we've been telling them not to, they keep cutting through."

"That has to stop." She crossed her arms, grateful for the sense of authority that her new skirts had given her. "We'll continue to have accidents if the sides of the camp keep mixing."

The lieutenant stood a little straighter. "We'll do what we can, Milady."

After dismissing him with the orders to restrict passage through the military side of the camp, she retreated to her tent near the center fire. Feeling worn out and far too on edge, she sat on a crate and tipped her face to the sun.

"Good mornin', Your Mightiness." Heather sat on the crate next to her. "And a fine day, to be certain." Her old friend's usually cheerful voice held a bitter edge.

"It was." Rose looked at Heather, whose Sea Wanderer shirt, flame-red sash, and trousers had been joined by one of the new navy uniform tunics. "What's gone wrong now?"

Heather pushed a curl out of her eyes. "Nothing new, love. Something still yet t'do. You know Violet was the healer at that accident, right?"

Guilt churned in her stomach. "I knew, but I didn't really *know*." She stood up. "I've got to find her." She gave Heather an appraising look. "I don't suppose you'd know where she's gone?"

Heather raised an eyebrow. "Think. Where'd she used t'hide when she got in trouble?"

Rose rummaged through her memories of their shared childhood. "Her grandmother's storeroom."

"Exactly." Heather slid off the crate, adjusting her tunic as she walked away. "I'd start looking somewhere like that."

AFTER CLEANING HER HANDS, restocking her bag, and having a horrible conversation with the rest of the healers, Violet had turned over the tent to Tora and left. The medical supply tent was stacked with baskets and crates of supplies, and there, in a quiet corner, she was able to finally let the tears fall. The shuddering sobs were beginning to die out when a gentle hand landed on her back.

"I thought you'd be here," Rose's voice said.

Violet tensed. "How did you know?"

"Heather told me what happened. She also figured out where you were." Rose paused before saying uncomfortably, "Oh, Vi, I'm sorry."

"Not your fault." Violet muttered into her crossed arms.

"But I *am* sorry."

"I know."

Across the meadow, the sounds of training had resumed as the men recovered from their shock. Rose's fingers drifted across her hair, smoothing its shortened strands away from her forehead as Violet let her shoulder muscles relax. "Better?" Rose asked after a while.

"A little." She relaxed her arms, but kept her face hidden. "This didn't need to happen. Most of the people arriving now are here to flee fighting, not join the army. With this many people, accidents will keep happening." She took a hiccupping breath, muscles trembling as the words kept spilling out in frustration. "I've tried to say something, but *everyone* has something they're trying to get fixed, or a problem comes up, or one tribal man says the other tribal man insulted his mother's cousin's great uncle's donkey ten years ago and 'how can he fight with such an honorless dog', and we haven't really been able to talk like we're used to anyway."

"Well, I'd say this will make everyone take notice. And, forgive me." The hand on her shoulder tensed along with Rose's voice. "I didn't even realize you were lonely. I'm so used to you always being there for me that I forgot I needed to be there for you." Pleading crept into her words. "Please, please forgive me."

Violet sniffed and looked up at Rose. "I forgive you."

"Thank you." Rose brushed down her dress. "I need to go collect the council." Her expression took on the flinty strength that was fast becoming part of her nature. "They'll listen to me this time."

"Wait," Violet grabbed the hem of her friend's dress. "Don't go yet."

Skirts shifted as Rose sat, putting her arm around Violet's shoulders. "All right."

When Rose called the council to order with Violet at her side, the young woman's demeanor made the battle-hardened men sit up and take notice of their words. That night, they began preparing to move.

"Attention, class." Clover tapped her stick on a barrel top. The squabbling continued as she raised her voice. "Hoy! I said 'quiet'!"

She surveyed the group of Shona, highland children, and refugees that had gathered to her and Heather. They were camped out in a supply tent today, as most of the other good meeting spots were being taken down in preparation for moving. Spread out on a crate was a bizarre assortment of items, and propped against a support pole was a plank on which Heather had drawn several diagrams. Clover pointed at one of the Shona boys with her stick. "You, there. What must you carry at all times?"

He bashfully stood, brushing a mop of brown hair out of his eyes. "Whistles."

"Righto, laddie!" Heather agreed. "And you use them whenever you have to. Sit. You!" She pointed at a broad-shouldered highland girl. "What does this mean?" She indicated a chevron, painted in soot on the plank.

The girl said, "It's a Lieutenant Commander, Lady."

"And who's above them?" Heather adjusted her new blue headscarf. Through some inventive use of the dye vats and several sacrificed bedsheets, they had managed to equip each of their newly minted message runners with a navy-blue vest.

"A Senior Commander, like Sir Erven."

"Well, he's not a Sir, and I'm not a Lady, but yes. Sit. You there," She zeroed in on a small refugee girl, "any idea who is above the Senior Commanders?"

The girl twisted the edge of her vest. "My Lady Rose, and the ones what sits on the council?"

"Very good," Heather leaned against the barrel. "Sit."

Clover dropped the stick and the silly mannerisms as she addressed them. "I know we've been joking with you, but I'm being serious as a badger now. Tomorrow we're moving to the battlefield. We need you, all of you, to carry orders'n messages to the battalion commanders an' their lieutenants."

She smacked the barrel top to emphasis her next words. "You need to be fast. You need to be smart. You need to know when the message you're carrying is important enough t'carry through dangerous situations, and when it's all right to fall back and let someone else deliver it." She looked over at her sister. "We've done our best to prepare you, but I don't think any of us *can* be prepared."

"Clover's right."

She looked up, startled, to see Erven leaning against a stack of crates. The Shona commander carried his sword at his side and was wearing armor. His helmet dangled by its straps from one hand. "None of us know what's going to happen."

Heather lobbed a pebble at him. "Bad form, interrupting the class, Sir!"

"I thought you said he wasn't a Sir!" one of the boys shouted.

An uproar followed as the children began arguing with each other and Heather. Erven silenced the din by walking to the front of the class and yelling, "Quiet!"

Most of the Shona knew to obey that voice, and the rest were learning quickly. They subsided as he said, "Thank you. Most of you understand what Clover is trying to say. Be quick, quiet, and brave. Stay with your partners and help each other. Understand that the messages you'll carry are one of the most important things to the Senior Commanders. You are our eyes and our ears on the field. Without you, we will not win this battle." He looked down at the runners, smiling a little. "If you go to the uniform supply, there are patches for you to put on your vests. Dismissed!"

As the children stampeded off amid shouts of excitement, Clover turned to Erven indignantly. "I had control of my own Rogue School, thank you! You had no call to march in and take over for me!"

He put up his hands appealingly. "I know, I know. Sorry. I needed to talk to the pair of you without thirty pairs of ears listening."

Heather elbowed her. "Be nice to the laddie, Ducky."

Clover sighed. "All right." She pushed her hat back from her forehead. "What did you have to say to the Headmistresses of the Rogue School?"

Erven sat down on the barrel that had served as her desk. "Some of the scouts are leaving today to set up a support camp a little way away from the battlefield. After seeing what you've done with your Rogue School, I think you'd be able to do a lot with a group of workers who don't argue with you all the time."

"Wait," Heather said from her barrel. "You're promoting us?"

"Sort of?" Erven said. "I need some people to put in charge of organizing where the healers will go, and where the food will go, and things like that. Violet's already agreed to help with the healers. She's the one who said to ask the two of you."

"Hmmm," Clover said. "What about our Da? He's not going to be happy with you."

"Your uncle's going, too." The corner of Erven's mouth had turned upwards as he said, "I feel your father would rather know that you're under supervision than gallivanting about by yourselves."

Heather cupped a hand around her mouth, whispering to her sister, "He's called our bluff, Ducky. We have to say yes."

"Well, then, yes!" Clover spat on her hand and slapped the top of the barrel, Heather following suit.

After a moment's hesitation, Erven did as well. "You'd better collect your things and decide which runners you're bringing with you." He picked up his helmet and started to walk away. "You're leaving in two hours, so I'd hurry."

After he left, the two girls stared at each other for a long moment. Then Clover whooped and started running for their sleeping space. As she stuffed clothing into her pack, her nerves thrummed with excitement. *They need us!*

AFTER A WHIRLWIND OF ORDERS, packing, organizing, and arming, the camp had diminished in size. From where Violet stood next to Rose, she could see many of the battle groups that were readying to move. The navy dyes donated by Rose's ancestral clan had helped greatly in bringing a sense of cohesion to the army. Embroidered insignias and flashings gleamed against sleeves and shoulders, the hard work of many village women's fingers. Each man carried a full pack, and a few carts stood laden with gear. Violet hoped that the carts would make it over the mountain passes. Division flags flapped in the air, the insignias standing out boldly against the navy-blue fields.

One of the captains jogged up to them and saluted Rose. It had taken many long hours of debate, but Rose had convinced her commanders to let her ride with the army as far as the advance camp. The young woman had her mouth set in a grim line as the runner addressed her. "We're ready to move, Lady. We await your orders."

Rose squeezed Violet's hand within the folds of her skirt, looking toward the east. When she turned back, her eyes were hard with the light of vengeance. "So be it. Let's move out."

The runners of Clover's Rogue School scattered, some to the commanders and others to the signal drummers. With a pounding signal from the drums, the army began to move.

23
OLDER AND SADDER

The *Mystic's* sails snapped in the brisk wind as the small vessel skimmed along the Illyn coastline. After a long, heated discussion with the Sea Wanderer commanders, Alder had convinced them to let him take Willow and a picked group of men with the advance guard. They'd sighted the Iorcan fleet two days previous, the ships unwilling to engage Sea Wanderer military vessels unless attacked. It was now imperative to move as fast as possible to establish a camp near the battlefield before either army arrived.

The *Mystic's* crew had been trying to eke as much speed out of the fishing boat as they could. Overhead, the ensign of the Sea Wanderers fluttered—a sea green field bearing two crashing breakers with a scallop shell between them. From the bowsprit, they flew a navy-blue pennant with a gold star. "The time for hiding is over," Alder had said as he handed her the flags. "The warlord already knows we're here and that battle is imminent."

Willow meandered over to the stern. Though it was high summer, the breeze coming off the water was chilly. Ethan was sitting with his back against the bulkhead, checking his armor and weapons. It was strange to see him with a sword, even though she'd learned over the last month that training with it was his refuge from the stress of espionage.

Willow sat across from him. "Are you afraid?"

He glanced at her between buffing the finish on an already pristine teal-lacquered chest plate. "I wouldn't call it afraid. Nervous, I s'pose. I think anyone headin' into what we are would be stupid not t'be nervous."

"Glad I'm not stupid, then. If I stop and think, I know I'll scare myself enough to be useless." Willow's voice came out in almost a whisper. "If I could, I'd take my sisters and my friends and run for it." She stopped. "That's cowardly. Sorry."

"It's not cowardly t'know when the losses will be greater if y'stand and fight." Ethan examined the sheen on his armor before pulling out a whetstone to begin working on one of many daggers. "If one battle is lost, you can still win a war." He angled the blade towards her, looking at her down its edge. "Rose wouldn't be alive t'lead her people if her parents'd made the choice t'stand and fight."

"That's why you're a spy," Willow sighed. "You see the bigger picture." Her boots scraped against the deck as she stretched her legs out. "Don't worry, I'm not going to desert. Well," She examined the deck. "Maybe I would if it wouldn't hurt anyone else, but we're too far into this to do anything but keep going. And I don't even know how I'd *find* my sisters without getting myself killed."

"Well, I know Heather." Ethan slid his dagger along the whetstone. "An' if your other sister is anything like her, we might start lookin' wherever there's th'most commotion."

Willow laughed. "Probably. One time, they managed to bring a whole pack of children home absolutely covered in mud." She covered her eyes, laughing at the memory.

Alder's yell brought them both to their feet. The rest of the crew hurried around the deck as they prepared to make landfall. Pebbles grated under their feet as the vessel landed and they prepared to disembark.

Alder turned the helm over to one of the others before joining Willow. "Ready?"

Willow hoisted her pack. "Ready, Sir."

"Don't call me Sir." The answer came automatically, as her father scanned the forest line. "Let's go!"

The water was only up to Willow's knees as she sloshed ashore. Still, it was bitingly cold. She hopped from foot to foot once ashore, trying to shake the water out of her shoes. Ethan laughed as he sloshed past, balancing a bulging knapsack along with his armor and weapons. "Y'look like a toad on a skillet."

She gave him an insolent cross-eyed look and stopped hopping. The others had followed, several carrying large bundles of tents and supplies between them as they waded ashore.

"There's bound to be a village nearby," Alder said. "I don't want them to see us." Her father pointed southwest. "If our timing's good, the others should've already knocked together some kind of camp that way."

"And let's hope the messages were clear, 'cause otherwise we'll be rushing t'set up healers an' supplies as casualties're flooding in," Ethan said in an undertone.

Alder gave him a stern look. "Let's not weaken morale even before battle starts, eh?" With an eye on the sky, he added, "We'll have time if we hurry. Hopefully, we'll be there before nightfall."

Willow cinched her pack straps around her waist. Her vest puckered under the straps, and she tugged it straight as she followed her father into the trees. A few hours later, she was beginning to wish that she had exercised more over the last few weeks. By the time the sun was low in the sky, she was more than ready for a break. They were in a gully by a creek when her father ordered a halt. Dropping her pack gratefully on the ground, she sat on a rock and wiped a sleeve over her forehead. "Tired?" Ethan asked as he sat next to her.

She nodded ruefully. "I'm not as fit as I thought I was."

He chuckled. "Should've been training in your off hours, instead of baking."

Willow was on the verge of educating her sardonic friend on the merits of baking versus hitting dummies with blunt objects when a shout came from the woods.

"Sea Wanderer patrol!"

Alder, sitting a few feet from Willow, looked up. "Who's there?"

A pair of men wearing weather-beaten jackets over navy tunics slid down the bank opposite them. Jumping over the creek, they came over to Alder and saluted. "Advance scouts of the Queen's Army, Sir."

"Good eve." Alder was slicing an apple, using a nearby rock as a table. "Sit down. Have some food."

The men came to sit near Willow. One of them pulled a kerchief out of his pocket and rubbed it over his forehead before accepting a piece of apple. "Good to see you, Sir."

"I'm not a Sir." Alder pulled another apple out of his pocket. "What's the news?"

The other scout bit into a piece of bread he had taken out of his jacket. Willow noticed that both the jacket and his tunic had the appearance of already having been worn for days. "You're less than an hour from the advance camp. Army arrives soon. I hope your lot didn't come alone."

Her father shrugged. "Alone for now. We're here to help

with the organization of th'camp. Fleet's moving into position now to engage the enemy ships."

"When are the ground troops landing?"

Alder took a bite of apple before answering the scout. "Not more'n another day or so. We wanted t'try and stop th'Iorca from landing too many troops."

The sun had hardly moved before it was time to march again. Willow wearily trudged after her father, wishing they would arrive at their destination soon. Her wishes were soon granted, as they passed through an outer fringe of sentries and came into a small meadow lined with hastily erected tents. A hard-faced woman came over to them. "Advance patrol?"

"As you see us," Alder agreed. "Seventeen elite fighters, three for camp organization, Ethan here for communication, and myself for command. There's a few more coming behind us; their vessel was a bit slower. Supplies—"

The woman pointed at a canvas awning shielding piles of bags and boxes. "Over there. Your men can set up that way, too. Who will they report to?"

"Myself, I suppose. Where do we need them for now?"

"Sentry commander for this watch—Captain Kelvar. He'll assign your patrols and sentry. Those of you for relief work can go see the cooks."

Alder raised an eyebrow. "The cooks?"

"Aye. You'll want to talk with Mistress Elisa. She'll give you your responsibilities for now."

"Cheers. All right, you lot." He turned to the men. "Those of you who're here to fight, go see this captain. Th'rest of you, come with me. We'll go see what we can do to help get things running smoothly here."

Amid muttered acknowledgements, the men who had been picked for front line scouting departed as Willow and the others followed her father. Ethan followed as well. "I need t'go see where they're setting up communications and command." He frowned. "I've got t'figure out how t'coordinate with an army I can't even see yet."

Willow patted his shoulder reassuringly. "Don't worry, I'm sure you'll have a band of squirrels trained to run messages in no time."

Ethan snorted as they wove between stacks of supplies. "Funny."

"Why thank you!"

"No, not you." Ethan pointed at the edge of the kitchen, where a smaller fire glimmered in the dusk. "Them."

Willow looked where he was pointing and saw two girls—one wearing a ridiculously ragged hat—talking with the workers. A grin spread across her face. "Ohhh, Dad's going to kill them."

As they approached, Clover spotted them. Willow found herself suddenly flattened underneath both of her sisters. Even Heather, ordinarily not the most affectionate of her siblings, swatted Clover aside to give her a long hug. As they let her go, she asked, "Have you stayed out of trouble?"

The pair grinned. "Well, y'might say so," Heather said, adjusting her scarf. "I mean, we're alive, we're not locked up, the food is still edible," she tallied on her fingers, "the blue dye does wear off after a few baths."

"Ah, so that's what happened," Willow laughed, examining her sisters a little more closely. Heather's left eyebrow was tinted blue, and both of their clothing bore unmistakable signs of misplaced dye. "Been playing in the dye vats? I'm fair certain that's something you were never allowed to do at home."

"And apparently that's not all you've gotten away with doing."

Heather and Clover jumped as their father approached, turning simultaneously with guilty looks on their faces.

"Da!" Clover squeaked, pulling her hat brim down.

Alder crossed his arms. "Hello, daughters." He nodded over towards one of the kitchen workers. "Mistress Elisa says that you managed to completely ignore what I said about staying in the village. And you organized the runners, *and* were put in charge of keeping track of supplies for the kitchens."

Heather raised her blue eyebrow winningly. "Yyess?"

"Runners?" Ethan interrupted.

"Aye!" Heather made a grand gesture, ignoring their father's stern face. "The Rogue School, highly trained runners for all your communication needs."

Clover cut in. "It wasn't our idea! We planned on them just running around camp. Erven's the one that asked us to bring them down here."

"Now that I didn't hear," their father sighed. "If he put you in charge, I suppose I'll have to let him."

The girls exchanged triumphant smiles as he said, "But you go no farther than here, understood?"

"Yes, Sir," they chorused.

For once, Alder didn't correct their use of 'sir'. Between the two of them, Heather and Clover showed Willow the rest of the camp. Encouraged by the news of a rudimentary communications system, Ethan quickly wandered off. When Willow next saw him, he was setting leaning on a worktable in the command area, the splintery surface already covered in charts, lists, and other odds and ends. Willow happily joined the kitchen crew to prepare food for the camp workers. Heather and Clover pitched in to lay out dinner, and during the course of the evening the girls shared their respective stories.

• • •

The following morning saw Willow where she was most comfortable—stirring a giant pot of oatmeal as her sisters fought for possession of a pot of honey.

"Let go or I swear I'll—hallpp!" Clover flailed as Heather recovered the pot. "Mine!"

"It's mine!" Heather retorted, swatting her sister away.

Willow dropped her spoon in the porridge. "No, mine." As her sisters struggled, she neatly lifted the pot out of Heather's hand. "Thank you."

The honey fell in a golden stream and melted into the porridge as Heather and Clover flounced off to collect their little Rogues for breakfast. Those of the advance guard not on sentry duty were soon streaming past, filling their bowls and spreading out around the eating area. The first of the main army were starting to arrive, and Willow found herself having to constantly update her calculations of how much food they would need for future meals. She hoped that there were more supplies coming along with the extra manpower.

Midmorning found her under a supply canopy, balancing a test bowl of spicy stew and noodles on her knee while making notes in charcoal on a list of supplies. "Nowhere to bake bread, let alone rise it." she rubbed out a line and put a question mark next to the words 'flatbread' and 'beans'. Deep in thought, she hardly noticed the noise level in camp steadily rising as more and more of the army arrived. Her concentration was only broken when a wet rag landed on the barrel next to her.

"Hoy!"

"Whaat!?" she snarled, expecting one of her sisters.

Instead, someone short in a navy dress hurled another rag her direction. Before she had time to react, the fabric splatted against her face. Peeling the wet rag away, she recognized the girl's hiccupy laugh. "Violet?"

List and charcoal were forgotten as the two friends

embraced. As they released each other, wiping their eyes and laughing at the same time, Willow could see that her friend had changed. Violet's long braid had been replaced by a neat cap covering all her hair, her dress was worn out, and there were shadows in her sky-blue eyes. It was a long moment before Willow could put a name to what she saw. *Older. She looks older.*

"You're safe!" she exclaimed.

Violet smiled, and to Willow's relief it was still the same smile she remembered. "You're taller."

"I am?" Willow stood straight and measured Violet's head against her cheek. "No, I don't think so. Could be you've gotten shorter."

Violet laughed again. "It must be something else, then."

"I think 'confident' is the word you're looking for." Rose stood at the edge of the tent, the sun making her pale skin glow.

Willow's eye measured her friend in a flash as they ran to each other. Like Violet, Rose seemed worn out, older, and sadder. *Confident, too.* She added to herself as they hugged. There was something in the set of Rose's shoulders, and the tilt of her chin, that implied she'd learned how to stand up for herself. "Confidence looks good on you, too." Willow brushed a hand over Rose's hair, intricately braided to show off her pale skin and blue eyes. "You never used to do anything other than stuff it in a scarf."

Rose mirrored the gesture, a hesitant smile turning up the corner of her mouth. "It's the first place I've blended in, and I didn't feel like I had to hide." The smile faded. "And then they needed someone to look to, so I decided I might as well look the part."

"Sorry if I—" Willow apologized, dropping her hand awkwardly.

"No, it's all right," Rose smiled, genuinely this time. "I didn't realize until I saw you how much is different." She surveyed Willow's Sea Wanderer clothes and apron. "You've changed too, but you probably don't realize it either."

Now that the initial meeting was past, Rose looked preoccupied. As Willow began acquainting her friends with everything that had happened since their separation, they were interrupted by a runner in a navy-blue vest.

"Milady!" The girl stopped and clasped her hands behind her back. "Milady, you're wanted in the tent. Lots of people have lots of things they need to talk to you about."

"And that's probably a direct quote." Rose sighed. "I'd better go."

Willow watched her go with admiration. "We've come a fair way from home, eh?"

"That we have." Violet carefully tucked her hair back under her cap, the sight of its short ends sending a pang of surprise through Willow's heart. "It's been interesting to watch. I didn't know how she'd take it all, but she's growing into things."

"What did she do when you found out about home?"

Violet shook her head a bit. "She was upset, but not for the reasons you'd think. She's more worried that it *didn't* bother her." She shrugged helplessly. "I don't know what to do about that, other than stay close and hope it doesn't eat her up inside."

"Hmmm." Willow recalled the bowl of stew she'd been letting cool. Gathering it along with her list, she said, "Let's go back to the kitchens. I want to keep talking, but this lot won't get fed from thin air."

24
GET READY

The remaining men continued arriving, swelling the camp as preparations began at the battle site. Earth fortifications were set up, screens for archers built on the ridge, and hollows deepened to provide more cover. Everyone kept looking anxiously to the southeast, watching for the first signs of their enemies. From the occasions when she helped Ethan in his cluttered communications area, Willow gathered that no one really knew how soon the Sea Wanderer ground troops would be able to land.

They're not here, but our enemies are. We have to go it alone.

As signal drums beat an alert, Willow went to find her father. She found him loading bags of sling stones into one of their few carts.

"What's wrong?" he asked as she approached.

So much for not being obvious. She handed him a jug of water. "Nothing. I'm nervous."

"Not that you have any reason to be," he pointed out sarcastically. "It's only war."

"Da," She took the water and set it on the ground after he finished drinking. "What if we lose?"

He put his arms around her. "Those of us who survive will flee into the mountains and find our way home from there. You and your sisters will be fine."

She narrowed her eyes suspiciously. "What about you!"

His chuckle rumbled against her ear. "I plan on living to a ripe old age so I can see my grandchildren. Assuming you ever give me any."

"It's not on the list right now." She loosened herself from his hug and stepped back. "It scares me that people I know may not survive."

"That's war," her father answered. "If we didn't take the risks, we'd be left with things the way they are. If we win, things will be better for everyone."

MERALD HUDDLED ATOP A LOG, trying to stay warm. After marching along the coast, his battle group had arrived at the battlefield, bone tired, late the night before. They had awoken that morning to the disconcerting sight of columns of smoke rising from the south. In the distance, they could hear war drums. This could only mean that Lord Kuma's army was closing the distance with their Iorcan allies. Merald sighed and hunched on the log again.

"Tired?" River sat down on the log next to him. The Shona captain was wearing leather armor and had a sling tied to her belt.

He shook his head. "No more than anyone else. Just cold."

She shivered in agreement. "These nights in the open aren't fun for anyone."

A horn blast came from one of their sentries, and the army rippled into life. The rise to the north of the battlefield fell steeply in a jumble of jagged rocks down to the grass, a river cut across the far edge, and the pinewoods ringing the meadow were interspersed with clumps of aspen trees. Behind them, the passes stood open to the rest of the mountains, and across the field, the first enemies were becoming visible. The horn call was joined by signal drums as tribesmen relayed the news to the commanders in camp.

"That sounds like it," River remarked. She looked up at Merald, who stood more than a head taller than her. "I'll go see what orders Erven has for me." She held out her hand. "Good luck."

They shook. "Good luck to you too."

He checked his armor as River darted off. The haphazard way that the army had come together meant that hardly anyone had full armor, and his was a combination of chain mail connecting hardened leather breast and back plates. He flexed his shoulders before pulling on his helmet and tugging the strap tight under his chin. Gathering his short spear and sling, he strapped his sword belt around his waist before heading to find his commander. Despite the weeks of practice, the sword still rode unnaturally at his hip.

VIOLET LOOKED up from her preparations as the drums sounded in the distance. She didn't understand exactly what the drummers were relaying, but she had a good guess. Around the tent, the rest of the healers also stopped what they were doing and began whispering. Tora, the straps of her medical bags crossed over her shoulders, came over to her. "That's it. The enemy's been sighted."

"Right." Violet shuddered. The rest of the healers gathered around her and Tora, waiting for orders. The divide between tribesmen, Sea Wanderers, lowlanders, and Shona had never existed among the men and women now gathered under the canopy. Half of the healers wore armor and carried bags for treating the wounded on the front lines. White flashes shone on their helmets and sleeves, stark against their navy uniforms.

One of the children from Clover's Rogue School came running up with her partner close behind. The girl's face was bright pink as she gasped, "Milady Healer, the commanders say for your people to take position with the men."

Violet nodded and brushed the girl's hair back from her sweaty face. "Thank you." She handed the pair cups of water from the cisterns set nearby. "Drink that before you report again."

Despite her entreaties, the pair only took a few gulps before running off again. With a sigh of concern, she turned to her healers. Lena smiled reassuringly from the front of the group. "Well, you heard them as well as I did," Violet said. "Battlefield healers, try to keep a soldier with you if you have to go beyond our lines. Don't be afraid to defend yourselves if you have to."

"Agreed," one of the field healers said in a serious tone. "Especially you younger ones." He shifted his pack over his shoulders. "Don't expect mercy just because you're a healer."

The command tent hummed with tension as the Senior Commanders discussed troop movements and gave orders to the runners of the Rogue School. Willow stood with her sisters, who were keeping track of their runners on a smooth piece of planking. She tapped Clover on the shoulder. "I'm going to go."

"Not into the battle!" Heather said hastily.

"No, not even close to the battle," Willow amended. "I'm going to go start people heating water and getting food for the commanders and your little Rogues. There's nothing here for me to do." She gestured at Rose and Erven, deep in their respective conversations. She had met the Shona leader a day or so ago, and had been deeply impressed by how he treated her sisters and father.

Clover blew a lock of hair out of her eyes and adjusted her hat. She'd put a scrap of blue fabric around the crown, holding the ever more bedraggled feather in place. "I'll come help you if I can."

"All right." Willow hugged both of her sisters before leaving the tent. As she went out, her father came in. "Da!" She hugged him as well, his lacquered Sea Wanderer armor hard under her cheekbone. "They're asking what's become of our reinforcements."

"I'm wondering that myself," he answered. "If what that intelligence chap is saying is true, the enemy ships were a tougher nut to crack than we'd hoped. They'll be here. I think they've been delayed."

Willow bit her lower lip before asking, "Will you stay here, or go out to the lines?"

Her father sighed. "I hope to keep myself out of things, but if I'm needed I will go." He examined his sword hilt. "I still remember how to use this."

Willow nodded, turning to go. A thought struck her as she left. *If I don't ask now, I may never have the chance to know for certain.* "Da?"

He joined her in the door to the tent. "Yes?"

"Sorry, I just have to know." She looked at the ground, not wanting to see his expression. "Those stories I heard—all of them—about the Fishhawks, the raids, the military command."

Alder sighed. "True. Most of them."

She scrutinized her father. "You left all of it. You had a future with them."

He shook his head. "I never wanted to be a great officer, with the awards and the promotions and everything. It was only ever a job. I was happier with you and your mother than I ever was among the Wanderers. That's why I left." He drew her into another embrace. "We'll be all right. I want to go back home."

"Hey, Sir. They need you!" Clover shouted from behind them.

Alder her let go and turned to face his younger daughter. "I'm not a Sir!"

FROM THE HEALER'S TENT, Violet heard a single horn blast from the ridge. This was followed by a roar as the Illyn armies launched arrows, stones, and javelins into the amassing enemy troops. The roar never stopped, and she knew battle had been joined. She took a deep breath and looked to her fellow healers. "Get ready."

25
SWORD ON SWORD

Battle raged as Merald darted onto the field. His stone pouch was spent, and his commander had given the order to engage hand-to-hand. The smell of blood and dust filled his head as he struggled not to be pushed backwards by the oncoming enemy. It was with a sense of fatality that he noticed how well armored their opponents were; the fortress soldiers in mail and the Iorcan in dyed leather covered in metal plates. Metal clanged on metal as spear met on sword, sword met axe, and hunting knife met short sword. With a chill, he noticed that men were falling all around him.

He ducked away from a curved sword blade that went whizzing by his ear. Whipping his head around, he stared right into the eyes of an Iorca foot soldier. The man's dark eyes glared at him from behind his face piece. Merald jumped back to avoid a crosscut slash that could have opened him right through the middle before dropping to one knee and slashing at his opponent's feet. His sword felt lighter than usual as he brought his blade up to block. The blade overshot and hit the Iorcan's throat, finishing him instantly.

Shocked, Merald turned away from the man he had just killed and looked for his comrades. His commanding officer was nowhere to be seen, and he suspected the man had been killed. Healers were running along the edges of the battle, defending themselves and the injured as they moved from person to person. A little way ahead of him, a Shona boy dropped his weapon and fell as a tufted Iorcan javelin took him through the shoulder. *No!!* Merald ran to the boy's side, shouting, "I need a healer!"

A Sea Wanderer heard his call and came to help him. Together they locked hands and carried the boy over to the woodland fringe. They propped him against a rock and turned to face the battlefield, hands on weapons as they continued shouting for help. Soon a girl accompanied by a tribesman dashed over. "Hands off. Let me help him." She examined the injury and clicked her tongue. "You're not going back out there any time soon. You men, hold him steady so I can get this out."

Merald did as he was told, bracing one of the boy's arms as the healer pulled the javelin head out. The boy screamed with the sudden pain and fainted against the side of the rock. "Well, at least he won't know anything else for a while." The girl wiped blood from her hands. "One of you, get him to the tent. This needs to be cleaned."

"I'll go," Merald volunteered. The other men helped him gather the boy up over his shoulder, and he staggered towards the camp. Shortly before he got there, he heard an explosion and screams coming from the field. A few seconds later, runners streaked through the trees past him, bolting for the command tent. He reached the canopy protecting the healers' area and was met by one of the novice healers.

"What happened here?"

Merald slid the boy off his shoulder and to the ground.

"Shoulder wound. The field healer says it needs cleaning and bandaging."

"All right." She draped an arm over her shoulder. "This way."

He helped her assist the injured Shona to where rows of men waited for their injuries to be attended to. Settling the boy in an unoccupied space, he accepted the water another healer brought him and drained the cup before heading towards the field.

"Merald!"

He turned to see Erven coming towards him from the command tent, wearing armor and carrying a helmet under his arm. They met with a firm handclasp as he asked, "What's happening?"

Erven's face was tight with worry as he answered, "Catapults loaded with firebombs. I came to get Violet. We need more experienced healers on the front lines."

"Does she know that you're coming to get her?"

Erven nodded. "I sent a runner."

"Erven, what's happening?" Violet came out from the supply stacks, adjusting the straps of her field satchels so they hung neatly. She carried a roll of bandaging beneath one arm.

"I need you to come with me to get a good idea of how many casualties we're missing."

Violet squared her shoulders under her navy dress. "All right. Lead on, then."

VIOLET FOLLOWED Erven towards the front, Merald falling in behind her. As they moved through their lines, she was forced to stop many times to staunch bleeding and pack bandaging into wounds. Her hands became covered with blood and grime as man after man died before her eyes, some mere moments after they had been wounded. Erven and Merald guarded her back, the pair of them working as a team to deter attackers who sought to take down anyone wearing a healer's stripes.

"Violet, help. Hurry!"

Violet looked up in surprise from another injured man as Tora ran up. The trainee was bespattered with blood and dirt. Her Sea Wanderer guard followed, also covered in gore. Violet followed to a spot not far from their shelter, where a pair of Shona fighters crouched over a prostrate form. It was a young man from one of the mountain villages, bleeding from a terrible throat wound. "We couldn't move him without him getting help first."

Violet gasped, "More bandages. Quickly!" Erven handed her cloth from her supplies. Even as she pressed another layer to the injured man's throat, she could see that it was no use. The man shuddered and died within seconds of her arrival. This death, like the others that she had witnessed, sent a choking sensation into her throat as she stood. "It's too late."

Tora scrubbed a hand roughly across her face. "He was my friend."

The Sea Wanderer laid a hand on her shoulder. "We need to keep going. There are still others that we can save."

Tora wiped away another tear as she slung her bags over her shoulder. "You're right."

A hand touched Violet's elbow. "Let's get you back to the tent," Erven said.

Violet swallowed hard. "We need to send more teams out here. Too many aren't able to make it to us."

"Agreed," Merald said.

They stepped out of the shelter of the trees, as across the field another catapult launched its payload high into the air. It landed and exploded as air hit the incendiary contents. Men screamed as another projectile landed nearby.

Violet stared wide-eyed as a trumpet sounded on the side of the enemy lines. For a moment, she didn't understand what the signal had been for. Then Erven dove and tackled her to the ground as a hail of arrows fell into the defenders. Men fell all around her, those who had not ducked in time and those who had been unlucky enough to get hit on the ground. Close by, a man cursed as he dragged an arrow out of his arm, blood trailing as he wadded a cloth against his wound.

Erven offered her a hand. "Let's go."

They had almost gotten behind the ridge when Violet caught sight of something out of the corner of her eye. A lone girl stood between an injured Shona and an Iorcan, a long dagger drawn in one hand and loaded sling dangling from the other. It was River.

Violet pulled away from Erven and Merald, running onto the battlefield. Behind her, she heard Erven shout, "Violet, no!"

The girl flung her stone into the face of the soldier. He cursed and lunged forward, swinging two long, curved knives as she readied her own weapon. As she tore towards her friend, Violet tripped over a helmet lying in the dirt and fell heavily. Merald grabbed her as she started to rise, pulling her backwards as Erven bolted past them. Violet yelled as Merald kept tugging her away, just as River's guard dropped and the soldier's blade tore through her chest.

The Shona captain screamed in horrified pain and fell back. The soldier came after her, but found his way blocked by Erven, who fought with a longer blade and more energy than his enemy. The Iorcan cursed and turned away, running into the thick of the battle. Violet scrambled out of Merald's grasp and ran to River.

River coughed. "Violet?" Her voice was hoarse. "What's happening?"

Violet bit her lip, unsure of how to answer. From what she

had seen, she knew that River had only moments left to live. She cradled her friend's head gently as tears made a soft film across her vision. Her voice was harshened from yelling, but she whispered, "Look at my eyes. Only my eyes."

The girl's grip was failing, her face turning white. She coughed again, blood appearing on her lips as she gasped, "Violet?"

"I'm here." Violet dabbed her cloth at the blood, a tear sliding down her cheek.

River gave her a ghost of a smile. "Oh, Violet. Don't cry." Her grip slackened and her hand slipped from her chest. Violet bent her head over River's and sobbed.

After an eternity, Erven shook her shoulder. "There are others to care for. Don't spend all your time crying over the dead." His face wet with tears, he lifted River's body and carried her to the back of their lines. Violet followed him, wiping her face with her sleeve.

CLOVER WAS ORGANIZING her runners into shifts. Too many of them were getting exhausted from their forays into the front lines, and several of them had been injured. One was dead. She wiped a hand across her forehead before turning back to her lists. Around her, the tent buzzed as runners came and went and the commanders conferred. There was a ripple of commotion as Erven came into the tent, his armor dirty and spattered with blood. He accepted the water Heather handed him and slumped onto a crate.

"What's happening?" Rose asked.

He shook his head, wiping his face with one of Clover's Rogue School scarves. "The men are starting to tire. They're saying that the Sea Wanderers have abandoned us."

"They're delayed," one of the Sea Wanderers maintained.

"I know that," Erven said. "But the men don't believe it." He came over to Clover, still shuffling lists on the floor, and knelt next to her. "Clover, I'm sorry to be the bearer of bad news."

"More bad news, you mean," she answered, pushing her bangs back under her hat. "I've already heard enough bad news to last me into old age."

"I know." He glanced at Heather, who must have caught something warning in his look. She settled next to her younger sister. "Look, Clover. River went out beyond our lines to protect one of the younger Shona. She didn't make it."

Clover's eyes welled with tears as the tent blurred. She turned away and buried her face in Heather's shoulder. Her sister rubbed her back as their father came over. "What's wrong?"

Erven sounded upset as he answered her father. "One of my captains is dead, Sir. She was one of Clover's good friends."

Alder sighed. "You didn't need to tell her that now." He pulled her away from Heather to fit in his arms. Disregarding his armor, she snuggled against him as he said, "Excuse me for a minute, please. I think we need to take a break." He carried her out of the tent and to the kitchens, where he set her on a log next to the fire. He returned momentarily with Willow, who was wearing an apron over her tunic and carrying a bowl. "Take care of her, please. I need to go sort out some morale issues."

"Sounds delightful. Goodbye Sir." Willow sat and put an arm around Clover as their father walked away, tightening the straps of his armor. "Hello, frog."

"Hello, fish," she answered numbly.

"Da told me what happened." Willow wrapped Clover's fingers around the warm earthenware bowl before handing her a spoon. "Here."

Clover took a bite, barely tasting what she was eating. "He's going onto the field, isn't he?"

Willow craned her neck towards the ridge, the noise of battle easy to hear beyond it. "I think so. The men need a reminder that hope is not lost yet." She tightened her arm around Clover. "He'll be all right."

Something clenched in her stomach that had nothing to do with the food. Her own voice sounded small and frightened to her ears. "But what if he's not?"

Willow was quiet for a moment. Then she settled her shoulders sternly and said, "Then we'll press on. We'll finish what needs to be finished, then we'll go home and find Mum. We'll do what he meant to do all along; have a quiet life and take orders from no one." She brushed back the feather from Clover's hat. "And I'll take care of you."

THE HUM of voices in the tent had somehow become louder than the noise of battle. Rose's feet hurt, and her mind ached from too many bad reports and worried voices. With increasing regularity, reports were coming in from the field of too few men, too many wounded, and of lines breaking under the catapult fire. The other commanders were starting to look at her more and more often with deep worry in their eyes.

They had drawn a map of the field on a cloth spread over a rough plank table, and as Rose surveyed it, she had to remind herself of what was what. After hours of looking at it, all the symbols were blurring in her mind. Erven hunched over the table next to her, eyeing the line that Ethan was tracing on the map. The intelligence agent's armor was still free of grime, and his sword leaned against the table as Erven said, "They're farther back than that."

Ethan smudged out the charcoal line with a hand already

covered in soot. He stabbed the charcoal stick in spots behind the previous line. "More like this, then." Some of the soot transferred to his face as he wiped his forehead. "At least five of them. All loaded with that special concoction the Iorca're famous for usin'. Explodes on impact." As if to punctuate, a faint explosion came from the field. "Difficult t'put out with water."

"I *know*," Erven snapped. "I've been out there, remember? We need to get rid of them."

"Can they be sabotaged?" Rose's throat was feeling raw.

"We can try," Ethan said. "It's possible that the projectiles could be detonated before they're fired."

"Or if we cut the ropes holding them to the ground…"

She lost track of their voices as she walked over to the crates where Willow had set up drinks. The water soothed her throat, and the distance from the conversation helped the ache in her head. Too soon, however, another runner came staggering in with more bad news. The line closest to the camp was suffering. She saw the panic in Heather's face, even as the girl hurried to comfort the young runner.

"Milady?"

"Sorry, yes?" She blinked at the Sea Wanderer advance commander, suddenly aware that she'd been standing as if frozen. "What is it?"

"Milady," The man cleared his throat. "Um, we've been discussing th'possibility of our lines breaking. It might be time t'start thinking about how you and other key figures'll survive if these lines don't hold."

"Other key—" She looked again at Heather, hugging her runner with tears streaking her face. "You mean retreat. Run."

"It's something we need t'think about," the man answered gently. "While we still have th'chance."

A chance to run. Run and hide. She clenched a fist around the necklace under her dress. *I've been hidden my whole life.* "If it comes to it, we'll discuss it. But for now," She marched over to the table and locked eyes with Ethan. "If the catapults go down, will we have a chance to survive this?"

The Sea Wanderer intelligence agent's eyes went wide. He studied the map for a long moment before nodding. "I think there's a way." He looked at Erven, ice blue eyes firm. "I need t'get closer t'know for sure."

The Shona commander picked up his helmet. "Let's go."

As they left the tent, Rose's throat went tight with anxiety. *I hope that wasn't a mistake.*

MERALD HAD LOST track of how long he had been fighting. Only the light suddenly blazing into his eyes made him realize that several hours had gone by, that the sun had moved beyond its apex and was on its downward curve. He had seen Erven on the field again, going in and out of the cover of the trees as the Shona leader attempted to shore up their lines. Firebombs from the catapults kept falling, bursting and sending drops of the liquid fire everywhere.

The men of the Illyn army were dying left and right, killed by the enemy or incinerated when a fiery projectile landed near them. Others moaned in agony on the battlefield, wounded too badly to crawl off under their own power. The healers, lessened in numbers as the casualties grew overwhelming, scurried here and there on the outskirts of the field, trying to save every man that they could before death claimed the lives of the injured. His stomach twisted bleakly as man after man went down, some whom he'd trained beside in the mountains.

Merald felt, rather than saw, a shadow loom behind him. He swore and spun, just as an Iorcan warrior knocked his feet out from under him. Lying on his back on the flattened grass, he stared, terrified, into the slanted eye slits of the Iorcan's helmet. The warrior raised his spear for a crushing stab. Merald shut his eyes.

"Leave him alone!" a voice yelled. Merald opened his eyes in shock to see the Iorcan fall dead. The Yarrow Leaf leader stood above him, holding out his hand, the other clutching his bloody sword. "Are you all right? Are you hurt?"

Merald gasped for air as he grabbed Alder's hand and stood. "I'm fine."

"We're getting too far extended." Alder wiped blood from his blade and gestured towards the woods. "We need to reform before the trees so they don't keep pushing us farther apart. If this line breaks, they'll have a clear path to the camp and we'll be lost."

Merald nodded breathlessly as they started pushing their way to the trees. Across the field, a fireball erupted as first one, then several of the catapults flipped over mid-launch. Their payload spilled out and exploded amidst the men operating the siege engines. Ragged cheers came from the Illyn side. As they reached the trees, Erven reappeared, Ethan at his heels. The Sea Wanderer's face was messy with soot, and his lacquered chest plate was slick with blood. "It worked!"

"What did?" Alder asked.

Ethan hooked a thumb across the field. "Destroying the catapults." He gestured at his blood-smeared armor. "We took off our uniforms to get close enough."

"Hm. Smart," Alder grunted. "Look, we need to get everyone back far enough to make one concerted push forward. We're too strung out."

Erven pulled his water bottle loose from his belt. "I'll get to one of the signal drummers. Grab any of your daughter's Rogues if you see them."

"Will do." Alder wiped sweat from his face. "Get going. And put your uniforms on before you get killed by our own side."

VIOLET PLUNGED MORE cloths into a pot of hot water. She noticed with a pang of worry that they were running low on bandaging. The casualties were coming in a steady flood, and she and her assistants were barely able to keep up. She called over to one of the women helping her, "How are we doing with supplies?"

The healer gazed into a jar of salve worriedly. "We're almost out of this. And a runner just came. We need to start sending the wounded back to the field."

Violet scowled and returned to putting pressure on bleeding wounds, stitching, bandaging, and cleaning cuts and burns. Her apron became so bloodied that she gave up trying to keep it clean. She finished tying off a bandage as a man staggered in, clutching a rag to his arm. "What's happening?" she asked as she handed him a flask of water.

"Those mercenaries fight as if it's their own homeland they're protecting! We're losing men left and right, and I think we're being pressed into the trees." He clenched his fist and cursed as she pulled the rag off his arm to reveal a long, shallow cut. "Where in flaming foxes are those Wanderers? We aren't going to hold out much longer."

She cleaned and dressed the cut with quick, precise motions. "Take a rest. You're not going to be able to fight at your best with an arm like that. And shut up," she said as she tied off the bandaging. "I don't know where the Wanderers are, but you gain nothing by spreading doom like that." He tried to stand anyway, but she pushed him back down. "Take a minute!"

He shook her off in exasperation. "No chance. We're losing!"

Violet turned her attention to the next patient, then the next. A noise from the battlefield startled her in the middle of refilling a water bowl. It was the sound of cheering, shouts, and battle cries. "What's happening?" She yelled over the noise to one of the healers.

He smiled as he grabbed another flask of water and dashed out. "It's the Sea Wanderers. They've come!"

THE DESTRUCTION of the catapults renewed the hope of the rebels and disheartened the enemy. The barrage of fiery projectiles ceased, giving the rebel army a much-needed breather. The arrival of the Sea Wanderers turned the tide of the battle so much in their favor that it became a matter of holding out to ensure victory for the Illyn rebels. The mayhem from before had died down to pockets of fighting surrounded by expanses of the dead. The healers were kept busy pulling wounded off the field and everyone was tiring, yet the rebels continued to press forward.

The sun was setting behind the trees as Merald and Erven took a break. Both exhausted, they sat next to each other on a rock at the bottom of the ridge, sharing a packet of food brought by one of the Rogue School. Two of the Iorcan commanders had already approached, requesting permission to retreat with honor. The other two, as well as Lord Kuma, had not been seen for quite some time on the battlefield. When Merald had last heard the commanders talk, he gathered that they were hoping an internal struggle had claimed the lives of the remaining enemy officers. In moments of conversation snatched with Erven during the chaos, Merald knew that his friend didn't think that this was the case.

"Well," Erven said with a sigh, dusting debris off his knees. He picked up his helmet. "Are you ready to go again?"

Merald stood and stretched. He was sore all over, and his left calf was stiff where a downed man had caught him with a spear point. "If you are."

Erven buckled his helmet. "Let's get back to the tent. I need to find out what's going on."

They skirted along the ridge, occasionally engaging with individual attackers. A good number of Lord Kuma's drafted troops still fought, joined by the remaining men from the castle garrison. Many of the Iorcan forces were gone from the field, retreating to their ships under the eye of Sea Wanderer troops. They stopped for a moment to catch their breath in the shade of the ridge.

Merald took a gulp from his water, keeping an eye on the battle while taking off his helmet to dump the remainder on his head. "Ready?"

A jolt went through his chest as he saw Erven looking wide-eyed at something behind him. Fear clawing at his mind, he turned to see what had the Shona leader so alarmed.

The warlord loomed behind him like a nightmare, battle armor dented and dirtied and sword mired. A morning star dangled from his belt, its spikes covered in blood and gore. Merald dropped his helmet and drew his sword, willing his hands to stop shaking. He and Erven instinctively spread apart, Merald backing towards the cliff wall.

The man was staring at Erven. "You again. They told me you were dead." He hefted his sword. "I knew I should have taken care of you personally."

Erven's sword flashed as the two men engaged, their swords meeting with a clang. Merald joined from the other side of the warlord, bringing his sword up to parry a blow that sent a jolt like lighting through his wrist.

"Back! Back!" Erven shouted, his eyes darting towards the rock where they had been resting. Between the two of them, they succeeded in pushing the Illyn warlord back another pace. If he tripped, they could finish the fight quickly.

On the level ground, Lord Kuma regained his footing. He roared and swung his sword in a scything sweep towards Erven. Their hilts locked, and Erven stumbled backwards to the ground, his weight no match for a man a head taller than himself. "Merald, move!"

Merald was already moving, his feet unfamiliar with the sloping ground at the bottom of the cliff. As the warlord rounded on him, he tripped over his helmet and fell flat. He jerked wildly away as the sword fell within a fraction of his skull. His vision clouding with sudden pain, he scrambled to his feet.

His vision flashed white, and he heard a crack as something knocked him backwards. Lord Kuma had drawn his mace and swung with devastating force. The spikes bit deeply into Merald's side. His head cracked against the rock and he fell to his knees, eyesight swimming black. Merald dropped his sword, clutching a hand over the wound. Then the darkness overcame him, and he knew no more.

"Stop!"

The morning star fell with a clank as Erven charged. Their swords threw sparks as the two men met, Lord Kuma's height and weight forcing him backwards once more. Erven glanced back at the cliff just in time to see Merald crumple to the ground. Gritting his teeth, he shoved on the locked sword hilts with all his strength and jumped a pace backwards.

Lord Kuma swung an armored fist at him, and Erven barely ducked a blow that would've certainly broken his jaw. His sword found a gap between the warlord's breastplate and backplate, and Erven threw his whole weight behind the blade. He heard Lord Kuma roar with surprise as the man's elbow came down on his wrist with a crack. Pain exploded up his arm and he let go of the sword with a scream. The warlord lashed out with his foot, sending him backwards to the ground. Erven clutched his wrist in panic, feeling his hand go numb.

Grabbing for his dagger with his left hand, he scrambled to a knee only to realize that Lord Kuma hadn't attacked. The man stood still, beginning to topple as his eyes emptied of life. With a crash of armor, the warrior collapsed on the ground, Erven's sword still jutting out of his left side.

Erven got to his feet, catching his breath in stunned gasps. A moan called his attention to the present and he turned to see Merald lying at the foot of the cliff with blood staining the ground around him.

Oh no.

He fell to his knees, gritting his teeth as the damage done to his friend's armor and side became clear.

"Hang on, mate," he muttered, clumsily drawing his knife with his good hand and cutting loose the sleeves from Merald's ruined tunic. Merald's eyelids flickered as Erven pressed the fabric into the wound, but his face remained still. "Hold on, I'm getting help."

Erven scrambled to his feet and made for the camp. As he ran, the men who'd seen the warlord fall began laying down their weapons. The confusion and surrender spread like ripples in a pond, until most of the fighting had stopped. Above him on the ridge, he could hear shouts of victory.

ROSE LOOKED up to hear cheering coming from somewhere nearby. As the sound filtered through the walls of the tent, the conversations in the tent dropped off one by one until the thin sounds of jubilation were all that could be heard. She beat the rest of the commanders to the door by a second, emerging into the golden light of the setting sun. Around them, runners streaked past to the medical tent, the kitchens, the rest areas—all yelling unintelligibly. She briefly locked eyes with Violet as the remaining healers hurried towards the battlefield. With burning curiosity, she rounded the supply tent with the rest of the commanders to see Alder hurrying towards them, his right arm bloody. "What's happened?"

Alder stopped in front of her and took a knee, bowing his head. "Lord Kuma's dead. The rest of his men aren't sure what t'do, but most're surrendering." He looked up at her and it took a long moment for her to recognize the expression in his eyes. *Pride. Like a father for his child.* "The warlord's dead." He pulled off his helmet and laid it at her feet. "Long live the Queen."

26

A NEW BIRTH

Pipes and drums sounded as the Illyn army snaked along the road leading to the fortress. Rose, mounted on a horse that had belonged to one of the Iorcan commanders, looked up to where the castle loomed above the landscape. The gates were still closed and barred, and there were sentries atop the walls. She laughed as she imagined what the guards had to be thinking as they saw the army approaching the castle. "We don't look much like a conquering force, do we?"

Erven, mounted next to her on a grey mountain horse with his wrist in a splint, turned clumsily in the saddle. "Carts of supplies, women, children, cooking pots, mismatched armor." His forehead wrinkled in a frown. "I have no idea. I thought this is what they all looked like."

At the gatehouse of the castle, the guards stood in awe. Some were in shock as the column came towards them with the blue and gold banner flapping, some clamped their hands tightly over their sword hilts, expecting to die fighting, and still others dropped their weapons in defeat.

One man did none of these, but instead took a deep breath and prepared himself to welcome the new ruler. The captain descended the steps from the ramparts to the courtyard, where he barked at the men guarding the iron-bound gates, "Open them." They stared at him askance, eyes wide with disbelief as he repeated himself. "Open them, men! And put down your weapons if you want to live!"

Hesitantly, slowly, they obeyed.

Rose tried to hide her nerves as the tribesman carrying her banner rode his horse to the main gates. He shouted, "Open the gates for the queen! Open them and surrender, or you will all die!" Rose closed her eyes apprehensively, praying that the remaining men in the fortress would acknowledge defeat. If the garrison was still set on fighting, it would cost her army many lives. There were many injured men in her company, they were hungry, and everyone was exhausted from the events several days before. She held her breath as they waited outside the towering gates. Nothing happened.

With a sigh, she turned to her advisors, ranged behind her. Alder, looking as uncomfortable on a horse as she felt, shrugged with the shoulder not hampered by a sling and resumed staring at the gates. "Well, any ideas?"

One of the Sea Wanderers sighed. "Building rams, waiting them out, trying to scale the walls—But all of those will take time."

"And we don't have time," Rose agreed. "The wounded need more care than we can give on the road."

"Milady!" one of the men called from the very front of the column. The sigh of relief could be heard across the column as the gates creaked open. The garrison soldiers sat miserably in groups, their weapons piled next to them. Men were coming down from their positions on the walls to sit, dejected, on the ground.

One of the commanders behind her gave orders, and a group of men fanned out into the courtyard. After a long wait, they waved them forward. Rose followed the other mounted officers into the courtyard, trying to look like she wasn't expecting an attack any moment. To her immense surprise, nothing happened beyond a handful of hostile glares.

Boots scraped against stone as one of the captains got to his feet, showing empty hands to the highlanders and Sea Wanderers. Before he got within ten feet of her, a highland guard moved his horse between them. "What do you want?"

"To welcome the Lady to her new home." The captain bowed towards Rose. "May I?"

The guard looked over his shoulder questioningly to his commanding officer. Erven nodded, and the boy stepped his horse aside to allow the captain to approach. He knelt on one knee before her. "If you see fit, accept my service. I have not acted as an honorable man these years, but I have found the truth. I offer my service as it is, in hopes that I can help you."

Rose cleared her throat twice before being able to respond. "Please stand up." She took a deep breath. "And thank you. If you are who I think you are, I owe you a great debt. If not for your compassion, we would have lost one of our best comman-ders." She looked at Erven before returning her gaze to the captain. "I accept your service. And I'm assuming even more thanks are in order. Was the gate being opened upon your orders?"

The man clasped his hands in parade rest. "Yes, your Majesty. I hoped that you would show more mercy to the men if they surrendered than if they stood and fought." He looked over her shoulder to Erven. "You're looking improved since the last time I saw you."

The corner of Erven's mouth twisted upwards in a smile. "If not for your help, I would not have survived the dungeons. Thank you."

He nudged his horse to the side and swung down, as the rest of the army began flooding into the courtyard. One of the Sea Wanderer commanders helped Rose from her saddle before turning to organize the takeover of the castle.

ALMOST A WEEK LATER, Violet had her hands full as she oversaw transferring the wounded from wagons and litters to a large dining hall on the ground floor of the castle. After so many days in the open, and too many lives lost, everyone had agreed to move the remaining wounded from the battlefield camp to the fortress. The tables had been moved out and cots brought in from the barracks. A fire crackled in the huge fireplace, and a long worktable was set over in the corner. The place hummed with activity as the healers set out their things and began treating their patients.

Violet caught Lena's sleeve as the girl went past. "Can you find out where they get their water from?" She pointed at the fireplace. "And see if we can get some pots heating over there."

"Yes, of course!" The younger girl rushed off. Violet followed her out into the afternoon sunlight, crossing the courtyard to help bring the next wave of wounded in.

Erven met her at the door. True to form, even with his wrist in a splint, he had been ignoring everyone's appeals to slow down. He held up a bag of rags in his good hand. "Found these while we were clearing out the slave barracks. Could your lot use them?"

"Oh, thank you. Yes, and whatever else you find." She beckoned to Heather and Clover. "Frogs, dear!"

As the sisters joined them, Erven asked, "Have you heard how Merald is doing? I heard he's one of the wounded that were brought from the field."

She tossed the bag to Heather. "Could you please take those to Tora and have her boil them, then go see if Lena needs help?"

Heather winked. "Naturally."

"Thank you." She turned back to Erven, shielding her eyes against the sun. "I haven't checked in a bit, but I was about to. He's been in and out, and I think the trip here was hard on him. We've put him in the healer's hall with the others who were worst off." As she crossed the courtyard with Erven following, she noticed that her apron had gotten stained yet again. *At this rate, I won't own any clothes that aren't covered in bloodstains.*

Stopping before the doorway to the healer's hall, she cautioned, "He might not be awake. And you might not like what you see."

"I've not liked anything I've seen since we got here." He shook his head. "I'll be all right."

It was quieter in this building, and still cool even though the day was warm outside. Lamplight flared in the corners of the room, competing with the light from small windows in the thick walls. Shona girls and village women moved from bed to bed, laying cool cloths on fevered brows and offering sips of water to those unable to raise a cup to their lips.

Arielle stopped what she was doing and greeted them as they came in. "I thought I told you to stop working for a bit," she admonished Erven.

"Yes, 'Mum'." He smiled, the expression quickly fading into uncertainty as he glanced around the room.

"I'm sorry I've been gone," Violet apologized to the older

healer. "I'm trying to get the dining hall sorted for the less critical."

"It's all right. We're holding on all right here." Arielle glanced at the ward of patients, lines of exhaustion and grief in her face. "Though for some, this is just a resting place before their last journey."

"What about—" Erven uncomfortably looked at the far end of the room.

"Merald?" Arielle set down the basin she'd been holding, its liquid tinged red with blood. "I still don't know. He took a hard blow to his head, on top of everything else."

"It wasn't his fault," Erven insisted. "We were resting, and he'd taken off his helmet."

"No one's blaming you for this," Violet earnestly said. "You were both taken by surprise."

Erven bunched a fist. "And he fought better than men with years more training."

"He'll need that strength." Arielle squeezed Erven's free hand. "If he survives, he'll be weak for a long time, and I don't know how long it will take for him to heal completely. It's not as if this was a sword cut." The older healer made a face. "We were pulling chain mail links out of his side."

"Is he awake?"

Arielle let go of his hand. "He's been in and out. You can go check." She smiled reassuringly. "If he's awake, he'd want to see you."

They left Arielle at her worktable and headed to the far end of the room. Merald lay sleeping under a coverlet on a corner bed. The former slave's skin was almost white, his breathing labored.

"I didn't realize he was that bad off." Erven's voice had gone quiet. He sank to his knees beside the bed, gingerly balancing with his bad wrist.

Violet picked up a three-legged stool. "You might not have realized, but you were almost as bad."

He reflexively touched his side. "Was I?"

"Maybe not quite," she said scrupulously. "I made a mistake there. But it *was* rather bad." She set the stool next to him. "Stay with him for a bit."

She left to get a cool cloth, leaving Erven sitting at Merald's side.

MERALD SWAM through a humming red fog, his thoughts twisting over and over in his mind. He kept reaching for his sword, trying to strike the giant who loomed in front of him, but his limbs refused to obey. As his fingertips touched his sword hilt, light shattered his vision and the world spun again.

He knew this time, as he woke, what had happened. He was on a low bed in the healer's hall where he'd so often run errands for the garrison healers. There had been a battle. He recognized Erven, leaning on the bed with his head buried in crossed arms.

His first attempt at words came out with a croak. Fortunately, the sound alerted his friend, who held a cup to his lips. The second time, he was able to make the words come out. "You survived."

There were lines between Erven's eyes that hadn't been there when they first met. "Barely." He shook his head. "He almost had me as well."

"I'm not much of a swordsman." Merald tried to shake his head, but the movement made the world go swimmy. "Sorry I was a useless battle partner."

"You need practice." Erven offered him another sip of water. "And you need to get better. There's a lot to still do, and we need your help."

"I'll try." He blinked hard. His vision was getting foggy again. "I'll try, but—" It was much easier to close his eyes. There was coolness over his forehead, and something bitter in his mouth. Somewhere, a voice called to him. *Mum?* As he drifted to sleep, he could hear the healers' voices.

"...working hard."

"Needs rest..."

"Just hold on, mate." It was Erven's voice, coming at him from a distance. "You saved my life, and I'm not going to let you go easily."

WILLOW and her sisters were on the cleaning crew for dinner two weeks later when their father came to find them. His right arm still wrapped in a sling, he nevertheless maintained an air of command. He pointed at the three with his good hand. "My pearls, I want a word."

Putting down the dish she was drying, Willow followed him obediently, tugging Heather after her by the apron. They followed their father out into the courtyard, where the summer night was still warm. He stopped and sat down on a bench against the wall of the great hall. "So."

Heather and Clover claimed the other two seats on the bench, and after a moment of indecision, Willow sat on the ground next to them. "So—"

"So," Alder repeated. "We need to decide what we're doing here, and how long we plan to stay."

"I'm sure you have your own plan," Willow said. "You're just trying to tell us without argument."

"Not true!" He fidgeted the knot in his sling lower on his shoulder. "I have plans, but I'm open to discussion."

"Hmph," Clover said. "What are your plans?"

"Our home is still in ruins," their father said. "That is, assuming the rest of the tribe hasn't started rebuilding. The others are asking me if we can leave and go home."

The girls were silent for a long minute. Heather finally said, "And you're telling us it's time for us to go home as well."

"That was my plan, and has been ever since I left." Alder sighed. "The process of recovering here will take years. I can't stay that long. We have our own recovering to do back home."

Willow fidgeted with her shirtsleeve. "So, when were you wanting to go?"

"Now, that's the thing," her father answered seriously. "I am giving considerable thought to taking the men home." He paused. "And leaving the three of you here."

All three girls looked at him with open mouths. "You're serious," Willow accused.

"Yes, I'm serious. But I wanted to know what the three of you think. It means you'll be here for another year—or more—before things calm enough for you to come home. Do you want to take that risk?"

Heather smirked. "Risk is my second name. Along with Danger, Trouble—"

"Shush." Clover elbowed her. "You trust us to take care of ourselves? I thought we were untrustworthy children."

"You know that's never what I thought. Different times call for different treatment. I think the three of you have seen and done enough to take care of each other until you decide it's time to come home."

Willow looked at her sisters. "What do you think, frogs?"

Clover clasped her fingers tightly together. "I want to help. There are so many little ones who follow me; I'd hate to disappear and leave them."

Heather yawned and sat back, resting her boot heels on the

ground in front of her. "The Rogue School still needs us, I'm sorry to say."

"I suppose that's them," Willow told Alder. "And I think I'd better stay too, to keep an eye on things. Who knows what trouble they'll be into if we both leave?" She hesitated, thinking of a conversation she'd had recently with Ethan. *No,* she decided. *Not while Heather and Clover are here.*

"Right then," Alder stood up. "I'll go tell your uncle. If you have letters for your mother and brother, give them to me before I leave. We're going after the ceremonies are over."

"Ah yes," Heather said. "The Ceremony of Memorial and Recognition. Big name, eh?"

"Why are you staying for the ceremony?" Clover asked. "I thought you tried to avoid those."

Alder grew uncharacteristically sheepish. "I do, but this one I can't avoid." He laughed. "Rose—erm—the queen is honoring a few of the commanders."

Willow and her sisters exchanged mischievous looks. "Honoring? Like, for instance, knighthood? Doesn't that mean—"

Clover swept off her bedraggled hat. "*Sir.*" She linked elbows with Heather, and the two of them pranced off towards the scullery, giggling the word 'sir' over and over.

Willow and her father watched them go. With a sigh, he turned to her. "Sir is correct, I'm afraid."

Willow hugged him. "It's all right. You dodged titles your whole life, so I'd say it's about time that someone caught up to you." She looked up at him as she let go. "Keeping things together at home isn't the only reason you're leaving, is it?"

He shook his head. "Enough of the Iorcan troops who survived know that I'm here. They might not think to look for me back home."

Willow frowned. "You can't hide forever."

"No," he conceded. "But I can try to stay out of their line of vision. At least I'm not going back with the Wanderers."

Willow nodded. "Ethan's leaving after the ceremonies too. He says he wants to see what type of mess his underlings have left in his office." She wrinkled her nose as a chilly breeze struck. "He's never said, but I gather that he's responsible for overseeing much more than I ever knew about."

"He's needed at Alcha Dar," her father said. "No one sits on the Council that young unless they've earned massive amounts of trust, and responsibility comes with it."

"I know. I'll just miss him." She clutched her wrist nervously. "And there's something else too…"

After only two weeks, the papers and inkpots had spread to cover the table and chairs in the small room Ethan had annexed for his work. "You know, you always insist this's how you stop intruders from finding anything—"

Ethan held up a hand, grinning. "Stop! Don't say it! This system works just fine for me."

Willow raised an eyebrow. "That so? Where's your pen case gone, then?"

"I—Er—Ummm."

"That's what I thought." She retrieved the case from under one of the chairs and handed it to him.

Ethan took the case without a word, and for a moment Willow was afraid she'd offended him. After moment, he tucked it into his pack. "Thank you. Thank you for all your hard work. If you hadn't been so committed to Rose and helpin' her, Illyn'd still be in th'grip of a tyrant, an' th'Sea Wanderers'd be conveniently ignoring a conflict buildin' under our noses." He deliberately smoothed out a handful of papers. "We could use someone like you, who's not afraid t'address things that others might overlook out of convenience. Well," He set the documents down. "I could use you."

"I don't know." She bent to begin collecting the rest of the documents from his desk. "It's tempting, to be in the warm sun, and eat rambutan with the sea breeze coming in through the window. I loved your home while I was there. It was the first place where I realized how much more of the world there is." She'd been avoiding his eyes, but finally glanced over. The longing in his eyes surprised her, and she wondered if it was homesickness or something deeper.

"So come with us," Ethan said. Now that they were looking at each other, there was warmth in his voice. "You'll be useful. And," He rubbed the back of his neck. "I'd love to spend more time with you."

Sudden cold and hot shot through Willow's chest. "Really?" Her voice was squeaky, and she cleared her throat to try again. "I mean, you really? I—" She clutched the documents to her tunic front. "I wouldn't mind that either." She looked down, not wanting to see what affect her words were having. "It's been nice, it has. I like you. And I'd love to come with you. It's just—"

"You have things that're keeping you here, too." He sounded sympathetic, and she decided it was worth the risk to look up.

"Yes," she said with relief. Seeing that he didn't look upset gave her courage to continue, "Rose only just figured out how to make her voice heard, but now she has to learn how to make people listen. She'll need help." She dropped the papers in the box and crossed her arms. "The Sea Wanderers feel like the family I never knew existed, but Rose has always been family. I don't want to set off on something new until things are settled here."

"Can I write to you, then? Until things're settled?"

She smiled, her stomach feeling quivery with nerves. "Yes, of course." She fished a stoppered ink bottle out of the mess and handed it to him. "Assuming you don't lose your pen."

"I can look after my own things, thank you!"

. . .

WHEN SHE FINISHED EXPLAINING, her father smiled. "He spoke with me later that evening."

The night air suddenly pressed against her, and she wondered if her ears were an unusual color. "What did you say?"

"I told him that you're an adult, and can make your own decisions."

She frowned. "Yes, but there's ways of warning someone off without warning them off. You didn't scare him, did you?"

"He doesn't scare easily." Alder fidgeted with the knot on his sling. "And I didn't try. He seems worthy enough of your attention, whenever you decide to give it." With a wink, he added, "Maybe grandchildren aren't that far off, after all?"

"We're only going to write to each other!" Willow exclaimed. "It could be nothing will happen! Don't try and pick the berries before they're ripe."

Her father raised his eyebrows. "Berry-picking at my age? Ha!" He sighed and shook his head. "Don't worry, I won't interfere. I trust your judgement." He straightened his sling again. "I'm going to go see if those healers will let me take this off before the ceremony. Maybe Violet will let me go home with two good arms after all."

Willow smirked. "I doubt it. She's very conscientious about things like that." She turned to go. "Goodnight, Sir."

"Goodnight, daughter."

SEVERAL DAYS LATER, Violet stood on the highest tower facing the mountains. The wind shifted, blowing from the sea and bringing with it a smell of salt and adventure. Above her the blue and gold flag fluttered in the breeze as it had in the days of the old dynasty, though this flag had a rose on either side of the star. Willow leaned against a battlement next to her. "What are you thinking?"

Violet braced her elbows on the wall, looking down into the courtyard. The torches lining the walls appeared as tiny as fireflies from where she stood. "I was thinking about my siblings. They're getting big, and I'm missing it."

Willow nodded. "I've been thinking about my brother, and my mum. I hope they're all right."

"Your father did say that they were safe. Soon we'll be able to go home, rebuild the village, and everything can go back to normal."

Willow spat a wisp of hair out of her mouth. "Well, I'm not sure how soon is soon."

"True," Violet agreed. "You said you thought it would be a long time—"

"Oh, *here* you are."

Both girls turned as Rose came up the stairway. "I needed to get away from everyone for a while." She smiled. "I have no idea of when to be a queen and when to be myself. Someday, I'm sure, the two will be the same, but for now I feel like I'm balancing on the highest point of the turret." She sighed and leaned against the battlements next to Willow. "I'm still having a hard time getting used to all this."

"I think we all are," Violet said, a sad smile coming to her face. "I still sometimes feel like there'll be a day when someone pops out of the air and says 'It's all done, you can go home now'."

"Except there isn't a home to go back to." The words coming out of Rose's mouth had a hard edge. "Not for me."

"And if there was, it's all going to be different." Violet heard the same resentful tone in Willow's voice. "Our lives'll never be like they were. It's gone from bad to worse to worst, and that's even *without* so many people dying at the end. What's worst's that even if we do rebuild, it's not going t'feel like home anymore. It'll feel like it does when you're outgrowing your clothes. It'll pinch." She angrily wiped her eyes with the edge of her sleeve. "And we'll still have t'carry on, because there's still so much left to do. We don't even have time to mourn what we've lost."

"You're right," Violet stuffed her hands deep in her apron pockets. "You're *both* right. But it doesn't either of you any good to dwell on it."

"No, it doesn't," Rose admitted forlornly. "I have to keep telling myself that some good *has* come out of all this." She turned to point at the flag, stirring faintly in the breeze. "There's that. That flag hasn't flown over this fortress in fifteen years."

"And it has your colors on it." Willow put an arm around Rose's shoulders.

Rose sighed. "Also, that." She ran her fingers over the braids circling her head. "Not that it's a comfort. If *these* are giving me a headache, I can't imagine what an actual crown will feel like."

"I don't know if you'll actually need one for a bit," Violet said. The braids had been her handiwork, a nice distraction from changing bandages and cleaning wounds. "I'm not sure how other countries think, but I hardly expect you'll have any formal occasions now that all the ceremonies are finished."

"I'll need one eventually." Rose leaned into Willow's arm. "The people will want to see that there's strength here, and a crown fits that image."

Violet wrapped her arm around her friends from the other side. Rose's shoulder was the perfect height to rest her head. "You'll have help. You don't need to do all this on your own."

Willow gave a very unladylike snort. "You'll have more

help than you want. Give it another few months; you'll have plenty of people comin' to tell you how t'run your country."

"You sounded like your Da right then," Rose said, a smile lightening her demeanor. "Or maybe Ethan. Is that accent leaving a mark?"

"I might be." Willow freed her arm. "I haven't noticed." She smiled sheepishly. "I really *was* tempted to accept his offer immediately. I was worried that Da would insist on us going straight home with him, and the idea of going t'fight with the elders about how to rebuild is still miserable."

Violet laughed. It was good to hear both of her friends sounding more like themselves again. "If I know your da, he'll have the elders sorted out, the houses rebuilt in stone, and a proper road laid to the forest's edge before winter sets in."

"She's right," Rose agreed. "I am glad he left you and your sisters here, though."

"It gives us all a chance to see how we feel about the world suddenly getting bigger." Willow hugged herself as the wind picked up. "We'll be all right."

"That we will."

Violet pulled the other two girls in for a fortifying embrace. Their breathing settled as they held each other for a long moment. As the flag overhead rippled and snapped, Willow shivered. "I think my blood's gone thin after being with the Wanderers. Let's go downstairs and see if we can find Heather and Clover."

"I'm sure they've been up to no good." Violet looked back at Rose. "Coming, dear?"

Rose shook her head. "I need some peace and quiet."

Violet opened the stairwell door as Willow gave Rose one last hug. "Don't take too long. We have lost time to catch up on." The cool air followed them down the stairs towards the hall, leaving Rose looking out to sea.

· · ·

ROSE SHIVERED as the breeze sharpened. A hint of moisture came with it, warning of approaching rain.

A noise from behind her made her stiffen with irritation. *Is the entire castle coming up here tonight?*

"I wondered if you'd be here." Erven joined her at the parapet. "It's the quietest spot in the whole fortress."

"It is." She shivered. "I'm finding that quiet moments are hard to come by."

"That's why I always made sure to lead a patrol or take one of my own every few days. It gave me time to think without everyone needing my attention." He leaned against the battlements. "It was something I had to learn as I went. Luckily, you picked it up faster."

"Oh..." Rose swallowed hard against the urge to correct him. Finally, she said, "The first weeks were so hard. I thought you made a colossal mistake, putting me in charge."

"I didn't." Erven turned to face her. "When I met you in the hollow, I knew that you could handle the responsibilities of leadership." The torches by the stairway doors reflected in his blue eyes as he added, "When I surrendered to the soldiers, I didn't know that I'd survive. In fact, I was planning not to."

To her dismay, the cold edge of tears stung her cheeks. She blinked hard, hoping he wouldn't notice. *Crying again. What's the matter with me?* "When Arielle told us you were still alive, I was so afraid. I didn't know if you'd turn us over to save your own life, or what they were doing to try and force you." She took a deep breath, which came out more like a sob. "And all that—and the expectations of everyone else, what was happening to you, the grief your clan was feeling, and that it was all my fault—"

"It wasn't!"

"Well, it's felt that way ever since the soldiers first came to my home." She closed her eyes tightly, hoping the tears would stop. "It's made me hate myself all the more."

"Rose," Erven's hand fell gently on her shoulder. "There are plenty of people who will hate you in this life. Don't add the weight of your own hatred to theirs."

Try as she might, she couldn't stop the tears from streaming down her face. She lowered her head to the stone face of the battlement and cried until something deep inside had settled itself. Erven didn't say a word, but his hand didn't move from her shoulder. When the tears finally subsided, she took a deep breath and felt like it was the first time her lungs had been clear in months. "You must think I'm pathetic."

"Not at all." He sat down with his back against the battlements. "I'm surprised you didn't do that sooner." He smiled. "Feel better?"

To her surprise, she did. "Lighter." She sat next to him, looking up at the sky. "Thank you."

He offered her a handkerchief, and she wiped her eyes as the stairwell light made shadows dance across their feet. She leaned her head against the battlement, silence settling around them.

"The stars are so clear tonight." As she said it, a streak of silver lit the sky.

"They say that for each dancing star, a baby's born," Erven commented, tipping his head back to watch with her. "I never made sense of that. There were always far more dancing stars than there were babies."

"I used to climb out onto my roof and watch them." Rose pulled her knees to her chest and wrapped her arms around them. "It helped me feel better."

She could hear the smile in Erven's voice. "I always loved night patrol for that reason. No matter how bad things were down here, they're always the same. It reminded me to keep hoping for better days. Look, there goes another!"

"Tonight feels that way for me." She accepted the hand he offered and scrambled to her feet. "Almost like a new beginning. A birth, I suppose."

"It's a new birth for all of us." Erven pressed her hand to his lips in salute. "Welcome to the world, Queen Rose."

CAST OF CHARACTERS

THE YARROW
LEAF TRIBE

Deep in the Gaillen Woods, the Yarrow Leaf tribe survives by hunting, fishing, and farming clearings in the woods. Fierce fighters when threatened, they joined other foresters to push invaders back during the war fifteen years ago. Since that battle, legends have begun to grow around the forest, telling of a people with magical powers who are in league with the trees. Reclusive in recent years, they now shun almost all contact with the outside world.

Alder

Yarrow Leaf tribe man, father of Willow, Heather, and Clover. Suspected to have been raised outside the woods. Commanded Yarrow Leaf fighters in the border skirmishes with a blend of approachable leadership and strong tactical sense.

Blackthorn

Blacksmith's apprentice, several years older than Rose and her friends.

Heather and Clover

Typically found together, the sisters are responsible for most mischief within their circle of friends. Despite their reputation, they have a knack for accomplishing tasks with efficiency and good humor.

Juniper

Violet's sister, the oldest of six siblings. Nineteen years old, she is married and lives apart from her siblings.

Kalina

Yarrow Leaf tribe healer, Violet's mentor.

Nyssa

Yarrow Leaf tribal leader, a grandmother figure to many children.

Oak

Yarrow Leaf tribal leader.

Rose Thinar

A foundling from the war sixteen years ago, placed with a childless couple and raised as one of the tribe. Different in appearance and build from her playmates, she has never shaken the feeling of not belonging.

<u>Rowan</u>

Willow, Heather, and Clover's older cousin.

<u>Sedge</u>

Husband of Juniper, sent to accompany children to refuge.

<u>Thorn</u>

Yarrow Leaf tribe man, Rowan's father and Alder's brother-in-law.

<u>Violet</u>

Trainee healer and one of Rose's best friends. Raised by her grandmother along with her five siblings after the death of their parents. While preferring to be in the background of things, she is very perceptive and gives good advice. Sixteen years old.

<u>Willow</u>

Older than her friends by two years, known for her dry humor and formidable will. Different in appearance from her tribe, along with her two sisters Heather and Clover.

THE SEA WANDERERS

Forming out of an alliance of tribes many years ago, the Sea Wanderers control the majority of the ocean with a network of trading and military vessels. A people defined by diversity, anyone can join them by living according to their laws and defending them in conflict. Their large area of influence places them in the unique position of having trade relationships with most nations around their borders.

Bysar

Captain of the *Fire Dancer*, father of Tiren and Kyli.

Ethan

Council Intelligence agent, with a crooked sense of humor and habit of misplacing things.

The Fishhawks

Renegade group of Sea Wanderers that raided and pillaged friend and foe alike, more than twenty years ago. Recruited to official capacity by Sea Wanderer military and instrumental in preventing full-scale war between Sea Wanderers and Iorca.

Kyli

Tiren's younger sister, approximately eleven years old.

The Speaker

Speaker for the Sea Wanderer High Council, the ruling power for the Sea Wanderer nation.

<u>Tiren</u>

Sea Wanderer boy, friend of Willow and Heather.

THE SHONA

In the aftermath of the war, the victorious army set their sights on conquering the Illyn highlands. In recent years, three of the key mountain passes have been held by the Shona, a group of young resistance fighters who rely on hit-and-run tactics to harass the occupying forces. While the Shona guard the passes, the highlands remain unconquered.

Annika

Whitecaps outpost leader, instrumental in directing Illyn deserters to Hold Eskel

Arrick

Thunderhead captain.

Carina

One of three main base captains, female. Blind in one eye from an old injury.

Erven

Shona commander over all three outposts. Very compassionate and protective of his clan, especially his younger sister. Nineteen years old. Known to the Illyn people as an 'uncatchable shadow' for how frequently the Shona have evaded capture by warlord's men.

Lena

Erven's younger sister, a sensitive trainee healer with a tendency to overestimate her capabilities.

<u>River</u>

Shona captain, originally born in one of the highland tribes.

<u>Soren</u>

The charismatic Thunderhead outpost leader, wary and hostile towards outsiders.

<u>Tait</u>

One of three main base captains, male. Often jumpy and nervous after a lifetime of living in a country on the edge of war.

<u>Tora</u>

Shona girl, one of Violet's trainee healers. Older than the other trainees by several years.

PEOPLE OF ILLYN

A country of mountains bordered by fertile plains and cold seas, Illyn was defeated fifteen years ago by an army hailing out of the northern edges of the sea. Since then, Illyn's riches have been depleted and its people broken in their ruler's quest to bring the entire nation under his command.

King Alaber Thinar

Last king of the Thinar line, Rose's biological father. Killed in battle when Illyn fell.

Arielle

Illyn village leader and healer, former nobility.

Lord Kuma

Warlord who conquered Illyn sixteen years ago, failing to wipe out the Thinar line. Rarely referred to by name.

Merald

Slave boy in Illyn fortress, born and raised in the Aubron highland tribe. Seventeen years old.

Captain Ricar

Guard commander in Illyn fortress, oversees dungeon and support workers. Unusually compassionate for a career soldier.

ACKNOWLEDGMENTS

The author would like to extend thanks to the following persons and establishments. Without their help, support, and occasional boots in the backside, this book wouldn't exist.

First, I'd like to thank Celestial Seasonings and the manufacturers of Yorkshire Gold Black Tea, for more cups of tea than any one person has the right to consume.

Warm regards to my family and friends new and old, who are no doubt wondering if I've based characters off of them. I have—some more obvious than others.

I extend my immense appreciation to Mr. Disney, whose depiction of chimney sweeps dancing on rooftops ignited the first 'aha' moment for this series. Even if the end result no longer appears as the inspiration did, the Shona will always feel madcap and daring to me.

My thanks to the people who've been intimately involved with this project over its lifespan. From the Big Obnoxious Advisors of drafts 1-5, to the betas of drafts 6-7, to the few die-hard fans of the first edition—thank you. Your re-reads, honest critiques, and unbridled enthusiasm have helped transform Star of Hope—and the entire Tales of Sea & Skies series!—in so many meaningful ways.

Ever and always, my most heartfelt gratitude goes to Amy, Emmy, Brittany, and Melissa, whose undying enthusiasm, sound advice, and fervent prayers helped me through more bouts of self-doubt than I care to remember. You, my dear friends, are the wind beneath my wings.

And lastly, to my characters. We've walked many paths together, but I've only fallen more deeply in love with each and every one of you. You opened the door to your world and welcomed me in, and in doing so allowed me access to an entire universe. Thank you.

~ BCC

ABOUT THE AUTHOR

Brigitte Cromey has been known to daydream so heavily that a gong must be rung to retrieve her. When not submerged in worlds of her own making, she can be found cooking with bizarre ingredients, reading entire books in a single sitting, dressing her children as fairies and knights, and occasionally responding to the world with kindness tainted by cynicism.

Brigitte lives in southern Arizona with her husband and children. Should you encounter her, the tea kettle will always be on. She can also be found on Instagram @yarrowleafauthor, and on her website www.wordsinmyblood.com.